THE SOLDIER'S DAUGHTER

FIONA MCINTOSH

Storm
PUBLISHING

Crime

DCI Jack Hawksworth crime series

Bye Bye Baby

Beautiful Death

Mirror Man

Dead Tide

Foul Play

Blood Pact

Epic Fantasy

The Quickening

Myrren's Gift

Blood And Memory

Bridge Of Souls

The Scrivener's Tale

Valisar

Royal Exile

Tyrant's Blood

King's Wrath

Percheron

Odalisque

Emissary

Goddess

Trinity

Betrayal

Revenge

Destiny

This one's for you, Dad.
I know how much you appreciated savouring a wee dram.
And for you, beautiful Mum, the original Violet in my life.

PROLOGUE
KNOCKANDO, SCOTLAND

July 1930

'Violet Nash!' It was a shriek.

Breathing through her anger, ten-year-old Violet turned around with a narrowed gaze to see Miss McKenzie bearing down on her. Of all the teachers, did it have to be *her* on break duty? Couldn't it have been her favourite, Mademoiselle Laurent? Why was she so unlucky? Her mother's words came to mind: *create your own good fortune.*

Miss McKenzie arrived, looming at her full, fearsome height. She was more brutal in her desire to punish than any teacher Violet had encountered and seemed to enjoy staring, hawk-like, down the bridge of her pointed nose, her lips stitched into a mean line. Violet's friend, Angus, quaked under that look, but she wasn't scared of Miss McKenzie, not even when she felt the pinch of the teacher's fingers around her arm. She winced as the teacher spoke to the boy on the ground.

'Get up, Douglas!'

'She shoved him, Miss McKenzie,' Ailsa Johns bleated, pointing at Violet, then cut her a smirk.

'I don't know how. Douglas weighs twice as much as Violet,' Miss McKenzie said.

'He pretended to fall,' Violet said.

'I was raised never to hit a girl,' Douglas said with false contrition.

'And you'd better not, laddie,' Miss McKenzie replied.

'But it's all right for him to hit the boys?' Violet wondered aloud. 'Angus will surely have a black eye.'

'I'll be all right,' Angus said, mooching on the fringe of the group of children who had gathered at the scene. It had all begun with Douglas picking on him.

'You might be, Angus,' Violet said, aware of his reticence at being the centre of attention, but unhappy about it, 'but Dougie is too free with his fists. And if he gets away with it, he's just going to get bigger and meaner.'

'It's not your job to deal with playground squabbles, thank you, Violet,' Miss McKenzie said in an acid tone, shaking her; she still held on to Violet, her fingers digging into the tender flesh on her upper arm.

'No, it's yours,' Violet replied with her trademark honesty. 'But you were too busy talking to Mrs Roper over the fence. You didn't see what was happening here. Angus could have been seriously hurt.'

'I'm all right,' he groaned again, clearly hating the attention. 'How dare you speak to me like that, you wretch!'

'I'm just saying—'

'I don't care! You can keep your thoughts to yourself and your mouth shut. To the headmistress's room!' Miss McKenzie pointed in the direction of the schoolhouse. 'Wait outside. And, Ailsa, you're on litter-bin duty from this afternoon.'

Ailsa looked horrified. 'But, Miss Mc—'

'No backchat, or you'll be in front of the headmistress too. Still here, Angus Munro?'

'Yes, miss.'

'Go and make yourself useful and ring the bell, please. Break is over. Dougie, you can go to the headmistress with your boxing partner for your trouble.'

Giving each other distance, Violet and Douglas skulked through the school's short corridors to the head's room and waited for Miss McKenzie to arrive, which she did in due course, sneering at Violet. She loved to gloat in front of the headmistress, Miss Chisholm, although Violet secretly believed that Miss McKenzie thought she should be head.

Miss Chisholm had only recently taken on the position of headmistress. In the school of eighty or so children, there were just two full-time teachers and one part-time teacher, so she also took classes with a smiling firmness and already knew each child well. She was far more likeable than Miss McKenzie, but just as imposing: tall with silver hair caught up in a tight, neat bun. She was often seen striding around the hillsides with a walking pole in one hand and the leads for two dogs in the other. The dogs were rarely on the leads but they were very obedient, as were her students in her presence.

Miss Chisholm saw Dougie first. He was shown out by a smug Miss McKenzie with a note for home; he grinned at Violet as if to say, *I'll get you later.*

It was Violet's turn to follow Miss McKenzie into the office. Inside, the afternoon sun was slanting across the polished wood desk where a number of small buff folders lay. It was reports time for the children.

The headmistress sighed. 'Well, now, Violet, tell me why I have a visit from you today.'

Miss McKenzie opened her mouth to explain but the headmistress gave a small hand gesture. 'Er, thank you, Miss McKenzie. I'll just have a chat with Violet alone.'

'But—'

'Thank you, Miss McKenzie.' Violet felt a small trill of triumph.

'You tell me what happened, Violet.'

'Dougie Baxter is a hulk who talks with his fists, and Ailsa is a bully who works hard at getting others into trouble,' Violet answered without pause.

'I see. So you're simply an observer?'

'No. Angus is scared of Dougie, but I'm not. Dougie punched him, and that eye is going to swell badly.'

'So you hit him on behalf of Angus Munro?'

'No, Miss Chisholm.' Violet dropped her gaze. 'I just gave him a push. My father used to box in the army, and he taught me to look at how balanced people are. Most often they're not and if you spot the right moment, a simple shove can send the biggest man down. Except I barely touched Dougie. He pretended to fall.'

Miss Chisholm tried to disguise the twitch of a smile at the corner of her mouth. 'Ah. So you simply unbalanced Dougie?'

'That's right. I didn't hurt him. But he hurt Angus for no reason. We were playing jacks together and he called Angus a sissy for playing a girl's game. He's not a sissy. He's kind and fun. He's just not very good at football, and he doesn't want to get into fights.'

'Which makes him far more sensible than you, Violet Nash.'

'Well, I don't have a black eye or a note going home,' she answered.

Miss Chisholm's gaze slanted at her. 'Not yet,' she said. 'So this was all about defending Angus's honour?'

'No. Dougie and Ailsa said I was an orphan, and she pulled my hair, and then Dougie accused me of being in love with Angus and told us that we're so poor we'd never get anywhere in life. Angus told him to shut up and that's when Dougie hit him, and so I got involved. But I just wanted to stop them saying those mean things. It doesn't bother me, but it does trouble Angus.'

'It *doesn't* bother you?'

Violet shook her head. 'I have plans.'

The head's mouth creased in a smile. 'If it didn't bother you, why get physical?'

'Because it hurt when Ailsa yanked my plait, and I suppose I was angry.'

'Anger is never a useful emotion.'

Violet shrugged.

'No, I want you to take this seriously, Violet. Anger is loud. Anger is destructive. You are by far the smartest pupil in this school – in this region, I would hazard – and you know it! So be smart, Violet. It's far better to take that anger you feel and turn it into something else.'

Violet studied the headmistress. 'Like what?'

'Well, ignoring bullies like Ailsa and Dougie is far more powerful than letting their words have any effect on you.'

'So I have to ignore them when they pull my hair, punch my friend, say mean things?'

'People say lots of mean things when they feel insecure. Do you know what that means, Violet?'

She nodded.

'I thought you might. But still you used violence instead of ignoring them.'

'I think that sometimes you have to surprise a bully, Miss Chisholm, stand up to them.'

This prompted an actual chuckle from the headmistress. 'Of course you do. You are an enigma, Violet, and I won't ask if you know what that means. I want you to work hard at your studies. I can see you flying through your scholarship exams to make us proud, finish school and go to university.'

'But I don't want to go to university. I don't even wish to finish school. I plan to leave at fifteen.'

'Don't be silly. You must finish and sit your exams,' Miss Chisholm said with a look of doubt.

'I can do what you ask, to please you, and of course to please my dad, but then I wouldn't be pleasing myself, would I? And it is my life, isn't it?'

Miss Chisholm looked astonished. 'Yes, Violet, but—'

'School is boring. Exams are meaningless.'

'You find school boring now because you're ahead of the others, but university will—'

'Not teach me how to make and blend whisky.'

She'd finally tested Miss Chisholm's patience. The woman looked at her in disappointment. 'I know you want to follow in your father's footsteps, Violet, but I think more study will give you a better grounding, broaden your outlook.'

'Why? I already know what I want to do. Most of the girls here have no ambition and just talk about getting married.'

'And you don't think about those things?'

'No.' Violet privately had no understanding of such an attitude. 'Maybe when I'm older I'll want to be married and have a family. But first I want to achieve my dream, and that is to be the best female whisky distiller and blender in Scotland – or even the world, as my dad says.'

'Violet, you're ten. Too young to be making such firm plans.'

'I know what I want to do, so I think plans are important. Very few of the other children know what they want to do. The rest will just see what work is around, and they'll never leave here.'

The headmistress frowned. 'Scotland, you mean?'

'Speyside. Some will never even leave Knockando.'

'But you will?'

Violet nodded gravely. 'This is the best place to learn about and make whisky, but I want to see the world too.'

'And you don't believe that university could improve your chances of making better whisky or...' Miss Chisholm trailed off, because Violet was already shaking her head confidently.

'Mum said practice makes perfect. She got better at nursing during the war because that's all she did – injured men came in by the dozen every day. And after the war she got better at sewing the more she sewed, she said. I won't get better at making whisky by learning at university, because I'd be studying music or art or writing.'

The headmistress blinked at the precocious remark. 'Well, you could study science. That would help.'

'Dissecting a frog will not improve my knowledge of whisky. Working in a distillery will. Because I'm a girl, the university would push me into biology, which is no help, and anyway, I am just not interested in chemistry or physics. I'd still have to start from the beginning and learn about whisky after university. I'd rather just start full-time in our family business as soon as I can.'

The headmistress frowned. 'Does your father know this?'

Violet grinned. 'Of course he does, Miss Chisholm. We talk about whisky a lot. It's when he's at his most'—she shrugged—'alive.'

'And he's agreed to teach you?'

'He's teaching me now. I've been learning for years. I think he would prefer me to aim for university – simply because it would make him proud – but I just want to be as good as he is.'

'Your father used to be a chemist, am I right?'

Violet nodded, knowing what was coming.

'So *he* went to university to qualify in his field.'

'Not in whisky distilling, though, Miss Chisholm. That he learned by watching others and trying it himself, much later in life. I don't want to wait that long.'

Miss Chisholm gave a long sigh as though she had been bested. 'You know, Violet, I've been doing a lot of reading about this region and, to my surprise and delight, I've learned that some of the earliest and most fearless moonshine producers... er, do you know that's illegal alcohol?' Violet nodded sagely. 'Well, some of the earliest and best whisky makers were women.'

That caught Violet's attention. She paused and stared at her. 'Really?'

Miss Chisholm smiled. 'Truly. You know where your father worked, at John Walker & Sons?'

'Yes.'

'The Cardhu Distillery was originally set up by a farming couple, and Helen, the wife, made moonshine. When alcohol became legal, her daughter-in-law, Elizabeth, through various circumstances, took over the whole company and made amazing single malt whisky. Her product was so good that lots of bigger companies wanted her to sell the business to them, but it wasn't until John Walker & Sons made an offer that she agreed. She was a brilliant woman during the toughest of times, and she blazed a trail for whisky making.'

Violet noted how Miss Chisholm's eyes sparkled with the ferocity of the woman's daring and determination. 'I want to be like her, then,' she admitted, captivated by the story.

'Yes, Violet, I believe you when you say that.'

They smiled at each other.

A knock at the door broke the magic of the moment. 'Come in,' the headmistress called.

Violet was surprised and embarrassed to see Charlie Nash step through the door, his hat in hand. 'Hello, Violet,' her father said in that gentle voice of his. He smiled tentatively at the headmistress, and Violet immediately felt ashamed for making him part of this. He looked so thin and hesitant, not at all the man she remembered from when her mother was alive. 'Miss McKenzie said you wanted to see me?'

'I do. Come in, please, Mr Nash, and take a seat.'

Violet said nothing while her father listened carefully to the story from the headmistress, who neither exaggerated nor toned down the facts. Violet didn't feel she was coming out of this very well, and she looked down when her father cut her an admonishing glance.

'I'm sorry she got into a fight. She's better than that.'

'The loss of her mother is obviously—'

'No, Miss Chisholm,' Violet interrupted, at once apologetic and firm. She knew she was rather young to take this tone with her headmistress, but she had promised herself she would never compromise on this. 'Please don't blame my mother's death for my actions or decisions.'

'Violet,' her father whispered in a plaintive tone.

She gave him a soft glare. 'I am how I am because this is who I am meant to be. Mum told me never to apologise for being Violet Nash. And, Dad, if you were not so broken over losing Mum, you'd be telling Miss Chisholm exactly the same.'

Her mother had been dead three years now. Ellen Nash was a

strong woman who had survived working on the frontline of the war as a nurse in the hospital tents. She'd seen death over and over – just as Violet's dad had – and defied it repeatedly; her only weakness was the 'balloon', as Charlie described it, in her brain, which had, one ordinary day, decided to burst and cause something called a stroke. Her mother was there one moment and the next only her dead body remained. She died instantly, according to the neighbour who had been sharing tea and gossip with her at the time. Ellen had been making baps – Violet's favourite bread – to go with dinner, her beautiful hair tied up in the scarf Violet had given her several birthdays ago.

That vision of Violet's beloved mother – lifeless on the flagstones, her hands still dusted with flour, while her father, white-lipped and speechless, cradled her head in his lap, groaning like a wounded animal – would live with her forever. Violet couldn't even cry back then; it had been too difficult to get her young mind around the fact that her mother was gone.

Now, she watched the adults share a long glance.

'I think that sums it up, Miss Chisholm,' her father said with a sheepish look. 'Violet walks her own path.'

The headmistress nodded. 'Indeed. I apologise, Violet, for mentioning your mother, rest her soul. I'm very sad for both of you, but I now understand that Violet is very determined to follow in your footsteps and become a whisky distiller and blender. She, er... has your support in this regard?'

'One hundred per cent,' he said, nodding.

'Well, then, I do thank you for coming in. Violet, you're on notice now; there will be no fighting in my playground. Use your hands against anyone again and you'll be sent home. Am I clear?'

'It won't happen again, I assure you,' her father hurried to say.

'No, I know. Violet's far too intelligent for that,' Miss Chisholm said, giving her a wise smile.

PART ONE

ONE

KNOCKANDO

July 1935

'When are you going to let me kiss you?'

'Never, Angus,' Violet replied matter-of-factly, inhaling the smell that blew across the barley fields on the soft wind, creating golden waves all around as the tall heads bent in ripples.

'Why not?'

'We grew up next to each other. You're like a brother!' She shoved him as they walked together.

'Och, no! Don't say that.'

'Already said it.' She grinned.

'But I've waited all my life for it.'

Now she laughed aloud. 'You liar! I saw you kissing Morag behind the school sheds.'

'Ach, that was nothing. 'Tis you I love.'

'Angus,' she pleaded.

'I can't help it if you're so pretty.'

'Neither can I,' she said, laughing again; it sounded boastful. 'Fall in love with someone else, please.'

'Is it because of my red hair?' he asked, frowning.

She had to stifle a fresh gust of laughter. 'No, you're very handsome.' He wasn't, but that didn't matter. She adored him all the same.

'Is it my flat feet or freckles?'

'No. Angus,' she began patiently, 'you're lovely in every way. And you're my very best friend—'

'So kiss me!' he said, before she could give him any more reasons not to.

Violet stopped walking. They'd arrived at the turn-off that would send Angus up the hill to his home. She reached for the basket he had been carrying for her. 'Angus, do you like having me as your friend?'

'I want no other,' he said.

'Well, surely you'd hate our friendship to change, wouldn't you?'

'I would hate that,' he replied, looking wounded.

She put a hand on her hip. 'Well, then. It *would* change. A peck on the cheek doesn't change much, but a kiss on the lips changes everything,' she said, hoping her tender tone would get through to him. 'And neither of us wants that. We want to stay friends forever.'

He frowned, unsure.

'Trust me.'

He shrugged. 'Doesn't stop me wanting to kiss your lips instead of your cheek, though.'

She gave him a friendly push. 'Go home, Angus. I'll see you tomorrow.'

'Don't leave me, Violet.'

'I've got to go home to—'

'No, I mean later. Don't leave. Say you'll marry me when you're older, and I won't chase you for a kiss now.'

She paused to summon the patient tone her mother had adopted as she'd told Violet she behaved like a much older person. Her mother had remarked on it so often that Violet believed it. And the truth was, she felt it, aided by her height, which often put her on par with the boys and a head above many of the girls her own age. These days, in the company of her peers, she heard herself speaking like a grown-up: sometimes dismissive or impatient with their antics, often bored. She had long ago accepted that she was different and needed to follow her own path.

'So?' Angus prompted, believing she hadn't heard him.

'Angus, if I'm not going to risk our friendship to kiss you, then I'm certainly not going to marry you.' She didn't add that she couldn't promise to stay in Knockando either, that it was too small and she wanted to explore more of Speyside... Gosh, she wanted to travel around Scotland, England and perhaps even Europe, where both her parents had been during the war. In her imagination that sounded so exciting.

Angus kicked at the dust. 'Maybe you'll change your mind.'

'I won't,' she said.

He ignored her assurance. 'I'll see you tomorrow, then.'

'See you, Angus. Say hello to your mam from me.'

'She worries about you – and your dad. He still seems so sad.'

'I think he is.'

'She feels...' He opened his palms, not knowing how to finish the sentence.

'I know,' Violet said, with a gentle smile. 'But she shouldn't, as I've told her so many times before. It could have happened at any time. And it happened a long time ago, so we all need to get on.' How pragmatic she sounded and yet, just last week, she had caught her father staring into space. She herself still had moments of melancholy that she would never again see her mum's smile or hear her voice.

Angus nodded. 'All right. Bye, then.'

She pretended to pick her nose and flick something at him. He grinned and returned the gesture they'd used since childhood, then began to trudge up the hill, while Violet continued on over the slight rise, towards the small cottage that she and her father now lived in.

Their big dream to forge ahead with their own whisky had been slowed by the death of her mother, and perhaps rightly so.

She couldn't expect her father to go at full speed with their new business venture amid the loss. But she was glad they had followed through and set up the distillery, because it kept them both anchored to a shared pursuit, and busy. While she was at school, he blended his own whisky at their tiny distillery, selling it to one of the biggest whisky operations in Scotland. It was sold under the impressive label, though he and Violet made a pact that one day they'd sell it under their own. She spent every spare moment outside of school learning at his side.

These last two years, they'd found a rhythm that had kept them close and there was a building sense of contentment, as though Ellen had slid fully into the past, allowing them to become more connected to life. From next week, Violet would be a full-time employee of Glen Corbie, their own label. The thought excited her. They could be more productive without school in the way.

She went into the cottage, not for a moment expecting to find her father there, but he was sitting at the scrubbed table, staring out the window with a faraway gaze. Her mood of moments ago, laughing with Angus, fell away. 'Dad?'

'Oh, it's you, Violet.'

She didn't know who else he'd be expecting. 'Are you all right?'

'I think so.' Even his tone sounded distant.

She frowned. 'Why aren't you in the distillery?'

He shrugged and then gave what sounded like a nervous chuckle. 'I don't know.'

'Dad!'

'Hmm?'

'Stop.' She banged the basket onto the table to get his attention. 'What's going on?'

He barely looked up. 'It's over, Violet.'

'What's over?'

'Glen Corbie.'

She blinked. They'd chosen the name together – it meant 'Glen of the Ravens' – and it fitted the landscape and their tiny distillery so perfectly, with their frequent, chatty black visitors. 'Dad, talk to me properly. Why is it over? What is this about?'

He turned and finally focused. 'We can't go on, darling girl. I haven't involved you in any discussion of the finances, but there's nothing to be done.'

'Och!' she said, sounding like Angus now. 'We'll make ends meet.'

'No, Violet, we're way past making ends meet. The bank is not extending any further credit. They want us to sell off what stock we have, and they're talking about selling off our equipment too.'

She blinked, not really understanding the intricacy of bank loans. She did understand that a bank selling off someone's equipment meant no more money could be earned.

It was the death of their dream.

'No! We don't agree, Dad.'

He shook his head. 'I'm afraid we have no further say.'

She hated how beaten down he looked. 'We'll find the money.'

'No. That's your mother talking. I know the reality.'

'Dad, one of the things Mum so loved about you was your fearlessness. You might not talk about the war, but Mum told me a little of your bravery behind enemy lines, and I can't imagine you ever really lose that sort of courage, surely?'

He smiled sadly at her. 'It's not about courage any more. It's about realism – what is actually possible, and what, no matter how hard I try, is not.'

Violet sighed. 'Did the Alexanders go back on the deal you struck?' She knew all about her father's agreement with one of the leading Scotch distributors in the region.

He nodded. 'But even if they hadn't, I think we were headed for gloomy days. I don't blame them for pulling out.'

She sat down heavily opposite her father. 'You don't know that about gloomy days ahead, Dad. This was a truly special blend – we agreed. You said it had the magic.'

He smiled again. 'You know, Violet, I forget too often that you're only fifteen.' He shook his head now. 'I feel embarrassed that I let you taste it. You've been tasting whisky for years, and your mother would be turning in her grave.'

'Don't be daft, Dad. She would be smiling. She always knew I was going to follow in your footsteps, and you can't make Scotch if you can't taste it. Besides, I don't drink it properly... yet!'

'The children's authorities would string me up for sure.'

'They'd see I'm well fed, well cared for, well loved... more than you can say for some of the other students at school.'

'Either way, we don't have the cash now to pay the coopers. No more barrels for us, and without barrels...'

'I know,' she said, not needing to hear it. She reached over to cover his hand where it rested on the small kitchen table. 'But please don't give up, Dad. We'll think of something.'

She watched the dust motes in the late afternoon sunlight, which streamed through the cottage's small windows, dancing around her father's thick head of hair. She imagined them as a magician's aura, sparkling around him like wizardly dust. Their latest whisky blend was distinctive; she might be young, but her palate was already well trained. She'd known it was special from the first sip, so she couldn't understand why the big houses weren't queueing up to buy it. 'Why did they go back on their word?'

Charlie stood, stretched to his full height and let out a sigh. He'd lost weight, she could see; the stress was taking its toll and his strong frame was leaner than usual. 'So many things were against us even before we started,' he said. 'The Great War put so many distilleries out of business – their workers gone, the barley held for the war effort or essentially to feed everyone, and the equipment being used for weapons. This was all before your time, Violet, but a year into the war, the government limited the amount of alcohol being produced, especially near the munitions factories up here, in Carlisle and at Invergordon.'

After a second she realised what he was saying. 'Oh, you mean so the workers weren't drunk on the job?'

'Sobriety – er, to be sober—'

'I know what sobriety means,' she said, hearing the tedium in her tone. 'Sorry,' she added quickly with a smile.

'Being completely focused is important around explosives,' he explained. 'The munitions workplaces were hazardous, and I understand that they had to protect the workforce. Each person – man or woman – was so precious, given so many lives were being spent daily.'

She could hear the emotion in his voice. This was the first time she'd ever heard her father talk about wartime in anything but a very general way.

'I deliberately made no friends,' he continued, 'because we couldn't be sure that the next day one of us wouldn't be lost. It's tough. I remember once, a young lad was so keen to help, perhaps ultimately take on the sniper role I held in my unit. His excitement frightened me. He was a good lad too. I thought if I kept him under my wing, and not going over the top into no-man's-land, running madly at the enemy and firing blind into a blizzard of smoke and explosives and whistling bullets, that I could keep him safe. His name was Hartley; I can't forget it.'

Violet didn't want to hear what was coming. Her father recounted how Hartley had been killed in the night, while he himself had lain in that space between safety and the enemy. Her father had been wounded but had taken the opportunity to feign death so he could get a shot at a German sniper who was taking out too many of his fellow soldiers. Until her mother had died, she'd never seen anything but affection and laughter from her father; she couldn't imagine him killing.

'Anyway, the war crushed us, and crushed the whisky industry in Scotland too. Men came home to no jobs, no income and not enough food to feed their families, and let's not even speak about the Spanish flu that raged around the world claiming the survivors.' He shook his head. 'We don't speak much of the Great War, Violet, because it's so painful. I count myself lucky to have survived with a healthy mind, but so many came home and were never the same.'

She hadn't heard him say so much at one time and wished he'd say more, but then he sighed. It was hurting him to speak of that time, she could see, and it was up to her to steer him away. 'But, Dad, that was a long time ago. Why is it still affecting the industry?'

'It takes a decade at least for the wheel to turn. Just about all the distilleries closed. The last small handful were there simply to supply industrial alcohol and perhaps grain whisky. Malted whisky was fully outlawed until the end of the war. I guess the industry was still finding its way back from that and then the General Strike knocked it back to its knees.'

'The distilleries look busy enough to me,' Violet argued. But, in truth, she didn't know. Her father took care of all the finances, while she concerned herself with making sure they had the necessary stocks and keeping his laboratory tidy, because he tended towards mess and she couldn't bear it. She liked labelling all the bottles they used and her greatest joy was being in their tiny barrel room, which she considered her space. It was a quiet, reflective area, where the oak barrels slumbered, allowing the alcohol within to develop its flavours over the three years required to be called Scotch.

She took her role seriously and often found herself talking to the barrels, each of which she named at the time of its filling. She'd called one Angus, thrilling her friend, who had come in twice to visit it, which made her smile.

For her most recent birthday, her father had ordered an ornate spirit thief to be made just for her. Until that point she had used an old copper tube from her father's first distillery to draw off – or steal, a more fanciful thought – tiny amounts of the spirit to taste and test. But she deserved her own, he felt.

'No cast-offs for you, Violet.'

The thief was fashioned in shiny copper and the top, which she covered with her thumb when dipping the tube into the barrel, was wrought in a beautiful pattern. On the shaft her father had inscribed

For Violet, Mistress of the Barrels. CN x

'You're the only woman right now in Speyside actually making whisky – not that anyone knows it – and, unlike my neighbours, I trust you implicitly. I know you can test the barrels for alcohol and choose the right moment for us to bottle and sell our product. That's why you need your own tools.'

If losing her mother was the saddest day in her memory, then opening that gift was easily the happiest. But now it seemed as though all her learning and skill development had been for naught.

'The strike hurt us all badly,' her father continued now, 'and you didn't have to be an accountant or banker to see that the Depression was coming for us all. And now, all it will take is one more punch in the guts and we'll all crumple.'

'How? Not another war?'

He shook his head. 'Never again, one can only pray. No, Violet, there's misery, but also greed everywhere, with the big buyers forcing us to sell our product cheaply. And a downturn may have nothing to do with us here in Scotland. We'll just be the victims.' He looked at her, grim. 'One more thing going against us, Violet: we're not even Scottish. Perhaps I was silly, thinking it wouldn't be a problem that we're English. I'd hoped that a great product would overcome the prejudice. But I'm still the Sassenach.'

'Dad, you always said the people in our industry take care of each other.'

'They do, yes.' He nodded. 'It's a very good industry in that regard, but when we're all hurting and there's a Scottish family and an English family to choose between...'

'The Alexanders are taking Jimmy's whisky instead?' she asked. Now the knock back made sense.

He shrugged. 'I don't blame them,' he repeated, then raised his head to look at her. 'But I'm tired of fighting, my love. I seem to have done it for a lifetime.'

She searched his features as he paused, looking as though he wasn't sure how much to say.

'I know you don't know much about my past, and your mother was perceptive enough not to pry, but my childhood was a hard one. And it's been one long fight ever since, apart from...' His gaze turned wistful again.

Violet wanted to ask where his thoughts had gone to earn that soft smile, but she stayed silent, considering his worn face. Nearing fifty, he was still a handsome man, but he'd worked himself near skeletal at one point, doing the work of several men, especially during malting, which was physically arduous and repetitious. She helped him in their endeavours as much as she could around school; she was a sponge, soaking up everything he shared.

She'd surprised him one day in the malting house with a random thought. 'Does the water we use affect how our whisky tastes?'

He'd smiled with pleasure. 'I certainly believe so. If the water has passed through heather or perhaps peat bogs in other parts of Scotland, or maybe near a forest, then I believe the water picks up potential flavourings on its journey, which can inspire the final outcome of our whisky.'

'How do you know, though?'

He was always happy to encourage her curiosity when it came to the chemistry of whisky making. 'Well, let's take Champagne. Wherever those grapes are grown, their vines are firmly rooted in the soil, and the flavour of the final wine is influenced by what the French call *terroir*.'

'The earth?' she translated.

'Violet, when did you get so clever? I know I've been teaching you French since childhood, but I don't remember teaching you that word.'

'You know the teacher I really liked, Miss Laurent?'

'Yes, a lovely person, I recall.'

'I hated it when she left. Although she was taking us for English lessons, she used to teach us some French as well, because she was fluent. I loved listening to her speak French, as I loved listening and learning with you. She took a real interest in me because I had a good ear for language. I remember hearing that word and she explained it.'

'French is perhaps the most romantic language to listen to… certainly to my ear.'

'Mine too.' A thought occurred to her. 'I've never asked you before, but did you hear it spoken during the Great War?'

'Yes. We would march through local towns and villages in France.'

'Mum said you were wounded badly behind enemy lines.'

He grimaced slightly, clearly not happy to be reminded. 'Yes, I was. I managed to get myself to relative safety and I was found by a French officer. He took me to a hospital in a place called Reims.'

'Where's that?'

'East of Paris.'

She considered the map of France in her mind. 'And were there vineyards there?' She watched her father blink slowly and wondered why he looked suddenly spooked. 'What's wrong?'

'Nothing.' He tried to smile. 'What were we talking about before we got sidetracked?'

'We weren't sidetracked. We were talking about terroir and Champagne. So I asked about the vineyards in France where you found yourself.'

'Yes, um, there were beautiful vineyards – exquisite, in fact – producing the three major grape varieties used in the making of Champagne at a place called Épernay, which is where all the famous brands call home.'

'Like all of us whisky makers here in Speyside?'

'Yes. The war took a terrible physical toll on their vines and their produce… and especially their people.'

'Who looked after you?'

'Violet, we'd better get on with—'

'Dad, I know nothing about this time. I want to understand. I only have you, and I want to know about your life. After all, you know everything about mine.'

He gave a sad laugh. 'That's the way of parents and children, Violet.'

'Tell me. I like these stories. They help me to learn, they make me want to see places like you have.'

'Well, I hope one day you do see Épernay, because you'll fall in love.'

'Did you?'

He stared at her open-mouthed.

'With Épernay,' she prompted. 'Did you fall in love with it?'

He cleared his throat. 'Yes... yes, I did. I think it was because of my time there that I decided to one day make something delicious with my science skills, rather than make something that could hurt people, like mustard gas.'

'Did you learn about making Champagne, then?'

'I did. While I recovered from my wounds, I learned from one of the best Champagne makers in the region.'

'What was his name?'

He cleared his throat. 'It was a champenoise, actually – a woman. Her name was... is... Sophie Delancré.'

Violet noticed how curiously uncomfortable her father had become, even though he'd answered her questions. She put it down to him being reluctant to speak about his past, but it was something more than that, though she couldn't put her finger on it.

'I'm glad it was a woman you learned from,' she replied. 'I'm going to be as good with whisky as she is with Champagne, so that people will say Violet Nash is one of the best Scotch makers in the region.'

She watched a smile break across his face. 'Violet, they're going to say you're the best Scotch maker in all of Scotland... the best whisky maker in the world.'

'Thanks, Dad,' she replied, feeling the familiar fizz of joy at his praise.

'Now, where on earth were we?'

'That water and the earth it flows through can affect the taste.'

'Exactly! Well done. I'm glad you pay attention. Now, I'm not suggesting it dominates the flavour, but I firmly believe that every influence, from water course and source to the season we malt in, is important to the complexity of the liquor. The malting really is the key to how the final whisky emerges.'

'Right. So what does our water taste of?'

He picked up a hoe and began to work on the rows. 'It comes down from the Cairngorms Well at Moray, one of Scotland's highest natural mountain springs. It flows over hard rock to become soft and low in minerals. It's perfect. One of the reasons Speyside whisky is so admired.'

Now, sitting at the table in their cottage, she realised she'd been musing for long enough to allow her father to lose himself in his thoughts. Violet cleared her throat, bringing herself back to their dilemma. 'So what are we going to do, Dad?'

'Hmm?'

'If we've run out of money, what shall we do?'

'Well,' he said, as though enlivened with fresh energy, 'we're going to close Glen Corbie, as I said.'

'Do we really have to?'

'You know we do.'

'And what then?'

'You'll go back and finish school to O-levels, perhaps even consider doing your A-levels to give yourself some time. I'll try to find some work with Glenfiddich or one of the other major distilleries.'

She could see by the set of his mouth that he'd resigned himself to a future he would hate. 'That is everything I do not wish to do,' she said firmly.

'Give me a better idea, then, Violet, because I can't see another way for us. We need time to, I don't know, reset ourselves. Decide what comes next.'

Her lips pressed together firmly as she ran her mind across what felt like a rather final decision about her future, one she didn't support and would frankly refuse. But her father was right; she needed to give him an alternative. He watched her, almost amused

– or was it fear she could see? She reached for the only salvation she could think of.

'Dad, let's pack.'

'Pardon?'

'We're going to London.'

'London? Whatever for?'

'I want to talk to my grandparents.'

She saw him make the leap in his mind. 'No, Violet. He's not going to give me money. Your grandfather doesn't even like me.'

'It's not you specifically he doesn't like; he has just never appreciated that his daughter and granddaughter were taken far away from them.'

'Well, he was right to be unhappy. His daughter died, and his granddaughter is now in danger of having few choices in life.'

'Both of those statements are rubbish, Dad. Mum would have died in London in their house if we were still there, or wherever she was.'

'But they'd have had her longer.'

'And,' Violet continued, ignoring his remark, 'I don't need others to give me choices.'

He shook his head. 'I don't want his money.'

'I know. It's not for you, though. It's for me. Now get packed. We'll take tomorrow morning's train.'

TWO
LONDON, ENGLAND

July 1935

Charlie had watched Violet thoughtfully parcel up a couple of bottles of their whisky for her grandad, and some of the bulbs that grew near Ellen's grave for her grandmother. They had tried to keep up annual visits since Ellen's death, but lately that had become harder with the heavy workload and lack of funds, and it had been at least two years since they'd travelled to London.

But Violet getting to skive off school for a couple of days was exciting, he imagined, and the time away to think clearly would be good for him. They'd shut the doors on Glen Corbie and ruthlessly walked away for a few days: a dress rehearsal for when he closed the doors for the final time in a few weeks.

They were now seated inside King's Cross station, taking a pause after a meeting with Violet's grandparents that had gone worse than either of them had anticipated.

Anne's expression had remained wooden during the visit, but Charlie suspected this was due to her illness rather than a particular attitude. She did emerge from whatever mist she lived in when Violet gave her the bulbs.

'Are these Ellen's?' she asked, surprising them.

'Yes, they are. Er, Dad dug them up last night for you.'

That was a fib. Violet had dug them up, but he could see what she was trying to achieve.

'Ellen grew the most beautiful flowers,' Charlie said.

'She was our beautiful girl,' Anne replied and then stood – Charlie thought it was to fetch a plant pot, but then she stopped, looking lost.

Ellen's parents had never recovered from their only child's early death, and Anne was now sliding into a world of her own; they called it senility. Charlie believed the shock of losing her daughter had destroyed something inside her, and she'd begun to slip away from reality. Ellen's father, meanwhile, had turned to anger. Retired, with nothing to hold them together except their despair, they seemed to move from day to day in their separate lonely worlds.

Dennis blamed him for Ellen's death, Charlie knew, but this was unreasonable and all raw emotion. The doctor in charge at the hospital had explained Ellen's ailment to Dennis, calling her parents in England while Charlie was there; the doctor had dismissed any suggestion that her death could have been avoided or had anything to do with geography.

'No, sir. No. You see, it was like a time bomb ticking down. No one knew when the timer would hit nought. Your daughter had lived with this potential killer probably since she was born. And the fact that she got past forty without it taking her life is a miracle in itself.' He'd listened and then responded. 'No, it would not have mattered if she was nearer to a hospital. The aneurysm is a force unto itself, sir. It chooses its own timeline and we have no control. There was, I gather, not even a sign that there was a problem. No dizzy spells, no headaches, no fainting. Ellen was a healthy, middle-aged woman. Her body behaved exactly as it should have until the moment the aneurysm decided it would take control.'

He'd waited and listened, glancing at Charlie with a soft nod. 'It is a mystery, yes. Affects more people than most of us know – it's where the saying dropping dead comes from. Forgive me for that bluntness, but it does give a very good description of what occurs. Your daughter would have had no idea.' Another pause. 'Yes, indeed. And I am deeply sorry for your loss.'

Charlie had tried to be compassionate in conversations with Ellen's parents, because he knew more than anyone what a loss it had been for them all. But it seemed Dennis was still blaming Charlie for all his pain, even eight years on.

'I'll fetch a box from Grandad's shed for those bulbs until you have time to plant them,' Violet jumped in, clearly sensing Charlie didn't know what to do. 'You sit down, Grandma.'

'You'll need to dig around at the back, Violet,' Dennis warned. 'I've been meaning to tidy up as your grandma keeps pottering around in there and moving things.'

Violet gave a smile and headed outside, leaving Charlie alone with Dennis and Anne, who had sat down again. Patting her hand, the older man wore the grim expression of someone who felt powerless. Charlie realised he had probably worn much the same look himself in the trenches, but no one could see it because of all the dirt and, besides, everyone had looked the same: beaten down and filled with despair and a sort of constant bafflement that this could happen. He fully understood the older man's mood.

Charlie searched for something to say. Without Violet's presence, the room felt hideously empty.

Dennis spoke first. 'Well, I suppose thanks are in order for bringing Violet to see us, Charlie,' he said. 'It's been a while.'

Charlie ignored the barb. 'She's making us all proud. She's her mother all over again. All of Ellen's smart, practical intelligence and wit.'

'But she looks like you,' her grandfather said, almost in accusation, and Charlie tried not to notice his grimace.

'I can't see it myself,' he said, affecting a self-deprecating tone, feeling stupid for lying in order to please Dennis and let him hold on to his daughter somehow. 'I think she looks like you, actually.' It was a stretch, but Dennis attempted a smile, looking slightly surprised.

Charlie was well aware that Violet was the spit of him, and he couldn't help feeling privately proud of that. As an orphan, he felt that one of the greatest favours he could do himself was to leave a small part of himself on this earth after he was gone. Make his mark. He'd thought maybe his Scotch would leave his name somewhere, but he had begun to believe that Violet would be his single great achievement.

She was his legacy.

'Has she finished school?' Dennis asked.

'Any minute. She doesn't want to go on to university, so she sees no point in taking any more exams. It's Violet's decision, and I won't push her, much as her mother and I had high hopes she would continue her education. She's certainly smart enough for university.'

'Are you saying she won't go because she'd rather make alcohol?' It sounded accusatory.

'Er, well, whisky – particularly Scotch – is so much more than simply alcohol. There is a chasm of distinction.' Charlie couldn't help the admonition. 'Your granddaughter is moving in an industry that can only grow and she with it; any major distillery would give her an opportunity when they realise what she's capable of. I've already begun talking to some of the bigger establishments about her potential. And it would be especially attractive to them as she's still so young. And, while I won't say she's the first of her kind, because Scotch is carried on the shoulders of some very strong and brilliant women, I will say that there is no modern woman today distilling and blending Scotch as Violet is. She is a modern trailblazer, and I would hazard that few men could hold a candle to her knowledge, even at fifteen. What she lacks in experience, she makes up for in a magical ability to taste and blend. I think Violet will be a leading light in her field and inspire a new generation of women. She just needs the opportunity.'

Dennis made a scoffing sound. 'Charlie, this is *your* dream for her. Not Ellen's. She hoped she'd become a nurse, too, get all the qualifications she never had.'

Charlie forced his rising hackles down. There was no point in antagonising a desperate and heartbroken father, and Charlie knew he would be inconsolable if Violet were snatched away from him. 'You know, Dennis, Violet left London at four and a half years old. She started her schooling in Scotland and spent the next five years working out how much she didn't enjoy spelling and arithmetic, and how much she did enjoy learning about what I do. She doesn't even know it, but she has a natural inclination for science. It was her mother who first said Violet was going to follow in my footsteps, no matter how good she became at her times tables.'

'But if she becomes a qualified nurse, her working life is assured.'

'Is that all you'd want for Violet? That she has secure work?'

'A vocation!'

'If I knew she was interested, I'd at least dream bigger and think medicine. As a nurse she'd still be answerable to doctors and surgeons, doing all the hard work with patients while they lorded it over them. If she were alive, Ellen would tell you that nursing is not what she wanted for Violet. I would hazard she'd have expected her daughter to go into medicine.'

'Well,' Dennis spluttered, 'if you're saying I'm thinking small—'

'I'm not saying that. But I think you're a man in grief, with a daughter taken too young and a wife slipping away into dementia, and you resent the fact that your daughter married a soldier with few prospects, who carried her and your grandchild off to Scotland and now makes whisky. And Violet wants to follow in her father's footsteps rather than benefiting from her grandfather's wisdom, which is to get a job and feel very happy to be employed.'

'How dare you!'

'Dennis, I've tried. Anne,' he appealed, turning to her, but she didn't even make eye contact. 'I've tried to absorb all the anguish you've levelled at me since we first met. I was never good enough for Ellen, in your eyes, and yet I certainly was for her... That's what should have mattered to you. All I did was love her.'

'Is that so?'

Charlie blinked. 'Meaning?'

'I overheard Ellen saying to her mother that she'd never match up to your great love. Some woman in France.' Dennis spoke the words as though they sounded dirty in his mouth.

Charlie was speechless. He opened his mouth to respond but nothing came.

Dennis hadn't finished. 'She loved you so much that she was happy to be the runner-up, she said, because you were married to her and you had a child with her and she knew you would be loyal. She said that in your own way you loved her.'

'What?' Charlie couldn't believe what he was hearing.

'She said to her mother that she had enough love for both of you. Broke my heart, Nash, to think my daughter was playing second fiddle to some French tart!'

Violet chose that moment to return to the room, the smile of triumph at finding the perfect box for the bulbs fading at her lips. 'What's going on?'

Charlie had to swallow his rage and plead to the gods that she hadn't overheard any of that. 'Dennis,' he said quietly, 'I don't think you and I have much more to say to one another. Anything we risk now is going to be ugly, and I'd rather we didn't go there... for Violet's sake.' He found the grace to hold out his hand. 'Let's shake and say farewell and that, unless our paths have to cross, they won't.'

The older man snorted. 'Suits me, so long as we see Violet. She's all I care about.'

'Right.'

'Grandad! Dad! What's happening? Don't do this, please,' Violet begged.

'You're the beneficiary of our wills, Violet, my girl. But he'— Dennis jabbed a finger towards Charlie—'doesn't get a penny.'

Charlie just nodded, unable to think of anything helpful to say in that moment, and the two men shared a firm, final handshake.

And that was it. Violet bade a tearful farewell to her grandparents, kissing Anne's cheek, and they left, making their way back to the station and taking two trains back to King's Cross, where they now sat in silence.

Charlie had left behind yet another chapter of his life, and it felt to him as though he was closing the book on Ellen as well. She'd always be in his heart, but there was something painfully true about what Dennis had accused him of, and it was needling him. He needed to think, take stock, breathe out.

'I'm sorry, Violet,' he said now. 'I'm sorry that it all went so wrong.'

'I'm ashamed for them. Grandad shouldn't speak to you like that,' she said. 'What happened? I'll sort it out with him.'

'There's nothing to sort. You stay close with him. I don't matter, and I want nothing from him.'

They fell into silence again, punctuated only by the announcements for one train or another. He really didn't know why he had brought them here. Their train didn't leave until tomorrow and they had nowhere to stay tonight. But it felt familiar, plus it was the most affordable place to get a cup of tea and think about their next move. He led Violet across the concourse to a lonely table outside the café, which was cramped and noisy, and surrounded by smokers.

He didn't smoke, which was an oddity, he knew, but for blending he needed his palate clean and unaffected by the effects of nicotine. He ordered a pot of tea for each of them, while Violet held her tongue; he could all but hear the wheels of her mind turning. He knew she was considering the situation before she acted.

Some minutes later, sipping from a cup, she spoke at last. 'Are you going to tell me what went wrong while I was out of the room?'

He shrugged. 'The usual problem. I was never good enough for your mother, according to him. It all just boiled up.'

She frowned. 'What did he mean by *French tart*?'

'What else did you hear?' he asked, feeling desperately disappointed.

'Just that. He all but yelled it.'

'He was being vicious, Violet. Obviously he needed to strike out and hurt me. He was referring to someone I knew in nineteen eighteen, before your mother and I got together, before you were born.'

'How does Grandad know about her?'

Charlie shrugged. 'Oh, I don't know. Your mother probably made a joke about soldiers and French girls during the war,' he lied. 'You can see he's hurting, and I think he just needed to hurt me too.'

'That's not fair, though.'

'No. But it's human nature. Later he'll see how unreasonably he's behaved, though I'm not going back there again, Violet. But you must not lose touch with them. They're your blood.'

'I'm really sorry, Dad. It was my idea to come. I thought I could persuade Grandad to invest in our distillery.'

'One day, when we open it again, it'll all be yours and you can ask him then.'

'Well, Dad, that would mean you'd be gone, and he would surely be gone too, so I don't want to think about such a time.'

'I shouldn't have said that. I just mean—'

'I know what you mean. But let's just forget that idea.' She sighed. 'We'll need to think of a new way to save ourselves.'

Charlie was twirling his cup, staring into the cooling, tarry brown of his tea, when a voice called out his name. A face that was both familiar and terrifying appeared in front of him. He was suddenly dragged back more than fifteen years to squalid conditions and a great deal of fear and loathing.

'Captain Nash, it is you, isn't it?'

The man's name erupted in Charlie's mind. 'Bob Bailey?'

'Yes, sir! Thank you for remembering me, Captain.'

'Just Charlie now, Bob. How nice to see you. You look taller – is that possible?'

The man laughed. 'Maybe I stand taller these days, sir. I have a good job, and I'm married with two little ones.'

'Oh, congratulations. That any of us made it out of there is a miracle. Um, Bob, this is my daughter, Violet.'

'Violet.' The man turned to her and smiled. 'How lovely to meet you. Are you aware of the hero your father was to all of us?'

'No,' she freely admitted. 'Dad doesn't speak about the war.'

'Well, we all looked up to him and that marvellously sharp eye of his.'

Charlie had told her he'd been a sniper, and he felt her own keen eye as she turned to consider him. 'Here, join us, won't you, Bob?' he said hurriedly, not wanting the attention.

'I will, for a minute or so, thank you, sir.'

'Can I order you a cup of tea?'

'No, no, I was just seeing someone off. I need to get back to work.'

'Where do you work now?' Charlie asked.

'I'm general manager at the Great Midland Hotel, sir.'

Charlie looked at him in surprise. It was so genuine, he didn't have time to hide it. 'Forgive me,' he said. 'I—'

Bob laughed. 'Don't worry, I didn't think I had it in me either, sir. But I grew up in those trenches. I think we all did. I was twenty-one when the war began, and I was determined to live a full life. I made a promise that if I survived the war, I'd go back to school and make a career for myself. I went to hospitality college, and I've spent the last fifteen years or so working in hotels.' He smiled. 'I was good at it, sir, and I climbed the ranks. Maybe it was the training in the trenches. I got some lucky opportunities and...'

'No, Bob. I think we make our luck.' Charlie glanced at Violet, who'd heard the sentiment from him often enough. 'Well, I hope you're not offended if I say I feel very proud of you.'

'Not at all, sir. I'm thrilled to see you. What do you do these days, if you don't mind me asking?'

Charlie grinned. 'I make whisky, with my daughter at my side. She's damn near as good at it as I am, and damn good Scotch it is too, although the industry is suffering for so many reasons at present.'

'Whisky – good grief. That's exciting.' He cut Violet a look. 'And very impressive, Violet – but you look so young.'

'I'm fifteen. Dad's given me good training.'

'Oh, I don't know about that. She seemed to grasp it almost from birth. I spend a lot of time staring at barley,' Charlie admitted. 'I, er, lost my wife – Violet's mother – so we're a tight team of two.'

'I'm very sorry to hear that.' Bob shifted topics quickly. 'Are you working while in London, sir, or is this a break?'

'We came to see relatives,' Charlie answered, 'but I suppose having some thinking time away from home and work is extremely good for the soul.'

The younger man looked worried. 'You looked very thoughtful when I saw you. I feel badly for interrupting you both.'

'No, please, I'm thrilled you stopped.'

'I suppose you're both headed back now, are you, sir?'

Charlie shook his head. 'No, to tell the truth, we're not leaving until tomorrow, but I rather like the anonymity of the train station and they do a decent strong cuppa.'

'So much for anonymity with me hanging around.' Bob grinned. 'Are you staying nearby?'

'I was thinking that it was time to go and find a room for the night.'

Bob blinked. 'Captain Nash, it would be my absolute pleasure to extend a night's stay – two nights if you need – at the Great Midland, sir, to you and your lovely daughter.'

'Good heavens, no. That's not why—'

'I know that, sir, but I can't have you both staying anywhere else but my fine establishment. I'd consider it an honour for you to experience it, and it is a very inadequate way for me to thank you for keeping me safe in those trenches. Your rifle was our last line of defence, sir. Without you...' He trailed off, his face solemn. 'Please', sir, and Violet, walk with me back to the hotel. Spend the evening as my guests. It truly is my pleasure.'

'Oh, say yes, Dad, please,' Violet urged with shining eyes, grinning alongside Bob. 'I've never stayed at a hotel.'

Charlie looked back at him, slightly flustered. 'I don't know what to say.'

'Nothing to say, sir,' Bob said, reaching down to grab their two small cases. 'Come on.'

Violet was at Bob's side in a blink. Charlie stood. 'On one condition.'

His companion waited with a question in his expression.

'No more *sir*. I am just Charles Nash now. Call me Charlie, as everyone does.'

Charlie and Violet soon found themselves being escorted beneath the colonnade of arches and across the tessellated tiles in the vast entrance hall of the Great Midland Hotel of St Pancras. Bob organised their check-in and showed them to the drawing room.

'We're preparing your room, so please have a drink and relax, and I'll have one of our staff find you shortly,' Bob said. 'And sir?' He won a glare from Charlie. 'Er, Mr Nash,' he settled on. 'I am your host in every sense. Please, both of you, enjoy your meals and drinks as my guest.' He gave a small bow and stepped away before Charlie could even form a word of rebuttal.

And so here they were, sitting beneath two great chandeliers in an elegant hotel drawing room, among hushed voices and attentive waiters.

'Dad,' Violet said, her voice filled with awe. 'This is incredible.'

He actually laughed. 'Someone's smiling on us, Violet. Let's enjoy ourselves, shall we? Forget all the bad stuff for a day.'

'It's a pity we couldn't share this with Mum.'

'She's watching and smiling, darling girl. One day, Violet, you'll live well and feel very at ease in places like this.'

'Do you think so?'

'I know it. Come on, let's order something.'

After considering the options, he ordered a pot of coffee for two.

'Really?' she asked, sounding flabbergasted.

'You're so grown up now, why not? Given that you taste

whisky for a living, I think you're well past warm milk or hot cocoa, don't you?'

She nodded vigorously.

'Besides, I don't imagine you'd get a pot of coffee like this just anywhere. You might as well taste a good cup and see if you like it.'

Her eyes shone. 'Oh, I'll love it, I'm sure.'

The concierge team found them half an hour later to say that their room was ready, with their suitcases waiting upstairs. Charlie crooked an elbow and Violet grinned, taking his arm as they followed the porter. Although the young man gestured towards the modern lift, Charlie nodded at the majestic, sweeping wrought-iron staircase that curved its way up the floors, in wrought iron.

'Let's savour the moment,' he suggested.

'We'll take the stairs,' Violet said, smiling back at the young man, who looked almost disappointed to see them leave his side.

Their footsteps fell silently on the plush, thick carpet as they ascended, and Charlie felt his mood shifting from dark to hopeful the higher they climbed. The chance to stay in a fancy hotel was akin to a gift from the gods for both of them. It gave him an indulgent setting to carefully think through their next steps, and he felt pleased that Violet had something exciting to enjoy – she deserved some lightness and fun in her life.

THREE

Their room was huge, and although there were no private facilities, Charlie was very happy to relax in the communal bathtub down the hall, particularly as it was not especially busy in the middle of the day. While Violet used the ladies' facilities, he sat on his bed with damp hair and a fresh set of clothes, wondering at his luck in stumbling across Bob Bailey.

Charlie had spent the last dozen years deliberately blocking any memories of the war. It wasn't easy; they crept up and could strike at the oddest of moments, and it was worst when his mind was relatively empty, perhaps involved in a repetitive task, like his work in the malting shed. Then images and sounds of the war arrived in full colour, at full volume, and it was all he could do not to shake. It was during those times that he'd taught himself to leap in his mind to Épernay, where he had found not only peace and healing but love. The memory of Sophie Delancré – her perfume, her smile, her teasing – could still undo him. Though when he thought of her, it made him feel like such a traitor to Ellen.

Dennis's hostility and accusation simmered angrily in Charlie's mind. Referring to Sophie as a 'French tart' was offensive, but perhaps Dennis had been right to criticise him. After all, he was thinking of Sophie right now rather than his dead wife. He banished her and filled his mind with Violet instead.

She was the one who mattered now. He needed to safeguard her future somehow, while their present felt so desperately threatened. Closing Glen Corbie was certainly on the cards. He couldn't see a way to avoid it.

Violet came blustering back into the room. 'That bathroom is enormous! I met a lovely lady who offered to take me shopping. When I said I didn't have any money to spend, she suggested something she called window shopping instead.' She grinned. 'It sounded fun.'

'You should go,' Charlie encouraged.

'No, Dad, I want to be with you. Or would you prefer to be alone?'

She knew his ways all too well. He shook his head. 'No, it's not that. But I was thinking of taking a stroll.'

'Go ahead. I have to dry my hair and get into some fresh clothes, and then I thought I might write to Angus on this lovely hotel paper,' she said, gesturing towards the desk. 'I'll never get another chance to be so fancy.'

Charlie found a smile. 'Oh, don't bet on it. All right. Give me three quarters of an hour,' he said, glancing at his watch. 'We can think about an early meal. We might even see Bob Bailey again to thank him... have a drink together.'

'Perfect. And take your time. We should send Bob some of our Scotch. He might wish to stock it,' Violet said in a wry tone.

'Always thinking broadly, Violet, well done.'

Charlie left, feeling brighter suddenly. The thought of this grand hotel ordering a year's supply of Glen Corbie's finest was a lovely notion.

Violet had also been thinking about her remark, and wasted no time acting on it. Dressing fast and with her hair still damp, she left the room, grateful that the young porter had given them two sets of keys.

'Miss Nash, how can I help you?' the man at the front desk asked, his voice full of charm.

'Is Mr Bob Bailey still here?'

'I saw him just a moment ago,' he replied with a smile.

'I would like to talk to him, please.'

'Er…'

'He's a friend of my father,' she pressed, and then told a small fib. 'We're meeting him later, but I have something I'd like to say to him before then.'

'May I pass on a message on your behalf?'

She shook her head. 'No, I need to speak with him myself, if he's free, please.'

The man's smile faltered; he clearly wasn't used to being spoken to quite so confidently by a teenage girl. 'Let me ring his office.' He picked up the handset.

'Thank you,' she said, smiling sweetly.

'Ah, Jennifer,' he said. 'I have a guest, a Miss Nash, here at the front desk, who is asking to speak with Mr Bailey.' There was a pause. 'All right, thank you. I'll let her know.' The man replaced the telephone. 'Mr Bailey said he'll be out here shortly, if you don't mind waiting.' He gestured towards the chairs nearby.

'Thank you,' she repeated, surprised. She had anticipated a polite excuse.

Bob Bailey was standing in front of her before she'd had time to arrange her skirt neatly. 'Hello, Violet. Is everything all right with the room? Is your father—'

'It's wonderful, Mr Bailey, thank you, and my father has gone for a stroll. I wonder if you might spare me a few minutes?'

He looked at her quizzically but didn't pause. 'Of course. Let's go over there.' He pointed towards a small sofa on the far side of the reception area. 'Away from the hustle and bustle.' Once seated, he regarded her, full of interest. 'How can I help?'

'May I be honest?'

'I'd like it no other way, Violet.'

She liked him so much for not treating her like a child. 'Thank you. My father has fallen on hard times – the Depression, as I'm sure you're aware.'

He nodded. 'It's a profound thing. No one is left unscathed.'

'My father told you he makes whisky?'

It was rhetorical but Bailey answered all the same, his face lighting with pleasure. 'He did.'

'It's incredible Scotch, actually, and I know you'll consider me biased, but everyone in the industry around Speyside tells me Dad is a genius blender.'

'Is that so,' Bailey remarked, his forehead creasing with interest.

'Before the war Dad was an industrial chemist – did you know that?' Violet asked.

He shook his head.

'Mum said the company he worked for was asked by the British government to make mustard gas after—'

Bailey held up his hand. 'I was there, Violet. And I'm not at all surprised to hear this.'

'So Dad joined up because he refused to use his skills to make something evil that could hurt or kill people, Mum said. He preferred to either die on the battlefield for his country or fire bullets at the enemy, which was a more honest way of killing, in his opinion.'

'Your father was a deadeye. He saved so many lives, mine included.'

She felt proud of her dad. She swallowed, then continued. 'After the war he decided he would use his chemistry background to make something people could enjoy. He took us to Scotland and found he was very good at distilling and blending whisky. But he wanted to be part of the whole process, so he farmed barley as well. He was good at it, and it meant that by the time he was ready to risk starting his own distillery, he could use his own barley, which he had carefully tended. That way he could be sure the liquor was of the highest quality.'

Bailey nodded. 'He is extraordinary. So did he open his own distillery?'

'He did. It's called Glen Corbie, and I'm learning from him.'

'Then you're even more extraordinary!' He chuckled. 'So tell me how I can help.'

There was no point in hedging, she realised. 'Dad is being forced to close. His product is beautiful, but being English, he's finding that the Scottish whisky makers are favouring their own while everyone's hurting.'

'Because he's a Sassenach?'

'Exactly!' She was thrilled he knew the term. 'So...' Here it was. *Do it, Violet,* she urged herself. *Nothing ventured, nothing gained,* as her mother used to say. She had been full of those inspirational phrases. 'Er... I was wondering if the Great Midland Hotel had a need for whisky?'

He smiled, understanding, and she sensed some admiration. 'Our guests consume a great deal of whisky, from tots on a cold night to a lot more for celebrations. We tend to stock the better-known labels.'

'Glenfiddich, Glenmorangie, Johnnie Walker...' She listed them to show she understood their worth.

'You're wondering if I'd stock Glen Corbie?'

Her eyes shone. 'A few bottles, perhaps. It would help.'

Bailey nodded. 'How many barrels is your father handling?'

Barrels? She had been hoping he might order half-a-dozen bottles. She kept a straight face. 'At the moment, he has three standard casks that will yield, say, three hundred bottles, depending on evaporation. And we have one quarter cask – also oak – that will give maybe seventy bottles. We call the evaporation the "angel's share", which I've always found very romantic. But then whisky *is* romantic, because it holds memories dear, bringing them back to the person sipping with the most vivid clarity.'

'Good grief, Violet. You're a born saleswoman. You know your stuff. I'm impressed. Have you had a hand in these barrels?'

She gave a proud smile. 'Yes. And I'm learning to blend under Dad's guidance. May I send you a bottle of ours to taste, perhaps? Maybe we can—'

'You can put Great Midland's name on the quarter cask,' Bailey cut in happily. 'We'll take all that it bottles.'

Her mouth fell open. 'Really?'

'Yes, you've sold me. I like the idea of supporting a small artisan distillery, and I am enamoured by the romance you've sold me regarding the Glen Corbie product. And frankly, Violet, this is a tiny thank-you for all that your father did and all that he risked for us. It's my pleasure, truly.' He held out his hand. 'Nice doing business with you, Miss Nash.'

She began laughing, holding back tears. 'Thank you. I... we'll get it bottled and sent.'

'Send me the paperwork as soon as you get back to Scotland. We'll pay upfront and in total. I'm sure that helps?'

'More than you can imagine.'

'And, Violet, I have colleagues in the hotel industry. I'll be glad to talk to them, so maybe send down some sample bottles too, and I'll see what I can do about shifting some more for you.'

It was too much. She flung her arms around Bob Bailey and hugged him hard.

Back in the hotel room, filled with fresh energy from her success, Violet grasped her father's fountain pen, which he'd left on the desk. It had been a gift from her mother, his name engraved on its shaft. She unscrewed the lid, then lifted a thick sheet of embossed hotel paper and let the ink flow onto its absorbent surface as the gold nib scratched the first words.

Dear Angus,

I'm writing to you on this very posh paper with nothing important to say except that I could get used to staying in fine hotels like this.

She paused to think about what to tell him that might make him smile. As her thoughts drifted, so did her gaze.

Her attention alighted on some hotel pamphlets, neatly stacked on a display holder, with information on tours out of London by train, as well as various museums and galleries promoting their attractions. Then her gaze caught on a pamphlet that looked slightly dog-eared, out of place. Tugging at it, she realised it was not only tatty but slightly torn. Perhaps the cleaning staff had tidied it into the holder, not realising a rogue pamphlet had been left behind by a previous guest.

`The call of the stars to British men and women!`

was proudly emblazoned across the front.

`Men for the land, women for the home, employment guaranteed, good wages, plenty of opportunity.`

Violet stared at the pamphlet featuring the Southern Cross and opened it to read more. *The stars which shine over Australia the land of opportunity.* She couldn't help but notice a comma was missing in that phrase but, even so, there was something stirring about it. She felt in the moment as though it were speaking directly to her.

Had her mother, watching over her, steered her attention to this pamphlet?

'I was meant to see this,' she muttered to herself, turning the patriotic red, blue and white paper in her hand. Someone else had read it too, going by its worn state. *But they left it behind*, a thought echoed in her mother's voice.

This was a sign, Violet fancied. An omen of the future. Her father had been a traveller. He'd had adventures.

She wanted to find out more.

Just at that moment, her father turned the key in the door and entered the room. 'Hello, beautiful.'

'Ah, you're back.' She stood, the news of her sale wanting to burst from her. 'Dad, guess what?'

'You look very excited, so just tell me.'

She did.

'You organised a meeting with Bob Bailey?' he asked, sounding incredulous.

'The idea came to me after we spoke, and I thought why not? I know you wouldn't want to ask because you're too proud, and you're too modest to let anyone else know how good you are.'

Her father looked amused. 'And?'

She actually jumped on the spot with glee. 'He's taking the quarter barrel.'

His brows shot up. 'Seriously?'

'I didn't push him, Dad. I just told him what we had and that he could rely on it.' She didn't mention telling Bailey about her father's struggles.

'But that's sixty-five bottles,' he said, sounding awed.

'Maybe seventy. But there's more.' Before he could ask, she told him about the sample bottles. 'I think he means it, Dad. We might not have to give our whisky to the other distilleries for a song. We might be able to sell it at a fair price down south.'

He looked impressed. 'I would love to be able to say we've found a buyer in England.'

'Even if we shift one more barrel before we close, it will feel satisfying.'

'Violet, this is wonderful, but I need to talk to Bob myself. It's not that I don't trust you, but I can't leave our business entirely to a teenager – even though you're better at it than I am.' He laughed. 'I'm incredibly proud of you. Just the quarter barrel is worth a good sum to us. It will keep us going for a little while longer – buy us some time – and if he really can help us move the rest... even half of it, then we don't have to make any rushed decisions.' He hugged her, still dressed for the outdoors.

She could smell smoke and metal on him from the city. 'Dad?' Violet began, releasing herself from his hold.

'Yes?' he said, removing his coat and putting his hat on the hook behind the door.

'What do you know about Australia?'

'Whatever makes you ask that?' he said, looking at her, amused but puzzled.

She grinned. 'You tell me first.'

'Well, er, I met plenty of Australians during the war. What a grand gang they were – always so optimistic. And what great-looking lads – strong, healthy, still bronzed beneath the dirt of war from their endless sunshine.'

'They sound wonderful.'

'They truly were, Violet. So many of them I met were farmers' sons, or drovers, as they called themselves, or journeymen shearers, with powerful shoulders and a seemingly tireless humour. I had nothing but admiration for the Australian brigades, who looked so strong compared to us smaller-built English soldiers. But, as invincible as they seemed, they died as easily as we did,' he admitted. 'The bullets and artillery did not spare them.'

Violet nodded. 'What else do you know about the country?'

'Australia, the continent, is vast. You only have to look at it on a scale map to see just how big it is. The men used to talk about endless skies and their enormous sheep farms – stations, they called them – that stretched for thousands of miles.'

Violet was intrigued. 'It's hard to imagine that when you think of our tiny farms in Scotland.'

'Actually, after the war ended, I worked with what was called a clearing party,' her father continued. 'Our job was essentially to follow in the wake of the retreating enemy and find our fallen men, mark their graves, retrieve anything we could to return to their loved ones. Anyway, I met a Tasmanian. He was a sergeant who'd stayed on as I did to help with finding and marking as many fallen Anzacs as he could. That's what they nicknamed the Australia and New Zealand force,' he explained. 'Lawrie Greene was his name, and everyone called him Greeny. And when Greeny talked about his home, I have to say I felt an envy, but what he described also sounded a lot like Scotland. It was a place called Richmond. He was a farmer's lad; they grew cereals.'

'Sounds English.'

'I think a lot of the towns were named for English towns.'

'Any whisky there?' Violet asked.

'I don't know. Didn't sound like there was. Plenty of breweries, though. Curiously, Violet, now I come to think of it, a lot of Australia's barley is grown in Richmond. I recall him saying you'd be hard-pressed to stumble across a finer spot in Tassie – that's how he referred to Tasmania. He told me, *It's full of the English anyway. It's probably the third-largest region on the island. Perhaps the most beautiful.* He was a great chap and said he couldn't wait to get back.'

Violet watched her father closely as he spoke. 'And did he?'

'No.' Charlie looked down. 'I'm very sad to say he died the next day. Caught a stray bullet from a retreating German unit behind enemy lines that hadn't fully understood the war was over.' He sighed.

'Oh, Dad, I'm sorry to make you remember that.'

Her father shrugged. 'I haven't thought about Greeny in a long time, nor the great land mass of the Australian continent on the other side of the world. What makes you ask after it, anyway?'

'I'm glad you say they grow barley there,' she began with care.

He nodded. 'According to Greeny, it was a successful crop.'

'Then we could too.' She held her breath now she'd dared to say it.

He raised his head to look at her. 'What?'

She took her chance. 'I've been thinking. We could go to Australia and grow barley there... and then make our whisky. It could be the fresh start we need.'

'Violet, what are you talking about?'

'This!' She thrust the pamphlet at him. 'Read it, Dad. It's a new opportunity. A chance for us. I'm not scared of adventure. I know you're not, and both of us need to change something, don't we? It's why we're here in London. It didn't work out how I hoped, but this is something amazing to think about.' Her father opened his mouth to speak, but she continued. 'And before you start shaking your head, think of all the odd little things that had to happen to make us have this conversation.' She began to count on her fingers. 'I had to come home to find you in the mood you were, ready to give up on Glen Corbie. We had to agree to come to London – against your wishes, but you allowed me to have my way. You had to have that bust-up with Grandad in order to come to King's Cross early and be seated in that exact spot for your old army buddy Mr Bailey to spot you. And then he had to not only recognise you, but feel he'd like to do something nice for you. And then you had to agree.'

'I get it—'

'No, there's more, Dad. You had to want to go out for a walk and I had to want to write a silly letter to Angus. That's how I got sidetracked reading this pamphlet that I might never have noticed otherwise, let alone picked up. But I did. That's a lot of things that had to all work out, one after another, for us to be here now and talking about Australia. It's fate,' she said airily.

'Are we really talking about leaving, though, Violet? Now that you've achieved something so incredible with the hotels?'

She considered his question. 'It's still going to be a struggle though, isn't it, Dad? We both feel grumpy about the industry turning its back on us in Speyside. It doesn't matter the reason,' she said, before he might jump to their defence. 'I don't really care. They've snubbed us, after all you and Mum have done while living there. All the kindnesses you've shown to others. How many times did you pitch in with harvest and not get paid? And what about when Albert couldn't do his work in the barley shed? You did it for two days and still gave him his wages.'

'He had five mouths to feed,' Charlie defended.

'Dad, I could go on. You're always there for others in need but when you need those people, they've looked away. I bet they'll be relieved when they hear we've left. They can let go of their guilt. I think if we stay it's going to feel uncomfortable... certainly for a while. And you should know, I probably won't forgive them, even though it seems like you already have.' She smiled sadly to show that she felt no wrath towards him.

'But, Violet, you want to go to the other side of the world? There'd be no chance to nip here to see your grandparents, or Angus...'

'I can write. And it wouldn't be forever. I think this sort of change is coming at the right time for us. And it would mean we were doing something positive to help ourselves rather than complaining about what we can't have. Remember how Mum always used to say to deal with a problem square on and not avoid it?'

He nodded.

'Well, we have a problem. Let's face it. You've told me the whisky business is all but impossible for us here, so why not start fresh somewhere else?'

He tilted his head and studied her. 'How old are you again?'

'Dad,' she bleated.

'I don't know. This is so daring.'

'Are you scared?'

'Not scared. Concerned that any decision I make will so profoundly affect you. We'd be starting over from scratch.'

'This is my decision too. We wouldn't even be talking about this if I didn't want to go. And I do. We can do what we're good at, somewhere new, away from all those folk who won't help and don't want us around. This pamphlet says that they want people to come and be farmers and business owners. That's us, Dad.'

He took the pamphlet and tapped it thoughtfully. 'I would be lying if I said I wasn't intrigued.'

Her expression lit up. 'We can go to that place called Australia House and find out more.'

. . .

Charlie scanned the pamphlet for what must have been the twentieth time. He'd sent Violet down to ask about dinner – was Bob Bailey available for a meal, where he could ensure the man hadn't felt coerced by his daughter?

Australia. Maybe it was exactly what they needed. He and Violet could run away to the southern hemisphere... run away from their problems. He could flee from memories of Ellen and the closing of Glen Corbie and, perhaps more importantly, cut his helpless, invisible tie to France and to one person in particular.

Ellen had been his safe harbour after a life of rough seas, but he had never fully allowed Sophie to leave his thoughts. They had not communicated since he'd left Épernay, though he wondered about her often and was sure he could sense her thoughts reaching towards him too. It sometimes frightened him that he found himself thinking about her... about them.

That was probably why the comment from Dennis had hurt so much. How sad that Ellen had somehow known but never once referred to Sophie in all their time together. It only made him admire Ellen's strength all the more. She'd known he was hers and that he would remain faithful, and so she'd found it within herself to allow him those memories without guilt. What an incredibly pragmatic woman he had been blessed to share his life with... and she had given him an equally pragmatic and searingly intelligent daughter. He owed it to Ellen to ensure, to the best of his ability, that their daughter's life was one of safety and prosperity.

So maybe starting afresh *was* the answer. Leave Scotland, England, Europe... all of life as he had known it. Leave it behind. Turn away from its challenges and sorrows, and begin again – for Violet. A new Charlie Nash.

Violet burst back into the room and he realised how tightly he was holding on to the brochure – as though it was suddenly his lifeline.

'Let's go to Australia, Violet,' he heard himself say.

FOUR
KNOCKANDO

July 1935

As much as Violet enjoyed Angus's company, she would have preferred him not to be mooning at the doorway of the tiny barrel room while she worked.

'Close the door, would you?' she asked companionably.

'Why?'

'You're changing the light.'

'Violet, come on.'

'Seriously, Angus. Look around you. Can you see the soft light coming through those high windows? It's like the gloaming in here. It always is. Look at the motes dancing about in that gentle golden shine. And soon the stars will sparkle through like a million gemstones.'

'So?'

'So I like to maintain that equilibrium in here.'

He cast her a look of umbrage. 'Big words. Have you got the hump?'

She grinned, shaking her head. 'No, Angus. I'm just working.'

'Well, you should be filling in those forms for end of school,' he said, sounding like a testy parent.

'I've already done it. I'm guessing you haven't, and that's why you're here.'

'Och, don't be rude, Violet. I'm here to see you.'

'And to see if you can copy my forms, perhaps,' she said, glancing up from one of the barrels. She was re-stoppering it with a large wooden bung.

'I'm offended you'd think that,' he said, and she could hear he was doing his best to sound injured. 'Do you want me to go, then?'

'Yes.' She laughed.

'But why? Aren't I fun?'

'You are. But I'm working. I have told you about this place, haven't I?'

'You blasphemed and said it was like your church. I dare not tell my mam you said that.'

'I'm just saying that the barrel room has a similar ability to humble me as a church does. You know how when you walk into church, you naturally fall silent or speak in a hushed voice?'

He nodded.

'Well, the barrel room can do that to me. I'm among the spirits here in more ways than perhaps you can understand. I feel like these barrels are my friends, and they're all at slumber, so we need to speak quietly so as not to disturb them.' She smiled softly at the next barrel in her line of sight.

'You're losing me, Violet.'

She sighed. 'That's all right. I actually don't expect you to share my feelings.'

'But I want to understand.'

'I'm not sure that you can.' She uncorked another barrel and dipped her spirit thief in further than she'd anticipated; it had lost more to evaporation than expected. 'Hmm, the angels have taken a bigger share from this one,' she muttered.

'Are you all right, Violet? You're talking to yourself.'

'I'm talking to my friends, Angus.' Before he could reply she said, 'Shh.' He was silent as she sipped, closing her eyes, allowing the potent spirit to roll across her tongue and slip gently to the back of her mouth and down her throat. She understood why the angels had claimed so much; this would be a mighty Scotch.

She could hear Angus scuffing around at the doorway and wished he would leave her to her communion. 'This has to be approaching sixty per cent alcohol,' she said. 'But when I get that down to where it needs to be – which is forty per cent, for your information – I can't tell you how amazing this barrel's contents will be. We are going to really please our buyers in London.'

'How do you know that?' Angus asked.

'By what I taste beneath the alcohol. The flavours are going to be immaculate.' She closed her eyes again and recalled what she'd tasted. 'Burnt sugar, simnel cake with—'

'What's that?'

She opened her eyes, slightly frustrated. 'Simnel cake is made at Easter, Angus. You should know that.'

'The one with that gritty yellow icing?'

'The one covered in marzipan.' She smiled. 'And then I can taste oloroso – that's sherry,' she explained before he could interrupt. 'And something herby, or maybe earthy, but I'll wait for that to develop to pinpoint it.' Violet re-stoppered the barrel, excited that the liquor was developing beautifully, and hung up the spirit thief. 'Right, you want to see the forms, Angus? They're up at the house on the kitchen table.'

He looked down. 'Thanks, Violet.' He followed her to the cottage and gratefully accepted the three pages she handed his way. 'Can I do it here?'

'No.' She was firm. 'Go home and do it properly. Actually think about what you're saying, Angus.'

'You used to say something like that about our homework. *Really learn while you do your homework, Angus,*' he said mimicking her. 'But I already knew that I'd never need to know the lifecycle of the bee or of grass.'

'Really?' She put a hand on her hip in exasperation. 'You're a dolt, Angus. Learning about bees is vital to anyone who wants to go into agriculture – which is precisely what you plan as a farmer – and just in case you didn't know it, barley is a grass.'

'No, it's not. It's a grain.'

She grinned. 'It belongs to the family of grasses. And was first cultivated thousands of centuries before Jesus walked the earth.'

'Ooh, you fibber. I won't tell my mam what you've said. She'd come here and wash out your mouth with soap.'

Violet just shook her head. 'Barley has been around forever, and you claiming you don't need to understand it, when you are very likely going to work in the industry that depends upon it, is very short-sighted.' She laughed. 'Maybe we should get you some glasses.'

'Marry me, Violet,' he said suddenly in a plaintive bleat. 'You're so clever. Smart enough for both of us. I'll grow you the barley you need, and you can make your whisky and we'll be—'

'Desperately unhappy,' she finished for him, but with an affectionate smile and a playful push. 'Please don't ask me again. The answer is no. But I will always love you. Is that good enough?'

He looked down. 'I suppose.'

'Get on with you, Angus. My father is due back today, and I want to cook something nice for his return.'

Violet met the train from Aberdeen at Dufftown railway station, taking the opportunity of being in town to gather up some groceries. She nearly bought a *Press and Journal*, but the newsagent dissuaded her.

'I wouldn't if I were you, Miss Nash. It's all bad. Save your pennies.' He smiled kindly, handing her the tiny black and orange tin of Nipits, the pure licorice pellets she bought for her father's night-time cough, which seemed to be getting worse as he got older.

'I'm going to take your advice,' she said, grinning back. 'None of us needs to read any more grim news.'

He nodded and turned to the door as the bell signalled the arrival of another customer. Although she saw the man hesitate at the door, she found her grace and walked towards him. He had no choice but to remain where he stood, holding the door open for her. 'Afternoon, Mr Alexander,' she said, making sure it didn't sound too bright but also schooling her tone so it was not accusatory. Her smile helped.

He lifted his hat. 'Miss Nash.'

She passed over the threshold.

'Er...' he began awkwardly.

She would save him the struggle. 'It's all right, Mr Alexander. There is nothing to say. It's done now.'

'You and your father are making a fine product, Miss Nash. We just cannot purchase it at this moment. Times are... well, I'm sure you know how challenging it all is in our industry right now.'

'I do, Mr Alexander. We'll be fine,' she said. 'Good day.' She left before he could say more, not wanting to look into his guilty eyes a moment longer.

What she wanted to do was yell at him that the Nash blend was far superior to what they were buying instead, but she wouldn't compromise her dignity in public. She kept walking, trying not to attract anyone's attention, although various people nodded or doffed their caps.

Dufftown felt like a saucer at the base of the great bowl that was the glen, surrounded by hills. It was a busy town, home of the famous Glenfiddich, which the Grant family had built in 1887 and whose distillery dominated the main street. Together with other distilleries it had kept the economy of the region moving, but Violet's father was convinced it was all caving in on itself now, and their own distillery was already a casualty. For that reason she didn't regret their decision to leave. Her father often had a sense of these things – of imminent danger. Was it due to his experiences in the trenches, or simply a knack of foreboding?

She wondered sometimes what had attracted her parents to each other: serious Charlie and her mother, who always found a smile for everyone. Two opposites, perhaps: two lonely people who were both deeply scarred by what they'd seen of the battlefield.

She was sure that part of her father's reticence and his seeming loneliness was that he'd left something behind in France. Her mother used to say it was his soul. But now Violet wondered if the 'French tart' her grandfather had flung in his face was the missing piece. She'd not had the courage to ask him again about this woman in France. But he'd been there a long time ago – before she was born, before he was married. Everyone was entitled to their past, their memories, their loves even. And she'd never felt her father didn't love them enough. It was true she had often caught him with that faraway look in his eye, and there was always a sense of pain about him. It seemed to travel on his shoulder, even if they were in a happy moment.

But here was the truth, she thought, confronting it: was she really any different?

When it came to malting, blending, even tasting, she didn't want anyone to share her experience or offer advice. She and her father tasted separately and compared notes later. They might help each other when needed, but when it came to blending, for instance, she wanted no one else at her side, and she knew he felt the same.

She was her father's twin in many ways, but in one regard she was different. She might be a loner, but she was capable of social interaction in a way her father found too difficult, even exhausting. People liked him, but they were wary of him, whereas people found it easier to interact with Violet. She could see a future in which he withdrew from all meetings and left dealing with people to her, because her conversations were warmer, more generous. That certainly came from her mother, for which she'd forever be grateful.

But now was not the time to be reflective or look backwards. It was a time to be excited, filled with anticipation and happiness at a new adventure... a new life beckoning. She looked up towards the clock tower. Her father's train was due in eight minutes. She made her way to the little stone railway station and sat on a small bench just outside the ticket office.

The bright whistle sounded from somewhere in the distance and soon enough she could see the billow of steam rising above the treetops and hear the engine's approach. She wished now that she had gone to London with her father.

Another teacher had had yet another conversation with her, even though everyone now knew she would not be finishing her final year of school. She had been stopped in the street by Miss Stewart. 'But, Violet, Miss Chisholm believes you could be such a torch for other girls to follow in your footsteps.'

'They can make their own decisions to further their education, Miss Stewart. I don't mean to be cruel, but surely they don't need me. I'm not even that popular.'

Her teacher gave her a soft glower of despair. 'Violet, a lot of them don't have choices. It's not always about money, you know. A lot of life is about education, knowledge, the ability to think intelligently. You're fortunate to be clever, so you can probably do anything you want. So at least get the education first.'

That irritated Violet, because it sounded so accusatory. 'I *am* doing what I want. Why is everyone so determined to tell me what I should do, what I should want, when I already know? I want to make whisky.'

'Och, that's for men, Violet!'

Her skin tingled with rage at the teacher's dismissive tone. She understood that Miss Stewart had her best interests at heart, but it did not stop the sting of the old-fashioned, head-in-the-sand attitude that women couldn't equal men in any intellectual or creative pursuit. No, she wasn't as physically strong as a man, but – and she dared not admit this out loud for fear of more derision – she could outwit a man in every other way.

And I can grow and birth a child! Top that! she said in her mind. But to her teacher she gave a sad smile and said in a neutral tone, 'History would disagree with you.'

The teacher shrugged, disappointed. 'Imagine what you could do for this region if you went to university, Violet. You would make us all proud.'

'Would you feel less pride if I became one of the best whisky makers in the world?'

'I would.'

That hurt, but Violet knew not to be surprised. The older woman simply couldn't imagine how whisky might possibly compete with biology, even teaching, or whatever else she might have had in mind for her top student.

'I should consider that a total waste of talent,' Miss Stewart continued. 'We have enough whisky makers going broke just in Scotland, let alone around the world.'

Violet tried a different tack; there was no point in arguing about whisky versus writing books or becoming a doctor. Miss Stewart would never see it from her point of view. 'I feel my greatest gift to myself is to pursue my dream,' she said instead. 'A whole generation of men – and women, whether they were involved in the war effort overseas, like my mother, or were keeping the home fires burning – have had their dreams cut short or destroyed because of war. Even the women who dreamed only of marriage and family have suffered. Miss Stewart, there has never been a more important time, in my opinion, for us to dream again and do our best to make those daydreams come true. We owe it to my parents' generation to do just that.' She could see that her argument had landed and she watched her teacher's lips thin and her shoulders tense slightly with contrition.

Violet tried to soften her argument. 'This is truly what I want. I don't want to be a doctor or a biologist, or a writer or a teacher. I want to follow in my father's footsteps and make one of the world's finest whiskies, to be known for that. This is what he daydreamed about when he was fighting to survive in the trenches, and I share that dream – it's not just his. It's mine.'

Her teacher had had no response to this and had looked at her with a little bit of awe above her disappointment.

The stationmaster's shrill whistle sounded and the train came chugging into view, great puffs of grey-white vapour folding and twisting in on themselves to disappear against the sky, which was the colour of used dishwater. She saw her father lean out a window, waving and grinning, and her spirits soared. Her father rarely showed his emotions publicly. Alone, he was funny and affectionate with her, but he always held himself together in front of others and made a liar of her whenever she assured friends that he could be most amusing. To see him like this, though, was plain joy. Obviously he felt energised from his travels.

The train slowed with a great sigh and wheezed to its final stop. Her father was one of the first off, striding towards her. Just for a moment he looked younger and, as curious as it sounded in her own mind, he looked inspired. There was no doubting his handsome looks; she knew several widows in Dufftown would gladly hitch themselves to Charlie Nash, but she loved him all the more for his indifference to all other women but her late mother.

'*You're* the love of my life now,' he had said countless times when she'd suggested – lied – that she would not take offence if he needed another woman at his side. He had stopped short of laughing, but his soft smile had told her all she needed to know. 'No one can replace my Ellen,' he'd said.

He swept her up into his arms before she could speak and twirled her around, both of them laughing. What had happened in London?

'Dad! What's got into you?' she asked when he finally set her down.

'Life, Violet. Life's got into me, and a new beginning,' he said, eyes shining with excitement. 'We're off to Australia!'

'We are?' Her expression was full of query and disbelief.

'We are!' he repeated firmly, and did a small jig of joy.

'Are you drunk?' She laughed, shaking her head.

'Drunk on excitement, yes!' he agreed, tucking her hand under his elbow. 'Come on, get me home. I have so much to tell you.'

Violet leant against the soapstone sink, looking at the counter her father had cobbled together using old timber floorboards. There were moments when she missed the old cottage they'd shared with her mother at Cardhu, but once her father had decided to go out on his own with a distillery, they'd had to leave the happy four walls they'd built around their small family to be closer to work. Violet still thought about those times, but she was quietly glad they were here in Knockando. Cardhu carried too many memories that still hurt.

And now they were planning to leave again. Were they mad?

She must have said it aloud.

'Probably,' her father said, frowning. 'But Violet, like me, I think there's a part of you that just wants to cut all ties here and go.'

'I do. I just keep saying to myself *Australia*, Dad. The other side of the world. It doesn't feel real.'

'My love, I wish you could have been there at Australia House with me yesterday. The things I read about made me so excited and there's a... a... how can I put it?' He tilted his head. 'There's an energy about this young country. It gives me hope for the future.'

'When I told my headmistress I was not returning to school and that we were going to Australia, she was not impressed.' Violet grinned. 'Apparently we sent our prisoners to Australia once upon a time.'

'Yes, parts of it were a penal colony for convicts – if you can call them that. So many of them were sent for stealing a sheep or a loaf of bread, for heaven's sake. Hardly deserving of what our government considered banishment. Now Australia is thriving as a country, and it's a beacon for freedom, for advancement, for the everyman, Violet. You don't have to be rich or powerful, you don't have to own anything. You just need the desire to go out and work hard. Like us, they've lost a generation of their men to the war and, as you read in that pamphlet, Australia is now actively looking for British men, women and families to become Australians and repopulate. I've been reading about how they want to get the agricultural industry going, and—'

'So you've definitely decided on farming?'

'I know we hadn't made a final decision together, but I feel we need to live up to what Australia needs and might expect of us. Plus, we'll do what we know, my love. But I do mean to build a new whisky distillery. The dream hasn't changed.'

'Can we be sure it's going to be easier than here?' she asked.

He sat back, studying her. 'I thought you wanted this as much as I did. But we won't do it unless you feel one hundred per cent committed. This is your life too, Violet, and my life is about giving you the best one, the best future.'

'I do want it. It was my idea after all,' she said, with a chuckle. 'I'm just making sure that we've asked each other all the right questions and that each of us is saying yes for the right reasons... not just to keep the other happy. Does that make sense?'

'It makes perfect sense. And you are being perfectly sensible too. But Australia wants us, I've discovered, and I really believe we can build something there.'

'Why?'

'We fit exactly what they're looking for. The government of Australia is offering all sorts of incentives for people like you and me to become Australians, to work and raise families over there. You're young, and I've got farming pedigree. There's also special consideration for people who fought for King and country.' He frowned. 'Are you worried about something in particular?'

She shook her head. 'Not really. But while you were away, I got to thinking about leaving Mum. Leaving Grandma and Grandpa. Leaving the only life I know,' she replied carefully.

'Mum is dead,' he said, not flinching at his blunt words. 'Her spirit has flown. All that's left are her bones rotting in the ground, Violet. She's not my Ellen or your mum any more. She's here now.' He placed a hand over his heart, making her swallow. 'Your grandparents; well, they don't like me. They never have, but the gloves are off now. Your grandfather's not hiding behind politeness or family duty any longer.' He put a hand up to stop her instinctive response. 'It's all right, I've made my peace with that. They love you, and I know you love them, but you need to decide whether to follow your own heart or follow theirs. After the war, you were the future for all four of us. But I want to assure you that, despite your grandparents' despair, your mother never resented leaving London. She wanted to go to Scotland too, and have an adventure, the chance to start again, away from miserable London.'

Violet nodded. 'I know. She told me that several times. She loved Scotland, and she loved you more than anything—'

'Except you,' he corrected her, and she gave him a sad smile.

'Then we don't hesitate. We go to Australia,' she said, touching the tickets of passage that sat between them on the table. 'And we'll make a go of our new life.'

Her father withdrew a package from the small satchel he had put on the table. 'These are our forms. They're carbon copies of what I've already filled out, Violet. But we need to apply for passports. I had an interview in London, and the man confirmed that I qualify for what's called the Soldier Settlement Scheme. That means help with passage, and I am feeling quite confident that they're also going to assist with getting us settled.'

'What does that mean? A roof over our heads?'

He gave a knowing smile. 'More than that. If all goes to plan, then the Australian government will grant us some land.'

She was happily shocked. 'So we can grow our own crops?'

For the first time since he'd returned, he looked uncertain. The soft clearing of his throat was a giveaway. 'Yes. Grain. Barley, and wheat, maybe, but barley's our thing and then...'

'And then we set up a distillery!' Violet joined in. 'We'll follow the same pattern as we did here. Do they make whisky in Australia?'

He nodded. 'Some. But where we're going there's none.'

'And where *are* we going?'

'Tasmania.'

Violet nodded. 'That's an island?'

'Yes, just off the southern coast of Australia's mainland, but it's one of the seven states and territories.'

'Even further away then,' she said, trying not to sound injured.

She was excited, but the whole idea still seemed daunting. 'Closer to the South Pole.'

'Is that supposed to encourage me?'

'It should. Tell me why.'

She regarded her father, whose features had hardened slightly, his gaze narrowing. It was such a rare expression for him, although she suspected he'd probably worn it throughout the Great War. Her mother had told her that you didn't make captain or survive the war itself unless you had real grit, and, most importantly, were not frightened of losing your life.

It's my belief that your father was reckless; he took lots of risks for his men, I think mostly because he didn't care much for his life. Violet remembered those words vividly; her mother had almost muttered them, perhaps not realising how Violet would absorb them.

Her father was waiting for her answer.

'Because it's colder and echoes Scotland's climate,' she said, watching his smile return and broaden.

'I've done some study and I am convinced that Tasmania is far more like Scotland and Ireland than we imagined. Warmer summers, and slightly warmer, shorter winters, maybe, but I believe its climate is similar enough for us to use what we know. And more importantly, it has what we need, including clean spring waters.'

'And you think Australians are going to treat us better than the Scottish have?'

'Yes,' he said, nodding emphatically. 'Because *they* want us there. They're not threatened by us. Almost everyone in Australia has come from somewhere else – only the Aborigines were there before it was discovered by the Dutch and other explorers. Every Englishman or woman has arrived either as a convict or a brave, entrepreneurial soul, keen to make their own way with new opportunity. And we can too.'

PART TWO

FIVE

RICHMOND, TASMANIA

April 1944

Violet Nash stood with her hands on her hips, her golden hair showing brighter traces from its regular bleaching by the Australian sun. Right now it was being stirred by the cold autumn breeze coming down from Brinktop and its surrounding hills. It seemed to match the swaying grasses of gold she was admiring.

The last harvest from this field had been strong, and she was sure it would make a memorable winter seeding in time for next summer's harvest. Her father would be pleased. He'd been away for the last week, but he was going to share her glee at just how good the soil was looking.

They had arrived during an Australian summer, sailing into Tasmania and taking a coach down to Hobart. She remembered the journey for its many shocks: the heat, the vast distances of empty land as they passed through what she would call, at best, villages but the Australians called towns, and most of all, the colours. It could almost have been a different world.

Green was sparsely showing, and its hue was not rich and bright like in Scotland, but a duskier shade in the trees and bushes. Olive? Was that the colour? The land itself was a crisp sort of gold, dry and scorched by the sun, which shone in the most dazzling sky she had ever seen. Where were the clouds? There was nothing shy about this sky, celebrating a loud, proud colour she couldn't describe if asked: 'blue' just didn't do it justice. She had remarked as much to her father, who was seated next to her on the coach and was equally absorbed by the countryside.

'Is it me or is the sky somehow bluer here? It's almost like that colour we saw on the Egyptian pieces in the British Museum.'

He smiled. 'It is.'

'How can that be? It's the same sky as home, surely.'

'Well, if you'd gone on to university and studied science, Violet, then you'd know a bit more about atmospheric conditions.'

She made a face. 'Don't start, Dad, just tell me.'

'I don't actually know for certain.' He grinned back at her. 'But I'd guess that these eucalypts we're seeing everywhere are releasing something into the air to create a sort of haze that we view the sky through.'

'I think you're making that up,' she said.

Now he laughed. 'I'm not – there's some scientific weight to what I'm saying, I'm sure I've read something about this – but Violet, we're so far south, and so far from industrialised Britain and Europe, that I think we're just looking at the cleanest, brightest air we've ever encountered.'

'That makes sense.'

'Anyway, I agree with you. The colour is incredible.'

'Don't they get any rain here? I thought Tasmania was like Scotland, but the countryside looks parched.'

'I imagine in winter it might resemble home. Have you ever felt so hot?'

She was fanning herself with a magazine. 'I feel like I'm cooking.'

'We'll have to get used to this.'

They'd looked at each other with a mixture of dread and excitement.

Now, nearly a decade on, Violet knew exactly how to live

beneath the hot Australian sun, how to take advantage of the winds when they came, and how to do her hardest work in the early morning or in the cooler periods of twilight. She always wore long sleeves and a broad-brimmed hat outside and had even attached some netting to it to keep the annoying flies at bay. If there was one thing she'd happily remove from Australia, it was the flies, but life was good here.

They'd taken over ten acres just outside the town of Richmond. Another returned serviceman had originally been granted the land, but he wasn't much of a farmer and hadn't done well in the intervening years when his barley should have been flourishing. Then, sadly, he had taken ill and died; Charlie attributed the man's ailments to the war, which the poor soldier had miraculously survived. The authorities had put Charlie and Violet in touch with his wife, who gladly agreed to transfer the barley fields to them on arrival, grateful they were taking the land off her hands.

'What will you do now?' Violet had asked, concerned, looking at the woman's two wide-eyed children staring back at her from behind their mother's skirt.

'The twins and I are going north – home, actually. Back to Victoria, where I have family who can help. We have no one here, now that Don's gone.'

She looked older than her thirty years; life had clearly been hard.

'I'm sorry this didn't work out,' Violet said.

The woman shook her head. 'I never trusted it. Don worked in breweries before the war, and he hoped that working with barley would feel a little familiar because of it. But I come from a dairy farm and I always felt he had it wrong – it would be a little like my family going into sheep farming and believing it would be much the same as dairy cows. Barley and brewing might be related, but they're two different worlds really. Don wouldn't listen... but then he wasn't the same when he came back.'

'What do you mean?'

'He was not the man I married. Looked like him, though he

was thinner, weaker, but here'—she tapped her temple—'he was different. I know he loved us, and he couldn't have been happier when these two arrived. He said we were blessed and life was beginning, but it was beginning to unravel for him. He didn't know how to grow barley or care for it. He tried, but the yield got smaller and smaller. In the end, I think he just gave up.'

Violet gave a sympathetic smile. 'I'm so sorry you lost your husband.'

'You know, I feel he's happier now, wherever he is. At peace.'

Violet nodded, hoping this woman would find her own peace back home with her family.

Charlie had taken over the farm, with its failing crop, and then he and Violet had set out to turn their land into a successful venture. There were few men available to work with them so, when they could, they hired transient workers – journeymen who moved up and down the state doing any jobs they could find – but mostly Violet worked as hard as any man alongside her father.

Their efforts were soon rewarded, with the barley fields flourishing. Charlie and Violet won the barley growers' competition of 1937 and were awarded a cup valued at thirty guineas. Except they couldn't take it home; it would only become theirs if they won another two times. Violet had her heart set on owning that cup, much to her father's amusement. Meanwhile, Charlie brought together a group of local barley growers and suggested they carve off a small piece of land between them and turn it into an experimental farm. Violet organised a picnic for the group so that her father could explain.

'You are all more experienced barley farmers than us,' he began. 'My daughter and I have only been growing barley for a matter of years in this country, but some of you are generational farmers. My scientific background tells me that unless we take steps now, our seeds are going to deteriorate and our crops risk failure or certainly lower yields.'

This caused a murmur of consternation.

Charlie held up a hand. 'Now, Bill Jenkins has given us two

acres to experiment with. What I'm proposing is that we incubate superior seeds and release them annually to see how they perform on this land. That way we can compare the results with what we're all producing in this region. We'd all have to contribute money for its upkeep but, from those joint funds, we can pay whoever among us would like to take on the physical care of the crop. Having the experimental farm might help us deal with any bad years on the horizon.'

Violet had thought it an inspired project, and it was her idea to feed and ply the group with local beer to encourage them to come on board. All hands went up, all voices said 'Aye' and her father overnight became a sort of leader in the region. They accepted him without considering his nationality or inexperience, and trusted him because he made sense and because the Nash family grew good barley. That she and her father had lost support in Scotland because they were English still stuck uncomfortably in her craw so many years on, and this felt like a balm to them both.

The experimental farm soon showed its value, the farmers watching progress carefully and noting how the crop differed depending on how it was cared for. Some parts were given less water or more hand-delivered nutrients, while others were deliberately shaded to get less sun or left to fend for themselves with just rainfall and sunlight.

While her father had championed the project, as well as garnering support from the group to appoint the services of a malting specialist, Violet had focused on their own fields, their barley, and on establishing a distillery.

She'd bought an old still from a farmer who said it had belonged to his grandfather, who'd distilled moonshine through the war years. It was an old copper machine, not much more intriguing to look at than a big pot with a chimney, and when the contents were heated, it could cool and collect the ensuing vapours. She had rebuilt the still, checking it was sound, and burnished the copper until it was shiny again. Together, she and her father had fixed up a shed adjoining their property, which would become their new barrel room. It was small – they didn't anticipate a lot of barrels would need to be housed – but it was a beginning, and when her father attached the new handle and lock to the door, they both stood back proudly, squinting into the sun and congratulating themselves.

'Glen Corbie lives again, Dad,' Violet said, helplessly proud.

Her father simply nodded. 'Feels satisfying, although now we're in the valley of the magpies.'

'Well, they're part of the crow family. It still works,' she assured him.

Those were happy days. But as the new decade approached, everyone's lives changed again. News of another war shattered her father, though he'd known it was coming, his attention glued to the newspapers or the wireless, listening to reports of the rise of the man called Adolf Hitler. It all felt so far away, even when Britain declared war with Germany in September 1939 and Prime Minister Menzies signalled Australia's involvement just two days later. Violet had nothing to compare it to, but she watched her father's expression darken and his body language change over the months leading up to that declaration; he'd become less interested in their distilling and the farm, too occupied with another war that would draw Britain into its jaws.

She liked to call their operation 'Moonshine', but her father didn't appreciate the jest, especially now they were close to applying for a licence and commercialising their whisky.

'You shouldn't say that. Someone might hear you and think we're running something illegal... The only reason I'm choosing not to make it public is that I want to wait until we feel absolutely certain about what we have and our licence is fully approved.'

'Dad, the whisky is brilliant and you know it.'

He frowned. 'I need it to be better.'

'We've tasted all the whiskies on the mainland, and you know ours is superior.'

He raised a finger and said, 'In our opinion,' which was one of his favourite cautionary phrases. 'Whisky is subjective, Violet, never forget that. What we taste may not be what someone in Melbourne tastes. Besides—'

'Besides what?'

He smiled. 'I want to see their expressions when they taste it in Scotland. That's my great aim.'

She thought about that now, watching the barley rippling under the sun. With war raging into its fifth year in Europe, would they ever have the opportunity to travel to Britain and show their friends and colleagues what they'd achieved? Violet wasn't sure, not in this climate of depression, fear and conflict.

Families had said goodbye to fathers, sons, cousins and uncles. And countless women had received the news that no mother, daughter, wife, fiancée or sister wanted to receive.

War. Violet had had no experience to draw on, and her father slowly retreated from life, from her. He had become so quiet, lost in his thoughts, holding himself so still she would have sometimes forgotten he was in the room, if not for the hum and clipped voices of the broadcasts on the wireless. She thought she was losing him to a sort of melancholy that had built over the war years, though she wasn't entirely sure why. At his age he was not required to fight, and besides, their work on the land was considered essential, especially since they grew cereals. And Tasmanian barley, she had come to appreciate, was superior in so many ways but especially because in Richmond they could grow the English variety with ease.

They supplied barley to Tasmania's leading brewer, the Cascade Brewery in Hobart, a wily arrangement by Charlie that meant they had a reliable income. Perhaps for the first time in her life, Violet felt her father had a sense of real financial security. Cash flow was finally on their side. She no longer fretted over how to make ends meet. It had happened gradually, almost invisibly, but now she could purchase whatever they needed for the business or their personal needs without counting down to the last penny. They'd even been able to buy their land officially from the govern-ment, so it was theirs, forever.

Just recently, though, her father had become strangely busy; not that he shared with her what his activity entailed. He was sending and receiving letters, all of which he was secretive about, and he'd made trips into Hobart – only for the day, so she suspected it was to make phone calls or send telegrams that he didn't want anyone local to know about.

She'd tried to speak to him about his agitation, but he wouldn't discuss it with her. A few weeks ago, he'd said he needed to travel to the mainland and, without explanation, he'd gone. When she pressed him upon his return, he said it was to do with licensing for the whisky. She had no obvious reason to disbelieve him... and yet she did. She left the administration of their farm and the new Glen Corbie distillery to her father, while she focused on the practical running of the operations, but, even so, something wasn't ringing true.

That had been four weeks ago, but now he was away again, with a similar excuse. This time she didn't even bother to question him; it would all come out eventually. She could accept that he often needed time alone; she thought of it as his 'reflection time' when, she presumed, he allowed himself to think over his war days and the time spent with her mother. Everyone needed time alone. She used to enjoy hers in the malting room at Knockando as a child, but now she walked their fields of barley and wheat, imagining that the grasses absorbed and reflected – and even somehow answered – her thoughts and ideas.

For the most part, she too was in a reflective state of mind. Even the launch of their own Australian whisky was overshadowed by the world at war. There wasn't much to look forward to, other than the fighting ending, but it was showing no signs of abating – intensifying, if anything, despite all the fierce opposition. But her father had said that now the Americans were involved, Germany would be crushed.

'Someone needs to tell Hitler,' Violet remarked.

Her father shook his head. 'He's finished. He just doesn't know it – or accept it, more likely. The Soviets are beating him back. I can't imagine what their rage will be like once the war on the Eastern Front turns... and it will.'

'I like your confidence, Dad. I want all our boys home.'

She was happy that Hitler had never managed to topple the small, resilient island of Britain. The cost to the Brits had been huge, but his staggering ambition to rule them too was in tatters.

Violet turned from her thoughts of war to an old stalk of barley, rubbing the dry and wispy seed head until it relinquished its grains. She thought about how each grain had the power to transform into beer or whisky... into food products, like malted milk or even bread.

'Clever little things, aren't you?' she whispered to them, pulling her woollen shawl tighter around herself. Winter was on its way, and they'd all be shivering soon.

A voice hailed her as she arrived home and Violet turned to see their employee Jimmy Lawton walking towards her. Jimmy was a hulking lad, good-looking with hair bleached by the sun, and his size belied his gentle way and his age of just fourteen and a half – the half being very important to him, apparently.

It was Violet who had found old Ben and his grandson Jimmy to do the malting work her father could no longer do alone. She'd wanted to take precautions against him developing 'monkey shoulder', as it was known in Scotland. The men who did the repetitive, demanding work in the malting sheds developed a strained shoulder that caused one arm to hang lower, like that of a monkey. Ben had been malting a lot of his life; he had the classic appearance, Violet could see.

'Are you sure you want Jimmy to do this work, Ben? Are we committing him to a lifetime of pain?' she'd asked, when discussing the job.

'Miss Nash, Jimmy needs to be doing something physical. You know how he looks – hard to believe he's not yet fifteen. If we're not careful he'll run off to war, pretending he's older, because he's got that sense the young ones have that nothing bad could happen to him. His mother has already lost his brother and his father, and I can't lose my only remaining grandson to that bastard Hitler.'

Violet understood. 'Amen to that. Let's keep him safe and working and away from all that. He's a good boy and a good worker.'

Old Ben had doffed his flat cap at Violet in thanks, and Jimmy had now been learning the work for the past five months. He and his grandfather both worked a few afternoons a week, but he was on his own today.

'Ben all right?'

Jimmy grinned. 'His team won the bowls competition last night. I think he celebrated a bit hard.'

Violet cackled. 'I can't imagine your grandad tying one on. He's always shied away from tasting any of the spirit in the barrels.'

'He's not one for whisky or gin, Miss Nash, but he likes his beer.' Jimmy pretended to stagger, making them both laugh.

'We can forgive him, because today he's a champion.' She nodded purposefully. 'Just us, then, Jimmy.'

They walked together back to the sheds. He stood as tall as her and the malting work had broadened his shoulders. He was all muscle, the plumpness of boyhood gone and a fuzz on his chin.

'Is Mr Nash not here either?' he asked.

Violet shook her head. 'No, he's gone to the city.'

'Again?'

Jimmy was observant. She liked that in him, even though he seemed to be echoing her own slightly alarmed thoughts about her father.

'Er, yes, getting our licence sorted.'

Jimmy nodded. 'Miss Nash?'

'Call me Violet, Jimmy. You've known me long enough.'

'Violet,' he tested, and gave his bright, sunshine smile. 'Did you finish school?'

She paused; was he thinking of leaving? None of them wanted

that for him. 'No, actually. I left at fifteen, but we're going back nearly a decade, Jimmy. Things are different now.'

'Why are they different?'

'Well, we want all our youngsters to have the best education they can. And school today is so much more comprehensive than it used to be, even when I was there. Why do you ask?' she said innocently.

'I don't enjoy school. It's not helping me.'

She kept her tone light. 'Few of us appreciate it while we're there. It's only years later that we realise they were very good days, and we had opportunity and our lives ahead of us to do exactly what we wanted. That's the point you're at now, Jimmy.'

'The thing is, Miss N— er, Violet, I already know what I want to do. And so I want to leave school soon. I'm nearly fifteen. I just don't know how to tell Mum and Grandad.'

'Oh, Jimmy, why?' She feared that old Ben's worry about him joining up was well founded, and prepared herself to talk him down from the dizzying heights of running away to serve his country.

'Because I want to learn how to make whisky.'

Violet blinked. She hadn't expected that.

He continued excitedly. 'I want to do what you do. I want to learn everything you can teach me. I want to be a distiller and blender for Glen Corbie and maybe one day I'll have my own distillery.'

'Jimmy!' Violet's jaw dropped.

He frowned. 'Don't tell me off, I know my—'

'I'm not going to tell you off,' she interrupted. 'I want to hug you. I haven't got a leg to stand on in terms of convincing you to stay at school, because I didn't, and I couldn't be told. I was absolutely sure about wanting to be a whisky maker. Are you as absolutely certain as I was... and that this isn't just a nice thing to do?'

He shook his head. 'Malting is hard work – it's not exactly fun,' he admitted. 'But I can see that when we do it well and exactly as you specify, then we get that perfect base for the next stage. Taking pride in that is important... but it's the same thing over and over. I want to do more.'

She nodded. 'There's a lot more to it,' she cautioned with a smile, 'but, yes, you're right. If the malting stage is less than satisfactory, we're setting off from a poor position.'

'Grandad told me you're the first people in Tasmania to be making whisky honestly, ready to pay taxes, have a proper licence and all that. He said people have made moonshine in the past.'

Violet shrugged. 'It's how the industry began in Scotland.'

He nodded thoughtfully. 'But it's new here in Tasmania, isn't it?'

'There is whisky being made in Victoria – but this is a first for Tasmania. I think most whisky drinkers in this state import the Scottish or Irish whiskies.'

'I like the idea that we're making Tasmanian whisky, though. I want to be part of it.'

'You are, Jimmy,' she said, wanting to ruffle his hair, but he suddenly seemed so grown-up.

'*Really* part of it, I mean. I want to start as young as you did. Mr Nash told me about you. He said you were better at making whisky in your teens than people much older in Scotland.'

She grinned. 'He's my dad – what do you expect him to say?'

'No, he meant it. Mr Nash doesn't joke much, so I take what he says seriously. He told me how clever you are with distilling and blending. He says your palate is so well developed that you've long since overtaken him with tasting the notes in the spirit and how best to blend them.'

'Well, I think my father is overestimating me and underestimating himself,' she said firmly.

Jimmy shook his head. 'I believe him. And I want to be that good too. And to do that, I have to start now. Will you teach me?'

Violet felt a mix of guilt and pride. 'If you stay on at school, I will.'

'That's blackmail,' he said, but he smiled. 'Would *you* have stayed on at school if your father had used the same argument?'

He'd trapped her squarely. There was no way she would have tolerated such a deal, so why should he? She sighed and looked at him, amused. 'All right, Jimmy. If this is what you want, I'll teach you. I can't pay you more – not yet – but I will when you start being useful around the distillery. Right now, though, it's all about the malting for you. Come on.'

He beamed. 'Thank you. I'll make you proud, Violet.'

They'd arrived at where they stored the barley.

'Start today. Ask all the questions you want,' she said, inhaling deeply. 'What do you smell?'

'Er... bread?' he tried, looking unsure.

'Good!' she said. 'I do too. What else?'

'Um...'

'This isn't a test. Close your eyes.'

He did so.

'Now smell the air gently. What can you sense?'

He took a moment to inhale. 'Sugar, something sweet?'

Violet smiled. 'Very good. Almost caramel, right?'

'Yes, like a toffee.' He frowned. 'It's a bit musty, though... er, like a cupboard that's been closed for a while.' He opened his eyes, perhaps expecting her laughter.

But she was impressed. 'You're going to do well, Jimmy. I know the aroma you're referring to – I smell it too, along with a nuttiness. So we've got musty, nutty, sweet, bread... these are all the notes we want when we walk into the malting room. The reason you can smell that mustiness is because we are now deep into the malting process.'

'So how would it smell in the early stage?'

'Sort of fresh, like newly mown grass, and then it becomes sweeter, like freshly baked bread. Now that it's been heated and the germination halted, it's smelling more musty, earthy.'

He took off his hat, hung it on the hook behind the door and reached for one of the paddles to begin raking the grain.

She'd learned how to do this watching her father wield the shield-shaped paddle with one hand, flipping the barley over his shoulder, keeping it aired and moving while it heated. Old Ben, who had been malting for years for the local brewery, had taught Jimmy well. But he perhaps hadn't shared a deeper knowledge of what he was doing, beyond the physical side of it. It was important for Jimmy to understand that too if he was going to seriously learn about making whisky.

'Turning the barley is vital, because it aerates the grain to keep the heat and cooling even,' she explained now, watching him. 'Your grandad and my father did that. And we must rake gently over the surface to create shallow grooves – this assists in the same process.' She'd taken great pride in learning the knack from the masters back in Scotland. Her father had told her that Iain McClelland, a well-known maltster, believed her rows of neat, humped barley were among the best he'd seen.

'This turning and raking is the hardest work of the whisky process. You keep going, and I'll make the rows.'

She watched Jimmy bending to scoop and toss the grain high enough to aerate it. She waited until he'd moved along before she started neatening and furrowing the rows.

'What we're doing here is making sure all the barley is at a consistent stage,' Violet explained. 'Germination for barley means the seed is sprouting to become its own plant. Do you understand what I mean by that?'

'Not really,' he said. 'I understand the warming and cooling but now you're going into science.'

She grinned, feeling like her father, who had once taught her. 'It's like it's coming out of a period of sleep, or dormancy.'

He looked back at her blankly.

'Have you heard of hibernation?'

'Like a snake, you mean?'

She gave him a big smile. 'Exactly. These little grains are asleep, and we want to wake them up.' She was pleased that she'd helped him understand. 'But just as they wake, we want to halt that growth.'

'Why?' he asked, forehead wrinkling with confusion.

'Because we don't want the sprout to actually grow. We just want to trick the barley grain into waking up, because we don't want them using all that lovely sugar; we want it for our process.' She grinned, seeing a perfect image in her mind of barley grains all yawning and groaning with wakefulness. 'So first we do what's called steeping, which is soaking the grains, and that begins the stirring of the grains from their slumber.'

Violet had loved these lessons with her father. He'd always found a way to make learning fun – not like most of her teachers, who sounded bored with themselves and their topics. She was convinced that her education in whisky making had saved them both, in the toughest months after her mother's death, when it had been so fresh it was like an open wound.

And now, it felt right that she was passing on the knowledge to someone younger.

Jimmy flipped another load over his shoulder. 'Right, so if you don't want the barley to actually grow, how do you stop it?'

'Well, once we've steeped it in water to begin the germination, we want to halt it at just the right moment, and that's when we do the kilning – heating the grain on the warmed floors. Heating it stops the process. All right, a bit more science now, Jimmy,' she said, smiling as she formed the rows as neatly as she could. 'If we wake it up to fully alert, this "baby" – if I can call a grain that – would get hungry and begin to eat the food store that the mother plant has left for it. That food store is essentially sugar, and the thing is, we want all that sugar for ourselves.'

'Why?'

'Because the more sugar we have, the bigger our yield of alcohol.'

'Right.' He frowned, not entirely understanding.

'Do it enough and you'll learn. Over the years I've stood side by side with Dad, considering the temperature of the barley that it generates as it sits here beginning to wake up. And together we would make the decision when it was time to halt the germination, and we do that by kilning and turning up the heat.'

'So I'll just watch.'

'To start with. The best way to learn anything is to observe and then practise alongside someone who knows a lot more than you.'

'Is it different doing this here in Tasmania than it was in Scotland?'

'Yes, good question, Jimmy. Irrespective of where you are, what does matter is the season. That change in temperature – even a slight change outside – can affect the speed at which the barley is germinating. It tends to be easier to control in cooler weather, so that's why we do this process in autumn. Tasmania and Scotland aren't as different as you'd think.'

'All sounds complicated.'

'It is. But you're learning the science of this process as an apprentice now, on the job, as I did. So you have to listen, watch, learn and do.'

She could see the young man was intrigued, as she had been, and remembered admitting to Angus that she felt 'connected' to the barley. 'To the whole process actually,' she'd said as they walked home from school one day. 'I feel I'm in it. My actions, my decisions, my body and my mind are all part of the chain.'

Angus had gently scoffed. 'You take too much pride, Violet. It's all just going into a vat with other liquor from the big distilleries.'

'Yes, but one day...'

'One day you'll be married with a host of bairns, and you'll have no time for your precious whisky making. It's man's work.'

'Well, Angus,' she'd said, bristling, 'I'll make you eat those words.'

That moment felt so long ago, and there was no husband, no bairns, yet... nor did she and her father have their own brand of whisky. But soon there would be the Glen Corbie brand once again. She smiled as she created her signature furrows in the barley: shallow, uniform grooves that allowed the heat within the grain to dissipate.

Jimmy looked over his shoulder. 'They look like they could have been made by a machine,' he commented. 'They're so even.'

She smiled at the compliment.

'You know,' he continued, 'this is probably going to sound daft, but why don't we just get malted barley from the brewery and save ourselves the trouble?'

She straightened, shocked at his remark, staring at his back while he worked. The barley lifted in a cascade of nuggety grains, the sun's reach through the small window painting them gold as they lifted and then dropped in a soft clatter.

Violet's mouth parted in astonishment. Jimmy might have stumbled onto something genius.

SIX

Violet was out in the garden, passing an hour before she left for the station to pick up her father. She heard the honk of a car and turned around to see Mr Jarvis, the local grocer, pulling up. Her father stepped out of his van.

'Found him lurking at the train station,' Mr Jarvis called with a grin, and waved farewell to them both.

Violet looked at her wristwatch, startled.

'I caught an earlier train,' her father explained, pulling off his hat as he stood in front of her.

'So it seems,' she said, sensing an odd tension between them. 'I hate not picking you up.' She hugged him through his big overcoat and he returned it.

'Albert was more than happy to give me a lift.' He looked towards one of the fields that they were working, behind the house. 'My gosh.'

Violet smiled. 'I thought you'd be impressed.'

'It's ready.'

'And magnificent, Dad. This year's winter harvest is going to be huge. I've already contacted Don. He reckons he can come in a few days and get this field harvested, which is perfect.'

Her father nodded, staring in awe across the wide field of bobbing barley heads. 'Time to sow the wheat, too.'

'Yes. I think we should start next week.'

'Good, good,' he said.

Violet thought he sounded distracted, saying what she needed to hear. She was excited to tell him her new idea but held off; he wasn't focused. 'It's lovely to have you home,' she said instead, hugging him again.

As he put his arm around her shoulders and they began to walk, her initial hunch felt right; there was a curious atmosphere about him. Something was not quite right with her favourite person. She paused and leant away to look at him. 'All well?'

'Yes, of course,' he said, a little dismissively and overly bright. He was also not making eye contact. 'Let's go up to the house.'

Their home was a small stone cottage with a verandah and two windows either side of the front door, surrounded by a picket fence that contained their garden and vegetable patch. In the kitchen, Violet waited for him to say something – anything – but he avoided her eye.

She would have to prise it out of him. Or would she? He looked nervous, pacing around. She decided to corner him, something she normally avoided. 'Out with it, Dad.'

'Pardon?' He looked almost frightened.

She couldn't understand it. 'What's going on? And don't say nothing,' she warned him.

He ran a hand through his dark hair, neatly slicked back and silvering around his ears. He looked far younger than his years, but he seemed deeply unaware of the effect he had on the women of the surrounding hamlets. They had no idea what an enigma he was and how distant he could be. Besides, her father had no intention of remarrying; he had made it clear he would die a widower.

She swallowed hard and intensified her stare. 'Dad? You need to talk to me.'

'Violet,' he began, his tone earnest, but with almost a tremor.

'Right, you're scaring me now. What is it? Are you sick? Has something gone wrong? Have you gambled away our savings? Sold the farm from under me?'

He let out a slightly shocked half-chuckle. 'No, nothing like that.'

'Then what?' Violet felt ready to shake him.

He finally looked up and met her gaze. 'I'm sailing for London shortly.'

The words had to pass through her mind twice more before they made sense. 'London,' she repeated.

He nodded, waiting.

'Why? What about the wheat?' It was such a strange response, but the shock was intense. Her throat felt like it wanted to close.

Her father let out a slow sigh. 'Violet,' he began.

'No. Don't do that. Don't try and soften whatever it is you've decided to do. Just tell me the truth. I'm not a child.' She squared him up with a defiant stare that begged him to test her.

'I've offered my help to the war effort,' he said, blunt and raw as she'd asked.

She absorbed this. Why wasn't she that surprised, when it was so alarming? 'In what way? Dad, you've done your bit for King and country – no one will ask more.'

'You'd be surprised. I know how war goes, Violet, you don't. A lone man, without a wife or young dependents, who doesn't pull on the uniform will be happily considered a coward, or a shirker at best. I'm lucky not to have received a white feather.'

Violet frowned. 'Is that what we're talking about? You're afraid of being called a coward after being hailed a hero of the Great War?'

'No,' he said, ignoring the edge of sarcasm. 'I want to help.'

'You're nearly sixty. The war has dragged on into its fifth year, and you said yourself it will soon end, because of the Nazi failure in Russia and the bombing of Pearl Harbor. Australia's not going to—'

'Listen to me,' he cut in. 'The war is *not* over, despite the Americans' involvement and Germany's defeat at Stalingrad. That

German lunatic would rather beggar his nation again – he'd now have every old man, woman and child pick up a weapon and die for his maniacal cause. But I do want to believe that we're in the final efforts to end this war. It's going to take all of the Allied effort to do so. I've offered my services to the Special Operations Executive in England.'

She frowned. 'I don't even know what that means.'

'Why should you?' He tried a smile but didn't win one in return. 'It's a division that sends spies out into Europe to gather information.'

Now her gaze narrowed. 'Spies? How are they going to help at this stage of the war?'

'Spies deliver crucial intelligence on the enemy, Violet, and information is what will equip us to end this – in Europe at least. If we can send the Nazis on the run back into Germany, then we can push from the west and the Soviets can push from the east. I can't bear the thought of all the people who have become casualties. I never thought we'd have to face this again and I've tried hard to quell my feelings over the past few years, but they've got the better of me. I had to do something... and so I'm going to London.'

'Tell me how this happened,' she said, an edge of despair in her tone.

'I've had some communication with people I knew a long time ago, and they've told me I'd be a good candidate.'

'For spying?' she said, sounding incredulous.

'Not necessarily. More in a liaison role. I had a phone call with... oh well, it doesn't matter with whom, but they're keen to get me over there as soon as possible. We have people on the ground who are feeding the Allies with all sorts of vital information, working closely with the Resistance.'

'Are you sure this is not just an opportunity to run away, to go be a hero again and put yourself in the line of fire? Mum said you could be reckless.'

Her father looked down. 'Why would I want to leave you,

unless I felt it was my duty? My life is yours, darling girl. Every bit of toil, every decision, every breath I take is for you.'

That made her cry. 'I couldn't bear it if you died as well, Dad,' she admitted, sniffing and wiping at the tears on her cheeks.

'We all die, darling.' His voice was so tender.

'Yes, but we don't invite it. I feel like this is your invitation, and you've just been waiting for it.'

'I have to go and do my bit,' he said. 'I will suffer here so much more if I don't. Surely you've seen already how hard it's been for me. I've been a bystander for years, and I can't take it any more. But I plan very much on coming home to you. I'll need to drink your whisky, at the very least.'

'I understand,' she said, meaning it. 'I don't agree, but I can tell you've already decided anyway, and I guess you're also well advanced in your private preparations.' She sniffed again, and banished her tears. It was time to be practical. 'So what's your plan?'

'I sail to England for training.'

'With your distinguished experience?'

He found a small grin. 'In spite of it. But my age and experience make me "organiser" material, apparently.'

'I thought you said you would be a liaison?' She frowned, trying to read him.

He moved his head from side to side. 'The same thing.'

'No, you're doing it again, Dad. You're shaking a hand over here,' she said, doing just that, 'so I can't see what you're doing over here,' she continued, raising the other hand.

It made him smile. 'Well, I might be liaising in a different sort of role.'

'What sort of role?'

'To help run a few spies in the region.'

She blinked. 'What sort of training will you be doing?'

'Well, most people doing this sort of work have to do paramilitary first. Guess where?'

'Scotland?' she offered, sounding astonished.

He grinned. 'Yes. Arisaig, in the north-west. But I'm too old to be tossed out of a plane, so if my credentials stand up, then I guess they're flying me in behind enemy lines. I have no other details. However, first I have to do "finishing school" at Beaulieu in Hampshire.'

'What does that entail?'

'It's spy school, Violet, and by its very nature is secretive, but I guess I'll learn modern communications using the wireless. Let me stress that my role will be support rather than in the field. I mean it when I say I'm planning to come home.'

She stared at her hands. 'Where will they send you?'

'Well, after England, maybe over to Paris, to—'

'Paris!' Now her heart was in her mouth. 'Dad, being flown into occupied France *is* the field. Please don't think I'm too dim to work that out.'

'You're not dim at all. All I'm saying is that my job is not really to spy, but to support the spies. I'm not in the sort of daily danger they are.'

She shook her head. 'I know you're lying. You won't be safe.'

'War is not safe.'

'You're safe here!' she protested.

'Safe and miserable.'

'Can't have that.' She was unable to disguise her disdain. 'I'm sorry,' she added quickly.

Her father waved the apology away. 'It's all right. This isn't easy for either of us.'

No, it is easy for you, Dad, she thought. *Off to foreign soil. Off to war, whistling at the thought of the adventure ahead. Off to do something heroic instead of being a simple farmer or fulfilling our dream to make whisky in Tasmania.*

'So you'll be based in Paris?'

'I don't know. The area I know best is outside Paris, actually. In the rural region... north-east.' She heard the false note in his voice, and she would swear in that moment that her heart gave an extra strong beat. She felt it pound in her chest and a whoosh of blood behind her ears.

North-east of Paris. Her father was going back to Épernay... back to see his champenoise. Her gaze felt white hot as it landed on him. 'Just a moment.' She left the kitchen to find a book in the lounge room.

'What's going on?' he called.

When she returned she saw him glance at the atlas she carried and could almost see his heart sinking deeper into his chest.

'I want to see where you're going,' she said with feigned cheer-fulness. 'Now, let's open this to France.' She turned pages point-edly until she reached the right one. 'Ah, here we are. There's Paris, so...' She traced a finger across the map. 'Heading east, where do you think you might be based?'

Her father cleared his throat. 'Um, the next big city is called Reims.'

Violet squinted, hardly daring to breathe at what she saw next. 'Épernay,' she said triumphantly. 'Champagne country. Now, that's where you recuperated during the last war, wasn't it?' She gave him a glacial stare.

'Nothing gets past you, Violet. I didn't know you even knew I was in Épernay.'

'You told me before we moved here. That's where the champ-enoise was, and you learned about making Champagne from her. You told me you became inspired to use your skills to make some-thing people enjoy, rather than going back into industrial chemistry.'

He shook his head with awe. 'Your memory is astounding.'

'I'm right, though, aren't I?'

He shifted uneasily in his chair. 'Yes. And it's one of the reasons they might want to send me there, because I'm already familiar with the region. I'll have to polish up my rusty French, but I was fluent, so it's like riding a bike. You don't forget.'

She nodded, watching him carefully. 'You sound excited.'

'Well.' He blew out a breath. 'I wouldn't say excited exactly, more that I'm relieved and filled with anticipation to finally be useful. We've watched all our fine young men bravely hug their families goodbye, with too many of them not realising it would be their final farewell.' He shook his head sadly. 'They all looked so fresh and energised by the adventure, keen to get away from sleepy Tasmania.'

'Just like you do now.'

'Violet, those lads had no idea what they were being sent into. They were going to hell itself. I *do* know. But when I was in the trenches, it was all artillery and sniper fire. Modern warfare is even more terrifying – I've read about the firepower involved. A lot fewer of our boys are coming back.'

'That's bleak, Dad.'

'All the older blokes like me won't say much. None of us do. None of us want to think about those times, but now we've been watching our young go off to the same, if not worse.' He gave a sound of disgust. 'But I can be useful.'

'So could I,' Violet protested. 'How would you feel if I trained as a nurse and signed up to go to the battlefront, like Mum did?'

'I would forbid you,' he came back fast.

Violet gave a shocked laugh. 'But it's fine for you to spring this on me?'

'I have to do this, Violet. I'm a man.'

'Oh, really? Yet I can do a man's work around the farm while you flit off to war?'

'I'm sorry, that came out wrong.'

'I don't think so. You feel it's your right to protect me, but I can't protect you.'

'I'm your father. I'm allowed to take that role. Besides, I can't let other men go off to war while I sit it out, all safe in my barley fields, sipping whisky.'

'You know full well, Dad, that we are growing grain to feed Australia, to feed our men overseas, to feed our cattle. There is no shame in working the land. It's still for the war effort.'

He shook his head. 'Cold comfort, I'm afraid. I hate to admit this, but I know war, and unfortunately I'm good at it. I can't sit back and watch any longer – even if this ends soon. I need to help.'

'And me?'

'You need to stay here and run the farm that's helping to feed Australia. And to continue the real dream and make whisky from that spirit we've had sleeping for three years. You're grown now. I know I can leave you alone to get it done. I didn't tell you yet – I heard that our licence has been approved. They're sending the paperwork.'

She shook her head; it was his turn to pin her down, like a butterfly specimen. 'We're so close to turning it into whisky. You're now giving up the dream.'

He sighed, turning to stare out the window. It was as though he'd known they'd have to have this dramatic conversation, and that he just had to survive it and she would come around to his point of view.

'And if I asked you not to go?'

He whipped his head around to look her directly in the eye. 'You wouldn't do that.'

She folded her arms. 'Wouldn't I?'

'I know you too well. You're as pragmatic as your mother. And she wouldn't try to change my mind any more than you will. This is not about us, Violet. This is about trying to save lives, and I have knowledge that can help.'

'Is that *all* it's about?' She had to ask the question that had been burning in her brain since he'd mentioned France.

He stared at her, open-mouthed, and she was sure she saw a flash of guilt in his eyes. 'What does that mean?'

'Sophie Delancré,' she said evenly, and yet it landed like a bomb. She watched his features rearrange themselves from a soft frown of enquiry into an expression so even and empty to the point of being blank.

'What did you say?'

'I said the name of the champenoise.'

'Why?' His voice was steel.

'Mum's dead. You're not letting her down if you tell me the truth. But you *are* letting me down if you lie to me any longer about this woman.'

'I—'

'You can hide from everyone, but not me. We're too alike.'

'Violet—'

'Think first before you try and talk around it, Dad. Because if you lie to me now, I will never forgive you. Is that what you want hanging over us as you march off to war, with no guarantee that you'll come back, or ever see me again?'

He leant his elbows on the table and put his head in his hands, like he was hiding from her.

'You're going for *her*?'

He shook his head behind his hands. 'No.' He looked up with pain in his expression. 'Absolutely not! But I can't help it if the fates push us together; if I'm in the region, maybe I will lay eyes on her again.'

'You loved her.' It was not a question.

'I love her,' he answered, and although this should have shocked her, she felt only sorrow.

'More than M—'

'No! Not more than you. Never more than you. You changed my life, Violet. You brought the sunshine.'

'I wasn't going to say "me". I was going to say "Mum". Did you love her more than my mother?'

He let out a long, slow sigh. 'I don't know how to answer that.'

She wouldn't let it go. 'With the truth.'

'Then, Violet, yes. Yes, I did. But only because I loved her first. She was, without a word of a lie, the first woman I have ever loved, and I did so with every ounce of myself.'

Violet scraped her chair back and stood, feeling desperately sad for her mother's memory. 'Grandad was right.'

'No. He wasn't. I was never disloyal to your mother. I was faithful every day of my life to her.'

'Mum worshipped you.' They could both hear the accusation in her voice.

'I know,' he admitted, sounding as forlorn as she did.

'Dad, just harbouring another love is a betrayal.'

'I don't know what to say to that. I loved a woman. I couldn't be with her. I returned home and got on with my life. Fell for and married your mother, had you, and we lived the happiest of lives as a family of three. You know the rest. I resent being held accountable for a love that was never consummated, from more than a quarter of a century ago.'

Violet had never seen her father this riled up, and if she was being honest, he was making perfect sense; it was unfair of her to lay accusations upon him.

'But you demanded truth from me,' he continued, 'and so I've given it to you. May I explain?'

'I'm not sure I want to hear it,' she admitted, shocked by her attitude given how hard she'd pushed him for it.

He shrugged. 'That's all right, I understand.'

'No, on second thoughts, tell me. I think I do need to know it all, or I'll forever wonder.'

'There's not a lot to tell, but here it is.'

The afternoon lengthened while Charlie told his story. As he spoke, he watched his daughter become as still as the vase of flowers she had picked to welcome him home. He knew he should feel guilty. Instead he felt unburdened. Not only was he finally coming clean about the one truth Violet didn't know, but it felt empowering, like a release from jail, to be talking openly about the woman who had been in his heart for so long.

He spoke while he filled the kettle and lit the stove to put it on to boil. He talked through the gathering sound of the heating water and as he busied himself warming the pot. Leaning against the kitchen counter, he took Violet on a journey through his life before he'd met her mother. He hadn't meant to tell her about the orphanage, the scholarship for the grammar school or even his dismay when the laboratories he was working at in Liverpool were forced to start manufacturing gas to use against the enemy at the start of World War I. As one of its chemists, he would have been tasked with this job.

'So you ran away to war?' Violet asked.

He nodded. 'It was the only answer. I told my boss that if I was going to be forced to kill people, I would rather kill them honestly, squaring off against them with a rifle, than with this insidious, cruel mass-killing agent.'

'The Germans used it against all of you, though.'

'They did. It was revolutionary and wicked. But I did not want to have that as my legacy.'

'So go on – what happened?' she said, as he brewed the tea. He placed a thick tea cosy, which he had made himself, over the pot. She often teased him about being a good mother as well as a father to her.

He continued the tale of his time through the war, becoming a crack sniper, and all the woes he had suffered as a result. He even mentioned his German foe, someone he'd nicknamed Adolph Topperwein, who'd been in an American travelling circus as a deadeye shooter, entertaining the crowds by creating impressive designs with the bullets he shot. The German sniper had terrorised their unit. He had been a cracking shot, and until Charlie took on a do or die mission to combat him, he had defied all attempts to be subdued. Charlie had disobeyed orders and gone 'over the top' before feigning death.

'I lay there for hours, Violet, not daring to twitch a single muscle. I listened to the moans of my fellow soldiers pleading for help, praying for death, begging for their mothers. It was heartbreaking, and I'm sure just as heartbreaking on the other side too, as their men fell. But I got him, Violet.'

'You did?' she said, daring to smile.

Charlie touched his forehead, right in the centre. 'He wouldn't have known a thing.'

Finally he shared the frightening series of dangers and decisions that had led him to Sophie Delancré. 'I found myself with the French, don't ask me how. I was simply running for my life from the Germans on their side of the trenches. They were hunting me, and I found myself in a canal, trapped beneath an upturned boat with a German infantryman.'

Her eyes widened. 'Did you have to kill him?'

He shook his head and smiled in memory. 'He was bleeding.

We were both in a bad way and couldn't think of hurting each other. I let him know his own side were near – I spoke some German, fortunately – and told him my name. His was – and I hope still is – Wilhelm Becker... Willi. He was from Bavaria. I told him I was tired of killing, and he admitted the same. I checked his injury – it was his leg, and not life-threatening, but obviously painful.'

'You didn't feel frightened?'

'Of course I did. We were both terrified and exhausted, but we discussed killing one another in an almost academic way. Willi said now that we knew each other, it would be rude. He was funny and lovely. We would have been friends in a different life, and yet we were forced to be enemies by our countries' leaders. Anyway, I bound up his leg, thinking he'd be fine, only to discover that he had taken a bullet to the side. I was so sorry and shocked to see it. He knew from my expression it was bad, and said he was not long for the world.'

'Oh no,' Violet groaned, totally absorbed. 'What did you do?'

'Well, the men were getting closer – we could hear them – and he told me I had to leave or they'd shoot me. He admitted that they were not taking prisoners but killing on sight. So we kissed each other's cheeks and told each other to stay alive. He said I had to visit his town, Freising, near Munich, and come share a beer with him. Best in the world, he claimed. I can even remember its name because he told me I must: Weihenstephaner. He made me promise we'd drink together in peacetime.' Charlie sighed. 'You know, Violet, I can remember thinking in that moment that I'd never felt closer to anyone than I did to Willi, who was my enemy but now my friend.' He nodded, remembering. 'He promised to distract them for as long as possible and then showed me how to get out without being seen. Then he gave me two minutes to steal away before calling for help.'

'And you did.' Violet blew out a breath.

'Yes.'

'Did you go to Bavaria and find Willi after the war?' she asked.

Charlie shook his head sadly. 'I hung back to help out with the clearing parties, so I didn't leave France until early nineteen nineteen. And then influenza was raging, and your mother so pleased to see me back home and safe, there was no way she was letting me hoof off to Germany anytime soon. You came along soon after. So it just never happened.'

'Sad. I hope he's alive.'

'Me too. I hope he made it home to his little girl,' Charlie said.

'And after Willi?'

Charlie sighed. 'After Willi, I was running again for my life.

I managed to run all the way into French territory, where I met another generous man called Gaston de Saint Just, an officer, who had me taken into Reims, where they had a makeshift hospital in the Champagne caves.'

'Caves?' Violet frowned.

'Think of them as cellars, except they're vast tunnels cut out of the limestone,' he explained. 'They stretch for hundreds of miles, and in some parts are tall enough to give you the feeling that you're in a cathedral.'

'And there was a hospital underground?'

'Yes, among cafés and classrooms, sleeping quarters and laundry rooms.' He smiled at the memory. 'The Germans were battering their city with artillery, so the French turned their city upside down and lived underground. Sophie Delancré was a volunteer at the hospital. When the hospital needed spare beds, she took soldiers into her home if they needed time to convalesce before rejoining their men.'

'Is that what you did?'

He shrugged. 'I needed to build my strength. Sophie took an interest in me – perhaps because I was a bit of an oddity, being English, but also because I was a chemist. And I took an interest in her because I enjoyed her intelligence and skill as a champenoise. We became friendly at a time when I needed a friend – life was feeling pretty bleak, with everything I'd seen, all the lives that were being wasted... She helped me to feel like living again, and I helped her to make her Champagne when there was no sugar and it seemed impossible to produce.' He found himself smiling. 'We were both so excited to find a solution and we...' Charlie didn't quite know how to explain what he'd felt around Sophie, nor was he sure he wanted to share it.

But Violet finished it for him. 'You fell in love.'

'I did. Yes,' he said carefully. 'I loved her on sight, I think, but I tried to ignore it.'

'And Sophie?'

'Sophie was married.'

Violet gasped.

'Married, but her husband had been declared missing and killed in action. There had been years of war – and life without him – when we met, though I don't think she gave up hope until...'

'Until what?'

Charlie shook his head, remembering kissing Sophie for the first time in her attic room. 'Until a new sort of hope presented itself. A chance at a different life... to be happy again.'

'With you,' Violet said.

'Perhaps.'

'What happened? It sounds like there was no barrier to you two...'

Charlie poured his untouched tea down the sink. 'Jerome came back from the dead, and that was that.'

'But what—'

'Don't, Violet. I've told you what you wanted to know. It's painful, because while you think I was unfaithful somehow to your mother, I never was. I left Sophie within two hours of her husband returning, and Épernay the following morning. The war ended. I left France about four months later. Your mother and I had met once, just briefly, at this point. She had stitched a head wound of mine and we'd chatted a little. I liked her, but it had felt like a lifetime before. She'd insisted I survive the war, though, and told me that if I did, I was to come and find her and take her dancing.'

'And so you did?'

'That's right. I went looking for her as soon as I came home from France. And I loved her. Sophie was locked away in my memories, and I was completely faithful to your mother. I told her about Sophie before we were engaged to marry, and I think she knew that I would never stop loving Sophie in my heart, but she married me anyway. She knew the love she and I shared was real. I promised her that the past was the past, and I kept my word.'

'Until now.' Violet was watching him carefully.

Charlie shook his head. 'I don't see it that way. We're at war. I am going to do my duty and help out where I can.'

'But you're going to France. What if you meet her?'

'What if I do? It's been nearly twenty-seven years. She's married, probably has grown-up children. Should our paths cross – which I doubt – we are not going to do anything but smile in fond memory and wish each other well.'

Violet nodded, looking thoughtful. What might she be thinking? He wanted to assure her that he was telling the truth, that he had no hidden reason for wanting to go abroad. He wasn't the one choosing where he'd be sent, but, if he was honest, Épernay did feel like it had a magnetic force around it, pulling him there. Perhaps he was always meant to return.

'Are you worried about being here alone?' he asked. 'You can run this place with your eyes shut and one arm tied behind your back, my girl, and you know it. You can call in help too – you've got old Ben and Jimmy around whenever you need them – and you can get yourself set up to blend and bottle the whisky.'

She shook her head. 'It won't be the same without you.'

'Maybe not, but tell me of a household – here, or in England or even Germany – that is the same right now. We all have to play our part. *This* is your task, to keep the cereals growing. Australia needs you. And I need you to follow through on what we began together. You're not a child any more, Violet. You are stronger than your mother and I put together. Make our whisky; make it in *your* name. You have my blessing.'

She shook her head sadly, but he knew she was starting to accept it, would no longer fight him.

He heard a rumbling noise outside. Violet looked up too, frowning. 'Whatever is that?'

It was something that he had not expected until tomorrow, but maybe this would help the sombre mood that had developed over the afternoon.

'I have a surprise for you,' Charlie said.

'Another one?' She shook her head again. 'I don't like your surprises, Dad.'

'Come with me.' He held out his hand.

She took it reluctantly and followed him to the door, which he opened, then grinned widely back at her, pulling her gently forward to look.

Outside was an automobile the colour of gum leaves. Her lips parted in surprise.

'What's this?' she asked, turning to stare at him.

'It's a beautiful big Buick.'

'But... Why is it here? You're not leaving n—'

'Violet, it's ours,' he said, enjoying her shock. He led her down the short path to where the car rumbled on the road.

As they approached, the engine switched off and a man wearing a white coat alighted. 'Hello, again, Mr Nash. Here she is.'

'Here she is, indeed,' Charlie murmured. 'Mr Collins, this is my daughter, Violet.'

She again looked shocked. 'Dad, what's going on?'

But he'd left her side to shake the hand of the newcomer.

'Here are your keys, Mr Nash. All the paperwork is done. Is there anything I can show you, take you through?'

'No, we did that before, and my memory is trustworthy.'

'You drove like a professional, sir, if you don't mind my saying so. Ah, here's my ride back to Hobart,' Mr Collins said, pointing to a black Buick arriving at a funereal pace. 'It's much jauntier in the green, if you don't mind me saying so, sir,' he added with a smile, then touched his hat in farewell.

As the black car retreated, Charlie turned to Violet, who stood in stunned silence. 'Now I'm going to teach you how to drive this beast.'

'Dad, this is madness,' she said finally, in a tight voice.

'No, my darling, it's the future.'

'How did you even get this? I thought new automobiles were on hold through the war.'

Charlie tapped his nose. 'It's who you know, Violet. I managed to get this one because of its colour. Defence has claimed all the available Buicks as its staff cars, but they only want black. I knew a fella who knew a fella.' He grinned. 'Wasn't cheap, but we're doing all right now, Violet. And when I go, you don't need to be hitching up a horse to a cart any longer. If it's good enough for the ambulances in New South Wales, I know it's safe for you. But you have to know how to drive this thing. Come on, hop in. We begin today.'

A few days later, Violet had finally toppled into the right mindset: she knew the rhythm of the Buick and was beginning to feel more comfortable. It had been nerve-racking to begin with, as her father explained how to move to second gear when she sensed the car was gaining speed, and then up to third, and she had discovered changing from third back down to second was potentially traumatic unless she gave the Buick time to think and adjust; she'd bump the gears gently until they slipped back down. But her left hand began to work independently of her awareness, in time with the car's rhythm, and she was making decisions through the gears without having to perspire with concentration.

'Violet, you're driving this Buick as well as I could,' her father said as they hit the open road in the Coal River Valley surrounding their town. Hills undulated around them in velvety mounds of rich emerald. She liked these cooler months most of all because the landscape reminded her of Scotland, but her father explained that the Buick needed time to get warm enough to drive or it would struggle. Now they were bouncing along, the spongy sensation of traversing the road to Hobart a pleasant experience.

'I never really know where the front of the car is, Dad.'

He chuckled. 'It is long, I agree, but you'll learn to judge it – you already are.'

'I'm not ready to take this into town. I'd have to park it in a wide-open space,' she bleated.

'You'll get there, Violet. Just try not to be scared.'

They passed clusters of sheep, normally white but now muddied by the rain and dirt.

'When do you leave, Dad?' The question had sat unspoken between them since he'd told her he was going, while they pretended to be cheerful about the car, about their winter planting ahead, about the quality of the spirit in their first barrel. Violet had been quietly laundering and ironing his shirts for him to take to Europe. It was just a small thing to do that kept her occupied, distracted, while he seemed to hardly focus on what he was about to do. He certainly hadn't raised the topic himself and wouldn't unless she pressed.

'Next week,' he answered bluntly.

They were both peering out of the split windscreen, Violet driving evenly now on the open road.

'When next week?'

'Tuesday.' He wouldn't look at her.

Her heart sank. It was now Friday – that was only a few days away. 'I see. And where do you go first?'

'To Hobart, then Melbourne. I'll take a ship from there.'

'To London?'

'Yes,' he said. 'Come on, let's call into the dairy on the way home. I want to eat some of that delicious cheese of theirs.'

And those, apparently, were his final words on the matter of his imminent departure. He shifted topics and would not gladly return.

EIGHT
BEAULIEU, ENGLAND

July 1944

Charlie had completed his training at Beaulieu, in the south of England. It was six weeks of challenge, but he would be lying if he said it was anything but completely absorbing. He had lit up inside when the trials began: first learning and then being tested on everything from how to pick locks to recognising German uniformed police and the national police of France, who were working with the invaders.

He was not allowed to write home with any details, but if he were, his first message to Violet would have been to tell her that he had a whole new respect for pigeons, having now learned how to use them to send clandestine messages. Given a lot of people considered pigeons a messy nuisance, he would from now on defend the birds loudly. *We've domesticated them and used them in two wars to protect our safety, and they have bravely trusted us and done our bidding. How dare we now consider them a pest?*

He found it straightforward to recognise German troops and weaponry, having been up close to both in the past, although he would be the first to admit that the modern kits and weaponry were dazzling. The days of learning felt endless but intriguing, and perhaps the most fascinating topic was morale warfare. The propaganda from both sides was astonishing, cunning and cruel.

At the end of his six weeks, he was called in to meet with SOE-F Section's Planning Officer, a man in his forties with a thick head of hair and a sympathetic smile. A thrum of excitement was weaving through Charlie's body like a current that connected him through time and space. He could feel it drawing him towards France and whatever awaited him there.

As excited as he was, he missed Violet fiercely. By the time he got home, she'd be producing and selling whisky in her name.

Would he get home?

Who knew?

He focused his attention on the man in front of him, who was consulting some notes in a file. 'Flying colours, Nash.'

'Thank you, sir.' Charlie was pleased. 'You seemed to take it all in your stride.'

'I wouldn't say that, sir, but I feel newly educated, as though I've just done all my school years again in a very short time. My head is full, and I feel ready to get on with things.'

'Subversion seems to be your strength. A natural aptitude, perhaps?'

Charlie shrugged. 'I just did my utmost in every part of the training.'

'Well, your suggestion that you be attached to the eastern circuit in France can work well for us.'

Charlie felt his insides twist with a helpless thrill. If they sent him south he wouldn't have even the faintest opportunity to see Sophie again. He'd mentioned his experience in the Champagne region before leaving Australia, but from the initial correspondence he hadn't held much hope that he'd be sent there – he'd imagined the closest he might get would be to work with the city circuits based in Paris. 'The east,' he replied, keeping his expression neutral. 'Good. Where exactly, sir?'

'Well, we know you have knowledge of the area around Reims.'

'I do,' Charlie said, his heart leaping with excitement. 'Reims, Épernay, above and below through the tunnels.'

'Yes, that's what we thought. We're going to attach you to Silversmith circuit, which works with the maquisards in that region.'

'Fine. Thank you, sir.' Charlie wanted to leap into the air and punch it. Instead he gave a conservative nod, privately delighted to imagine himself working with the French Resistance fighters.

'You'll link up with Captain Borosh, whose nom de guerre is Hippolyte.'

'Do I report—'

'We're aware that you demobbed with the status of captain. We're also aware of the selfless risks you took in no-man's-land to save your unit from a particularly crack sniper.'

'Yes, sir.'

'Good man. We also know that you volunteered to remain behind in France when many of your peers went home, and that you worked diligently with the clearing parties. Very impressive.'

'I was young, sir. I'm almost twice that age now.'

'Indeed. While you will technically report to Hippolyte, you'll really be working alongside him in a liaison role between Silversmith and ourselves here at HQ. We'll be expecting reports from you regularly.' The officer looked at Charlie intently. 'I can't say much right now about forward plans, but north-eastern France is obviously a region of intense activity from all sides. Hippolyte has been in the field regularly, most recently after the Normandy landings earlier this year. His team's role now is to support all that was achieved at great cost to the Allies. We lost something in the order of ten thousand men during Operation Neptune, and we can't let it be in vain. All circuits are now actively working to capitalise on what was achieved. I hope we never forget just how vital Fortitude North and Fortitude South were for Neptune.'

Charlie frowned. He knew what Neptune was – known to most as D-day – but he didn't know what his superior now referred to. 'I'm not aware of those ops, sir.'

'Good job too – they were operations of pure deception. We managed to point the Germans towards an attack on Norway but, even more importantly, we set up a fictitious First United States Army Group located in Kent and Sussex, convincing Hitler that the main Allied attack would take place in Calais. A truly beautiful deception in so many ways. I could talk about it all day, but you have places to be. Silversmith can use your expertise and extra hands in every disruption the team can achieve towards ending this bloody war. We want to sabotage German plans, we want to interfere with their advance, to confuse and disrupt communications and especially to prevent them from gathering any reliable information.'

'Yes, sir.' Charlie nodded.

'You've requested a specific nom de guerre, I see?'

'If I may, sir.'

'Orge?' The man smiled. 'Most unusual. Barley, is it?'

'Er, yes, sir. I grow barley back home, alongside wheat. Barley is also the key ingredient used to make a single malt. I see you favour Glenfiddich, sir,' he said, nodding towards the drinks cabinet behind the military man.

His smile widened. 'I do.'

'Can't make it without barley, sir.'

'Right, then.' He chuckled. 'Orge it is. You'll be leaving here for a base near Chichester.' At Charlie's frown, he explained. 'The home base is Tempsford in Bedfordshire, but we've been based out of Tangmere for clandestine missions. We drop and pick up from behind enemy lines using the nimble Lysander aircraft.'

'Where am I landing, sir?'

'Within the Angers to Tours area.'

'And I'll make my way to Paris?'

'No, you'll avoid that, Nash, at all costs. Far too dangerous, with all the checkpoints and random searches. No, I would recommend that you make your way directly – as best you can – to Reims. You've learned your backstory competently? Know it, feel it, believe you've lived it?'

'Yes, sir. I believe now after six weeks that I actually *am* Pierre Dupont.' He grinned. 'And the surname checks out as northeastern French, too. It makes absolute sense to me that I'm an itinerant worker from the vineyards at Épernay and therefore have knowledge of the Champagne cellars. It is all very familiar, and I can ad lib if I'm ever cornered.'

'Excellent, excellent. Well, Captain Nash – or should I say Monsieur Dupont – I'm going to hand you over to my colleague in the office next door, and he will make the final arrangements for you to leave here. I have briefed your contacts, especially the emergency ones, and you've been assigned a safe house. Please note the emergency people may not be in Reims or Épernay.'

'Very good.' Charlie held out his hand. 'Thank you, sir.'

'Nash, I'm sure you'll work diligently and make us as proud as you made us in the previous war.'

'I hope so, sir.' Charlie gave a salute.

'Good luck, Nash.' He saluted in return.

Next door Charlie met an older, ruddy-faced officer smoking a pipe. 'Ah, Captain Nash. Come on in.' The officer gestured to a seat.

Charlie settled himself and waited. Suddenly this was all feeling terribly real. He'd never imagined he would have to go to war again, but he was ready. He might have a pistol on him, but he was reassured that he would never again have to look down the sight of a rifle. He also had a very firm hope that he could play his part for the Allies without having to shoot a bullet or injure anyone, given his role was liaison. Maybe that was a hollow hope – he was being sent in to help injure the Germans after all – but it was something to hold on to.

Besides, he told himself, it was stalling the Germans. Not killing. Subversion was his game now. And then he'd go home to Violet.

It had been heartbreaking saying goodbye to her, but she'd been brave, even as she was unable to disguise or banish the tears in her eyes. 'Come home, Dad,' she'd told him. 'You don't have to be heroic. You have nothing to prove.'

Charlie had realised, on that cool autumn's day, that in spite of all the sadness of his life, he was truly blessed. And his legacy didn't lie in his heroics or his cunningly blended whisky, or his bountiful barley or wheatfields.

His legacy was Violet Nash.

'You'll find all your papers in here,' the man said now, sitting opposite Charlie and puffing gently on his pipe. His tobacco smelled of Sweet Virginia and, though Charlie was not a smoker, he found the smell comforting. 'You've impressed all your trainers, none more than me, in how convincingly you present yourself as Pierre Dupont.'

'Thank you.' The man was not in uniform so Charlie had no idea if he should be addressing him by his status.

'After you leave here, you'll be changing into new clothes and, as invasive as it may feel, someone will check everything on your person. Please do not carry any personal items. I understand it may be comforting to have something on you from home, but if you are stopped at a checkpoint or searched by the police, that item could get you arrested. I might add, they are holding public executions for any resisters or traitors they can get their hands on. No trial, nothing, just taken into the town square and gunned down. So make sure there's nothing on you that even smells of England, or indeed Australia. I gather you're leaving a daughter behind?'

Charlie nodded. 'She's in Australia.'

'You might like to call or compose a letter straight after our meeting, because there won't be time once you leave for Tangmere. I'll make sure it's sent immediately. All items given to you will have been vetted and checked, down to the buttons on your shirt, so I can't stress enough the importance of taking this seriously. Your life and, even more importantly, the lives of your fellow circuit members may depend on it.'

Charlie was solemn. 'I'll be diligent.'

'Good, good,' the officer said. 'Well, I think that's it, Nash. Can I offer you something to toast to your success in the field?'

Charlie was going to decline but that felt suddenly churlish. 'Whatever you're having, thank you.'

'Well, you're my last appointment of the day and it is past six, so I think I'll have a nip of Scotch. Know anything about good Scotch, Nash?' He gestured behind him to a drinks cabinet similar to that next door.

Charlie smiled. 'A little, sir.'

'Oh, really? What's your favourite poison, then?' The officer reached for a bottle of Glenfiddich.

Charlie couldn't help himself. 'Well, sir, that bottle's this year's, is it?'

'It is,' the man said.

'That one has quite a complex aroma. It's at once vibrant and uplifting. I'm guessing you like it very much?'

'I do, as a matter of fact – it's got something going on that is slightly different to my usual Glenfiddich dram.'

Charlie smiled. 'This year's has a faint hint of floral – perhaps rose and even violets – but I imagine what you're responding to is the green tobacco leaf, as well as oak and smoke.'

'Good grief, man.' He looked amused.

Charlie held his finger up, forgetting himself momentarily. 'There's a toffee flavour because it starts so sweet. I might even describe a zesty marmalade.'

That made his companion chuckle. 'I've never heard Scotch described this way. How do you know all this?'

Charlie shrugged. 'I used to make Scotch in Speyside. I was a chemist originally, but I turned my attention to distilling after the Great War, probably at least partly due to my experience in Épernay, learning about Champagne.'

'Marvellous. But don't show any affinity for Scotch in France. They don't understand it.'

Charlie nodded his agreement as the man handed him a squat glass with a syrupy slug of liquid gold.

'Well, here's to it, old man. Bottoms up, safe landing and a successful mission.'

Charlie raised his glass. 'Cheers.'

Charlie arrived in France in a Lysander aircraft, painted a matte black, which carried him up and over the English Channel. The pilots used the simple navigation tools of a compass and the moon, which is why, he learned, they traditionally only flew these spy missions in the dead of night, and only five days either side of the full moon. One of the fly boys explained to him that the pilot also used the Loire River for navigation because under the silvery light of the heavy moon it was illuminated 'like a girl's ribbon for us to follow'.

Charlie would be lying if he said, looking down at that silver ribbon, that he wasn't excited. But, perhaps more to the point, he also felt useful. For the past couple of years, he'd been allowing Violet to make more and more decisions. Her awareness of business, selling, buying and even forecasting was now far superior to his, and she would soon outclass him on the blending too. Violet had an uncanny knack for knowing how to manipulate people, which sounded sinister, but she weaved her magic with a smile that was as generous as her attitude. She might outwit the person on the opposite side of the desk, but he was sure she would not do anything sly, unlike many others in such a situation.

He had chosen not to telephone her before flying out for fear that hearing her voice would somehow undo him. He'd been able to leave her in Tasmania because she was smart and capable, but to be so far away, knowing he was walking headlong into danger once again, made every moment feel exquisitely precious. He didn't want to second-guess his decision, so it was easier to write. Although it felt cowardly, it was the right decision if he was to remain committed to carrying out his duty.

And so, hours before he climbed up into the Lysander, he wrote to her, keeping it as understated as possible and as vague as would be demanded, but feeling happy she knew where he would be.

My dearest Violet,

By the time you read this letter I will be in France. Please do not fear for me. I am feeling extremely confident in my role compiling regular reports for the folk at home. I am, you could say, the eyes and ears in the region they have sent me to, though I am not allowed to mention where that is.

He was sure that would pass muster. It was all appropriately vague and didn't mention where, when or British Intelligence.

I hope this note finds you in good spirits and that the barley did indeed deliver the bumper crop we anticipated. My fingers are crossed that Cascade paid you handsomely for all your hard work.

Before I left England, I shared a farewell dram of Glenfiddich – this year's. It is delicious but honestly, my girl, I think you're going to make a drop that will not only announce you on the world stage but have some old men in Scotland very worried. Ha! I hope to taste that special first bottling with you on my return. Don't sell it all!

All my love to you, Violet. Keep making me proud.

Ever your loving Dad, xx

So now here he was in France, carrying nothing but his identity papers. His name belonged to a real person from southern France – recently dead, apparently, but a name like Pierre Dupont felt common enough. Since he was supposed to be a vineyard worker, he'd taken the added precaution of roughing up his hands, but with his years of working in Tasmania, they were likely convincing enough anyway, with various scratches and tiny scars.

He had even taught himself to walk with the slight stoop of the labourers who'd worked with Sophie in her vineyards. He hadn't shaved in days, and he'd splattered his trousers with some mud and used a blade to nick a hole or two in his jacket so he looked like a journeyman.

He hadn't spoken a word of English since leaving the Lysander and felt amazed at how easily the beautiful language of the French had returned to him. It felt natural and easy, although he was a little concerned that colloquial French might have changed over the past couple of decades. He listened carefully to the local lilt as he travelled, keeping his own words to a minimum, like the gruff old worker he presented as. He'd also taken up smoking again, but that mostly meant having a lit cigarette in his mouth, smoke curling at his eye; he rarely inhaled unless he was talking to someone and they were close enough to notice. He'd done a lot of walking as he slowly made his way to Reims, thumbing lifts wherever he could. He'd caught one bus and travelled in the back of a truck, and now he had a bicycle that he'd found lying in a field. He wondered at its story: who owned it, why it was abandoned, and why there? Ideas swirled and kept him entertained for a short while, but he never let it enter his head that the owner had been killed, perhaps as part of the Resistance he was supporting here.

He found himself seated in a café, taking a welcome break from the summer heat, drinking a thin, cold soup that was tastier than English fare despite having no meat, its onion and garlic humming around a few chunks of potato. A heel of bread cooked that morning made all the difference. Since the 1914 war he was no longer greedy about food, and was sure he wasn't alone. Years in trenches with a hollow belly had taught him how to survive on slim choices and manage cravings. Ellen had complained repeatedly that he ate like a bird, and once Violet began to cook for him, she took up her mother's lament. He'd kept his figure trim despite their efforts, and now he was losing weight again, the appearance he needed to blend in with the so-called Free French. They were doing it tougher in Paris, he'd gleaned, living on who knew what, but out here in the countryside it was easier to find fresh food – if the Nazis hadn't commandeered it – including the odd egg as a rare treat. A thin soup with a crust of bread wasn't exactly a feast, but it was more than adequate to stop the grind of hunger.

During his meal, he fell into conversation with the owner of the café, a middle-aged woman who was polishing wine glasses behind the counter.

'I haven't seen you around here,' she said, not exactly suspicious, Charlie thought, but being careful. He accepted it. Everyone behaved this way.

'I'm on my way to the vineyards at Épernay,' he said easily, 'to see if I can find work.'

'You know vineyards?'

He nodded and took a deep spoonful of his soup as she watched him. 'Any grapes, I'm your man,' he replied after swallowing. 'Though it may seem to the untrained eye that it's quiet this time of year.' His softly amused expression said otherwise.

'*Pfft!*' she said with a grin. 'And hell breaks loose soon.'

A young man entered and sat at the bar. His hair was neat, his clothes quite new and modern.

The woman gave him her attention and spoke in rapid French. 'Good day, sir. What can I get you?'

'Coffee and baguette,' he said.

Poor manners, Charlie thought, but he kept his gaze firmly on his soup bowl. He was aware of the man looking his way, but did not look up, listening to the woman going through much the same conversation as she'd had with him. The young man was vague in his responses.

'How's your soup?' she asked Charlie, returning to him.

'Everything I needed,' he replied with a smile.

She smiled back. 'I wouldn't have thought they'd be worrying about the vines up north. Lots of troop activity there.'

He wished she hadn't returned to the subject of his work, but he shrugged in the Gallic way that he recalled so well. 'The vines aren't at war. They don't understand guns and bombs,' he said sadly. 'They keep bravely growing. These are critical weeks.'

'You're headed to the vineyards?'

Why wasn't he surprised the younger man was joining in? Charlie gave a slow blink. 'I am,' he replied, feeling he would come across as surly if he ignored him. 'I was just telling madame that I travel there, hoping to find piecework in the wine regions.'

'What do you do?'

Again Charlie shrugged. 'A little of everything. I've been involved with vineyards all of my working life. And you?' he asked, looking at the man directly, hoping to change the direction of the conversation.

'I am a merchant. I'm from Paris,' he said. 'It's nice to be out of the city, though.'

Liar! Charlie thought. *Too young, too forward, and you're not Parisian either.* He sensed an Alsatian accent, with its Germanic trait of accentuating the first syllable of a word, and was immediately on guard. 'A merchant of what?'

'As a matter of fact, of wine,' the younger man said with a smile. Another lie. 'Surely there is not much work in vineyards at this time of year.'

Definitely not a merchant of wine, then, Charlie concluded, or he would know what a stupid remark that was. Work never stopped in vineyards, even when they looked quiet. 'In the Champagne fields, especially at Épernay, this is the time when everything is full of life, including the weeds... but you probably know that. It's a full-time role for several people in each field.'

'Why aren't you in the army, or...'

'In a work camp?'

Yes, this man was definitely an agent provocateur. Charlie had been warned about informants like this, who were paid to roam around spying on everyday folk, hoping to provoke an unguarded comment or entice the spilling of information to uncover Resistance members.

He despised their role, but were they all that different from him? He too was working clandestinely, telling lies, pretending to be someone he wasn't. Except, he reminded himself, he took on this role honourably, for the protection of life, and with no money involved. He was still a soldier, in effect, following his sense of duty. But maybe this young man had family he was protecting... or maybe he was being coerced by the Germans, blackmailed in some way. Maybe he was originally from Germany. Or maybe he just needed the cash to buy his family some food to survive another week or two. Charlie wanted to feel generous. Even so, he had to be very careful now.

'I imagine in most other occupations I would be in a work camp,' he said now, sounding resigned. 'I was working in the vineyards of the south last summer, around Avignon. You know Châteauneuf-du-Pape?'

The man's eyes widened. Yes, he knew of it.

Charlie didn't know the region well, but it was the only impressive region he could think of in the moment. 'It's very particular down there. So many grape varieties used in their blends. I counted thirteen grapes,' he said, digging into the deepest recesses of his memory for what he'd learned from Sophie. 'They all ripen at slightly different times, but I won't bore you with the details.' He grinned, having decided a more friendly countenance was required. *Be open, wear him down with conversation, if necessary,* Charlie thought, even though his natural inclination was to remain silent and blend into the background as much as possible. No, this fellow was looking for strangers, anything that might give a person away as a foreigner on foreign soil. *Not today, my friend,* he thought. *I have important business in Reims, and I'll be damned if you are the man who stops me seeing Sophie again.*

'Anyway, they like my work and I come with good recommendations,' he continued, tapping his pocket to suggest he carried paperwork attesting to this, then flexed his fingers. 'My hands are still strong,' he said. 'But I know about making wine too. They liked that I know the right moment to harvest all those different grapes.'

The woman, who had been listening, gestured to his soup plate. 'May I?'

'Thank you,' Charlie said. 'That will see me all the way to Reims.' He smiled and started digging in his pocket for francs.

But the inquisitive newcomer was not ready to let him go yet. 'Do you mean they categorise you as essential?'

Charlie gave a long shrug. 'All I know is that neither the French Army nor the German Army want me for their needs. Too old, too stooped. But I can help provide something our German masters in Paris are very keen for.'

The café owner laughed. 'Yes, monsieur, the German officers do love our wine and Champagne, so it is that skill that encourages them to leave you be.'

Charlie grinned. 'Can you imagine the higher powers without their Champagne?' He knew he was taking a risk speaking so openly, but he wanted to extricate himself now.

It worked; both of his companions laughed.

'Have a good day, monsieur,' Charlie said politely. 'I hope your work goes well.'

'Oh, the wine business flourishes during war as you suggest, monsieur... er...?'

'Dupont.' Charlie was pleased the name had flowed naturally from his tongue.

'Dupont,' the fellow repeated. 'It's my family's business. I am but a small part,' he said, sounding modest all of a sudden.

Charlie wasn't sure whether to believe this fellow had any family connections to wine, but then he didn't really care. All he wanted to do was get out of this café now, out from under the gaze of this nosy customer. '*Au revoir*,' he said, replacing his flat cap on his head.

'*Bon journée*,' the woman and the nameless spy said in chorus.

Charlie left the café but did not go to the train station as he'd planned. It was annoying to stray from his intended route, but every instinct told him not to trust the overly curious man he had been speaking with. Instead he took the backroads and resigned himself to being on a bicycle for a little bit longer.

NINE

HOBART, TASMANIA

July 1944

The Cascade Brewery manager whom Violet had travelled to Hobart to see had been held up at an appointment. She was told this by a man, John Cameron, whom she judged to be around her own age, neatly dressed and obviously part of the management team. She wondered why he wasn't away fighting, but immediately admonished herself, hating that some men were made to feel guilty that they weren't in uniform.

Mr Cameron was smiling. 'Mr St Hill sends his deepest apologies. He may be another half-hour, I'm sorry. I wonder whether, in the interim, you might like a quick tour, Miss Nash? I gather you haven't been here previously. I'm very pleased to meet you – I know *of* you, of course, through your father.'

'Yes, I too am sorry I haven't been here before. My father has always taken the lead with your brewery.'

'Is he unwell?'

'Er, no. He's gone off to war, Mr Cameron.'

Her companion looked mortified. 'Oh, forgive me, I—'

'It's all right. He's far too old to be off on this adventure, even though I know there are plenty of Australians who fought in the Great War still doing their bit. He insisted on going but, I hasten to add, he is working as some sort of liaison officer out of London. He's not at the front.' She was careful not to give any specifics; her father had warned her she was not to mention him being in France to anyone.

The man in front of her looked intrigued. 'Oh, what does that entail?'

'I have no idea,' Violet said, with a laugh. 'Pushing paper around a desk, no doubt. I can't imagine he'll enjoy a second of it, as my father is someone who likes to be very busy, usually outdoors, or certainly doing something with his hands. Staplers and reports are not for him.' She smiled, hoping to move Mr Cameron away from the topic of her father's absence.

'Is he safe in London?' he asked, and then shook his head. 'Apologies... I know no one's safe, and you must be worried. I tried to join up, but was rejected.'

'Oh, that must have been distressing. I know a couple of the younger men out our way were turned down when they volunteered.'

'Considered essential?'

She nodded.

'Well, I hope people are kind to them. I have found some to be less than generous in their attitude. I am considered an invalid,' he said, looking down at his foot, but offered no more information and she was not one to pry. 'I do hope your father remains safe. We all like Mr Nash. And I'm sorry to have enquired and perhaps stirred up your emotions.'

'I imagine he's not actually in Central London, where the bombings continue – I think he's based somewhere outside it, but I haven't yet learned where,' she fibbed. 'Now, if you apologise to me once more today, Mr Cameron, I shall have to leave.'

'Oh no, don't do that,' he said, looking worried. 'I promise I shall have no reason to again. Please call me John. I feel like my father when you call me Mr Cameron.'

'Then I'm Violet. And, yes, a tour would be most welcome, thank you.'

John looked delighted by this and gestured that she should follow him. 'We'll start where all the action takes place. Actually,' he paused, grinning, 'everything happens in one busy space.'

Now that he'd relaxed, Violet couldn't help but like him and his easy manner. As he moved ahead of her to lead the way, she noticed a pronounced limp, which explained more fully why he would not have been conscripted or allowed to enlist. But there had been disappointment in his tone and she suspected, with some sadness, that John Cameron would have taken any role – even pushing paper around a desk – just so he could play his part.

They moved into the factory building and started down an open staircase that wound into the brewery. They paused halfway down so she could view the whole expanse. 'We consider the Nash barley the finest we use in our beer,' John said, with a bright smile that turned his countenance from earnest to handsome.

'We're very proud of it,' she said, then remarked, 'I smell resin.'

He looked at her in query.

'Um, that woody smell – it's vaguely fruity... and perhaps even like licorice.'

'That smell will disappear as we go deeper, where it becomes overwhelmed by much more powerful aromas. But for now, well done – that's the fresh hops you're registering. A load came in today.'

'It's a pleasant smell,' she assured him.

'It needs to be. We like our hops to be very fresh, harvested at the right time too. We make high-quality beer here, so we insist on the very best hops to match your barley.'

'What do you want to smell in your hops?'

'Exactly what you describe. I grew up on a farm, where we had hops. It's that resinous aroma, leaning into sweetness and an equal balance of spice. And then, of course, we want that strong fruity note... slightly citrus, rather than anything floral or herbal. We avoid those last two. All our hops presently come from the Derwent Valley up north.'

She smiled. 'Thank you. I've learned something today, including that you're a farmer at heart.'

'Love of the land never leaves.'

'Would you do it again?'

He nodded. 'I think I would, but our farm went to my elder brother, so it's not an option.'

Violet gave him a sympathetic shrug and returned to their previous topic. 'So the hops give your beer its bitterness?'

'Well, it does depend on when you add it. If you do so early in the process then, yes, you turn up the bitterness.'

'And if you add it later?'

'It's complex. If you hold off, then it's more about what the hops brings in terms of aroma rather than taste, although I'm assured that taste and smell function together.'

Violet nodded. 'They do.'

'Oh, you know that?'

She didn't want to admit that she made whisky yet. 'Er, yes, my father used to work as a chemist in his early career. He told me about this sympathetic partnership of senses years ago.'

He grinned. 'Ah, well, there you go. I thought it was an old wives' tale.' Now, as they left the stairs behind, he gestured at the large space in front of them, around which were huge white vats. 'So all of this was rebuilt nearly two decades ago. At the time, I think Cascade laid claim to having the most modern ale, beer and lager plant available in the world of scientific progress.'

'Because of the equipment it had?'

'Because of everything. We use what's known as the Nathan Process, and that was installed here.' He went on to explain. 'Ale and beer are susceptible to infection from all manner of outside sources, and until this method was invented, there was no known process by which infection could be wholly prevented.'

Violet gazed around. 'Well, it all looks so clean and spotless, it's worthy of a hospital.'

'I think it might be even more sterile.' He grinned again.

She felt fortunate that such a pleasant man was helping her to fill this time. She was beginning to realise that this had been missing from her life; she had no company. She was friendly with everyone and never found it hard to generate conversation or get to know people, but she lacked close friends. Somehow, perhaps to avoid pain, she'd persuaded herself that her father's company was sufficient. They shared so much, with her father taking their farming and whisky ambition so seriously that he ignored the women who looked at him with yearning. But she now realised that she too had quashed all desire for companionship and had ignored so many invitations from young men that they'd given up asking her out.

So many dances missed. A chance to be in someone's arms. She sighed. Oh, she'd dated a little bit – met someone at the local fair, gone into town to see a film with another kind fellow – but they were all a little intimidated by her, she could tell. She really didn't mean to be scary, but perhaps she was, with her opinions and no-nonsense attitude – and her drive. She figured that was the dampener; she'd soon worked out that most men didn't seem to appreciate women with too much ambition for themselves.

Most of the local men she met had marriage and children on their mind, hopefully some sons to help run their farms, and daughters who would look after them into old age. When the few brave souls did pluck up the courage to kiss her, it had felt hollow, because her heart wasn't in it. She'd always been looking for something else. She wondered now, what was that something? Love, yes, but more. Something invisible and important; something that didn't need to be spoken but was understood... that was shown in his actions.

Next to her John cleared his throat.

'Er, sorry, I missed that,' she admitted.

'You seemed a long way away. Probably in England with your father? He's always talking about you, so it's not hard to imagine you are close.'

'Yes, thank you. We are. Forgive me, what did you say before?'

'I was talking about the wort... er, sorry... do you know what that is, Miss Nash?'

She thought for a second. 'The sugars? What I call mash, or the malt extract.'

'Exactly.' He smiled. 'You're knowledgeable.'

'In Scotland, where I lived as a child, I couldn't help but pick up some pointers on distilling whisky. Wort is just an old-fashioned derivative of "wyrt", which means plant, herb, root, that sort of thing.' She couldn't help mentioning Scotland and knew he'd react.

Now John looked even more impressed. 'Whisky,' he breathed. 'I wish we made it here – they do on the mainland.'

'Tasmania is built for it. Dad and I have always felt that Richmond feels like Scotland at times,' she said. 'Actually, I've not been wholly honest, John.'

'Oh?'

She smiled. 'Dad's begun the whisky process. He's been granted a licence too, but we haven't talked it up anywhere. It's early days.'

John's impressed look turned to surprise. 'That's brilliant news. Truly. Congratulations. I'd love to see the set-up.'

'Well, please visit, by all means,' she said, meaning it.

'I will,' he promised. 'I want to hear all about it. But I suppose we should get back to our tour?'

Violet nodded. 'Please.'

'At Cascade we take great care in keeping the malt extract and the beer well guarded against any sort of contamination.'

'Do you mean contamination by wild yeast?'

'By wild yeast, by anything at all.'

'Do you use all the malt?'

He shook his head. 'No, we always have plenty left over.'

She tucked that fact away, thrilled to hear it.

'And now,' he said, raising his voice as they moved further into the main factory, into a central, noisy section of men hammering and sawing, backlit by the orange glow of braziers, 'we've almost reached our in-house cooperage.'

'You make all your own barrels?' Violet shouldn't have been surprised, given how large the operation was and how many barrels they'd need on a weekly basis, but she'd thought they'd use a cooperage somewhere outside of Hobart.

'We have to, just to keep up with the production. Our cooperage is just around that corner.' He pointed. 'All the men work with the tanks and brewery equipment tucked all around them, and the braziers make it very hot.'

'That must be dangerous.'

'It is, yes, particularly in summer. We have very strict protocols for fire. The last thing we want is for the tinder-dry grass and timber all around this region to catch a spark.'

Violet nodded. 'But I notice everyone is smoking?'

He grinned and gave a shrug. 'Try stopping them. We'd have a mass walkout.'

'What do you make the barrels from?' she asked.

'Blackwood from the north-east coast.'

A new idea struck her, catching her breath. 'May I speak with one of your coopers, please?'

'Er, I suppose. Let me see... Frank?' John called, and an older man straightened from his toil. 'He's been here the longest,' John explained.

Frank came over to where they stood, removed his hat and gave a small bow as John introduced them. A lit cigarette hung from his lip, and Violet wondered again at the fire risk.

'I won't shake your hand, miss. My hands are filthy,' Frank said in a genial tone. He took a drag from the cigarette and expertly flicked it out of the huge factory door behind them.

Her gaze turned and followed its burning.

'It's midwinter, Violet,' John said. 'It's fine. Frank, Miss Nash supplies the barley we use.'

'I hear it's the very best, Miss Nash.'

She smiled. 'Thank you. We think so. It's nice to meet you,

Frank. John has been telling me about the barrels you make from blackwood. I was just wondering, could you make a barrel from other wood?'

He nodded. 'Yes, of course.'

'*Any* wood?'

Frank shrugged. 'I don't see why not.'

'How about applewood?'

He grinned. 'I haven't done that before, but happy to have a go.'

'Would you? Can I send or buy the wood to—'

'No, no. I live next door to an orchard, miss. Plenty of timber lying around. Let me have a go first, and perhaps Mr Cameron could let you know how we get on.'

'Thank you, Frank, I'd be really grateful. Your timber smells wonderful. I'm so impressed that all the barrels are made on site.'

'Thank you, miss,' he said, touching his head with a finger and nodding. He replaced his cap and moved back to his work.

John turned to Violet with a smile. 'Applewood barrels?' he quizzed. 'What are you thinking?'

'Well, if I'm going to make Tasmanian whisky, I want to give it some notes from this glorious island. In Scotland we used to brag among ourselves about the earth giving notes of heather or peat. Our barrels were usually leftover from fortified wines – you know, sherry or port – which made an enormous contribution to the flavour of the whisky. So I was thinking, why not apples?'

John's eyes lit up as he took that in. 'I know someone making apple liqueur. Maybe that could add something?'

'It would!' she said, delighted. 'I'd have to consider how to handle that flavour, which might be less subtle than what the actual timber would give but, even so, it's an exciting thought.'

'Tasmanian whisky *is* exciting, Violet. And you're going to make it, even though your dad's away?'

She nodded, laughing. 'I've actually been making whisky with my father since I was a little girl. So, yes, I hope to be bottling our first batch very soon.'

He looked at her with fresh awe. 'I can't wait to see what you do.' He glanced at his watch. 'Er, we have another five minutes. Would you like to see outside?'

'Is there something to see?' She caught herself with a soft chuckle. 'Sorry, that sounds rude.'

'The mill wheel,' he said. 'It's rather lovely.'

Intrigued, she followed him outside, trying not to shiver despite all the warm outer clothes she was wearing. Walking silently by his side, she admired the bush landscape that surrounded the brewery, the rushing stream, then gasped as she saw the mill wheel. 'My gosh.'

'There used to be a mill here,' he explained. 'I suppose one day they'll dismantle the wheel, but for now it's nostalgic, and no one is of a mind to change that.' He paused. 'If I told you the history of this water and how there came to be a reservoir you may know as Mountain Lake, would I risk boring you?'

'Nothing you say is boring, John.'

He gave her a grateful nod. 'This is the purest water in Australia, we believe.'

'I could argue that ours is the purest in Richmond.'

He smiled. 'I wouldn't debate you.'

She returned his smile warmly. 'You really should visit, and I can show you around our farm and the distillery. It's called Glen Corbie.' She surprised herself at how flirtatious she was being, but dismissed it. She was an adult, so was he; why shouldn't they flirt?

'What does the name mean?'

'Valley of the Ravens,' she explained. 'It doesn't entirely apply to where we live now, but it's romantic and beautiful. I don't wish to let it go. Valley of the Magpies doesn't sound quite as mysterious.'

'They're both of the corvid family, so I think you're fine.' He winked. 'It's a shame that your father left just as you're about to bottle.'

'Well, it's a long process. He'd been working on the licence, and it just happened to fall into place when he had to leave.'

John looked at her carefully. 'How exciting. I don't think we've ever had a single distiller of alcoholic spirit in Tasmania.'

Violet laughed. 'Not one who'll own up to it, anyway.'

He smiled. 'I do hear about moonshine.'

'Far more prevalent than you imagine. But our whisky is superb quality, and I have no doubt we'll be able to export it. Dad would like to sell it back to Scotland.'

John didn't let his gaze waver. 'It seems the apple has not fallen far from the tree.'

'You could describe it that way.'

'I don't know what to say, other than I am in awe. I find whisky quite thrilling actually. It's such a complex experience just to drink it, and I can't imagine what it takes to make it.'

She beamed at him. 'Thank you. Most people seem to be scared of a woman tackling what is primarily considered a man's role.'

He shook his head. 'No. I think you're all the more amazing for it. I would love to take you up on your invitation to come and visit, see what you do.'

'It's very simple. There's not much to the equipment. It's actually all in the know-how and a couple of key elements.'

'Which are?'

'The quality of the barley, the malting and the barrels,' Violet listed. 'The rest is science and Mother Nature.'

His eyes were shining with interest. 'My father drinks whisky, and I do too. So I know the beauty of a single malt, and I also know the magic of an incredible blend. I reckon you're being too modest.'

She gave a small shrug. 'Thank you. Should we head back?'

'Oh my, yes. I forgot myself.'

'Glad to know you like whisky,' she said, turning to follow as he hastened back up the incline towards the tall façade of the brewery.

. . .

Violet walked back through the brewery as John went in search of his manager, now on the floor. She moved slowly around the men, who were like worker bees, all busy at their particular jobs. It wasn't noisy with voices – just the odd yell to attract someone's attention, or the bellow of a laugh – but their industry was loud. She took in the bang of mallets being used to drive in the shives, which acted as bungs in the barrels once they were filled. The constant chime of glass bottles being filled and packed into wooden crates. The sound of wood being sawn and the clang of metal hoops being forged by the blacksmith. The hiss of the identifying numbers being burned into the barrels. She could taste sawdust along with the bitter, tarry smell of hot pitch that pervaded this part of the brewery.

It was an assault on her senses, which had been finely tuned over years of barley and whisky production; there was nothing gentle or refined about the process of brewing ale. Unlike whisky, which seemed to enjoy peace and quiet, the ale seemed powered by furious pace and energy. She thought about the single-use barrels the Scots preferred for whisky. They were the polar opposites to these beer barrels, used again and again, treated with indifference for most of their life, left with their dregs at the back of pubs and their insides smeared with pitch to protect the beer from infection. Was there anything she could learn from this process for her whisky? She wasn't sure.

Soon John appeared with a plump, older man at his side – probably her father's age, but not nearly as fit or handsome.

'Miss Nash,' the man said, extending his hand, his moustache straightening across his mouth as he smiled at her. 'I'm so sorry for your wait and grateful for your patience.'

'Oh, don't worry, Mr St Hill. I've already worked out compensation.' She gave a wide smile.

He frowned momentarily, then returned it. 'How intriguing. Please, let's go to my office. Er, thank you, Cameron, for taking care of Miss Nash.'

'Goodbye,' John said, offering a hand to Violet. 'It was a pleasure to meet you.'

She shook it gently. 'Thank you for your time. I'll look forward to seeing you in Richmond.'

'I can't wait,' he said and withdrew.

As Violet followed Mr St Hill to the offices, she glanced back over her shoulder and noticed that John had paused and was still watching her. She turned away, smiling to herself.

A moment later, Violet was making herself comfortable in a chair opposite the manager. He gave a cursory glance to some notes that had been left on his desk. She counted four, presumably telephone calls. A little of the noise from the brewery filtered through, and she imagined it was a comforting background to his work. She wanted to ask if it felt strange at the end of the day to return to a quiet home, but maybe he had a house full of children.

He looked up. 'Forgive me.' He undid the straining buttons of his suit coat and sat down opposite her.

Mr St Hill had been reluctant about having this meeting, so she wanted to keep him on side. 'It's fine. Mr Cameron gave me a lovely tour of the brewery. I'm sure the war has put all sorts of new pressures on you.'

She'd said this to be polite and was surprised when he shook his head.

'We're short-staffed, obviously, but the men remaining – mostly older – are pulling their weight amazingly well. I'm very proud of our team, who are doing their best to fill all roles.'

'Has production dropped?'

Mr St Hill shook his head again. 'It's hard to explain. Since the Depression, and after the new plant came in, we've been steadily increasing our output. A couple of years ago we were able to tell our board that beer sales had doubled.'

She gave the obligatory sound of awe, and he continued.

'The brewery is running as efficiently as ever and, in fact, we are holding steady through these awful years of war, although I will admit to everything getting a lot tighter in terms of supply. Last year we began rationing beer and the Department of War has since prohibited the interstate shipment of beer and ale, which I know is now seriously hampering our ability to trade. Even so,' he said, sounding cheerful, 'I'm told we still paid a twelve and a half per cent dividend to shareholders.'

'That's very impressive,' Violet said.

'We do donate plenty to needy causes, too,' he said, moving into promotional mode, or perhaps he thought that as a woman she needed to hear about charitable donations. 'Just recently we gave almost seven hundred pounds to the Red Cross for its efforts abroad. It's the least we can do. Now. Let's get down to business.' Mr St Hill regarded Violet. 'It's very nice to meet you at last,' he said. 'Of course I've only ever dealt with your father.'

'Who has abandoned us, Mr St Hill, in the pursuit of supporting King and country once again.' Violet gave a polite smile.

He nodded. 'I'm quite surprised they agreed to take him.'

'So am I. But he's cunningly presented himself as a pen pusher with all the right experience from the Great War.'

'Safely behind a desk, presumably?'

'I'm afraid I don't believe that for a moment. I know my father too well,' she said, deciding to be more honest now. 'He's acting as some kind of liaison between London and the European allies, but he's been circumspect with the details.'

'Good grief.'

She shrugged.

Mr St Hill nodded, his face grave. 'He was surely essential services, though?'

She sighed. 'The farm is running, so that essential service continues.'

He looked thoughtful. 'I admire you, Miss Nash.'

'Good, because I have some favours to ask of you.'

'Oh?'

'Given our barley is reserved for Cascade as a priority client – and I must say, you have negotiated some stunningly modest prices for that premium barley – I would like some brewer's yeast as a goodwill gesture.'

He frowned at her. 'Yeast?'

She nodded with a polite smile.

'Whatever for, Miss Nash?'

'To make whisky, Mr St Hill.' Over the course of this morning, she'd decided to tell anyone who asked and not keep the plan a secret any longer.

His confused expression rearranged itself into enquiry. 'What do you mean?'

'Has my father told you what we did before we arrived in Australia?'

He shook his head.

Gently she explained about their whisky production.

'Both of you?'

'Yes. I was just telling John Cameron that I learned the business of distilling and blending at my father's knee.'

'But *you* personally distil whisky? Is this what you're telling me?' He couldn't help the astonishment, it seemed. The idea almost seemed to offend him.

'I do,' she said, wanting to laugh at his shock. 'Actually, between us, I don't see myself as a distiller so much as a blender. Distilling is straightforward if you follow the right protocols and practices. It's blending where the magic happens. As I said, I have learned at my father's side since childhood, and he was nothing short of a wizard. His blends are stunning, especially given the short apprenticeship he had.'

'And now that he has enlisted, he's passed the baton to you?'

'I'd rather he hadn't. I'd rather be working side by side with him this minute, but, yes, I am now our family's distiller and blender, with a newly minted licence.'

'I'm speechless.'

'But why? Do you think women can't distil as men can?'

'Do any women even drink whisky?' he asked.

'Perhaps more than those who drink beer,' she said mildly.

'What I mean is, do you *like* whisky?' He shook his head. 'Mrs St Hill would no more drink whisky than—'

'Down a pint of ale?' Violet smiled, to let him know she was not offended. 'I understand your point of view, Mr St Hill. Given a choice, perhaps most women would rather sip a bright, sweet sherry than a challenging, somewhat smoky single malt. But that doesn't mean a woman is incapable of enjoying whisky. As for me, I love its taste and complexity, which speaks of ancient lands and waters, of memory.'

As he stared at her with a look of total bafflement, she grinned again. 'Anyway, I need brewer's yeast to make my whisky. And Mr Cameron tells me you have yeast to spare. Can I count on you, Mr St Hill?'

He nodded, looking somewhat helpless.

'Marvellous. Now, to my next favour.'

'Another one?'

Violet didn't hesitate. 'Would your coopers make some barrels for me?'

'Er...'

'Given I will continue to favour Cascade with our pricing and supply, this would be most gratifying. I only need half-a-dozen.' She had chosen her words carefully to make St Hill feel as though he was still in control; he was still the one granting the favour, but there was no mistaking the slight edge of uncertainty that the word 'continue' suggested.

'Well... er, yes. What did you have in mind? We can probably find some old barrels around the brewery that we can—'

'No, Mr St Hill. These need to be new barrels. I will buy and supply the wood.'

'But why make them new when we have spares? I don't see the point.'

Violet held back a sigh. 'Your barrels are old – battle weary and coated with pitch. I don't want any of those flavours coming through into my whisky. I want it to age naturally in freshly made barrels, taking on the scent and flavours of new wood.' He frowned as Violet continued. 'You see, if I could get hold of old sherry barrels, perhaps even port ones, that would work – we're using one now. I talked to some winemakers in Victoria and South Australia who fortify wine and they're generous enough to supply some more to try, but I also want some new barrels, and it occurred to me that we have an abundance of apple trees just down the road in the Huon Valley.'

'Good grief.' Now he sounded impressed. 'That's splendid thinking.'

'Thank you. So I'd like your coopers to make me some barrels. Frank in the cooperage has already agreed to do a trial. They're not huge, Mr St Hill, and I will supply both materials and the correct dimensions. They'd knock them up in no time.'

He scratched his head. 'Well, this is all quite unusual, Miss Nash.'

'I know you're not used to dealing with a woman, Mr St Hill. I do understand that it probably feels awkward, but we are now in the fifth year of war, and women are shouldering many of the burdens at home that their men would never have thought them capable of. But here we are. I'm running a farm and haven't missed a beat on production, so I am all you have if you still wish to be supplied by Nash Barley. I don't know when my father will return home, and I'm pushing on in his stead so that when he does come home, he returns to a thriving farm and a new working distillery, which will please him beyond all measure.'

She could see her speech landing as Mr St Hill's eyes widened and blinked. It was time to go for the jugular and request what she'd really come to this meeting for. Jimmy's remark had been burning in her mind; it was audacious but also so sensible and practical. Why go to all the effort of malting the barley themselves when their own barley was being malted right here?

'I also want some malted barley. I'm sure you don't use all that you have with each malting, so in exchange for my continued good-will with our pricing, I would like whatever you can spare for my whisky.' She smiled, moving to sweeten her tone. 'Of which, of course, you will be one of the first recipients.'

'I don't know quite what to say.'

She stood. 'It's very simple, Mr St Hill. Just say yes. Nothing I've asked for costs you much. You'll barely notice the yeast and the malted barley, and the use of your coopers will be minimal and a once-off. It's a very fair deal and just a slight balancing up of the scales. In this time of tightening, as you mentioned, I'm sure you'd wish your barley prices to remain the same.'

He grimaced. 'I'd like to lower them.'

She smiled again and gave a small shake of her head. 'Not just now. We need that goodwill working. There are other breweries very keen to get our grain and...'

'All right, Miss Nash. I don't want our arrangement to change in terms of supply, but perhaps you can sharpen your pencil too.'

She knew he needed to feel like he'd won. 'All right, Mr St Hill. You give me all that I want until March, and I will take a look at our barley prices then and see what can be done.'

He nodded, looking satisfied. 'Good. You can speak to Mr Cameron about the new arrangements.'

'Excellent,' she said, far preferring to deal with handsome, pleasant John than his superior. She held out a hand. 'Thank you for seeing me today and for your generous attitude. I'm really most grateful.'

He shook her hand gently. 'I'll hold you to that bottle of whisky, Miss Nash. I enjoy a tipple very much.'

She grinned. 'I'll deliver it myself.'

TEN
RICHMOND

July 1944

Violet had ended up inviting John Cameron for a picnic. She met him at the train station at Colebrook, not far away from Richmond town. He stepped off the train onto the platform, stomping his feet and blowing into his hands from the cold. She laughed as she greeted him, watching him dig in his pockets for gloves.

'It's not a typical day for a picnic, I know,' she said, shaking his hand once it was gloved. 'Nice to see you again, John.'

'These are for you,' he said, handing over a small tin of chocolates tied with a ribbon. Before she could express surprise or feel awkward about the gift, he continued talking as though the chocolates were irrelevant. 'Are we really going on one?'

'Well, I thought I'd show you the distillery, and then I'd take you out to our famous Richmond Bridge. I've got rugs and, besides, I want to test out my new Thermos.'

'What's that?' he said, sounding suspicious.

'You'll see,' Violet said, amused, 'And you'll be so impressed. Come on.' She gestured to the green Buick.

'Wait! What?' he said, astonished. 'We're going in that?'

She regarded him. 'Are you allergic to automobiles, John?'

His eyes were wide, drinking in the sight of it. 'This is your father's?'

'No,' she said, amusement in her tone. 'This is mine. Meet Gertie. She goes like the clappers once she warms up.'

He stroked the round fender and walked around the entire circumference of the car. 'Violet,' he breathed, 'she's beautiful. How do you come to have this?'

'You'll have to ask my father that. "A fella who knows a fella, apparently." He insisted. I certainly didn't ask for it or even dream of owning a car. But he taught me to drive before he left. Don't look so nervous, by the way, I drive Gertie really well.'

She let him open the driver's door for her, and then she relaxed into the familiar seat, the leather sighing beneath her as John clambered in. She put the chocolates between them.

'It's cold enough they won't melt. Thank you.'

He lifted a hand as though waving the small offering away, and they set off.

'It's not a very long drive,' she said. 'Comfy?'

'It's brilliant,' he said, sighing. 'Gosh, you're so fortunate.'

She steered away from the station with practised ease and gave a soft snort. 'This was all my father's idea, not mine.'

'But you love it, right?'

Violet smiled. 'I do. It gives me such independence. I drove it to Hobart a few days ago.'

'You did not! And you didn't visit the brewery?'

'I didn't want to interrupt you. Besides, I think I frightened Mr St Hill last time I was there.'

He chuckled. 'I think you did too. But we're about to send the barrels from Frank. He's quite happy with how the applewood works. I'll be glad to see them in place next time.'

Next time, she thought, with a small smile. He was moving things along. 'Oh, that's wonderful news. I was going to ask after him.'

· · ·

Arriving at the cottage, Violet put the chocolates on the table and picked up the picnic basket she'd packed.

'Can you put this in the car for us, please? I'll just get the Thermos ready.'

'Sure,' he said, reaching for the basket and watching her boil the kettle. It was whistling in under a minute. 'Oh, a flask,' he said. 'I've heard about these.'

'The latest thing. Great for when we're out in the field and desperate for a cuppa. You do like tea, I presume?'

'Who doesn't? I'll get this into the car.'

When the Thermos was ready a minute or so later, she met him outside and packed it into the car with pride. 'Now, how about a walk through the distillery? Over in a blink, I must warn you.'

'I thought you'd never ask.'

She walked him around to the sheds at the back, keeping up a running commentary. '... and we've rebuilt an old still into a shiny new one.'

John let out a whistle of admiration. 'Cor, Violet, that's amazing. And you make whisky from this?'

'We make raw alcohol spirit and then the magic happens in the barrels. We'll need a bigger still very soon. Follow me.' She led him into the barrel room, where it was peaceful and quiet. 'I once claimed this was like my church – where I come to worship.' She smiled at the memory. 'My friend Angus accused me of blaspheming.'

'Your boyfriend?'

'I think I was about twelve,' Violet answered in a droll tone. 'But, yes, Angus loved me. If I'd stayed, I think he would have got worse. It wasn't healthy.' She spoke more to herself than to John.

'Worse than being in love?' he mused.

She blinked out of the memory. 'Er, well, I loved him as a friend through our teenage years, but that's as far as my feelings stretched. He wanted more. It would have ended in sorrow.'

John nodded, then met her eyes. 'Violet, I think everyone who meets you falls in love a little bit.'

She waved her hand at him. 'Surely not. I think I scare off most men.'

He smiled. 'You don't frighten me.'

'Well, that's good.' She wasn't sure where this conversation might lead and was not yet prepared to find out. 'So,' she continued, brightly, 'let me show you what we do with the alcohol.' She explained the process, how she loved the creative side of it especially, and their plans for the barrels the room held.

'I envy you, Violet.'

She looked back at him quizzically. 'You do?'

'All this... well, drive and ambition. You clearly have so much passion for what you do.'

'You don't feel the same about beer?'

'Not at all,' he said, amused. 'What we make doesn't have the same complexity as whisky – it's more about quality control. We use good ingredients, make sure our protocols are rigorously observed – hygiene is paramount – and ensure we keep delivering the same taste that the people who drink our beer appreciate. It's really just a matter of repeating this process over and over.'

'What do you feel is missing for you, John?'

'Well, that creativity you speak about. And...' He shook his head. 'When you talk, I can feel that emotional connection... to the land, to the barley... even the cask.' He laughed. 'You seem so connected to the spirit as it develops, to the excitement of blending and wondering what flavours you can add by juggling the notes within.'

She nodded. 'Yes, all of that is true. In that respect, it's a sort of art, isn't it?'

'Definitely. You and your father are artists, but you produce a bottle of something rather than a sculpture or a painting.'

Violet smiled, feeling a warm sense of pride. 'Thank you for seeing it that way. It's quite a compliment.'

He shrugged. 'I enjoy whisky, but I had no idea of the craftsmanship behind it.' He sighed. 'So I envy you.'

'Then *you* should make whisky,' she said, mimicking his shrug.

'What?' He grinned helplessly.

'You heard. Come and learn – there's enough room for another whisky producer in all of Australia. We're the first in Tasmania. You could be the second.'

He stared at her intently for a protracted moment but she was not daunted. She held his stare, almost insolently, daring him to back down. 'I don't have your talent,' he said finally.

'How do you know if you haven't tried?'

He frowned in thought. 'I've never been artistic.' Before she could jump in to reassure him, he raised a finger. 'But that's all right. I know my weaknesses, but I also know what I am good at – processes. And just listening to you, I've learned that whisky is also about processes... getting it right from the very beginning, from growing top-quality barley to using clean, fresh water, to the malting process and onwards into the still. All of that really does interest me.'

Violet laughed. 'Weirdly, to me that's the boring bit. I feel all my lights switch on inside once we have the spirit in the barrel. That's when I feel fully connected to the whisky that will eventuate.'

'We make a good pair, then,' he quipped.

She deliberately did not react to his insinuation. 'John, I mean it. Come and learn. What you're talking about, the processes, is all rote stuff. As you say, it's like the beer, being rigorous with the protocols. All the creativity happens much later in the blending. If it's processes you love, then you'll breeze through learning the early stages of making whisky. What a boon you'd be to any operation.'

'You'd teach me?'

'Of course. I've already got an apprentice learning the ropes, and he's just a lad. He knows how to flip the barley during germination and everything to do with that stage. He picked up that side of it so fast. Now that the brewery is going to send us malted barley, he's thrilled, because he wants to start blending whisky – learning that is going to take years. Really, he needs to learn that from my father.'

'You're selling yourself short, Violet.'

'Maybe. But Dad's a good teacher. I think I'm more the person who says, "I'll show you and you can learn," rather than knowing how to teach someone. But for now he can learn single malt production, which doesn't require all the blending and balancing to achieve consistency. Single malt is complex in a different way, though. You have to pursue a single character... to me it's like the whisky sort of throws its gauntlet down. *This is me, this is what I taste like now. Love me or leave me. Next year I won't taste precisely the same.*'

They both laughed at her act.

'I'd love to learn more,' John said, looking earnest.

'Then you'll need to visit again.'

'I'd find that very agreeable, actually,' he said, maintaining his gaze on her in a way that she found slightly disconcerting.

'Good. Now, come on, our picnic awaits,' she said, switching topics. She didn't yet know how she felt about this man, but his company was pleasant, and she ought to give him a chance. She moved to the door, and John followed her like a faithful puppy. Anyone observing would have already presumed he was smitten.

The Richmond Bridge could show many colours in its sandstone construction: a prison grey on miserable days, a light gold, like a sandy beach on a bright morning, and sometimes a fiery hue at sunset. Today, in the afternoon light, it glowed a rusted blond.

'We're all rather proud of it,' Violet said, laying out a blanket for them to sit on. She knelt to start unpacking the food she'd packed.

John shrugged. 'It's just a bridge.'

'Well, they don't say that about Sydney Harbour Bridge.'

He smiled and joined her on the blanket. 'No, it's very pretty, especially from this angle,' he said, propping himself up on one elbow and looking at her.

She glanced at him in warning. 'It's more than pretty. The

Richmond Bridge is the oldest stone span bridge in the country. It's special.'

'Built by convicts, I suppose?'

'Yes.' She turned to regard it. 'A jailer was murdered by those convicts – pushed off the bridge. The story goes that one of his duties was to flog the prisoners and he was brutal about it, so they took their revenge when he was found in his cups. It's said that he was hardly aware he was being dragged to the bridge.'

John chuckled. 'Are you going to tell me his ghost walks the bridge each night?'

She threw a napkin at him but laughed. 'No.'

He straightened, looking at the spread. 'This is all very lovely, thank you.'

'Well, we'll need to eat fast, because I can feel the bite of the cold coming on. Here, let's see how good this Thermos is.' She poured two cups of rich, steaming tea. 'I hope you take sugar? I took the liberty of sweetening it, but only lightly.'

He took a cup and sipped. 'Mmm, delicious,' he said. 'Yes, I can feel that nip too. My leg likes to protest at the cold.'

'Oh?'

He shrugged. 'Arthritis has got me a bit early. My leg's like an early forecaster of cold wind or rain.'

'How did that happen, John?'

'I was injured in an accident on the farm. And then my mother and younger brother died in a separate accident... a drowning. That's when my elder brother took over the farm and I came to live with Nan. Dad never recovered from losing Mum.'

Violet looked down. 'Oh, forgive me for asking about such a sad subject.' Not wanting to intrude, she changed the topic by handing him a pie on a small plate. 'Freshly baked this morning and the perfect temperature now for eating. The gravy won't burn your mouth, I promise.'

'Thank you. And don't apologise. I was seven – two decades ago. I've often thought of getting my own place, but I'm a help to them both, especially Nan, and she's one of those fun old girls, you know.' He tapped his head. 'She's ninety. Still so sharp, and her memory supremely intact. Actually, she puts her good health down to a tot of whisky each night, can you believe it? It's where I developed my habit.'

'Good grief. How marvellous.'

'I've told her about you and what you're setting up here. She's most impressed.'

'Well, then, I'll make sure she's one of the first to taste the Australian Glen Corbie.'

John nodded in thanks. 'She'll be even more thrilled to hear I am going to learn about whisky making. Violet, this pie is brilliant. You should sell them!'

Later, they packed up their picnic things, and she led John down into the main street of the Georgian town.

'It's a lovely old town,' she said. 'In winter, it reminds me so much of England – patchwork fields and the view over the bridge to the Catholic church. That's the oldest in Australia, by the way. Dad and I have been made very welcome and we're happy here. The Coal River is lovely to live near, and it gives us that crystal clear water we crave, like in Scotland.'

'Do you miss it?'

She smiled. 'Every day, I think. But we've built a life here.'

'Will you go back?'

'Yes, I'm sure I will. Not right now with what's going on in Europe, but I do yearn to go back... hopefully with a bottle of Australian Glen Corbie tucked under my arm.' She grinned.

'You'll do it – I can feel it.'

'I hope so. It's Dad's dream. And I intend to make it come true.'

PART THREE

ELEVEN

ÉPERNAY, FRANCE

August 1944

Charlie and two other men were seated in a café, at separate tables. He was horrified to realise one of them was Otto Klaebisch, whom he'd heard plenty about from the Resistance. The German was hated for his pillaging of the cellars and frequent blackmailing of the heads of the Champagne houses. He was a former Champagne agent for Lanson, but he strutted around as though he was Gestapo. These days he was officially known as *sonderführer* – special leader – by the Germans, but the locals referred to him in whispered tones as the Champagne Führer, who controlled the golden liquid war chest of the Nazis.

As soon as Charlie had made the connection and tamped down an inclination to flee, he adopted a morose expression, let a cigarette burn down between his fingers and nursed a second black coffee. He had ordered the second cup in order to quell the panic but also to have a reason to overhear Klaebisch, who had been lauding the delights of the outstanding vintage from last year. Fortunately, he was speaking French, rather than German, with another fellow – one of the Champagne merchants who had climbed into bed with the Nazis. The merchant was lamenting that it felt like the previous war, with glass shortages, bottles having to be reused and buyers being required to return them when reordering. The obsequious Frenchman was apologising for this fact, and Charlie had to work hard not to show his disgust.

He glanced at the German. He was wearing his usual outfit, which was a bit of a joke to the resisters, who jested that he had created his own uniform so that he resembled a German officer of the Nazi hierarchy. In profile, his nose looked like a great wedge, angling out from his thick brow, and he had the kind of mouth that turned down in repose; right now, though, he was laughing, his slicked-back hair gleaming with the oil that kept it neatly in place. Clearly this man just loved dressing up and ordering people around.

He was also called a *weinführer*, Charlie's Resistance contact had told him, but the other nickname had stuck when he'd arrived in Champagne, chosen a mansion that appealed to him, banished the owners and made it his. He'd led the ransacking of the cellars of some of the finest brands and sent their product to Paris for the officers there. He also sent countless crates of the very best Champagne to Berlin and Munich – even all the way to the infamous mountain hideout where Hitler apparently liked to spend his time plotting and barking orders, far from prying eyes and surrounded by sycophants.

Charlie had learned that when the German Army had arrived in Reims and Épernay, they were soon drunk on Champagne; hundreds of soldiers swilling directly from the bottles, with no respect for the glorious drink. They didn't care about the sharp cut of the bubbles or how they effervesced to form that all-important 'necklace' around the flute; they barely paused to taste the exquisite combination of grapes, to know the 'three women' who danced within to create the spangled flavour, or to admire the beauty of the colour. No, they just drank to become inebriated, perhaps to forget the bloodshed and despair. Charlie could forgive them that much, perhaps.

The systematic and concerted pillaging offended him hugely,

though, and he wondered how much Sophie's Champagne house had lost to the marauders. She would be devastated.

He was finally allowing her to enter his thoughts, he realised. He had been moving around Reims and Épernay for three weeks and had not spotted her, and so began to believe – with some relief, he might admit – that she had likely left the region and perhaps headed south. It would have been wise, but then again he couldn't imagine Sophie leaving her Champagne house or abandoning her workers, their families or even the people of Reims to face occupation. No, she was far more likely to tough it out alongside them, eating little, sharing everything she had, and subverting the German cause wherever and whenever she could. In fact, he wouldn't be at all surprised to learn that she was knee-deep in helping the local maquisards. If she was, she was using an alias, because her name had not come up once via the Silversmith circuit. He never let himself truly consider the possibility that she might no longer be alive, even though it had been so many years since he'd seen her.

So far, he'd resisted mentioning her to anyone. He had tried not to think about her and just put his head down, to become worthy of the role he'd been asked to perform. His work had begun in Reims, but in the last few days he had shifted into Épernay proper, staying with a local family known to the Germans for taking in journeymen who worked the vineyards. Hopefully, what they didn't know was that the family also helped the brave maquisards, who moved in the shadows. If the family knew he was a spy, they had never let on.

He had found casual work clearing weeds and excess vegetation in the local vineyards. Although he was not in Sophie's fields, they were not far away. The magnetism of that thought fuelled him, allowing him to think of that ridiculously happy, and yet equally dangerous, time of a quarter of a century ago.

By day he would bend his back and feel grateful for the physical exertion. He had to admit to enjoying the time with the vines again, admiring their bounty, which was just about ready for harvesting. Straightening periodically to stretch his aching muscles, he'd look out over the undulating landscape of leaves, their brilliance beneath the sun lifting his spirits, and he'd think about the vines, which did not understand or care about war. This was the calm before the chaotic days of harvest, when perhaps even bombs and artillery could be forgotten, when all that mattered was gathering up the ripe grapes in that perfect moment, on the perfect day. It helped him forget what he'd left behind, and what might lie ahead.

He was sleeping in the family's barn with two other vineyard workers, who he presumed were genuine, and so far had had very little to do with the family members themselves other than to share the pot of food the woman made each day. One meal, that's all they got. Anything else was up to them to forage or beg for. They also had no coffee. People were drinking a strange version that tasted of chicory and perhaps acorns, but he dared not ask for fear of showing his ignorance. He simply thanked them, sipped it slowly and tried not to wince, allowing its warmth alone to comfort.

This café had the real thing, which he sipped appreciatively now. He looked up and berated himself for allowing his thoughts to wander. He hadn't noticed that the two men he'd been eavesdropping on were now looking at him. Even worse, the Champagne Führer seemed to be waiting for him to respond.

'Sorry, sirs,' he said in the most casual form of French he could muster. Being too polite here would give him away. He shrugged, giving a smile. 'I was daydreaming as I enjoyed this real coffee.'

Klaebisch didn't smile back. 'I asked you a question.'

Charlie crushed his smoking butt in the nearby tin ashtray, left some coins next to it and then stood, giving a sort of deferential bow, his cap in one hand. 'I didn't hear, sir. I'm sorry.'

'Who daydreams during war?' the French merchant asked, perhaps hoping to impress Klaebisch, who was leaning back and regarding Charlie as though he were a strange insect.

Charlie shrugged again, rolling his cap in his hands. He didn't have to feign nervousness. 'Don't we all? I look forward to the vineyards being at peace again.' He said this to deliberately avoid taking any side, but also to hint at his work. Maybe he could push them into a conversation about Champagne and shift their scrutiny.

'You work in the vineyards?' Klaebisch asked, then gave a nod. 'I thought as much. Where?'

Charlie turned languidly to point over his shoulder, and said, 'Moët et Chandon and, er, Delancré, sir.' He would later wonder why he'd said the second name; it slipped out easily.

Klaebisch had nodded at the first name but it seemed Charlie had caught his interest with the second, as he raised his eyebrows. 'Really? So if I speak with the vineyard manager at Delancré, he would know you?'

Charlie gave a sort of upside-down smile of uncertainty. 'I don't know if he even knows my name, sir, but...' and here he paused, suddenly terrified that Sophie might have taken her husband's name once he'd returned. He didn't know if she'd ever been known as Madame Méa – perhaps in some circumstances she was. He felt an icy pulse zigzag through him.

'Monsieur?'

'Sorry.' Charlie gave a meek expression, surprised he could still act out the role of such humility, scared as he was. 'I did not feel it was my place.'

'Speak,' Klaebisch commanded.

This was it. *Say it.* He knew her as Delancré. She was proud of her name and it was her brand, after all. He couldn't imagine she would have cast it aside in her professional role. He drew a deep breath. 'Sophie Delancré knows me.'

'The beautiful Madame Champenoise, eh? Is that so?' the German said, sounding doubtful and threatening at once.

The zigzag of terror halted. She was alive; she was still here.

'You know her?' Klaebisch pressed, his tone derisive.

Charlie nodded, feeling the scrutiny heavy all over him. Why oh why had he uttered anything about her?

'What's your name?'

'Pierre Dupont,' Charlie murmured, filled with regret, fully aware that this situation could develop into something deeply dangerous, not just for him, but for the circuit as well.

'Papers,' Klaebisch demanded, clicking his fingers.

The Frenchman sharing his table sat back and smiled, seemingly enjoying the theatre, and Charlie tried not to think about how much he'd enjoy wiping that smugness off the man's face. Instead, he nodded and dug inside his pockets; no one moved around without their identification papers. He handed them over. They'd been checked several times since he'd arrived, so he felt mildly confident, but why did he get the feeling this man wanted to make an example of him? Did he resent that a mere vineyard worker might know a Champagne maker personally? Did he resent that Charlie was sipping coffee at the same café as the mighty Champagne Führer? Did he want to impress the wine merchant? Or was it just a desire to bully anyone and everyone he could?

'You're from the south?' Klaebisch asked, studying the papers.

It was time for Charlie to play his role and be convincing. This was what they had trained for and he'd proven himself good at it. *So be Pierre Dupont*, he thought firmly. *You are Pierre Dupont.*

'Originally, yes, sir,' he answered.

'So why are you here?'

Charlie shrugged, trying to maintain a calm façade. 'I go anywhere there are vines, sir.'

'You have a stamp for essential worker, I see. How did you buy that?'

Charlie gave him a look that was openly surprised. He deliberately stammered, as though quaking beneath such an accusation from someone so powerful. If he was being honest, it wasn't hard. 'Er, no, no, sir. I did not buy this status. I can't.' He turned out his pockets. 'But I am a good vineyard worker.'

'You look a bit scrawny for physical work in the fields.'

He couldn't help shrugging again. 'At this time I weed and keep the rows clear as we prepare for harvest, but I suppose my skill is during the crush. I know how to make wine, sir.'

The imposing German frowned. 'Are you suggesting that Moët et Chandon do not know how?'

Charlie had known it was a mistake as his words had come out. He shook his head. 'I did not mean that, sir. I simply meant I can be helpful around the vineyards during harvest, at the crush and then at the more delicate time of—'

'Yes, yes, don't bore me, man!' Klaebisch waved a hand.

'Is that all, sir?' Charlie frowned, hoping to be cut loose from the café.

'No. I suspected you were a vineyard worker, though why you're here dawdling and not with the vines is a mystery.' He stared at Charlie, his eyes narrowing in suspicion.

'My shift—' Charlie stopped as Klaebisch raised a hand to suggest he didn't wish to hear anything tedious about shifts.

'"How is the harvest this year?" is my question, and the only reason I can think of to address you, Monsieur Dupont.' Klaebisch's voice dripped oily condescension.

Charlie had done his homework. 'As you know, sir, the nineteen forty-three vintage was memorable – it might even be talked about in years to come. Perhaps this was due to the reduction in mildew last year and, while that's a major contributor, there were other factors...' He shrugged again – this was becoming a habit, he knew, but it seemed to be helping him stay in character. 'Er, we had only one frost, little or no harvest worms, and—'

'I didn't ask for a lecture, little man!' Klaebisch spat, and Charlie bowed his head in apology, saying no more. 'I asked about *this* year's Champagne.'

Charlie's gaze darted between the men. He'd not had enough time in the fields to know, so he'd have to hedge. 'This year won't be as memorable, but it will be plentiful.' He suddenly went off script. 'Forgive me, Herr Klaebisch—'

'You know my name?'

'Everyone knows you and respects you, sir,' he replied, the fawning words nearly trapped in his throat. What he wanted to do was spit in the man's face, then pulverise it until the sneering expression was gone. Instead he forced himself to smile.

'What were you going to say?'

Charlie nodded. 'Only that this year's Champagne all depends on the supply of sugar... but I imagine you already know that, sir.' It was a throwaway line; just another way to shore up his fraudulent persona beneath the scrutiny of this suspicious man.

'I presume you are going to begin your next shift soon.'

'I am, sir.' Charlie nodded, then touched his hand to his head in a sort of polite salute, unsure whether he was required to perform the Sieg Heil. Some did, some didn't. He turned to smile at the merchant, hating him just as much as the German, and made to leave.

'Not so fast, Monsieur Dupont,' Klaebisch said in an unhurried manner.

Charlie turned back, feeling the hairs at his neck standing on end, a frisson of fear taking fresh hold. 'Sir?'

'I don't believe you.'

Charlie made sure his expression was one of confusion. 'Pardon, Herr Klaebisch? I don't understand.'

'I don't believe you are who you say you are. Yes, you have papers and, yes, you speak like a vineyard worker, but are you really? There's something about you that isn't convincing me, but I can't put my finger on it.'

'Yes, sir, I am a vineyard worker, I promise you,' Charlie said, not having to fake the nervous stutter. There was nowhere to run.

'Come with me,' Klaebisch commanded, as he picked up a telescopic cane. Charlie wondered if perhaps he carried it in order to smack down any French civilians who weren't paying him enough deference.

His heart felt loud in his chest, sounding a thump behind his ear in its suddenly irregular pulse. 'Where are we going?' he asked.

'Well, as it happens, I am visiting a couple of Champagne houses today. I was due to meet with Delancré next month, I think, but it doesn't matter. Why don't we pay Madame Delancré a visit together? And then you can be on your way into the fields.'

Charlie watched with dismay as Klaebisch clicked his fingers and two henchmen, who had been leaning in a doorway just outside, suddenly leapt to attention. 'Bring him,' the German said. 'No need to be rough.' He glanced at Charlie with a sly twist at his mouth. 'Monsieur Dupont is accompanying us to see a Champagne house about our order.' He shot a smile at his companion that only just stopped short of contempt. 'I'll let you pay the bill,' he said to the merchant, who had been largely forgotten. 'We can talk next week.'

The merchant stood with such deference that Charlie had to force himself to resist sneering. He had no respect for the Frenchman, who was so openly collaborating with the Nazis while others, much braver, died to protect France. *You'll get your comeuppance,* he thought viciously.

But the moment of self-satisfaction passed in a blink as he contemplated the exquisite danger he was now in. The two henchmen bundled him into a car and he sat silently between them while Klaebisch signalled for his driver to set off.

Charlie nearly said, 'It's only around the corner – we should walk.' But he held his tongue; the self-important man clearly enjoyed people looking at the car. The driver must have been trained to move at a glacial pace so the Champagne Führer could be seen and acknowledged.

They were going to Delancré. It hit him hard.

This was terrible on so many levels.

Charlie was surely walking into a trap that Klaebisch, the self-appointed law of the region, had set, primarily for his own entertainment. He couldn't know Charlie was lying and he was yet to voice his specific concerns about Charlie's story.

Had Charlie been too confident? He'd been polite, but had he shown enough deference, enough fear of the uniform to satisfy the bully that lived within this small-minded man? Should he have given the Sieg Heil – was that it? He closed his eyes with a final sickening thought: he had just brought trouble to Sophie's door. If only he had never mentioned her name. He pretended to himself that it had been necessary to sound authentic, but if he dug deep, he had simply wanted to say her name out loud in Épernay... to wonder if he could contact her.

But this was not the way.

He had been working nearby... if he'd wanted so much to prompt a meeting with Sophie, he could have tried to achieve it in another, less fraught, way. Perhaps, deep in his conscience, he hadn't wanted to meet because he felt he was somehow letting Violet down – or proving her right. If not, surely he would have tried sooner? But he hadn't even asked about Sophie.

Why?

He took a deep breath. It was the fear.

Fear of seeing her again, and what it would do to him.

TWELVE
RICHMOND

August 1944

John had visited twice since his initial tour and picnic, and Violet had kept those meets on a wholly professional level, always ensuring that Jimmy was present to signal the platonic nature of their budding relationship. As much as she liked John, she got the sense that his romantic inclinations were far stronger than her own.

It worried Violet from time to time that no man had ever properly intrigued her romantically. If her mother had been alive or if Violet had another wise woman in her life, she'd discuss this nagging thought. What was wrong with her?

She'd mentioned it only once to her father, back in the new year, before any talk of him joining the war effort. He'd likely been thinking about it, though, secretly working on his plan; her mother had always said her father was private. She'd never used the word secretive. 'Contained' was Violet's favourite way of describing him; it was hard to know what he was really thinking.

It had been in late January, one evening when they were walking the rows of barley. The summer sun was dipping below the horizon, setting the sky on fire and lighting the crop with a dazzling gold as the barley heads dipped and swayed. Both Violet and Charlie, unaware of the other doing the same, held out a hand so the tops of the stalks might caress their skin with a feathery touch.

'Any day now, Violet,' he said. 'We'd better get the lads all lined up.'

She nodded. 'I like to think we're communing with the crop, letting it know it's loved and appreciated,' she said.

Her father didn't snort in dismissal, as she'd expected, but smiled. 'I think it's healthy to talk to the barley, or to any plant. And it should know that it has a higher purpose beyond cereal and beer.'

'Whisky being the zenith of any barley's ambition?' she joked.

'Of course.'

They shared another smile as they continued their stroll, the day's warmth finally cooling and a sense of peace settling over their quiet field on the outskirts of town. Small moths, their wings made transparent by the golden light, flitted around them.

'Dad, do you think I'll ever find someone to love, who loves me back? I worry that it will never happen for me.'

He waited a few beats, perhaps realising that this was a conversation a girl might normally have with her mother. 'You've stepped out with a few lads, Violet. What's to worry about?'

'Stepped out?' She grinned. 'Dad, what century are you living in? Yes, I've been on some dates.'

'And?'

Violet shrugged. 'They were nice men, but...'

'Let me guess. Boring?'

'That's a bit unfair.'

'Call it how it is, Violet.'

'They're nice enough,' she said, 'but they have no dreams. They seem content with being farmers or government workers in the city, and their ambition runs only to getting married, settling down to family life—'

'Giving that family a good start in life,' her father interrupted. 'It's honest. Nothing wrong with that.'

'Nothing wrong at all. It's just... Dad, I think I'm hard work.'

That made him laugh. 'Surely that's no surprise to you. You would intimidate most men, Violet – including me if I was a young man going out on a date with you.'

'But why?'

'Oh, you're very pretty, everything a young man could dream of...'

'Until I open my mouth?'

He laughed again. 'Yes,' he said with a sigh. 'Until you start sharing your opinions and talking about your plans and your dreams. It's wonderful – I don't want you to ever stop – but I can see how it might be daunting for a chap who is looking for the simple life.'

She shrugged again. 'I'm not simple to be with, though, and I don't sit happily in complacency. So I'll probably be an old maid.'

'No, you won't, my love. You have to stay patient, though. Don't settle.' He put his arm around her as he said this, but then he pulled back to meet her gaze steadily, pausing their stroll. 'Do *not* settle, Violet,' he said, pointing a finger in emphasis. 'Because if you do, you'll be unhappy, and you'll make *him* unhappy – through no fault of his other than wanting a simple family life that doesn't match your ambition. And that's how problems begin. If you're honest now about needing a man who is at least as ambitious as you, as strong as you, and as challenging as you can be, then you'll stay patient for him to arrive.'

She wasn't sure. 'What if he doesn't?'

'He will.'

'But how can you be sure?'

Her father just smiled. 'I can't, not categorically, but life has taught me he probably will.'

'Because you waited for Mum – and the woman before her?'

'No, I didn't know they were going to arrive in my life, but I didn't settle for other women, Violet. I let the sort of love I needed find *me*. And I was blessed, because it found me twice. I'm not sure

I deserved it the second time around, but it came all the same with your mother.'

The question still lingered in her mind, even though her father's words brought some hope that she wasn't destined to live a lonely life. The conversation loomed large now as she considered John.

It was becoming very clear to her that his knowledge of farming and brewing would be a genuine help to their fledgling operation. While the similarities between whisky and beer ended at the barley mash stage, the quality control and processes that were so important to John were as key to producing high-quality whisky as to producing beer. His attention to detail was valuable, but she did not wish to give him any hope that they might become more than friends with a shared interest.

Today he was umpiring a cricket match in Richmond; apparently the local players had managed to field a motley group to play against a team from the brewery, equally cobbled together. John had sent a short note a few days prior since he'd be in the area.

I wondered if I might visit before the game for half an hour. It would be most pleasant to see you socially.

Sincerely, John (from the brewery)

She'd smiled at the modest qualification and accepted; he truly was becoming a good friend and she was happy to see him.

'Who plays cricket in August, anyway?' she asked when he arrived.

'It doesn't make sense,' he agreed. 'But it's more of a distraction, a bit of entertainment for the boys left behind. We all feel pretty useless, as you know.' He shrugged. 'It's a jollying feeling for the community, and good practice for the summer.'

'Do you think we'll have our boys and girls home soon?' She tried to keep the question general, but she was always thinking about her father.

He blew out a breath. 'How can Hitler keep going? Surely he realises it's over for him?'

Violet nodded. 'His Russian push is all over, which means they're on retreat everywhere, I would imagine. I'm going to cling to that.' She smiled. 'These are lovely, thank you,' she said, looking at a bunch of daisies he'd brought, wrapped in newspaper. 'I'll just put them in some water and we can go for a walk.'

'They're from my nan's garden,' he said. 'She's very keen on her plants.'

'They're beautiful, John. So cheerful for this time of year.'

'She was overjoyed that I was cutting flowers as a gift. She mostly donates them to the local church for Sunday services and was very happy to move some on.'

Violet deliberately did not ask him inside, concerned about him becoming too familiar, yet she felt churlish for taking this attitude. Leaving a man who had just presented her with flowers kicking his heels at her front door felt awkward, but she was quick, rushing back with her woollen shawl. 'Come on. I know your time is short.'

They walked down the lane behind the town, Violet's land stretching before them. The winter planting was in, and the barley was already up to ankle height – little green shoots of promise for the summer.

He whistled. 'All looking good.'

She pulled a face of uncertainty. 'I'm not sure. We were given a small parcel when we emigrated and we haven't bought more because our intention was always to fulfil our role to grow cereals – it's why Australia let us come. But now I'm wondering if it's enough to supply the brewery's ever-increasing demand as well as our own needs.'

'Well, those are what really interest me. Are you happy with the malted barley we're sending? I still don't know how you wangled that.' He chuckled.

Violet laughed too. 'Oh, I just let Mr St Hill know how committed we are as a supplier.' They exchanged a wry look. 'To answer your question, the malted barley is brilliant. Actually, it's changed my life. Changed the whole situation for the distillery. No longer having to worry about the back-breaking work involved in malting frees us up to get on with what really motivates us. But'—she held up a finger—'I, for one, know how important the quality of the malted barley is, so we did that work gladly. The brewery is sending us exceptional quality, thank you, and I have no doubt you have some involvement in that.'

He winked but said no more.

She led him back to the small shed that they had effectively grown out of. Her father would build another, bigger one on his return, but Violet had her own plan now. 'When Dad gets back, I'm going to talk to him about moving.'

'Moving? Away from Richmond?' John sounded startled.

'No, just out of the town. We're going to need a lot more room for our whisky operation.'

John followed her in. 'Oh my. I'd forgotten how it feels in here.'

She smiled, glad he felt arrested. It was pleasing to experience this place, so special to her, through someone else's eyes.

His expression was creased with awe. 'Our beer barrel warehouse doesn't feel like this.'

'Tell me what you mean.'

'Well, ours feels workmanlike. It's all practical storage and constant movement. But this...'

'It's the opposite here,' she agreed. 'Firstly, I never think of it as a warehouse – that practical storage you mention – though it did feel like that a short while ago. Now it's exactly how I want it, which is more like a dormitory, in my opinion... a nursery even. I want it to feel like a library or, dare I say, a small chapel.' She chuckled at his amused look. 'I probably shouldn't say that aloud as the local reverend might be offended.'

'I agree with you, though. In here you've achieved the sort of peaceful space I might bend my head to say a prayer in.'

'Oh, John, you've made my day, but we'd better not share that thought. They're quite pious around here.'

He shrugged. 'I think we can pray anywhere, don't you?'

She nodded. 'I've always thought so. I think this building is a celebration of nature. It was just a rundown shed that had been built using odd-shaped stones taken from the area – the person who built it was probably a convict.'

'Almost certainly,' John agreed.

'But he was also a craftsman – look how solid it is.' She turned around on the spot, her arms wide. 'This man took pride in what was likely an old livestock shed to keep a cow, some goats or old tools. But this was a dwelling that thanked nature for her goodness. Isn't that spiritual?'

'Yes. Definitely true.' He wandered around the barrels stored there, looking at the date written on their round faces.

Violet smiled to herself. What else could he say to her remark? Her slightly wild way of thinking had amused her parents: her mother said her spirited attitude might get her into trouble, but she told Violet she admired it and hoped she'd never change. Her father simply told her to always follow her own path.

'Never be a sheep, Violet,' he'd counselled. 'You may not be popular, and you may unnerve others, but you will always be happier if you stay true to yourself.'

She wondered now about her father, a daily, if not hourly, occurrence lately. She'd just heard from him, but the letter was already a few weeks old when she received it. What was he doing? Taking risks, no doubt. Her mother's words – her father was reckless – rang in her ears regularly now. He'd always been so careful with her, but then she was his to take care of. Now she understood that what her mother referred to was his carelessness with his own life.

'Have you heard from your father?' John asked, eavesdropping on her thoughts, it seemed.

She shook her head. 'I have, but nothing recent. I'm not surprised. He warned me it might be like this. Even so...'

John smiled gently. 'He'll know you're thinking of him. You told me your mother was a nurse, but how did your parents meet?'

Violet leant against the wall of the shed and told him the story.

She liked being able to talk about them, and her explanation came
so easily that her mind was able to wander into memory.

'I liked your father from the moment I met him,' Violet's
mother had told her, 'but I saw a loner in him as he lay there
wounded. I don't know, Violet, I just sensed he was miserable. I
know that sounds obvious, given it was wartime, but your father is
an emotional man. To me it seemed as though he felt everyone's
pain in his bones, like he was responsible for doing everything,
helping everyone, giving his life if asked, to end the war. Perhaps
you don't see it, but he feels everything very deeply and makes
decisions based on that emotion.'

Violet had nodded. 'Not sensible like you, then, Mum,' she'd
said, with a gentle smile. 'Isn't he lucky to have you?' She had
hugged her mother tightly.

'I like to think so. After we met, I tried to keep track of his
movements, but I had to rely on odd reports that often contradicted
one another. But then I heard about an English soldier in the
tunnels of Reims – in its hospital. I asked several people how an
English soldier could end up there, and I became convinced it was
him. I just knew if I ever saw him again I would marry him.'

They'd both laughed at this.

'So forward, Mum.'

'Well, yes. Good men were falling all around us – a whole
generation of potential husbands dying all over Europe and,
besides, I was already in love with this man. I barely knew him, but
he intrigued me.'

Violet's eyes had shone to hear this. As young as she was, she'd
always felt that her parents' story was romantic and this only
confirmed it. 'What did you say when you saw him again?'

'I couldn't speak, Violet. I was so shocked. After we all came
home I went back to my old work as a seamstress, not really
wanting to see another wound, but I volunteered at the hospital.
There were still so many wounded needing to recover, so I realised
my nursing days were not yet over. And one day I came out of the
hospital and there he was, leaning against a wall. He didn't smile.

He looked so earnest and broken and desperate for arms around him. But he winked at me, and that was it. I ran – someone in a van sounded the horn at me because I ran in front of it to get to him.'

Violet had giggled. 'Tell me you threw yourself into his arms.'

'I did, shameless thing I was. I flung myself at him and wept. I couldn't believe he had survived, that he was whole. That he'd come to find me and I was in his arms.'

'And you kissed him in broad daylight?'

'Yes, Violet. I kissed him long and hard, tears streaming down my face. I didn't have to ask him to marry me – he asked me – but first he asked me to the local social so we could dance in each other's arms as we'd promised we would.' Her mother had sounded wistful retelling this story, almost like the lovelorn teenagers at Violet's school, and she'd sighed with pleasure.

'What are you smiling about?' John asked.

Violet blinked, slightly embarrassed at having gone missing for a few moments. 'Sorry, I was just remembering how good they were together.'

She had never known such a feeling for herself, but she craved it. John was lovely but as much as she liked him, that passionate connection wasn't there; he didn't make her feel how her mother had described feeling about her father on their first meeting. And that's what Violet wanted. She wanted the man she fell for to be like a long cool drink of water to her parched throat. She realised how silly and swoony her thoughts were and cleared her throat to cover the concern that this kind, very pleasant man, smiling slightly longingly at her, might somehow read her thoughts.

She had unconsciously moved back to the barrels and was resting her hand on the smooth oak of an old Rutherglen cask. 'This barrel once held wonderful, syrupy sherry and now it's holding our single malt close.'

'You make it sound romantic.'

'It is, John. Everything about whisky is romantic. It's a marriage. The oak and its former guest have years of flavour to share with our whisky, which arrived in its new home as a brash, colourless spirit... like a newborn. The wood of the barrels, the season and, of course, just how much of the spirit the angels choose to claim – it's all part of its growth.'

'Now what does that mean – the angels?' he asked, intrigued.

'It's folklore in Scotland, called the angel's share. From each barrel we have to share some of its contents with the angels as the spirit evaporates and becomes more concentrated.' She tapped a barrel. 'This will be around sixty-three per cent proof.'

'Oof,' he said, pretending to stagger. 'Really?'

She nodded. 'Would you like to see how it looks and tastes now after three years of being loved by oak and sherry?'

'Really?'

'Of course,' she said, delighted by his excitement. She reached for the copper tool that hung on the wall. 'This is a valinch. Do you know what that is?'

He frowned, shaking his head.

'It's a French word that comes from the word *avaler*, meaning to swallow. But in Scotland we called it a whisky thief or spirit thief.'

'I like that notion of the theft... just a tiny amount to taste.'

'This was crafted specially as a gift from Dad... to sort of herald my career as a whisky distiller and blender.' Violet unstoppered the barrel closest to them. Fiery fumes wafted up through the dark hole, making her eyes water pleasantly. She dipped in her spirit thief and covered its tube with her thumb, then withdrew it, smiling. 'This is where it all begins.'

She let the spout hover over a small tulip-shaped glass her father had brought from Scotland, which she kept on a nearby barrel. 'Now, most Australian makers tend to use brandy balloons for tasting, but my father taught me that the whisky's fineness might be hidden beneath a haze of harsher alcohol with those.' She released the thief's contents into the small glass.

'Oh my,' she said aloud, surprised by the richness of the colour; she hadn't anticipated it after only three years. She held the glass up against the whitewashed wall to admire it. 'Dad, you will be pleased.' She sent a smile up, hoping it might reach him, wherever he was.

'It's certainly not colourless any more,' John said, sounding impressed.

'No, that's the magic of the barrel. It lends its colour as much as its flavour as the spirit rests and develops.' She grinned at him. 'We drink with our eyes first, Dad drummed into me.'

The colour matched the local honey she favoured, and it looked perfect. She felt suddenly teary, and wondered whether the long silence meant that her father had made her an orphan.

'Here, you try first,' she said, clearing her throat of the swelling emotion and handing him the glass.

He blinked as the fumes of the alcohol reached his nose and eyes.

'I should have warned you that sixty-plus proof is eye-watering. Don't worry, we take it down plenty, but that's how it begins. So... just a small sip.' She laughed.

As he tasted it, his eyes widened and he coughed. 'Oh, that's harsh. A lot of raw power.'

She shook her head, still smiling. 'Oh, you can do better than that. Sip again, come on. Let it sit in your mouth.'

He followed her urging, taking his time now that he knew what to expect and rolling the liquid around his tongue. 'That is potent, Violet, far too strong for me. But as silly as it is, I think I sense the flavour of an Anzac biscuit. Is that crazy?'

She gave a soft gasp of pleasure. 'John, your love of whisky is serving you well. Whisky will always echo its original ingredient, and malted barley does give off a biscuity flavour.'

'You're saying that as though other ingredients would give different flavours. What do you mean?'

'Well, consider wheat, for instance. We could make whisky from wheat grain and that would give you a more honeyed note. Corn, which they use in America, will add some spicy undertones. And rye... well, you know that makes famous American bourbon?'

He nodded.

'Well, if you use that for whisky, you'll get a sort of dried fruit flavour, which adds real complexity.'

'I had no idea,' he admitted. 'It makes sense, of course, but I'd never really thought about it.'

'I hope I'm not boring you.'

He shook his head.

'Well, this one we've just tasted is one hundred per cent malt, but if I start to play around with other spirits from other grains, you can imagine the range of flavours we might achieve in the final whisky. We can blend from one end of the flavour spectrum to the other – from sweet to citrus, to spicy to almost savoury. We can go as rich as licorice or as light as mild honey. And that's the fun part – what my father and I both love most of all is the blending. Yeast is present, of course. And my father believes its contribution goes beyond the simple science of converting sugar into alcohol. While many dismissed the notion, I support his idea that the type of yeast used will contribute to the aroma, flavour and complexity of the final product. Those are all the traits we're chasing and playing with when we blend.'

'I'm amazed. It's far more complex than what we do at the brewery.'

She smiled. 'Single malt is a precious thing, revered by many. But blended whisky is where all the true creativity begins, and my father is something of a wizard with blending.'

'And you said the type of oak barrel you use changes the flavour?'

'Yes, that's right. Traditionally, the great winemakers of France – those who make Champagne, for instance – prefer to use oak from the Limousin region in the south. But we whisky makers have always favoured Spanish barrels, because Britain used to have a roaring sherry trade with the Spaniards – they unloaded their sherry casks at the port of Bristol, and at Leith in Scotland. Those sherry barrels imparted the flavour of their previous contents.'

'And now I fully understand your request for the applewood barrels.'

She shrugged. 'Just trying something that might make it uniquely Tasmanian.'

'It's brilliant, Violet. I'm astonished by your knowledge.'

'Information is power, my dad always says, although that's really his take on war... But it does apply to life. The more you know about a subject, the better informed you are to make decisions. You know, John, a true whisky aficionado would have a go at breaking down a single malt in his mind, paying attention to all the clues from his nose and palate. And if he's good enough – I say he, but it could equally be a she – he can probably have a very good guess at where the barley was harvested, perhaps even the valley where the water they used was flowing.'

'You're joking.'

She shook her head. 'They do it with great wine, so why are you surprised they can do the same with great whisky? In fact, Dad told me there's a fellow in Scotland – a "nose", they call such people – who could even guess where the oak that made the barrel was felled.'

John laughed. 'You're pulling my leg now.'

'I promise you, I'm not. You need to watch a whisky nose do his tasting. It's quite a thing.' She took the glass again and blew on it gently to chase off the top alcohol, then smelled the bouquet once, twice and then a third time to conjure its early notes.

Aware that John was watching her intently, Violet sipped and then paused, closing her eyes to let the spirit in her mouth speak to her, then she spat it out into a small bucket. 'Mmm, this is so much better than I thought it could be. It needs time and I need to cut it back to around forty-three per cent proof, but it's got very good bones. Once more.' She sipped again, lost to her task now, and tasted the alcohol speaking to her.

Hello, she said in her mind. *You're complex... and strong.*

Give me time and love, her whisky replied. *Leave me to sit around for a while in the open. We could become very good friends. Fill your memories as you sample... you know who I am.*

She smiled at him – she always thought of the whisky as a man. In truth, she thought of him as her father.

She sloshed the liquid around her mouth and beneath her tongue and then brought a tiny amount back into the front of her mouth to allow the true nature of this dram to come to life.

There he was. Charlie Nash had arrived.

Her father's spirit was with her.

But was he alive?

THIRTEEN

ÉPERNAY

August 1944

Charlie was alive... for now.

The shiny black vehicle felt all the more sinister for how slowly, almost arrogantly it moved, like a softly growling panther, aware of its strength and power, unthreatened by anyone or anything. The pompous Nazi had attached the red flag with its black swastika to the car's front, just in case any of the folk of Épernay were not already cowed by his presence.

The area around the Delancré house hadn't changed much, the wide boulevard so familiar as the car rolled him closer to those familiar gates. As the metal hulk began to slow, Charlie's pulse began to quicken even further. There was the fear that he would be found out as an impostor and potentially shot against some random wall on Sophie's property. The stain of his blood on this house he loved... forever. Was that poetic? He tried to convince himself it was.

And then there was the fear of seeing Sophie again. Perhaps his heart would do him the favour of simply stopping at the sight of her, saving the Germans the trouble.

The car pulled up and the driver hurried around to open the door, executing a perfect Sieg Heil to his master.

'Shall we go, Monsieur Dupont?' Klaebisch asked.

Nobody waited for Charlie to answer. He took a moment to pull his tool pouch to the front of his body. He had to use every opportunity to stop Klaebisch from catching Sophie in any sort of lie. He cast out a hope that she was not home as he was pushed out of the car by his minders and manhandled to the gates. A woman, who had hurried over from where she was tending a vegetable patch, opened them, keeping her head low in deference. She curt-sied, but Klaebisch barely noticed her.

'Bring him,' he said and strode ahead, crunching over the gravel that wound a small path through the vegetable garden.

Charlie noticed the front of the once grand house had been given over to growing food. Another worker bowed her head as they passed. Charlie hated this; he felt his spine straighten and his step become bolder. A moment later he shook off the henchmen. 'I can walk,' he growled.

As they approached the front door, Klaebisch whipped his cane to its full extension and used it to rap on the door.

It was only a brief wait, but for Charlie it was the passing of a lifetime.

Sophie Méa was surprised to hear a bold, loud rapping on her front door. She was not expecting any callers and, in fact, was dressed like a man in loose, flared trousers. She'd only stepped into the house because she realised she hadn't eaten breakfast and the smell of the midday vegetable soup on the stove had lured her indoors.

'Now who can that be?' she said with a sigh, looking longingly at the broth in the big pan, dotted with chunks of their harvest. It kept the workers' bellies full for the day.

'I'll go,' Jeanne said. The younger woman had taken it upon herself to cook each day for the group of women who helped Sophie keep the Champagne house productive.

Sophie frowned as she listened to a brief exchange at the door. She recognised the voice; it was the vile Klaebisch, who often ogled her – mentally undressing her, no doubt – whenever he found an excuse to visit. He did this from time to time, fashioning reasons to discuss Champagne, which then led to a suggestion of dinner or some other treat he could access for her. She despised him, refusing all concessions, and she was sure that if not for her Champagne, he'd find some reason to clap her in chains and send her off to a work camp.

Jeanne was back. 'It's Herr Klaebisch,' she said, not daring to use the nickname they all preferred when he was out of earshot.

Sophie nodded. 'I heard his voice,' she whispered, stirring the soup now with yearning. 'What does he want?'

Jeanne shrugged and shook her head. 'He's brought some man with him.'

'Who?'

'He didn't say. But the fellow looks unhappy, so I'm guessing a prisoner of sorts.'

Sophie's shoulders drooped and she sighed out her despair. Who was in trouble now? Would she have to bribe Klaebisch with Champagne to look the other way? She put the ladle down. 'Save me a tiny bowl, Jeanne,' she said, touching the other woman's arm. 'It smells lovely. I don't know how you do it with so little.'

Sophie left the kitchen, presuming Jeanne had shown Klaebisch into the main salon. The room was divided by magnificent folding doors that could open it up into a large space for grand entertaining. She remembered a ball of sorts that her grandparents had held when she was a child; she'd been sent to bed, but she saw the parade of women in beautiful gowns and men dressed in their black formal wear with starched white shirts and waistcoats. Her parents had entertained, but not on that scale, and she and Jerome had not had any reason to open the doors since their wedding day. As she pushed one of the double doors that led into the salon, Klaebisch drew her attention immediately, clicking his heels together where he stood on the soft, smooth floorboards.

'Madame Delancré.' He nodded. 'I hope that it is not offensive to refer to you by your professional name? I am presuming because you're in your working clothes.'

'Are we conducting business today, Herr Klaebisch?' she asked, forcing a genial look she didn't feel. What she actually felt right now was fear; this man loved to intimidate, and there was no likely reason for his visit other than to stir up trouble. 'You'll have to forgive my appearance. I was in the cellars.'

He made an annoying tutting sound but she couldn't care less about offending this man.

'Oh, I know you pretty women like to look your very best at all times.' He smirked. 'Please don't concern yourself.'

No fear of that. 'How can I help you today, Herr Klaebisch?' She kept her disdain in check, knowing he was likely here to pillage more of her product. He didn't know about the finest stocks she had hidden, but she had already sacrificed plenty of bottles for the Nazi hierarchy. Klaebisch had once told her – a finger to the side of his mouth, as though they were fellow conspirators – that some of her vintage magnums and jeroboams were destined for the Berghof, Hitler's home in the Bavarian Alps, where he liked to entertain. As if that might impress her.

'Well, yes, I have brought my men and someone to see you.'

She frowned as he pointed behind them.

'I've had them wait around the corner so we have some privacy.'

'This all sounds rather cloak and dagger, Herr Klaebisch.' She tried to smile and sound light-hearted but neither her tone nor her mouth would oblige.

He fired off some order in German and she heard movement behind the doors. This was a test; she sensed it immediately. Nothing about this visit was friendly. He was about to challenge her, but she had no idea why or how.

And then she did.

Understanding arrived, accompanied by a thud in her chest, which felt as though a percussion master in an orchestra had just pounded on the bass drum, so hard she felt the pain of it in her throat and at her temple.

Charlie felt his composure slip a little as he heard her voice from the other side of the salon, where the two thugs still flanked him. That voice had walked with him in his thoughts all these years, invading his dreams, and he would sometimes wake guilty when Ellen kissed him good morning.

He had to save Sophie. Even if he were taken out into the garden and a bullet fired into his skull, he must not take her with him.

Think! *Think!*

He heard her trying to be diplomatic and then Klaebisch barked an order and Charlie was being marched around the doors and into her presence.

His knees nearly buckled. In the space of a heartbeat he noted her face, now far older than in his memory, though time had been kind to her, and her thin, near hollow frame, which was a shock. Even so, he smiled and helplessly uttered her name, as though time was compressing and it was perfectly normal for them to be in the same space in this moment. Then he caught himself, changing the dreamy tone to one more business-like. 'It's Pierre Dupont,' he said, making sure his tool belt was visible as he stepped forward and bowed before Klaebisch could take command of the conversation.

Sophie blinked twice, her mouth slightly open. He knew he hadn't changed so much that she wouldn't instantly recognise him, and shock was likely shaking through her like a thunder-crack too. Like him, though, she betrayed nothing in her expression, just a fixed smile. 'Pierre,' she said, ever so slightly breathless, and quickly shifted her gaze to look at Klaebisch with fresh puzzlement. 'Why have you brought Pierre Dupont here?'

'I was just coming for my vineyard shift—' Charlie tried, moving his hand deliberately to rest on the handle of his secateurs, hoping she would notice, before Klaebisch whipped around and cut him a look of pure threat.

'Say another word without my sanction and there will be consequences.'

Charlie formed an expression of horror. 'Please, Herr Klaebisch, do not subject Madame Delancré to this undignified scene. Her husband knows me well, and she has known me in her team for many years gone.'

Klaebisch actually raised his hand, but Sophie interrupted.

'What is this about, Herr Klaebisch?' She sounded appropriately offended, almost angry. 'Why is one of my favourite workers standing in my house under threat from you?'

She had followed Charlie's lead, understanding the only protection he had between survival and death was her.

'You know this man?' Klaebisch demanded.

'Know him?' she repeated. 'Yes, I know him,' she said, feigning vexation at a stupid question. 'I've known him for more than two decades. We go back to the early days of my marriage, Herr Klaebisch; Monsieur Dupont worked with me during the last time your people decided to make war on us. He's a trusted worker – a hard worker.'

'That's it? A vineyard worker of old?' Klaebisch snapped.

Charlie gave the most imperceptible shake of his head, which he hoped Klaebisch, who was looking at Sophie, would not notice. The thugs were standing behind him, probably used to confrontations of this nature.

Sophie blinked again, buying time, but it added to her portrayal of confusion. 'No. That's not it, Herr Klaebisch.' Now she managed to sound deeply offended. 'He is a trusted member of my team. He's versatile and knowledgeable. So much experience cannot be wasted, and he often helps out in the crushing room – anywhere he's needed. He's very informed regarding production, and I have often relied on his wisdom.'

'And how well do you know this man, madame?'

'How well?' she again echoed Klaebisch. 'I have known him

long enough to consider him a friend of this family and welcome in our home whenever he is in the region. And in terms of my Champagne house, Monsieur Dupont has become a highly regarded member of this family's seasonal team. Is that what you wanted to know, Herr Klaebisch?' She never broke eye contact with Klaebisch as she was speaking, and Charlie wanted to smile at her perfect response. She was magnificent.

'And what do you know about him beyond his work?' Klaebisch asked, frowning.

Sophie opened her palms. 'Well, I have never pried into his background. If you know Monsieur Dupont as well as I, you might know he's private and modest. What I do know is that when he works at Delancré, I can wholly rely on him.'

'And how do you contact him?'

'I don't,' she answered. 'My vineyard manager does, but you've sent him away to work in a German camp, so I can't even ask for you, if you need a complete answer.'

'Would your son know him?'

Sophie gave a nonchalant shrug. 'Probably. He has more to do with the few older men left behind from your work camps to work the vineyards. Monsieur Dupont is considered essential by your superiors, Herr Klaebisch, because they enjoy our French wines and spirits and we need people like him to keep providing it. Without him and others like him, there is no Champagne, or Burgundy, or—'

'How long has he worked for you?' Klaebisch interrupted, looking angrier by the minute.

'I couldn't say. My husband probably employed him originally. Jerome was head of the vineyards until—'

This time he waved a hand to cut her off. 'So you vouch for him.'

Sophie all but rolled her eyes, and Charlie again admired her composure under the weight of this man's gaze. 'Of course I vouch for him, Herr Klaebisch! Please tell me, what is this all about?'

The German shrugged. 'I don't trust him.'

'Well, I can't imagine why. He works the vines, he helps to make Champagne – has for decades. What did you think he might do?'

'There are French rebels everywhere, madame, and they are especially busy in the north at this time. We cannot be too careful.'

'Herr Klaebisch, I've told you before. I know nothing about all of that.' Charlie knew she was lying; there was no way that Sophie wouldn't be doing anything and everything to sabotage the invaders, from giving money to possibly even hiding the resisters.

'You have, madame.' Klaebisch suddenly switched topics, as though no one else was in the room. 'Er, perhaps you'd like to have dinner with me next week as my apology for the interruption to your day?'

Her eyes narrowed slightly. 'What I'd like is more food for my workers, Herr Klaebisch.'

He nodded. 'I'm afraid my hands are tied when it comes to food rations, Madame Delancré. The stringency, as I've explained, is because Berlin didn't like what the French did to them in the last war.'

'They're starving a nation, sir. We're no good to you dying of hunger.'

'Well, you might be pleased to see what I've brought for you today.' He glanced across to one of his henchmen. 'Go fetch the basket,' he ordered.

Charlie had seen it in the car, brimming with what he presumed were black market goods. 'A little gift for my favourite champenoise,' Klaebisch continued, clicking his heels again and nodding, his attention greedily back on Sophie.

She gave a shallow bow of thanks. 'I hope you won't mind if I share that food, Herr Klaebisch.'

'It's for you, madame, but it's your choice what you do with it. Now, you haven't answered my question about dinner next week.'

She cut a look at Charlie. 'Monsieur Dupont. You may leave. You'll be wanted in the cellars today. Please go through the back door.'

Charlie nearly touched his hand to his forelock but that wasn't a French gesture. Instead he cautiously nodded. 'Thank you, madame.' He turned to his captor. 'Herr Klaebisch.'

'Get out of my sight,' the man said with unwarranted disgust.

As Charlie left, he heard Sophie offering Klaebisch a bottle of an interesting drop to taste, adding, 'In the previous war there was a blockade, and the only way we could add sugar to make the Champagne was using the wine we call ratafia.'

Charlie smiled to himself as he ducked out of Klaebisch's reach. It had been his idea to use the ratafia that fateful year.

He knew his way down to the cellars. Nothing much had changed. The garden still looked much as it had, although he spotted a fine row of rose bushes – new to him – that looked strong, sturdy and established. However, the grass and its edges were neglected and overgrown; everyone surely had more important business on their mind.

He passed first through the riddling room, which was deserted. It was just after midday, he realised – the workers would be eating. He touched one of the pupitres, remembering how the wooden racks had felt like furniture around him during his days here. They held bottles and the skilled 'riddlers' performed remuage, shifting each bottle a quarter turn to the left or to the right, depending on what the riddler decided was best for the Champagne within, changing the angle some-times in one skilled motion. These decisions were made in less time than it took for his heart to beat, and Charlie had always found it breath-taking to watch: there were thousands of bottles to attend to. The aim was to gently guide the sediment of the wine to the neck of the bottle in its own time. He had marvelled at how this sediment would later be drained off in another skilled procedure to leave a perfectly clear wine.

Post-war mechanisation had crept into this most agile of processes and Sophie had likely embraced it over the past quarter of a century. Bottles, side by side, could now be cranked into a raised and angled position rather than requiring the skilled touch of a riddler's hand. He felt sad that the romance was disappearing from this most romantic of all beverages, but there was no obvious sign of automation here. He walked deeper into the cellar, also empty of people, and took his time, admiring the impressive lines of bottles held in their wooden shelving. He lifted one to blow off some dust.

'You have good taste, Charlie.'

He swung around at the voice, startled. Her English was perfect.

'Please don't drop that,' Sophie said, smiling. 'It's one of our finest vintages – nineteen twenty-nine. Despite the state of the world and its global depression, we made one of the best Champagnes in Delancré's history that year. Everyone did. It was a magnificent year for Champagne.'

He carefully put it back before gazing at her, hardly daring to believe they had turned back the clock. 'You remain as magnificent as your Champagne, Sophie,' he breathed, in French, because it was a language made for love. He rather liked the way they dipped in and out of each other's languages.

'Handsome Charlie,' she murmured, and he revelled in hearing his name pronounced once more as *Sharley*. 'I like this,' she said, touching just in front of her ear to indicate his greying temples. 'You look... debonair.'

He grinned. 'Well, that's just called age. Whereas you've matured like your vintage twenty-nine here into something extraordinary.'

She smiled, but smoothed down the front of her shabby working trousers. She felt self-conscious, he realised.

'Even how thin you've become can't hide your beauty, Sophie. Nothing ever could.'

She nodded, meeting his gaze again. 'They allow us so little food. We adults try to give more to the children, but my people need nourishment to work. The rationing is far more severe than in the previous war. I am raising rabbits, growing vegetables on every spare patch I can, and I keep chickens so we have fresh eggs, but it's not enough. If the Germans decide they want my eggs, they take them.'

Charlie blinked. There was nothing to say to that, given how well he and Violet had lived through the early war years by comparison. But Australia was a world away.

For several heart-lifting moments they simply stared at each other. He was lost for what to say next and presumed she must be too – there was so much to say, but he couldn't imagine where to begin. The stand-off lengthened until Charlie couldn't hold the spell any longer; in two strides he was in front of her, taking her into his arms in a long embrace.

She didn't resist, and he held his breath, trying to drink in every moment as they stood in each other's arms, saying nothing. He could feel her holding him tight as they buried their faces in each other, and he felt her frame shake with gentle sobs.

FOURTEEN

After a long moment, Charlie finally pulled away, missing the feel of her immediately. 'Don't cry, my darling Sophie,' he whispered.

'Charlie... Charlie, I'm so sorry about...'

'What?' he asked, although he knew precisely. 'Don't be. It was a long time ago. It was no one's fault. Your husband came back. I know you never stopped loving him – I know I was lucky to even have your attention, let alone affection.'

Tears ran down her cheeks via lines that hadn't been there the last time they'd stood like this. There was a slight softening to her face where there had once been angles, but her exquisite prettiness still shone through.

She was studying his face too, and she reached out a hand to touch his cheek softly. 'It really isn't fair. Men are like good wine – they just get better. You are still so handsome. Did you marry?'

He nodded. 'Her name was Ellen.' And before she could ask more he said, 'She died many years ago.'

Sophie looked mortified. 'Died?'

'It was a terrible shock. A blood clot in her brain. But it was quick. One minute she was there, and the next she was gone... so I'm grateful for that.'

Sophie sniffed, moving away slightly to lean against a nearby barrel. 'Charlie, that's too sad. I so wanted you to find happiness.'

'And I did. Ellen was a wonderful woman, the very best of wives, but I have to admit that I was unfaithful.' At her startled expression, he gave a sad smile. 'Only in my imagination. You see, I never fully gave you up. I knew we could never be together, but I refused to let go of my memories.'

'Oh, Charlie.'

He held up a hand to ward off any further apology. 'The war threw us together and then ripped us apart. We were helpless and even more so when Jerome returned. You must understand, Sophie, I was happy for you; I still am. Just sad for us.'

She nodded. 'That day of Jerome's return I wanted to split myself in half. I was distraught.'

'I know. That's why I had to leave immediately.'

'Do you have children?'

He smiled. 'A daughter. Violet. She's the best of both of us – I adore her. And you have a son?'

'I have two. Had two,' she corrected, and then swallowed. 'One was killed over a year ago. His name is Leo.' She used present tense, and Charlie took a breath. So they'd both had their griefs. 'The youngest was injured, sent home,' she continued. 'Raphael works here now. His wound wasn't too serious, but our invaders consider him essential for the Champagne because of his surname and skills, and they let him stay. I couldn't do it without him, or his ferocious loyalty.'

'And what about Jerome? Is he here?'

Sophie shook her head. 'In a work camp in Germany. He was too old to be called up immediately, and then after invasion he was rounded up and sent away.'

Charlie was shocked. 'Not considered essential?'

'He's a grower, not a winemaker. So no.'

'He's come full circle,' Charlie said, then grimaced.

She gave a low chuckle. 'Yes, we try and keep some humour about that. I accuse him of liking being away in prison camps.'

'Do you hear from him? Is he all right?'

'I think he'll be fine. He was taken away four years ago and continues to survive. Letters do get through, and his humour and love are intact.'

'He has many lives.'

'As do you, Charlie.' She paused. 'How is it that you're here?'

'Oh, that's a story.'

'I want to hear it. I want to know all of your life since the moment you walked away. Come with me.'

'To where?'

'To somewhere you know we are safe.'

She led him back into the main house and to the attic room: where else? He smiled with a deep pleasure as they found their way to the top of the house: no longer a storage room with a single beautiful chair but a glorious space that fulfilled Sophie's promise. It was her study, her private sitting room, a place where she indulged her creative side, it seemed, as he stood in front of a canvas depicting the view from the main attic window in pastels. He knew that scene so well; it was imprinted on his heart.

'I didn't know you were an artist,' he said with a grin.

'I used to draw when I was young. Even though I gave it up when I was married, I rediscovered it after I had the boys.'

This room held so much memory for Charlie that he suddenly felt awkward. He picked up a stick of colour. 'I'm glad. Is this alizarin?'

'Oh, very good. I'm impressed that you know this crimson.'

He grinned again. 'From the madder root. I can probably dredge up the Latin name, *rubia* something or other. I'm not a complete dunce.'

'Dunce?' she repeated.

'It means stupid. We English like to have lots of words that mean the same thing.' He stared at the pastel. 'It's intense.'

'The Roché way is to include no foreign elements in their pastels to fix the colours, which means you need a light touch when you use them, or you'll very quickly crumble away the world's most expensive stick. My father, keen to encourage all artistic pursuits in his children, took me to a courtyard, almost hidden, at rue Rambuteau in Paris when I was small. There we walked into a tiny shop, and I fell in love.' She smiled at him. 'I still am in love with these pastels,' she added. 'They have no equal.'

'Why are they the best?' He was eager to watch her move within the abandon of a time when there was no war.

'Oh, Charlie,' she sighed, 'the trays and trays of colours are breathtaking. They've been made the same way, by hand, for generations. Nothing comes close to their pigment. It's a secret recipe that pulls together colour in such a way that they become almost... I don't know, luminescent. They seem to find the light, and that's every artist's dream. They have pumice stone in them so they can grab onto the surface and maintain this brilliance of colour. Degas insisted upon them for his works.'

'You paint so well.'

'We *draw* with pastels, Charlie, we do not paint with them.' She grinned at her correction.

He couldn't keep his eyes from the canvas. 'I like this very much.'

'Why?'

He shrugged, reluctant to explain.

'Tell me, Charlie. It means more to hear your rationale.'

'I don't think I should, Sophie. Let's just say because I think it's beautiful.'

'Does it remind you of us?'

He couldn't meet her gaze, shocked at her directness. 'Yes,' he admitted. 'You explained this view to me, as I recall, and then...' He trailed off as the memory of their kiss flooded his mind. He tried to convince himself he had nothing to feel guilty about, but the feeling lingered as he stared at the drawing.

'Charlie, we can talk about this. It was more than twenty years ago.'

He nodded. 'But you were married the first time I kissed you at this very window, and you still are, so I do feel somehow... devious by referring to it again.'

She shook her head gently. 'I am secure in my love for Jerome, but I have never forgotten how you made me feel all that time ago when I most needed to survive my terror, my grief, my lack of confidence. Charlie, you made me feel strong and optimistic for a future beyond war. I see you as a sort of special angel who came into my life for a short time. You took nothing from me, from my marriage.'

He relented. 'Well, this scene has walked with me ever since I first saw it. In my imagination it is the happiest of memories. Forgive me for still holding the memory so close. I know who you belong to, and I know that you never stopped loving Jerome.'

Her blush came furiously, surprising him – given her candour – and he was touched by it; it proved she too had not forgotten that moment either. 'Then you should have it,' she said, to cover her momentary fluster.

'I couldn't—'

'No, I want you to. It's finished, and I'd like to think of it in England with you.'

'I don't live in England.'

She blinked, confused.

'I live in Australia now.'

'What?' He didn't think he could have surprised her more. It took him several minutes to explain that after returning to England and marrying Ellen, they'd had a child and moved to Scotland to make whisky. That raised her eyebrows, but she didn't interrupt as he continued his story of losing Ellen and, in an effort to escape the painful reminders, taking Violet to grow grain and make whisky on the other side of the world, where the small island of Tasmania reminded him often of Scotland. He finished his tale by explaining how he had joined the war effort from Australia and was now a spy for the Allies.

Her eyes became wider with understanding. 'Violet is left behind in Australia?'

He nodded. 'Unhappily. She's a very independent spirit, and threatened to join up as a nurse and come to the frontlines to spite me for my decision to leave.'

'I completely understand. With her mother gone and no siblings, you're all she has.'

'Don't make me feel any more guilty than I already do,' he pleaded.

'In this role as a spy, do you work with the French resisters?'

He nodded. 'I do. The local British circuit and the local French Resistance members.'

'I have so much fear they'll lure my son into their cause.'

Charlie shrugged. 'It's a good cause.'

'No, Charlie. This war is not taking my remaining child.'

He wanted to say many mothers had given up all their sons, and some their daughters, but that wasn't what Sophie needed to hear. 'We're close to the end now. Word is that the Americans have this region in their sights for liberation. They'll get here before any of the other Allies can. You and Raphael will be safe, and then Jerome will be home soon too.'

'I only hope that's true.' She closed her eyes for a moment. 'Charlie, I want you to meet Raphael, so that if he ever turns up around you and the resisters, you can send him home.'

'How old is he?'

'He's only twenty-three.'

'Sophie, he's older than many were in the trenches. I fought alongside boys as young as eighteen.'

'I don't care, Charlie. I've given my husband twice to the Germans. I've given them my beloved Leo. They will not have Raph. The Champagne house needs him.' She swallowed. 'I need him.' Her voice shook. 'Promise me.'

'I promise.' He gave his word without hesitation, without even knowing the fellow.

It calmed her. She walked to his side to stare out of the window, and easily began speaking in English again. 'Forgive me. I couldn't see Leo, hold him once more. I couldn't bury him. He was just gone. That lovely, calm, innocent, ever-smiling young man has simply disappeared, while I agree to have dinner with monsters like Klaebisch. I want to spit in his face.'

'I'm sorry. That was my fault.'

'No, don't feel responsible. Klaebisch is always pressing me to share his company. I want to tell him he makes my flesh crawl but instead I smile and make polite conversation, laugh at his jokes and give him more of my Champagne. He offers a thin protection for my workers.'

'He's never expected more?'

She visibly shivered. 'No.'

He half-whispered in French. 'You could poison the Champagne.'

'What? I couldn't. No.' She looked back at him half horrified, half amused. 'Think of what might happen to my workers. It wouldn't come back on me, Charlie. It would be them and their families who paid the price. No, I find other ways. I've hidden all the very best Champagne. Before Jerome was taken, we built a *mur faux* – er, how do you say, false wall?' He nodded. 'We did this in the cellars and then stacked thousands of the cheaper bottles in front of it. The Germans are too stupid and drunk on the idea of being able to raid our cellars to look any further than what's right in front of them.'

'Klaebisch included?'

She shook her head. 'Well, no, he's a former Champagne agent. He knows his wine. He even knows his vintages. He keeps asking for the nineteen twenty-nine and the nineteen thirty-four, which were both such extraordinary years. I tell him we sold all our stocks. I kept two of the nineteen twenty-nines out just in case, to show I wasn't hiding it.' She gave a wry smile and moved into English again for no reason; he loved it. 'One you found by chance. He has never noticed it, and I hope never will.'

He followed suit in English. 'I hope he appreciated the other one.'

Now a mischievous grin creased her face. 'Raph fetched it for him. As he came into the back garden, where Herr Klaebisch had arranged himself and his guest, and had ordered a lunch from my staff and the twenty-nine, Raph pretended to trip. I let out a small shriek, quite genuinely, and we all watched the bottle topple and smash on the flagstone path. Klaebisch was on his feet, all but...' She waved her hands, trying to find the right word.

'Apoplectic?' he offered in French.

'Yes, yes! Exactly. Red-faced, fuming.'

Charlie laughed. 'I'd like to have witnessed that. What a fine thing for your son to do.'

'It was. Raph made it look like such a clumsy accident, and I thought Klaebisch was going to hit him.' At Charlie's surprised look, she continued. 'I don't think Raph would have cared if he had. It would have been a sort of trophy for him. He told me later he'd rather watch the wine be swallowed by our grass than go down that man's throat.'

He gave a low whistle. 'Daring.'

'This is why I'm afraid for him. The whole notion of the Resistance, any sort of sabotage of the Germans, is seductive to this boy. He's far more daring than his cautious elder brother was – as reckless as his father used to be.'

'He'll mature, Sophie.'

'Well, that's what I want. I need him to survive this war so he can mature and can appreciate how sweet life can be. But right now he's angry, wanting to fight back against the people who stole his father, killed his brother, his friends... the people who are putting me into difficult situations every day.'

'Like today,' he admitted. 'You were very good, by the way. You would be a good cards player with that empty expression you managed to find.'

'Oh, it's been well rehearsed, Charlie,' she said in a weary tone. 'Anyway, that's the story of the twenty-nine. But Klaebisch is no fool. I can't keep tricking him; sometimes I have to let him have what he demands so he feels he is in control.'

'How many of your people are part of the Resistance?'

'In some shape or form, I would say all of them.'

'No bad apples?'

She frowned, not fully understanding.

'You trust them all?' he clarified.

'All the regular workers, yes. The transient ones I'm more wary of. We all are.'

'And Raphael?'

'He's forbidden from participating. He is the future of this house. Should anything happen to me, he alone has the ability to take Delancré into its new era, beyond this hateful war.'

Charlie couldn't imagine any hot-blooded young man, stinging from loss, being able to ignore the temptation to join the resisters in some way, commanding as Sophie was. He stayed quiet, though. She needed to believe that her son was as safe as she could make him. Instead, he turned the conversation away from war and resistance.

'I met someone after I left Épernay who became a friend,' he said. 'He was a fellow soldier, a captain too, who remained behind after the end of all the fighting to lead clearing parties through northern France.'

She frowned. 'What does that mean?'

'Well, there were always small pockets of the enemy who hadn't been able to get out, or were slow to move, or too determined to stay, and so I joined Captain Harry Blake's clearing party, which moved through the region, forcing the enemy to flee back into Germany. But our most important job was to mark the fallen, gather information, bury the dead and pinpoint those graves, that sort of thing. It was depressing work, and yet there was something comforting, even affirming, about knowing we were looking after our fallen. For each dead soldier there was a family back home yearning for news, even if it was news of the worst kind. It meant they could allow themselves to grieve, and somehow move forward.'

'I did wonder where you went.'

He shrugged. 'My mind was blurry. I needed some time to let

the reality settle that Jerome had returned and I had to leave you behind... to sort out my feelings and find somewhere to put them. This work was a perfect distraction, and it was helping others. That's not why I'm telling you this, though.' He chuckled, surprised at how melancholy he suddenly sounded. 'I mentioned Harry because one evening we were talking about what would come next for us. Harry had a bee in his bonnet about a tin of chocolate we found on a fallen soldier, with a note from his sweetheart, and he got it into his head that he was going to find her and give her the tin of chocolate and the news of her beloved in person.'

She frowned. 'Was that how it was done?'

'No, not usually,' he said with another laugh. 'It was to do with the chocolate. You see, everyone who received those tins of chocolate – they were special, they came from the royal family – all but fell on the chocolate itself. It was such a treat, and smelled and tasted of home at a time when we all felt like we were living in a sort of relentless hell. Anyway, it was rare to find an unopened tin, and this one had the note. Harry felt moved to take the tin home to the girl, who apparently worked in the chocolate factory where all of these tins were packed.'

'How romantic.' Sophie sighed.

'It *was* romantic actually... for Harry. But that's another story. I'm telling you this because it was Harry who encouraged... no, insisted that I follow through on my dream – which was inspired by you.'

She looked surprised. 'Making whisky was inspired by me?'

'Definitely. I wasn't going back to being an industrial chemist. I wanted to use my skills to make something that brought people pleasure. I would have tried Champagne if I thought we had the right climate to grow the grapes, but I realised I needed to make something that Britain was good at. Harry loved whisky and was drinking a single malt at the time of this conversation. "Make this!" he demanded. "I'd have to live in Scotland," I replied. "So?"' Charlie let out a chuckle. 'I'd drunk my fair share of whisky in my time, but I'd never really tasted it in the way I did when I shared it with Harry, who had a great palate for it. When I got back to London, I read everything I could. I tasted as many different whiskies as I could from all over, including Irish and American whiskey. And then I chose a region called Speyside in Scotland, where perhaps the most famous brands had set up their operations. I wanted to be among them. After a year in London, I knew I didn't want to be in the big smoke much longer and the idea of making whisky was overwhelming me, so I took my wife and daughter north, settled in a tiny village and learned from the best. I was counting on everything I'd learned from you coming to the fore to make a difference.'

'And did it?'

'Did it ever!' he said with a grin. 'Learning about the sugars was vital – learning from you about the natural ingredients of the grapes and, in this case, the barley or wheat, added so much... well, background knowledge to what I was now taking on board in whisky distillation. I learned fast because of what I'd experienced at Delancré. And, if you'll forgive a small boast, I found my real skill in blending. I had a nose and palate for it, to the point where I knew I could go out on my own and be successful. But then Ellen died and years passed miserably; then the Depression arrived, killing off so many small distilleries, and rather than be among them, Violet and I decided to start over in Australia.'

'Charlie, this is an amazing story,' Sophie said, smiling widely. 'I'm very proud of you. I would like you to send me a bottle of your whisky.'

'That depends if I get back safely...' He trailed off.

Now her expression darkened. 'Don't talk like that. You will go home to your child.'

He shrugged. 'I have to be realistic, and now Klaebisch has me in his sights.'

'You have my protection, for whatever that's worth.'

'Once again,' he replied, making her smile.

'And whenever you need it. Now, I need you to meet Raph. Have dinner with us. All the workers are coming this evening. I try to do a communal dinner each Friday, with whatever we have to share. It's good for morale.'

Charlie frowned. 'It wouldn't be seemly for a stranger to be dining with you.'

'Don't you worry about that. You'll be explained as a friend from the past – that's true after all. They trust me, especially if I suggest you might be working with us now. Please come. We dine in the garden, beneath the stars.'

'Sounds marvellous. Thank you, that would be lovely.'

'Good. Where do you stay?'

'With a local family. Best I don't say their name – the less you know, the better.'

She nodded. 'Why don't you go and wash up downstairs? I'll roll this up for you,' she said, pointing at the landscape drawing.

He hated to leave the space he thought of as a sanctuary, and perhaps she sensed that because she simply looked at him. Was she anxious that he might try to kiss her, rekindle that moment they'd shared in this room so many years ago? But Charlie's heart was already aching. Jerome was alive, and he would never wish to compromise her in that way.

'I'll see you down there,' he said. 'Er... thank you for showing me how you've turned the attic into your private space. It's lovelier than I imagined it could be. And thank you for the drawing.' He wanted to say more about what it meant to him, but he looked down, unable to find the words.

She was suddenly at his side, shoulder to shoulder, linking her fingers through his. 'I know. I feel it too, Charlie... even after all these years.'

She turned and he looked into her eyes, searching for even a flutter of appeasement. Was she just saying that to soothe him? He found instead her most naked and sad truth.

'Our timing is always wrong,' she said gently, with a soft smile. 'But know this. There was war, grief, uncertainty and despair during those weeks you spent in Épernay, but I found happiness with you. I saw a future again, and I felt loved and I loved you in return. But it was a dream; it couldn't be then, and it cannot be now. I just want you to know that I mourn that too, in spite of loving my husband very much. As in your marriage, there was an invisible third person after we met. Let that be enough, because it has to be. There is no other way.'

He nodded, and then lifted her hand and kissed it before departing down the ladder, aware that she watched him, silent tears falling from her face to dampen her blouse, as he disappeared, step by heartbreaking step, away from her again.

FIFTEEN

Charlie sat among the other workers at a series of scrubbed pine tables that had been pushed together, where they had gathered for supper. There was no fuss. No fancy linens, silver cutlery or precious crockery. Simple food on large communal platters was placed directly on the tables and everyone helped themselves. Meat, other than some rabbit, was not on the menu. It rarely was, he gathered. Sophie had probably used a lot of rations to bring this together but he'd taken a stroll around the property earlier and noted the well-tended vegetable gardens that were helping to keep her people fed through these toughest of times.

Sophie welcomed everyone. 'I thought we should celebrate the harvest, which is why we're drinking this very good wine this evening.'

Everyone cheered and banged on the tables.

'We welcome newcomers'—she named three others before introducing him—'Monsieur Pierre Dupont, a much-loved family friend and member of our team from earlier years, who hasn't been back for a while. It is a tonic to see him again.' Her gaze alighted on him only for a moment, but he felt its affection as those around him raised glasses of Champagne and smiled generously in welcome.

'Now, please eat, and enjoy!' she finished and sat down, immediately bending her head towards the nearest diners to engage them in conversation. The seat at her right was empty. Charlie assumed this was for the elusive Raphael.

'We have not seen you before, Monsieur Dupont,' one of the women opposite said.

'I travel around all the vineyards,' Charlie replied, 'but I haven't been back to Delancré for a while, as you heard. I used to come regularly, but these days I always seem to get trapped in Burgundy.'

Others around him chuckled. 'A good place to become trapped,' a different woman admitted.

'Indeed. Even when I'm ready to leave and head north, these last couple of years they've asked me to stay on and help in the crushing room.'

'A man in demand,' a third woman remarked.

'Are you all vineyard workers?' Charlie asked the group. He took a bite of the rabbit terrine they were sharing.

'No, we work in the cellars,' the first woman replied and made a twisting gesture with her hands.

'Ah, yes. Remuage?'

She nodded. 'Yes, that's all of us here.' She gestured to the group near Charlie. 'We take care of the bottles and the sediment.'

He realised Sophie had deliberately sat him among this group as they were not in the vineyards regularly and were less likely to question his presence. He was grateful for it.

Conversation moved to family and ultimately the war. Sophie had assured him that all her regular workers were reliable and trustworthy. Even so, he was cautious. When the woman next to him asked if he'd heard anything about liberation, he gave a shrug. 'I probably know as much as you.'

'It's just that my two sons have survived this long, and there's talk of this area being liberated soon,' she said, searching his face. 'I want to believe they'll make it through.'

'I have no information.' Charlie shook his head. 'But Germany has been losing its war for a long time,' he added, a hand to the side of his mouth as though speaking conspiratorially. 'They just don't know it.'

She smiled. 'I thought with your moving around you might have heard something.'

'I am just a worker and, like you, I hear on the grapevine'—he smiled at the unintended pun—'that this region might be liberated soon.'

As much as he wanted to reassure this woman that it might be mere weeks before the Americans pushed through, he remembered the warning to never drop his guard, to never speak openly to anyone – even someone who seemed innocent and trustworthy. He'd broken that rule with Sophie, but he could hardly maintain the lie with her. Besides, he trusted her wholeheartedly, even telling her which circuit he was attached to, whereas this woman might be a spy for the Germans, despite Sophie's assurances, or the Germans might have something with which to blackmail the woman. For all he knew, they could have one or more of her children captive and have made promises with regard to them – good or bad – depending on her co-operation. So he gave her nothing more, simply adding, 'I do hope so.'

He felt a touch on his shoulder and realised Sophie had arrived. Charlie desperately wanted to cover her hand with his; in fact, he wanted to stand up, turn around and take her in his arms. Instead he absorbed with joy the warmth of her skin through his shirt, looked up and smiled. 'Good evening, Madame Delancré. Thank you for the welcome.'

'Good evening, Monsieur Dupont.'

'Pierre,' he insisted.

'I don't believe you've met my son. I'd like to introduce you.'

'Of course. Will you excuse me?' he said to the women around him.

'Thank you for the protection of the riddlers,' he murmured once they'd moved away.

'Nearly all of them are widows. I knew you would be welcome among them,' she said, guiding him to where a strapping young man was serving wine. 'He insists on doing that,' she said with a shrug. 'He believes in finding ways to serve those who serve us.'

Charlie nodded, saying nothing, but he was impressed as he watched Sophie catch her son's attention. He motioned that he would just finish pouring the bottle and, a few moments later, strode over on long, sturdy legs.

Sophie put her hand on his arm. 'Raph, this is my friend, Pierre Dupont. We've known each other a very long time.'

The young man gave an easy smile that reminded Charlie of someone, and offered a large hand. 'A pleasure, Monsieur Dupont.'

His grip was strong and confident. 'You remind me very much of your father,' Charlie said, unable to help himself. As he glanced at Sophie, she blushed.

'You know him?' Raphael asked.

'Yes, indeed. We met only briefly many years ago on his return from a Swiss internment camp, but I felt I knew him through your mother, who never believed he was lost, as so many others did.'

Raphael looked down. 'And now he's in prison.'

'Again,' Charlie and Sophie said together, then chuckled awkwardly. It was vaguely alarming at how easily they had fallen into complete synchrony.

Raph seemed to find their overlapping words amusing. 'My brother looks like my beautiful mother. Looked,' he corrected, with apology in his tone. 'He was blessed.'

Sophie squeezed her son's arm. 'Your father's the most handsome man I know,' she said, cutting a subtle look of regret Charlie's way, but he refused to acknowledge the glance. She was clearly nervous, and he didn't want to trigger the youngster's suspicions or prompt any difficult questions.

A woman came up and asked Sophie something. 'I'll be back in a moment or two,' she said apologetically, and left the men standing together.

Raphael met Charlie's eye openly. 'How do you know my mother?'

Stick as close to the truth as possible, the team who trained

Charlie back in England had cautioned. 'From Reims,' he said. 'I got caught behind enemy lines during the last war and somehow, though I'll never quite remember how it all unfolded'—that part was a lie—'I found my way back to the French side and was taken to the hospital where she volunteered. People were giving up on me, but she didn't. I think my physical injury was not the problem.' He tapped his temple. 'I'd had enough of the killing. She brought me here to Épernay, had a brace made for my injured arm, saw to my rehabilitation and gradually worked on my mind to retrieve my belief in the world when I felt I'd lost it. I try to repay her kindness by returning as often as I can to work in her vineyards.'

He frowned. 'Why haven't I seen you before?'

Charlie carved his lie deeper. 'I was coming regularly when you were probably too young to know all the workers in the fields, but I haven't been back for maybe two decades. Certainly not through the war years because, as I was explaining earlier to some of the women from the cellars, I seem to get trapped in the vineyards south of here.'

It appeared to work; Raphael nodded and moved on. 'Have you heard anything about liberation?' he asked, his tone full of hope.

Charlie shook his head and lied again. 'I haven't.'

'My mother spoke to me about you earlier, assuring me that although you might seem like a stranger, you are one of the people she most trusts in the world. In fact, she says of all the people here, you are the *most* trustworthy and loyal.'

Charlie lifted a shoulder slightly. 'I can assure you that's true, though I'm flattered she would say it. Perhaps that's because she knows I would die for her.'

It was a stupid thing to say, and he saw the shock flash in Raphael's eyes.

'What I didn't say,' he hurried to add, 'is that she saved my life in that underground hospital in Reims and here at Épernay. So it would be only fair.' He tried to temper the emotional outburst with a wry smile.

'Saved your life? She has never mentioned you,' Raphael said.

'But while I wouldn't go so far as to call my mother secretive, I would call her a book that prefers to be closed rather than read.' He smiled. 'Learning anything about her younger years is a painful task... for her, I mean. She doesn't like to talk about when my father was imprisoned and how she coped through those years of the last war.'

Charlie gave a sad smile. 'Don't hold it against her. None of us like to recall those days. I have a daughter who is frustrated by a similar silence.'

Raph nodded. 'If my mother trusts you, I can trust you to speak my mind?'

Charlie frowned. 'Absolutely you can.'

Raphael gestured for Charlie to follow him further away from the tables. 'I hate that I'm here.' He paused. 'That's come out wrong. I mean I should be fighting. My brother died heroically. He will always be remembered that way. But me? What am I doing? Making Champagne for the Germans to steal and swill? I feel like I'm aiding the enemy, rather than standing up to them. I want to do something.'

'Raphael—' Charlie began, his tone cautionary.

'I have no one to talk to,' the young man continued. 'All of these people are as trustworthy as you, but I dare not speak the truth to them. And I can't speak to my mother. It would hurt her and frighten her.'

'What are you saying?'

'I'm saying,' Raphael said, shrugging, 'that all of these people are loyal to France and to this family, but first and foremost to my mother – to the name Delancré. I can't confide in anyone, because they will report to my mother.' He ran his hand through thick hair so reminiscent of his father's, with its slightly reddish tinge as the dying sunlight caught it.

Charlie didn't know what to say. He stared at the young man, waiting for more if he wanted to say more but not encouraging him; he could already sense what was going on behind those brooding eyes. 'What do you need to confide?'

Raphael pulled him further away still and dropped his voice. 'I need someone to know in case something happens to me.'

'Know what?' Charlie said.

'I am joining the Resistance.'

He grabbed his arm. 'Raphael, no!'

'I have to. I cannot sit by so uselessly and—'

Charlie was shaking his head. 'Can you begin to imagine what that would do to your mother? She's already lost a son, and her husband is in a camp.'

Raphael gave a heavy sigh. 'I adore my mother, but she has to imagine what this is doing to me. It is destroying my soul to be here, so protected and pampered, while other sons put their lives on the line for France.' He waved a hand towards the tables, where the women, lots of them widows, chatted amiably to one another. 'All their sons are fighting. They sit there and, while no one means to, I feel the accusation like another guest, staring at me, pointing at me, jeering at me.'

Charlie shook his head again. 'That's in your imagination, Raphael. *You* are one of the things that keeps this Champagne house going – keeps *them* going, keeps the mouths of their families fed, keeps them safe. You are contributing in your own way. And it's important to your mother that you're safe.'

'I don't want to be safe!' The young man's voice was louder now. 'I want to avenge my brother and all the French who have died in this war. I want to fight back!'

'Raphael, please.' Charlie gestured for him to lower his voice. It was a young man's attitude, that fearless bravado and sense of invincibility... knowing death came to some but secretly believing it would never come for you. He had to stop Raphael for Sophie's sake. 'You cannot follow through on this plan.'

'It's too late. I've agreed.'

Charlie frowned. 'Agreed to what?'

'There is a group in Épernay,' Raphael started.

Charlie closed his eyes for a heartbeat to decide how much he could reveal.

'I have offered my involvement. There's a parachute drop at—'

'At the clearing of the small forest on Monsieur Gauchet's farm,' Charlie interrupted. 'Yes, I know.'

Raphael blinked with consternation. '*You know?*'

Charlie nodded. It was too late now to back out. 'Raph, you must not get involved.'

The young man's mouth was open. '*You're* Resistance?' he murmured under his breath. 'Show me your badge.'

Shaking his head, Charlie had to give the truth. 'Everything you've been told about me is a lie. I'm British,' he admitted in a tight whisper that only Raphael could hear.

The youngster looked at him in soft bewilderment. 'A spy?'

Charlie nodded, refusing to drop his gaze.

'Does my mother know?'

Charlie nodded again as Raphael swung away and then twisted back.

'She's helping you?'

'Not through choice. I don't want to bring any trouble to her life.' Charlie quickly explained about Klaebisch.

Raphael narrowed his eyes. 'I'd kill him if she'd let me.'

'It won't do you any good. There are plenty who would take his place and kill both you and your mother for your trouble. Then they would confiscate the Champagne house or simply burn it to the ground. You've got to think this through, not be so hot-headed and selfish.'

Raphael looked shaken at the harshness of his words, but Charlie was convinced it was the only thing that might bring him back to reality. 'You think the Resistance is romantic? That it shows your bravery? Wrong. It's stupidity right now. The end is so close now, you have to trust me.'

'Listen,' Raphael hissed.

'No, you listen to me.' Charlie resisted prodding Raphael's chest, even though the gesture tingled in his fingertips. He moved so close that any observer might have thought they were sharing a secret. 'Smile as though I am telling you a joke.' He waited a beat and watched Raphael falter momentarily before forcing a grin. 'Few others know this, but the liberation is coming. If the Americans continue as they are, they'll break through the lines in a matter of weeks. You have to hang on. Look after your mother. Look after this Champagne house, continue to dance to Klaebisch's tune and wait for the release that will be here shortly.'

Raphael stepped back, staring at him. 'I... I can't. I hate him, and I hate what is happening to my home, to our life, to my shattered family. I can't just sit by and—'

'You can. It's happening to everyone. Look around you. You are not special, Raphael. Except to your mother. If she means anything to y—'

Raphael shook his head. 'I'm going to be at that drop.'

'You have no idea how dangerous it is.'

'And you do, old man?'

It was Charlie's turn to blink. 'I know what it is to stare death in the face.'

Raphael shrugged, defiant. 'Well, then, I have the right to do the same while defending my country. If you tell my mother to stop me, I shall never forgive you, or her,' he warned.

Charlie had no answer for this because he didn't disagree with Raph. He and Raph's father had not been that much older when they went to war to defend their nations. Why shouldn't he?

'Everything all right here?' It was Sophie, breezing back into their space. Charlie could tell she was concerned, but she covered it with a smile.

'Everything's fine. But I have told Raphael that I'm not who we said I was.' He could feel Raph's glare and decided not to test the younger man's threat, for Sophie's sake.

She schooled her features so well, the smile only brightening. 'Really? Was that helpful, do you think?'

'You should have told me... trusted me,' Raph said to his mother, accusing.

Charlie looked at her. 'He deserves to know, Sophie.'

Sophie looked down and her voice lowered. 'I thought if you

knew who Charlie is you might feel emboldened... but I can't lose you too, Raph.'

Her son softened, bending to kiss his mother's hollow cheek. 'I'm going to do what I have wanted to for a long time. You won't lose me. I'm like Papa – I have lots of lives.' He nodded at Charlie and left them, clearly happy to escape.

'Hold it together,' Charlie said softly, watching Sophie.

She swallowed hard. 'Meet me upstairs,' she said, then turned her back on him and departed.

He found her at the top of the house. It wasn't the attic this time, but the highest landing, where she stood on a pale rug on the floorboards. Several doors led off from this landing and Charlie was struck by how prophetic this felt: which door would they take?

'I'm sorry to have made you cry,' he said, feeling instantly ashamed. It was obvious from the way she was still dabbing at her nose, but her tears had dried, mercifully. Sophie, he knew, would never feel sorry for herself for long.

'You've always made me cry, Charlie,' she admitted ruefully. 'Sometimes happy tears, mostly sad ones.'

He nodded; he didn't know what else to say.

'You shouldn't have told him about you. You had no right.'

Charlie shook his head. 'Sophie, your son is going to do what he wants and neither you nor I nor the man in the moon is going to change that.'

She looked at him, bemused.

'Sorry, that's a saying from childhood.'

She ignored him. 'He's so young.'

'He's not, you know. I fought with lads much younger than him. I wasn't so much older when I was leading a group of men to their deaths.'

'Would you like your only child to be threatening this?'

'Of course not.'

'She's lucky she doesn't have to face it,' Sophie said. 'She's safe and you can count on that.'

Charlie looked at her, serious. 'I hope she's safe. But she's alone. I abandoned her to go and fight the war in my own way. She has no other family. And she's trying to keep our business running. It's hard work. Growing and harvesting like you, and then making whisky as you make Champagne, but she's doing most of it herself, with just a couple of workers. She has no idea of where I am or what I'm doing, or whether I'll even come back.'

Sophie bit her lip. 'I apologise.'

'You don't have to. But Violet is blameless here.'

'I know. I'm frightened, Charlie.'

He risked stepping closer, and then he risked holding her again. She melted against him, shedding silent tears. Eventually she sniffed, composing herself, but didn't let him go.

'It's nice to hold you again after all these years,' she said.

He chuckled. 'Nice? I'd call it dangerous,' and he looked down at himself to make her laugh. 'I've carried this throb around for more than twenty-five years.'

'Throb?' she repeated with helpless laughter. 'I don't know this word.'

He pointed. 'It's this!'

That made her laugh harder and she had to cover her mouth for fear of being overheard. 'Shhh,' she warned, still smiling. 'I'm flattered at this age,' she murmured through her amusement and then her face fell again and the atmosphere sobered around them. 'What is he actually talking about doing?'

He couldn't lie to her, even though he wanted to. 'There's a parachute drop nearby. He plans to be part of the retrieval team. I'm not sure what's coming in, but I can find out.'

'Where is the drop?'

He shook his head. 'I'm not going to tell you. It would betray too many. Not far from here. North.'

'Will you go with him?'

He looked at her, aghast, as she searched his face.

'Please, Charlie. I know you'll keep him safe.'

'I don't know if my team will permit it. I'm not in the field.'

'Of course you are. You're in France, aren't you?'

'You sound like my daughter. Yes, but my role is not to be dashing around with parachute drops. We have specific duties. I would be compromising—'

She clasped his hands. 'Charlie, I'm begging you.'

He pulled back. 'And what about the next time? He's not going to stop at one dangerous situation.'

She shook her head. 'I'll worry about next time when it happens. All I care about is right now and this crazy idea he has to do something heroic.' She pulled Charlie close again and kissed him on both cheeks. 'I am pleading with you to keep my child safe.'

He nodded unhappily. 'Of course I will.' It would mean going against orders, but he was helpless in her presence.

'Thank you. One day I will return this generosity, I promise.'

As a chill passed through him and settled in his gut, Charlie nodded, hoping Violet would never have to learn that he had broken his promise to her and was deliberately putting himself in danger.

SIXTEEN
RICHMOND

August 1944

The two men seemed to fill the space around Violet with their hungry gazes and fetid aura. She could smell them: old sweat, unwashed clothes, the dust and dirt of the road. One limped and the other favoured an arm. Returned soldiers, maybe? She could grasp their motivation; it seemed obvious they'd heard about a distillery in this region, run by a single woman. This probably equalled easy pickings in the estimations of men who had seen ugly things and likely participated in death and destruction. No doubt the thought of disappearing into some liquor, for which it appeared they had no money, overrode even basic sensibilities.

They'd arrived a few minutes earlier. She'd seen them out of the window of her barrel room, loping across her field like a pair of watchful wolves. She felt angrier for the newly planted barley being trampled than for what might be coming. They were predators, all right. She sensed it immediately, even though they might claim their arrival was innocent enough. Internal alarms were ringing just from the way they were looking around as though nervous of being seen.

She picked up the knife she kept in the shed and put it into her apron pocket, thinking about the rifle in the cottage, unloaded and in the laundry. Her father had been very unhappy about being told to keep a rifle when they'd taken over the land here. He made sure it was separated from the cartridges and its breach broken, but he accepted it might be necessary when a local farmer gave him some advice.

'Never know when one of them bastard tiger snakes might cross your path,' he was told. 'This ain't England, mate, where you might get bit by a squirrel if you're unlucky.'

The grim humour wasn't lost on Charlie, who had explained to Violet in less sarcastic terms that having a gun would be necessary. 'I'll teach you how to shoot it, but I'm here, so I'm hopeful you'll never have to raise it against anything.'

'You're not here, though, are you, Dad,' she murmured now.

The men had swags slung around their bodies; they were probably journeymen workers looking for a hot meal and perhaps somewhere to sleep in exchange for work. That was the intention, no doubt, but Violet's instincts sent the darker message that work was likely not on their minds, not from a woman who lived alone. She had none to give them or even to distract them with, anyway. The fields were quiet now, beginning their process of nurturing.

The pair were too close to ignore, and too close for her to make a run for the rifle, load it and then threaten them. She took a deep breath and filled the doorway, wiping her palms on her apron, feeling the reassuring bump of the blade in the pocket. 'Are you fellas lost?' she began, as brightly as she could, trying to keep her language as friendly as possible.

'We're looking for work,' one drawled predictably, though neither of them pulled off their hats in any polite manner.

'Your timing's a bit off for work around here. We've only just finished planting and won't be doing so again until the end of October. Harvest isn't due until next February.' She gave a friendly but confused look to show she meant no disrespect, but they weren't paying attention to her words. They were simply watching her, lasciviously, she thought. If she ran, they would chase her down easily enough. If she backed into the shed, there was no other door and she'd give them the privacy to do as they pleased.

Her mind fled to her father once again, but it was a useless thought; this was her frightening situation to handle. To capitulate was the easiest solution and it would be over soon, given their wolfish leers, but she heard advice in her mother's voice: *You fight them, Violet. You claw and bite and scratch and scream. Do not give them what they want easily.*

A woman is powerless, Violet thought. *So fight anyway,* she told herself. *Respect yourself and give them nothing; they'll have to steal it... and the hard way.*

The man who had addressed her shrugged. 'We thought there might be some odd jobs around.'

'I'm afraid not.' Her voice shook slightly, but she hoped only she heard it.

'Where's your husband?' the second one asked, with another leer from his dark eyes.

Now she knew they were here for anything but work. They would have asked around and have already discovered she wasn't married and that there was no man on the farm. The one who'd spoken first leant lazily against the side of the nearby shed while his companion with the darker looks and hooded brow simply watched. He was definitely the more dangerous of the two. She sensed he knew she wasn't buying their story. He sighed. 'Get on with it, Arty.'

'Get on with what, Arty?' she said, turning her gaze on the first man, finally finding rage as it pushed through the fear and the trembling. 'What are you really here for?' She needed them to say it.

The dark-eyed one gave a soft snort as Arty pushed off the shed wall and joined his friend. 'Well, rumour has it you're making moonshine, sweetheart,' he drawled. 'Me and my mate, Billy... well, we could sorely use a drink. You know, drown some sorrows.'

'No moonshine here,' Violet said, standing as tall as she could to bar the entrance.

'Then what's in the shed?'

'I'm licensed by law to make whisky.'

The man she now knew as Billy stretched lazily. 'You sound posh. What is that accent, darlin'?'

She regarded him with the most withering look she could muster, given her distress. 'What's it to you?' She sounded strong, but she felt her insides churning with anticipation. She'd never felt as alone as she did at this moment. This was about to turn bad and she couldn't see a way out of it. No one would hear her scream, even if she could drag enough breath in to do so.

And they knew it.

'Well, now,' Billy said slowly, sounding amused. 'I like you. The fiery type. How about we sit down together and you pour us some of that whisky?'

'I'm afraid not, lads. It's not ready.'

'Aw, we don't care,' Arty said. 'We don't need good stuff.'

'But this *is* the good stuff.' She couldn't help feeling affronted, though she knew it was stupid to bother with this detail.

'Don't make us take it, lady,' Billy said.

'It's just not ready. It would—' And then it struck her that she was being foolish. There was a way out of this. She paused. 'How come you're not fighting like the rest of our men?'

'Oh, we're injured,' Arty said, full of mock self-pity. 'Sent home.'

She nodded. 'They say the devil finds work for idle hands... and cowards.'

She saw Billy bristle at that. 'I won't wait much longer for a sip of your whisky,' he said. 'Or you.' He ran his tongue over his lips slowly. 'I'm a man starved of liquor... and women.'

Violet swallowed. 'Well, I'll tell you what I'll do, Billy. You can help yourself to a drink. Drink as much as you like, but if you so much as touch me, at least one of you is going to feel the keen edge of this blade,' she said, withdrawing her knife. 'That I promise you.'

That stopped their cocky smiles for a moment. Then Billy smiled. 'We can drink as much as we like, eh?'

'On the house,' she said, sweeping her free hand to gesture behind her. 'But don't test me. I'll stab you without mercy.' She was already moving in an arc as she let them into the barrel room so that she could come full circle and edge back to the doorway. At least she could try making a run for it if she needed to.

'We can drink a lot,' Arty promised.

'Here.' She pointed to the barrel that was around seventy per cent proof. Close up, the men looked red-eyed from a previous evening of drinking; she could smell the alcohol wafting from them, and they looked so tired that she imagined it wouldn't take more than three or four shots to have them legless and helpless with the pure alcoholic spirit in that barrel. 'There's a couple of shot glasses over there.' She gestured to a ledge where a small assortment of tin cups and glasses were gathering dust. She didn't want them touching her tasting glass.

Billy stared at the barrel. 'How do we get it?'

At that moment Jimmy arrived, and everyone looked suddenly alarmed, especially Jimmy.

'Violet? Er, are you—'

'We have guests, Jimmy,' she said quickly, pasting on a smile. 'Some visitors to these parts who wish to taste our whisky.'

'But...'

'They weren't invited, which is why I'm waving a knife around, but let's get them a taste of our best, shall we?'

Jimmy looked between them as if they'd all lost their minds. 'Violet, you know that—'

'Just do it, mate. Or we'll kick your head in,' Arty growled.

Jimmy looked frantically at Violet, who nodded firmly. 'Use the valinch. Give them as much as they like. Two big glasses, Jimmy. Though I doubt they'll be able to cope with much more than a few.'

'I'm going to drink as much as I choose,' Billy said, 'so shut your mouth, you gobby bitch.'

'Or we'll fill it with something you can tell your friends about, if you have any,' Arty added, laughing through broken, slightly blackened teeth.

Jimmy mercifully caught on and began opening the barrel.

Violet tried not to shudder. 'I wouldn't if I were you, Arty. Because I bite, and it looks as though I would do it better than you can.' She laughed, sounding brave, feeling terrified. 'And I won't let go, no matter what you do.'

Billy slapped Arty sideways. 'Shut up, will ya? Just let me drink in peace. Miss, we can drink more than you can imagine, and you did say as much as we want.'

'I did. Don't say we're not hospitable here in Richmond.'

They watched Jimmy draw two slugs from the barrel using the spirit thief.

'That's clever,' Billy remarked.

'Tell me what you think of the whisky,' Violet said, almost conversationally as the two men knocked back their shots. They were big slugs and, as she anticipated, both men winced, their faces screwing up in concert.

'Whew!' Billy groaned almost in celebration, releasing the fumes of the alcohol. 'Now that's some spirit.'

Arty let out a shriek as the burn hit his throat; she didn't know if it was pain or pleasure, nor did she care.

'And again, Jimmy,' Violet said.

He refilled their glasses.

'What do you think?' she asked again.

'Kicks like a fucking mad mule,' Arty said.

'What do you call this stuff?' Billy asked. 'That ain't the whisky I'm used to.'

'This is Australian whisky,' she said. 'Nothing like the Scotch you might have had before or the American rye. This is made with all sorts of things,' she lied.

Jimmy handed them each another full glass of the amber liquid. She hated to see her treasure wasted on them, but she didn't think it would take much longer.

'The second shot is usually smoother,' she lied again, her tone reassuring. Anything with that much raw alcohol was going to hurt.

They knocked their next glass back. This time they both coughed, Billy shaking his head as though he could somehow banish the power of the liquor.

She nodded at Jimmy, mouthing, 'Quickly!' And while they were still clearing their throats, he refilled the glasses.

'Can I get you some bread and cheese?' she offered as though she'd invited them for a meal. It would almost be amusing if the situation wasn't so dangerous.

'I've got all I need here,' Billy said, his eyes beginning to swim as he took the glass proffered by Jimmy.

'Well, I'm hungry,' Arty slurred.

She nodded brightly. 'So let me fetch—'

'You stay right there!' Billy warned.

She thought they would move slower than her now, but there was Jimmy to think of, so she stayed where she was and watched them take the third slug, which Arty swallowed in one gulp, but she noted Billy took his time. They'd now had the equivalent of seven normal drams and Arty, she reckoned, would be useless shortly.

It happened sooner than she imagined.

'Billy... I can't feel my fuckin' legs.' Arty began to laugh.

'You're all right, mate. What's in this?' Billy demanded, his gaze now unable to lock squarely on hers.

Violet nudged Jimmy back a couple of paces. If either of the men noticed, they didn't react. 'This is whisky in the barrel. It needs some refining,' she said, still conversational, and privately amused by her understatement. They wouldn't need another slug; Arty was already sliding down the shed wall, and Billy had begun to stagger.

'Have you poisoned us?' were his last words as his knees buckled and he too fell down.

'Go, Jimmy!' she urged in a tight whisper. 'Get help!

SEVENTEEN
ÉPERNAY

August 1944

The Resistance called them *parachutages*. There was no equivalent word in English, and Charlie simply thought of them as 'drops' from the RAF Halifax Bombers or those often dangerous US Air Force B24 Liberators, which flew heavily and leaked fuel. Whichever type of bomber was coming their way, it would drop their packages from around three hundred metres above ground. Up to twelve parcels of around one and half metres in width would fall from the sky to land in a designated area.

Charlie had only been involved in one of these drops and that was because one of the regular men had taken ill on the evening in question. It was early on in his role as a spy in France and while he found it exhilarating, it also felt as though he was back in the trenches of the previous war, with the gut-twisting and limb-numbing tension of his fellow soldiers going over the top into no-man's-land while he remained in relative safety. Watching the brave members of his group drop dead or get wounded – one moment yelling their war cries, the next felled, some dead before they hit the earth, others left to die slowly and painfully.

So much blood spilled on both sides, swallowed by the soil of

France. And for what? To do it all over again, this time encompassing all of Europe through the Middle East to Asia and the Pacific? It seemed as though the world collectively had the brain power of a lemming in mass migration, blindly following urges, or in the case of the human species, following orders to commit war and atrocity and bloodshed.

He couldn't imagine that anyone who had ever stood in a trench, watching fellow soldiers dying in large numbers daily, would ever sign off on going to war. Much easier to do it from a position of power without being required to face the reality. And so, here he was, engaged in yet another war that had already raged for years on the ambition of a persuasive lunatic and bigot.

Charlie's team, Silversmith circuit, had been involved in setting this particular drop, in league with the Resistance. His team had liaised with London once the people with the right knowledge – usually their French counterparts – had chosen the site. This one was a quiet field at the bottom of a shallow hillside, with thin woodland that hadn't seen much destruction from the scorching rage of bombs because of its isolation. It was situated halfway between Épernay and Reims, on a route that was dotted by the odd village but could hardly be called busy, even before the war. It was a reliable drop spot that had only been used twice over the course of the fighting in the region, the last time two years ago, so this made it a wise choice, Charlie felt, not that it made him feel safe. Nearby was a small hut that hadn't seen use in years. It was not a good hiding spot for the Resistance: the trees only gave minor coverage, and beyond were rolling fields of vines with far too much exposure.

His offsider, known only as Arthur, was using the new Rebecca/Eureka transponding radar that had been developed for SOE operatives working behind enemy lines so they could communicate with friendly aircraft. The transponder, requiring fiddly nickeliron batteries, was stored in a biscuit tin and buried in the ground. Charlie marvelled that it ever worked, given it often sat idle for long periods. Quite an incredible innovation, considering all the previous, more cumbersome methods. He didn't understand the clever technology that transmitted pulses between the unit on the ground and the one on the aircraft; he was simply grateful for its accuracy.

Even so, he preferred to rely fully on visual confirmation.

Waiting now for the telltale drone of the arriving bomber, he remembered the first time he'd done this. Although that drop had been successful, with packages full of weapons, uniforms, radios and tents, he had not imagined ever being part of the drop team again. But he'd made a promise to Sophie, and he knew what it was to love a child to distraction. His was safe. Hers was not. He had to help. He had loved Sophie too long and too deeply not to respond to her anguish, and so he found himself dressed in black clothing with his face covered in dirt, so no features could be lit easily, crouching in the dark at the bottom of a hill.

Charlie was the liaison, ensuring the Royal Air Force had the co-ordinates of the drop zone ten days ago. The unique code phrase he chose for this drop was 'Three dancing women', which made him smile because it referred to the grapes Sophie had taught him about – chardonnay, meunier and pinot noir – which were under harvest now, getting ready for their big dance.

Charlie had waited anxiously to hear the evening broadcast from the BBC, which, during its messages personnels, would repeat that seemingly innocent phrase in French within the context of a false message at some point during its airtime. It was the signal to his team that the supplies would be dropped tonight. He'd requested weapons and medical supplies, but of course nothing was guaranteed. They'd be grateful for whatever fell from the sky.

It was a mild summery night – neither too warm nor cool – and he would have sworn he could smell the salt of the ocean. Maybe he was being fanciful now that the tension was beginning to build. The moon was full and bright, providing good visibility for the pilot. There was no obvious wind gusting, so the drop should be relatively straightforward too, Charlie thought; with no effective wind speed, the pilot could probably even drop from lower, perhaps two hundred and fifty metres, and not risk the goods ending up in woodland.

One of the Resistance members sidled up to him. He looked desperate for a cigarette, clutching one unlit in his lips; it was too dangerous to throw any light on themselves until the final moments, when the plane needed to sight the drop zone.

'Thanks for coming tonight,' the man rumbled in a low mutter. They spoke in French. 'I was told there were only seven of us.'

'Who told you that?'

'Jacques. At the bar.'

The leader, a man Charlie only knew as Philippe, which was probably an alias, stepped in close to where they were skulking. He wasn't happy to see Charlie. 'You! I don't know you.'

'No,' Charlie said. 'I set up the drop, but it occurred to me that an extra pair of hands in this situation – especially if they do send us weapons – is always welcome.'

'I don't like surprises and I especially don't like strangers.'

'Then ask him,' Charlie said, tipping his chin towards Raphael, who was just arriving, looking even younger for some reason in the dark.

'Who is this?' Philippe hissed, prodding Raph. 'You know him?'

Raphael hadn't even noticed Charlie until now. 'Pierre?' he whispered, sounding shocked. 'Why are you here?'

'So you know him?' Philippe asked Raphael in nothing much above a murmur.

The younger man nodded, looking dumbfounded. 'Yes. I can vouch for him.'

'Good. I don't like unfamiliar people being here,' Philippe grumbled low beneath his breath.

The guy with the unlit cigarette gave a sad grin and whispered, 'Well, I'm grateful for an extra pair of hands. Let's hope we get it all away from here without a problem and are in our beds soon enough.'

'What time is it coming?' Raph murmured.

'We understood two o'clock or near enough,' Charlie's companion whispered.

Charlie checked his watch again, knowing barely a minute had passed since his last glance. Eleven minutes to go.

'I hope they bring sten guns and plastic explosive this time, and not chocolate and nylons,' Cigarette Man said with disdain. 'I know the chocolate and stockings please our locals, but me and my men need ammunition.'

'Quiet!' Philippe spoke so low everyone had to crowd in. 'When we hear it get close enough, let me repeat that we keep the circle tight. The pilot, because he's not landing, only needs to aim for the target and account for drop distance, wind speed and so on. Me, and you, and you'—he pointed, including Raphael in that group—'will light the lamps. You others, get ready to grab the gear and haul it into the two carts. Remember not to disturb the plants and soil that we've lined the sides of the carts with. If we're stopped for any reason, we are moving vines.'

Raphael gave a snort of dismay; Charlie knew this was ludicrous in late summer. 'And they'll believe it?'

'German soldiers rarely know anything about vines or vineyards. If we sound confident, they'll accept it. I'm hoping we don't meet anyone, of course, but it may just get us through a light inspection. I doubt you have a better suggestion, first-timer.'

Raphael scowled. 'And what if Gestapo are around?'

'At this time of the morning? Unlikely.' Philippe dismissed the younger man, unknowing of or perhaps unmoved by his wealthy status. 'Besides, all they'll care about is more Champagne for the devil they bow to. Let me do the talking if it comes to it. And you,' he pointed at Charlie, 'I don't recognise that accent, so don't speak at all.'

Charlie nodded. He didn't think a German would differentiate, but he wasn't here to rub anyone up the wrong way. 'Not a word,' he replied.

Raphael moved closer to Charlie. 'Are you here for me?'

Charlie shrugged. 'Like you said, everyone at your Champagne house is deeply loyal to your mother, myself included.'

'So you *are* here for me.' He sounded disgusted.

'I'm afraid so.'

'I don't need babysitting,' he hissed.

'Hey!' Philippe growled under his breath. 'We can make good use of him. Now be quiet. Hear that?'

The soft, unmistakable drone of an approaching aircraft was evident in the near distance, flying in fast, Charlie deciphered, likely keen to make the drop and leave enemy territory swiftly. A fast drop was also for the retrievers' protection, so they could gather up the gear and melt away as soon as humanly possible.

Everyone fell silent and crouched low, like animals in the grass, watchful, nervous. Charlie felt the familiar tingle of both anticipation and dread activating like a drug, racing through his veins and making him feel as though he were teetering on a tightrope, with danger of the worst kind on either side. He couldn't flee, although his sixth sense screamed at him to straighten and run away. But the fear of letting Sophie down rooted him to the ground, where he clung on like one of her old vines – faithful, always prepared to give.

He banished the thought. *You've been here before*, he told himself. *Find the sniper's calm. No trembling. No thinking. No breathing, in fact.* Stillness washed over him. Some of his soldiers had said they found him scary when he was like this, his jaw set tight, stare intense, his body like a statue... his rifle poised.

No rifle this time. No weapon at all.

The bomber was nearly upon them.

'Ready yourselves,' Philippe ordered. He waited another fifteen seconds or so, and then growled the command. 'Go!'

Eight men, including Charlie, ran low and fast. They moved like wraiths across the landscape, running down to the field in silence. Charlie was impressed at how quietly everyone scrambled, and within another thirty seconds a small circle of lamps were placed and lit to create an illuminated target. Arthur was performing his role, in touch with the pilot, and Charlie was glad to see the plane approaching them accurately. It should be a successful drop.

The reception party, as they were known, stood back and awaited the plane. It finally arrived, black shapes dropping from its belly before it passed overhead and disappeared, lifting away from any ground-to-air capability by the enemy. Charlie and his companions worked furiously to douse the lamps and started hefting the packages back to the carts, where patient horses were harnessed and ready to pull their load. No vehicles were used; engines at this time of the night might arouse suspicion.

It was hard work and there was nothing to say, even if they weren't trying to stay quiet – it was taking everyone's committed effort to lug each heavy package, which weighed up to one hundred kilos, Charlie estimated. One container was mercifully designed with five separate cells so they could break it up and carry twenty kilograms each.

'Where's it going?' Charlie whispered.

'A cave,' was all Philippe would say. He was taking no chances with anyone. He turned to Raphael. 'Collect the lamps and take them back with you. Hide them for now.'

'I don't know how to carry those on a bicycle!' Raphael protested.

Philippe jutted his chin in Charlie's direction. 'Use your friend. But come up with a reason for carrying them in case you're stopped.'

'Arthur, you all right?' Charlie murmured in French to his SOE colleague, who nodded, also carefully answering in French.

'I'm fine. You go. Help with the lamps as he needs. I'll get our precious Rebecca back to her hiding place.'

'Don't take the same route back.'

'The other way's the long way. I'd rather not,' Arthur admitted.

'Follow the training. Promise you'll go the other way.'

Arthur sighed his obedience, clambering onto his bicycle. Charlie watched him wobble off, hit his rhythm and disappear into the night – in the right direction. He was relieved. Now their transmitter could be hidden again.

Everyone left swiftly and Charlie and Raphael raced back down the hill to collect the lamps. He was feeling the effects of all the dashing about, only highlighted by the fact that his younger companion wasn't even vaguely breathless.

'We can hide them in that broken-down hut,' Charlie said. Raphael was right – even with the two of them, getting the lamps back safely would be dangerous. Better to do it in daylight with a horse and cart and a lot of other goods on board. The youngster nodded, looking relieved. 'Go, don't wait for me,' Charlie urged. 'Get them hidden. I'll pick up the others.'

Sophie's son loped back up the hill. It took him no effort and he was soon out of sight, even in the moonlight. As Charlie grabbed the final two lamps and began the journey uphill, which he tried to assure himself was not steep, he heard a sudden flurry of voices.

Shouting now, and a crack of gunshot.

He ducked, shocked, and then, realising their entrapment, straightened and began to run as bright torches and car lights were switched on behind him. Heedless now of his fatigue, he ran blindly; he had to get to Raphael.

A voice yelled into the night over a bullhorn. 'Stop! We will shoot!'

Whether that was directed at him or the others trying to escape, Charlie kept running. Behind him he heard more sporadic fire and his heart felt like it might explode from his chest, not simply from exertion but from the realisation that someone had surely leaked their activities and location. The German voice bellowing through the horn sounded smug and calm; they had likely arrived with stealth while the team was busy watching the plane deliver its load.

'Damn!' he growled, arriving at the hut. 'Raph?'

The young man stepped out. Charlie didn't have to see his face to know he was scared, but the jut of his chin suggested he was resigned to some heroics this night.

Well, not after what he'd promised Sophie. No. Raphael would not be dying.

'They know we're here,' Raph said dully. 'But they'll have to shoot me in the back, because I'm not putting my hands up and dying like a helpless victim to any German.'

'They're not army. They're Gestapo!'

'How do you know?'

'I know. Now listen to me. I am out of breath as it is, and can only say this once. For your family's sake and because I am going to die tonight, I want you to hide.'

'I will not—'

Charlie threw down the lamps and grabbed Raph's shirtfront. 'You will do exactly as I order! If you take a bullet tonight, you will not be a hero. You will only be a hero if you live to tell this terrible tale and warn others. You will be a hero if you return home, appearing innocent and never admitting to any involvement tonight.'

'Pierre, you can't expect—'

'I can. I came here for you. So do this for me. Live to explain to my daughter what happened. Be a witness for us when these bastards are held to account for not taking prisoners but simply executing us.'

'Pierre...'

'It's Charlie. Charlie Nash. And my daughter's name is Violet. This is for her,' he said, releasing Raph and slipping an envelope from his pocket. You make sure she gets this.'

'How?' The young man's eyes were wild.

'That's your problem. You owe me this much. Look after her heart as you explain what occurred tonight. I know Violet; she'll come hunting for answers. You will give her those. So you have to live for me, so she never doubts my love for her. Now hide.'

'What? They already know—'

'They know nothing!' Charlie glanced over his shoulder and saw men hurrying in their direction. His voice turned into a low, commanding growl. 'Whoever betrayed us would have told them seven men. No one was expecting me to be here.' He heard a shot in the distance from the other direction and knew that was Arthur giving his life; Charlie felt something within himself give as well. 'I'm begging you, Raph. Stay silent. Even when they kill me, you stay silent. And you wait for the dawn. Don't move or twitch a muscle. Now go!'

Raphael nodded, tears forming in his eyes. 'Charlie, I'm sorry.'

Charlie nodded and pushed him. 'Hurry!'

As Raphael fled, Charlie turned and watched the men approach and then made to run away, as if realising he had been seen. Another man coming in from the other side ran him down easily enough and waited for the others to arrive.

Charlie said nothing to their questions, just squinted into the light of the torches trained on him. A car drove up and a man who was clearly in charge strolled towards him: an officer, presumably, but he ignored him. It was his final defiance.

'Ah, another rat,' the man said in German. Charlie knew enough to understand. 'So how many is that accounted for?'

'He makes seven, sir.'

'Excellent. All the sewer rats caught. It was seven we were told, am I right?'

'Yes, sir.'

Bastard! Charlie wondered who had turned them in. There were always leaks. No one could be trusted; this was why he'd admired Philippe's reluctance to share any details. It could even have been Jacques from the bar who'd betrayed them, for all he knew. Treachery was everywhere, and it seemed the death he had gone hunting for all of his life, which simply wouldn't come, had finally arrived to take him. He was glad that Violet didn't have to watch him die at home, finding him in a field of barley or slumped over a barrel. Perhaps this was easier all round. Just gone... becoming dust in the fields of Épernay, which he loved.

Someone kicked him. 'Name?' the man said in French.

'François Dagot,' Charlie lied.

'How many of you were here tonight?'

'Seven,' he mumbled.

'Six are dead,' his tormentor said with a hint of glee.

Charlie spat. 'Then get on with it and make it seven, you dog!'

He got a full swinging backhander for that, which sent him flying. He saw stars, but glimpsed the moonlight and decided it was time to escape this. He wanted his death to happen quickly – it was inevitable, he knew – because the longer this took, the more likely it was that Raphael would reveal himself, even by accident. He was frantic that the young man remain silent, undiscovered.

'Shoot your gun,' Charlie said. 'You'll get nothing more from me.'

The German scoffed. 'Your radio man pleaded for his life.'

That hurt – it was meant to, of course – but in the next heartbeat Charlie's good sense told him this was likely untrue. Arthur was as brave as the next fellow and had, like all of them, accepted the consequences of their actions.

'So what?' he said, sounding as if they'd just told him it might rain later.

'You're, as they say, a cool customer,' the man said.

'I know what is about to happen.'

'Don't want to bargain with us?'

'For what purpose? You'll shoot me anyway.'

The man laughed.

Charlie knew he was right, so what the hell, he would remain defiant. 'I'll tell you this. You've lost the war – you know that much. And one day, they'll catch up with you all. I don't know why you aren't already fleeing to Germany... oh, that's right, the Russians are coming for you too, as well as us.'

The man gave an order in angry German, and Charlie braced himself.

'Tell me,' he said suddenly. 'Did Klaebisch send you?' He had to be careful in case they were on Sophie's scent, knowing somehow that she was helping the Resistance. At least if the man answered, Raph might hear and be able to warn her.

The German shook his head. 'I don't know the man. But I can't imagine it's of any consequence to tell you that he's left the region.'

'Fled?' Charlie laughed. 'Of course he has. He's a coward.'

The man shrugged.

'I just don't know why you and your men are bothering any more,' Charlie continued. 'The war is lost to you.'

'So you say.'

'Paris will fall any moment. You know the Americans are rebuilding railways, and once they break through from Brittany, you'd better be running fast all the way to Berlin.'

For the first time the man looked unsure and Charlie felt a spike of triumph that lasted all of a few seconds. He could now count his life in a couple of heartbeats, and he wondered why he was wasting his breath on this man, rather than thinking of Violet, Ellen and indeed Sophie. But maybe he could help just a little more and save more lives. He was sure Raphael was hanging on every word being shared, crouched somewhere near in the darkness.

'Before you kill me, may I ask who betrayed us?'

The German chuckled. 'Well, most men are granted a final wish before execution. I shall grant you yours. It was a man called André.'

'André?' Charlie frowned. He didn't know an André.

The man who would order his death gave a *tsking* sound. 'You rebels really should do your homework better. He is the cousin of the owner of the bar that your group meets in. Your people think the bar is safe.' The Gestapo officer gave a bitter laugh. 'But the newly arrived cousin likes this too much,' he said, rubbing his thumb and fingers together. 'Too easy, monsieur. We'll let the bar owner live just to keep your people unaware of the danger.'

'Well, I gather my people are all dead anyway, so they're not going back there.'

'Others will, though. They'll trust the bar owner because he is a loyal patriot, but he has no idea his cousin collaborates with us.'

The German laughed again. 'Now, Monsieur Dagot, I think it's time.'

Charlie closed his eyes. 'Will you allow me to walk down the hill?'

'Whatever for?'

'I won't run.'

'You wouldn't get very far if you did. You're a dead man.'

'I know. So let me walk in silence. The moon is bright enough, so you can hardly fail to see me. I would like to say a prayer before you kill me. Will you grant me that?'

The man sighed. 'Off you go. I don't know why I'm feeling generous tonight. Make it a quick prayer. You'll be seeing your maker very shortly.' He reached into his pocket. 'I'm giving you three drags on my cigarette.'

Charlie nodded as his tormentor opened a cigarette case. He didn't wait a second longer, keen to get well away from the young man in the shadows. He was afraid Raphael would cry out in shock and give away his position if he witnessed this piece of vicious theatre.

'Goodbye, monsieur. Your war is definitely over.'

'And yours too, sir,' Charlie said, surprising himself with a smile. He turned away, no longer interested in the German or his cruelty, or their war. He walked slowly, suddenly peaceful, knowing the end of his life was just moments away. He'd already dodged plenty of bullets in his time, and he'd lived a much longer life than he'd ever anticipated. He had loved, and been loved. He'd had a good wife and been the best husband he could be to her. He had a child he adored and had set her up for success. He was sorry that he was leaving her this way, but her memory of him would be of a man still with all his capacity, dying for something he believed in. She would mourn him, of course, but she would be spared seeing him withering into old age.

And he had held Sophie again. That was a gift he hadn't expected.

Time was short. He allowed his mind to drift away from death and bloodshed, from tension and fear, from war and despair. Instead he let it land in Knockando and the barley shed, where the work was monotonous and back-breaking, yet rewarding.

The smell of the warmed cereal wafted around him and spoke of what he would turn it into. His mind roamed to the blending room where he and Violet would taste from their various barrels full of whisky, slumbering in oak. Impossibly, he smiled into the night as a final vision came to him of his darling girl, Violet, swinging on the garden gate at Knockando and promising him that one day she would make a whisky that would make all the men of Scotland sit up and take notice.

You do that. You show them what Violet, the daughter of Charlie Nash, is capable of.

It was his last shiny, happy thought.

He didn't hear the shot of the pistol.

He didn't feel himself hit the ground and kiss the soil of France.

He didn't know that the Germans carelessly walked by his body and left him where he'd fallen.

But before he died, Charlie did know that Raphael would have heard every word and could warn everyone who needed to be warned, and that Sophie would know what had happened and demand his body be brought to her.

And that was enough.

Sophie found Raphael under the oak tree in the midst of the vineyards. They had always worked around it; Charlie had called it a 'giant' when she'd explained it had been here for generations, providing shade for the workers.

Her son was solemn, his head bowed. As she drew closer she could see he appeared unruly, unshaven, his shirt torn and dirty. He looked like his father had as a young man after a day of toiling in the fields. Except Raphael had not been working. He'd been missing.

'Raph?'

His head bent lower at her voice. He clearly hadn't heard her approach, or he might have melted away into the vines.

'Michel said you were here.'

She won no reply.

'Where have you been?' she asked. 'I was worried when you were not home last night.'

Again, she earned only his silence. It was then she realised he was weeping silently and his face was stained with tears that had cut narrow rivulets through the dirt. What had he been doing?

'Raph,' she repeated, her voice thin and stretched. 'Are you all right? Are you hurt?' She crouched before him, checking his arms and hands for injuries. 'Please look at me.' She forced him to lift his chin, looking past the mud on his face into eyes of the deepest sorrow.

'I'm sorry,' he murmured.

She shook her head. 'Why? What's to be sorry for, my darling? Please speak to me. Tell me what has so upset you.'

'He's dead.'

'What?'

'They're all dead, but he died for me.' His expression was blank, his voice a monotone.

Sophie blinked as her mind raced and then she felt the chill creep over her. Her throat began to tighten, but she didn't need her breath; she was holding it, waiting for his explanation.

'They knew we were coming,' he said, barely audible. 'We were betrayed. They let the drop occur, let us do all the work and then they pounced, slaughtering everyone.'

'Charlie's dead?' she asked in a thin voice, not wanting to hear the answer.

He simply nodded.

The chill reached her heart. 'You saw it happen?'

He shook his head like an obedient child answering questions at school. 'I saw him walk back down the hill, a man from the

Gestapo following with a gun. I heard the gunshot. I couldn't see from where I was hiding.'

Sophie's hopes soared. 'Then—'

'But I saw his dead body. I touched it.'

She stood and twisted away, tears coming helplessly. It couldn't be true. A small sob escaped her as she dug in her pocket for a handkerchief. Charlie... her Charlie.

'He gave me this for his daughter.' Raphael's hand trembled as he passed her the envelope.

She turned, hastily dabbing at her eyes. 'Oh,' she said, staring dully at the handwriting.

'Can you keep it safe?'

'Of course. Raph, you're absolutely sure Charlie is—'

'He's dead, Maman. I stayed in the dark with him for a long time. He had told me not to move, but I couldn't bear it. I had to sit beside him.'

'Tell me what happened,' she said, gathering up her pain. 'And then tell me where to find him. We must bring him home.'

'It's dangerous.' His eyes grew wide with fear.

'I am bringing him home,' she said with vehemence, surprised at the strength she found in her voice. 'I sent him to his death. I sent him to protect you, which I presume he has done because you are alive, and he is not.'

He hung his head again. 'He knew he was going to die. He knew his death would save me.'

She wept openly now and, through her tears, spoke in a trembling voice. 'And I knew he would keep you safe at all costs. It's why we will not leave his body to rot in some isolated field. We will find him a resting place in Épernay. In fact,' she said, looking up into the oak's limbs, 'perhaps somewhere right here.'

EIGHTEEN
RICHMOND

August 1944

Violet locked the door of the barrel room behind her as Jimmy's legs pumped hard, driving him down the path before he exploded into the street to get help.

She ran to stand by the gate and waited there, her heart pounding as she tried to calm her breath. She was far enough away to feel somewhat safe and could keep an eye on the barrel room door in case the journeymen came staggering out. But there was no sound from within.

It took several long minutes, which felt like an eternity, but then she heard distant voices and saw Jimmy racing back with the local police officer.

Constable Peterson wobbled to a halt on his bike, with Jimmy stopping alongside, both of them breathless.

'Violet?' Jimmy gasped.

'I'm fine,' she reassured him. '*They're* not, though.' She pointed her thumb back towards the barrel room.

Peterson nodded. 'I heard about a couple of louts hanging around, but when I looked for them they'd disappeared. I reckoned they'd left town.'

She shook her head. 'Came looking for free whisky, so I gave it to them because it was better than paying any other price, although I fear for their organs. They've both drunk seventy per cent proof spirit, which is going to make them very sick indeed.'

'Good!' Jimmy scowled. 'They were threatening Miss Nash.'

'You were wise to comply, Miss Nash. Stupid fellas. They can go into the lock-up and sleep it off.'

'They might need a doctor, Constable Peterson. That kind of spirit could poison them.'

'Leave it with me. They can suffer for their troubles.'

They followed her to the barrel room where both men had passed out, as she'd hoped.

'Best we turn them on their sides,' she said, and Jimmy reluctantly helped the policeman and Violet. Billy groaned, but Arty made no sound.

The constable scratched his head. 'Right. I'm going to handcuff them so they can't do much more damage, but then I'm going to need to get the van and some help to move them in this state.'

Richard and Nellie Jones, her neighbours, arrived at that moment.

Violet gave them a weak smile. 'Hello, Nel, Dickie. You've caught me in a drama, I'm afraid, but it's all over now.' She turned her attention back to Constable Peterson. 'His name is Billy,' she said, gesturing to the dark-haired man, 'and the sidekick is Arty. Brains and brawn.'

'I saw them earlier,' Richard said as Nellie put her arm around Violet's shoulders. 'We saw Jimmy fetching Constable Peterson, so we assumed some trouble and wondered if we could help.'

Violet didn't need comforting but it would have been churlish to shake the embrace away, so she patted the woman's hand gratefully. 'I'm fine, unhurt, but thank you.' She didn't know them to be nosy people.

'They came skulking around our shop,' Richard explained, 'but I didn't like the way they looked at our niece, who is working with us. I sent them away. I'm sorry, Violet. I'm so sorry they found you.'

She understood their alarm and haste now and shook her head. 'No harm done. They came looking for whisky and found just what they needed.' She actually laughed. 'They're not feeling so well now, though.'

'Did they hurt you, love?' Nellie asked.

'No,' Violet said with relief. 'Didn't get close enough.'

Constable Peterson finished handcuffing them and then tipped his finger to his head. 'I'll be back soon enough to collect them, Miss Nash.'

She nodded and watched Richard take the extra precaution of tying their ankles with their own belts. 'We can leave them sleeping,' she said.

When he was done, the Joneses stood back, waiting. Violet noticed they kept looking over at her, then at each other, perhaps debating whether to take her to hospital or to their home... possibly to the police station to make her statement.

'Truly, I'm fine,' Violet said. 'They didn't touch me.'

'I'll come with you to the station in case they need a statement from me,' Richard offered, and Violet nodded. 'Nellie, you go back to the shop.'

'Please, Nellie, do go. I'm fine,' Violet urged.

After making her statement at the police station and agreeing to press charges against her attackers, Violet had refused further help from her neighbour and gone home alone. The incident had perhaps demonstrated to her just how alone and potentially vulnerable she was, but she didn't dwell on it. The ruffians weren't worth her time or wasted anxiety over what might have been; in fact, she reached a point a few days later when she found the whole thing amusing, even joking with Jimmy about their combined cunning, working with the greed of the two journeymen.

She thought that was the end of any upheaval in her predictable life until there was a knock at her door. She was making bread, her hands covered in flour, which she wiped on her apron as best she could, frowning as she moved to answer it; she was not expecting anyone.

'Oh, it's you, Harold. I could have picked up my post. Have you brought me a letter from my father?' she asked eagerly, now wringing her hands clean on her apron, no longer caring about the mess.

'Hello, Violet, er no,' he began, shuffling awkwardly on the threshold. 'I came to give you this.' He sounded grave. He withdrew a small envelope from the breast pocket of his uniform.

For just an instant it felt like the whole of Tasmania suffered an earthquake. Violet didn't know what that might feel like, but the ground beneath her suddenly rolled, tipping her off balance. Did she stagger? Why was Harold reaching for her?

'Violet? Violet... I have to give you this telegram,' he bleated. 'Perhaps I should have waited, given what you've been through recently with those men, but I am bound by law to deliver this at my earliest opportunity.'

Violet stared at the envelope, its buff colour not giving anything away and yet its very presence giving her all the information she needed. Telegrams never brought good news... not in wartime.

Harold stepped slightly closer with the communication, urging her to take it. She had to, or he'd just stand and watch her, she knew, and was it better to get this over with, if the inevitable was coming? It might not be what she feared most... but something inside her told her it was.

Finally she commanded her unwilling hand to take it, clutching it tight as her legs felt suddenly weak and she crumpled inwards like a party balloon with a tiny leak, slowly exhaling into a small, lifeless version of itself.

Time passed, but she couldn't remember it. Water was never wasted in their house, or in any other household that she knew of in Australia, but at one stage Violet filled the tub to nearly full and climbed in to sit in its womb-like, weightless warmth, pressing hard on the bruise of the news.

How had her father died?

When had he died?

Who had killed him?

What was he doing when he died?

Where had he died?

And why did he have to die? Did he choose it, or did someone else place him in the situation that caused his death?

Questions knocked against her mind like skittles disrupted and scattered by a bowling ball. She soaked in the bath for hours in an effort to calm herself, losing sense of time. She refilled it twice, not caring about the extravagance of using so much water. Who was watching? Who cared anyway?

Her mother was dead.

Her father was dead.

She might as well be dead.

No, that was stupid, she corrected herself. That would mean all their lives were meaningless. And her father had often said she was the best of him and her mother put together.

'Everything that's good about you is from your mother, Violet. And everything that's good about me lives within you,' he'd said.

Tears flowed. Over the course of the longest bath she had ever taken, they came in shaking sobs and in a small silent stream. They wet her cheeks and dried and then began again until she was sure she had cried enough to fill the bathtub with her tears. Finally she drained the tub, knowing it was time to emerge from her sorrow, but still she sat there, knees pulled tightly to her chest, arms wrapped around them, her face buried in her knees. It lifted only at the sound of a door knock.

She didn't want to see anyone, or explain how she was doing, or thank anyone for their concern. It was probably a meal being left on the doorstep for her from a friend; there had been a couple when they'd heard the news.

Violet sighed. This was no good any more. She had to start

facing the reality of life alone, make some plans, even though they would be cursory. Sell the farm? Sell the whisky? Move back to England? Her grandparents were both gone now, and the house had been left to Violet; she could go and live there for a while, make a new life where no one knew her. She felt like a glass marble, unable to be still each time the ground tilted.

She might just roll away.

Nowhere felt like home. Australia had been welcoming, but Scotland was still part of her soul – and yet it held the cruel memory of her mother's early death. And now Tasmania, which had tried so hard to embrace her, represented another cruelty in her father's.

There was nowhere safe from grief.

She had no home.

Remembering the knock, Violet stepped out of the bath and pulled a towel around her. Her fingertips, she noticed absently, were shrivelled.

'Violet?' She recognised the voice. 'Violet, it's Harold. You don't have to open the door, but can you just answer, so we know you're safe? Everyone's worried.'

'I'm all right,' she called out to the postmaster, and she heard him sigh with relief. 'I just want to be left alone for a while.'

'I understand. I'll let the village know.'

'Thanks for everyone's concern, but I don't need anything. Just some time. Would you tell them, please?'

'All right, Violet love. You take care. I'll knock daily and check on you, but I'm happy to talk through the door,' he said gently. 'Everyone's very upset for you. He'll be missed.'

She leant her head against the door and began weeping softly again, surprised she had a drop of moisture to give.

'Righto, I'll be off.'

'Bye, Harold. Er, what day is it?'

'It's Thursday, love.'

'Thank you.'

'I'll stop by tomorrow.'

She heard the gate close gently and moved to the window to watch as he climbed back on his bicycle and rode across the street.

She'd lost two full days and nights to the blur of grief. It wasn't disbelief; she believed it all right. She had believed in the possibility of his death from the moment her father told her he was joining the war effort. But he'd batted away her protests and anxiety, constantly reassuring her that he was too old to be an active soldier. How many times had he soothed her fears, saying he would be in some dark and dusty back room simply lending knowledge or advice?

He'd lied.

Maybe not intentionally. Perhaps he'd believed what he said, but no doubt that rush of blood had hit at some point and he'd put his hand up for a more dangerous task. Surely he loved her more than England? Couldn't he have paused, just for a heartbeat, to consider the potential repercussions of walking into danger – that he was risking her life too in his bravado?

Afternoons became evenings, and evenings became nights. And nights, the hardest hours, were finally banished as the first streaks of light began to slash open the sky. She wasn't aware of the days passing; they simply blurred into time and weeks passed.

The sun tried to bring her back to life and the days stayed lighter for longer. Eventually she began opening the door to people, letting in the kind souls who wanted to comfort her and make her tea and see that she was managing – at least as well as she could under the circumstances.

'I'm so sorry you're alone,' Nellie said on one of her and Richard's visits, putting her hand on Violet's.

Violet nodded at the older woman's sentiment, mugs of tea steaming between them; her own remained barely sipped.

'Your father was a good man,' Richard added. 'A brave one too. He didn't have to go, had nothing to prove.'

'He felt it was his duty.' Then Violet felt ashamed. 'Oh, Richard, I didn't mean—'

'I know you didn't, love,' Richard said in a soothing tone. 'I'd have gone too if I thought Nel could handle the farm and the family, but the kids are still so young. Jamie's just a toddler, and there's the store to manage too. I would have let my country down if I didn't stay and make sure our farm produced food. And I was told I'd probably be rejected anyway.'

Again Violet nodded, her body responding mechanically. Her mind was still awash with pain.

Nellie patted her hand again. 'It's just such an appalling pity. And so close to the peace. The wireless says the Germans are now on the run, retreating east.'

Violet didn't want to think about that. If only he had waited a few more days.

The telegram had said her father died in action. What action? Wasn't he supposed to have a liaison job? That sounded like it needed an office and a telephone. But she was being naive. Of course he wouldn't have stayed safely behind a desk.

He'd have run straight into danger.

Violet refused to move in with her neighbours, even for a short while. She couldn't tell them that she wanted to feel the grief and suffer through it. It wasn't that she was masochistic or incapable of allowing others to help, but the grief kept her father real in her mind. She had no proof of his death. She had no body to cling to or funeral to occupy her, just a few words typed on a piece of paper. It wasn't that she didn't trust them – she did – but she needed to live alongside them, around them, in them. She didn't want any platitudes or comforting words about her loss getting in the way.

Nellie and Richard meant well, she knew, but they would do all they could to distract her from her grief, when the pain of it was precisely what she wanted.

At some point Violet dressed herself in working clothes and ventured once again to the barrel room. She feared she might feel repulsed by the space, after the drifters had been there, and she tentatively stepped back into its quiet. To her deepest relief, the barrel room felt safe. It was full of the warmth she'd anticipated, as though it had the uncanny ability to hold the sunshine, to store it and deliver it back to her. She hadn't expected this, had imagined herself pausing at the threshold and turning away until she felt stronger. But it had the opposite effect. To Violet – and she knew it was fanciful but she didn't care – the barrels felt like friends. The two drifters were nothing, just awful, desperate men with little to strive for, and that made them forgettable in her mind. She was able to put away their potential to disrespect or injure her world. The image of Billy's leering could disappear into memories that didn't need to be re-examined.

A couple of butterflies had followed her in and were dancing around, flashing a magnificent iridescent lime green amid their black and tan wings. She wished she knew their scientific name. She'd seen them before; her father called them swallowtails, she recalled, because of the shape of their wings. They looked happy flitting among the motes of dust, highlighted in the morning sunlight streaming into the room, which cast yellow-white stripes across her oak barrels.

An applewood barrel carried her newest spirit. The wood had come up a light reddish brown, which, she was told, would soften to a greyish brown over the years that the whisky needed.

She stepped fully into the shed's embrace and murmured aloud in this hallowed space that Billy and Arty were to be forgotten, but her father's death was not to be let go. His loss was something to be experienced, to become a part of her. It would sit beneath her skin and grow old with her, as her lovely mother's memory had. Her mother never did though: Violet carried her mother's image as that thirty-something, laughing, affectionate, intelligent woman who always knew how to comfort her and her father. Her mother had been the noisy one of the family; she created the fun. Both of them had joined in, but her mother instigated every game of cards, every picnic and every long walk through the woods.

Still, Violet dared to admit only to herself that she loved her father more. He was her and she was him, although no one could see that when she was young. They'd all thought she was a carbon copy of her mother. She looked a lot like her, but in her ways and her mannerisms – and now her personality, she realised – she was Charlie Nash's girl, all right. She was even beginning to look more like him as she matured.

And that pleased her.

The barrels already knew it, even if others didn't. The whisky held knowledge. Her father had always told her this. *Whisky is memory, Violet. It remembers.*

And so the barrels would remember her pain, and the man who they too had lost. Without further thought, she moved over to the whisky thief and removed the bung from her favourite barrel, which had once held the richest, most syrupy of sherries from the Pedro Ximénez grapes that flourished in Australia. They had been introduced well before the turn of the century and were used mainly for fortifying wine or blending for dessert wines.

Think of the whisky, she told herself. *Lose yourself in its flavours and your first bottling, now only weeks away.*

She poured some of the alcohol into the small glass she kept in the shed and sipped, rolling the intense liquor around her mouth before taking a second sip that she would properly taste.

Go, Violet, she heard her father's voice. *Go into the barrels and hear the song of Scotland in them.*

Vapours lifted from the glass and moved invisibly around her mouth before dissipating, leaving behind the venerable spirit. She closed her eyes and allowed herself the whimsy that she was entering an ancient world of flavour and knowledge – and memory. She had chosen not to add water, but would suggest a splash of fresh spring water to enhance it when poured from the bottle. Right now the alcohol needed to be reduced by a third. But Violet's tasting experience could get her past all of those technicalities.

In her imagination, with the powerful spirit awakening her senses of taste and smell and perception, she travelled deeper into its barrel, to its heart, where the true taste lived and would deliver itself, with the right handling and care, into the bottle. Together she and the whisky remembered Charlie Nash: father, husband, chemist, distiller, whisky blender... soldier. Always the brave soldier, prepared to sacrifice his life to save others.

She sat on the dusty floor next to the barrel that now held the spirit from their barley, nearing four years in the cask. This was to have been their first, the one that would launch their whisky distillery in Australia. But she would do it alone.

The name of her whisky, which had eluded her, came to her now. She would call it the Soldier's Dram, in honour of the one man she loved above all. *Wherever you are, Dad*, she wailed in her mind, *know that I love you.*

Violet felt her mind loosen. She hugged the barrel as though it were him, and could have sworn she could smell the angel's share around her.

NINETEEN

RICHMOND

December 1944

Violet continued to keep to herself, but as summer took hold, she began to be seen more often around the town. Now, when people waved, she lifted a hand in response, even finding a soft smile.

No one intruded, though. She and Charlie had always been friendly and liked, but they were also known as generally quiet people who preferred to keep their lives fairly solitary. This had been respected through the months of grief.

Now, though people were kind, no more meals were left. So many others were suffering the same sort of losses – she was not special, simply a young woman alone as many young women who had lost husbands were. At last they could meet each other's gaze and swiftly pass the time of day with a polite salutation. She rarely lingered, though, not keen to get into conversation.

Dear John had tried several times to reconnect: first with two disappointed visits when Violet did not answer his gentle tapping or pleas, and then with three earnest letters requesting to meet, not for anything more than friendship, he assured her. He was worried about her; he wanted to get her out of the cottage, perhaps for an excursion to see a film in the city. He'd even tried a more subtle approach, checking to see if she needed more applewood barrels.

On each occasion she'd been polite but responded with brevity, explaining that this was a difficult time and that she preferred solitude for a while. She'd come to the firm conclusion that as lovely as he was, John was not a suitable partner for her, as much as perhaps they both craved one. She would not make him happy, nor he her, hard as he might try to bring her happiness. She could imagine him all but turning himself inside out to make her smile, to give her all that she needed, but what she needed he didn't have. Her attraction to him in any romantic way had been fleeting and what was between them had fast become a friendship; this was a dangerous scenario for a kind and generous man like John.

Even when she'd been a little girl counting the stones in her prunes or plucking petals from daisies, murmuring, 'He loves me, he loves me not,' her mother would talk to her about husbands.

'You'll know when you meet him, Violet.'

'How?'

'Well, if you have to work at it – and by that I mean, if you have to ask questions of yourself regarding him – then he's not right.'

'Isn't it wise to be sure, though?' Violet had asked as she got older and they continued to have these conversations.

'Love isn't wise, Violet. It is powerful and all but impossible to trump.'

'So I shouldn't marry sensibly, you mean?'

Her mother had laughed. 'There is no such thing as sensible when it comes to love. It is overwhelming. When I met your father, he was bleeding, unresponsive, clearly wanting to die. And as I cleaned his face and attended to his wounds, I fell in love with him.' At Violet's look of despair she'd held up a hand. 'This is what I'm saying. It's not rational – the opposite, in fact. I firmly believe you have no say in it, Violet. Now, you can make it more academic and choose someone who suits your needs in every way, and that's fine – plenty of women do. But just as many marry simply for the way the man makes her feel. And if he's a good man to boot, then it can't be topped. I was in love with your father by the time we spoke. I didn't know if we'd ever meet again, but we made a pact and he stood by it. He came and found me, and I can't tell you how my heart did somersaults in my chest when I saw him again after the war. I want *you* to have that feeling one day.'

'So if I don't feel like my heart is dancing around inside, then whoever I'm standing in front of isn't the man to marry?' Violet asked.

'Precisely, my darling. Make sure he makes you catch your breath.' Her mother had winked at Violet. 'Make sure he accepts you for who you are, that he isn't going to try and change you. Oh, and when you're satisfied with that, then check his bank account.'

That had made them both laugh. As young as she was, Violet had understood the message her mother hid behind the jest, and as an adult Violet was clear that she needed someone driven, a man who could share her passion, match her sometimes fiery ways and not feel battered by her strong personality and motivations. Yes, she wanted to be taken care of, but never patronised. She knew that John was not right for her, so she kept him away, but she wished she could tell him this was a kindness to him.

Jimmy also stayed away. There was no work to be done right now; it was all about waiting.

In mid-December, the sun's heat was burning into Violet's back as she tended some determined weeds in her front garden. Her father had taken great care of this garden so that she could always have fresh flowers on her scrubbed table – just as he had for her mother in those happy years in Scotland – but she'd recently allowed it to grow over. She was attacking the beds with a vengeance, a huge straw hat covering her neck and shoulders, her father's gardening gloves, which were far too big for her, keeping him close, when a youngster from the post office arrived on a bike.

'Oh, hello, Robbie,' she said. 'How are you today?'

'I'm great, thank you, Violet. You look very busy.'

'I need to get out into the fields soon, but more than that, I need to get rid of these weeds.'

'Not much to plant at this time of year,' he remarked.

'Well, I was thinking of planting some vegetables. I know they're not exactly pretty, but then I'd have something to exchange with all the people who have been so kind to me.'

He nodded. 'Well, I've got a letter for you.'

She presumed it was another from John, imploring her to come out of her cocoon and meet him in the city. 'Is it from Hobart?'

'It's from France,' Robbie said, digging into the satchel slung around him.

For a blinding, joyous moment she allowed herself to believe that a catastrophic mistake had been made, that the telegram had been sent in error and her father had been found alive. Had they got it wrong?

'It's from a woman,' Robbie continued, flipping it over, oblivious to Violet's galloping heart and hopes. 'Sophie something. I can't pronounce her name.'

Sophie. Sophie Delancré? The champenoise! Why was she writing?

Robbie held out the envelope, grinning. 'They say the war is going to end soon.'

'We live in hope, Robbie,' Violet said, covering her disappointment with a contrived smile for the optimism of teenage years. She took the curiously bulky envelope and stared at her name. It was written by a firm hand in extraordinary violet ink.

'Bye now.' Robbie waved and cycled off towards his next delivery.

She took off her father's gloves and went indoors, sighing with relief at the relative cool. She found her letter opener and carefully slit the envelope. Inside she discovered two letters and a second, smaller envelope with handwriting she instantly recognised. On it her father had written *For Violet* in pencil.

She breathed in. Again her hopes were triggered. He couldn't be alive, could he?

The most sensible part of her told her this was not possible, but she held back a sob as she opened his envelope and unfolded the single sheet of paper.

My darling girl,

I write this in haste, forgive.

If you're reading this, it means I didn't make it.

The disappointment turned to pain... even her teeth ached from it, and she folded the letter back on itself hurriedly to allow the tears to fall freely. *Let them come and then let them go,* she told herself. Seated at her table with the letters before her, she counted three of them.

One from Sophie Delancré.

Another from someone called Raphael Méa-Delancré.

And, of course, the note from her father.

She was torn. Her father's was correspondence from the grave, she knew that now, and had to accept he'd written it for someone else to send in the event of his death. Sophie's would presumably be to commiserate, but Violet wasn't ready to read a letter of sympathy from a woman who'd held her father's heart in her palm since before Violet was born.

She reached again for the letter from her father, believing it was a moment of madness to read it first, but he was the only person she cared about in the trio; his were the only words that mattered. She took a long, slow breath and reopened it. She would not cry again. She was done with tears. They would not return life to how it once was.

My darling girl,

I write this in haste, forgive.

If you're reading this, it means I didn't make it. I am writing this in a hurry because something is happening that is beyond my control. Well, most of it is. One aspect I can and will control is conserving the life of Raphael Méa-Delancré to the best of my ability. I wish I had more time to explain all of this, but suffice to say, he is the only surviving son of Sophie at Épernay. Her other son has given his life to the war. Her beloved husband, Jerome, is in a German prison camp. Raphael is young and passionate, like you. He is determined to play his part, and he is stepping into peril on behalf of the Resistance – the group I am involved with – so I am going to do all in my power to protect him.

I cannot imagine my life without you, Violet, and so I can put myself in Sophie's place and understand her great fear. She has no idea of the danger her son will be in, although she senses his impulsive need to play a part in defending France. I am choosing to involve myself, and if things go badly for me, that's why you're reading this. I can only say I'm sorry that you have been left alone by both of your parents. You deserve better, but war is cruel in every way. No father, mother, son or daughter should die for one man's campaign of the acquisition of power across the world. And that's what this is – a madman's crusade, with hundreds of thousands of brave, obedient soldiers and helpless innocents dying around the world as a result.

Peace is so near, though. I feel Paris will be reclaimed very soon and that means this region will be liberated, but it may not come soon enough to save Raph, so I must. And before you think it, or allow any seed of thought to grow, I am not choosing Raphael over you, Violet. I am choosing life for you both. You are the next generation. You and those like you who survive will be the people who change this world for the better... towards harmony and friendship. We're all the same, you know. One of the best men I've known is German – remember Willi? He refused to kill me, and I refused to kill him. All any of us want is to live and raise our families safely. So I'm going to make sure that Sophie keeps what family she has left, because I know you are safe.

I also know that you are brilliant, Violet. I know that you are resilient too. Hold my memory close, darling girl, but make your own life exactly how you want it to be. Everything I own is yours, and whatever you choose to do in your life, I will watch and cheer you on from afar. And whomever you choose to share your life with, don't worry about money or status or what anyone else thinks. You find yourself a man who worships you, Violet, who is worthy of you and whom you love and respect... and who makes you laugh.

You deserve to laugh and be loved.

I do love you so much, and I'm sorry I'm not coming home. I am thinking about your mother right now and casting my sorrow her way too. As you read this, know that we're together and watching over you in joy and pride.

My love to eternity, Dad x

Violet swallowed the clog of emotion as she put the letter down and stared out of the window, feeling utterly adrift.

The one constant in her life, writing from the dead.

She thought about him. Quietly gone. He'd left for England, dropped out over the skies into France, presumably, and disappeared into the Champagne region to bleed into the soil far from their home. *Did* he bleed? Was he stabbed, shot, hit in the head? Or did he die of a heart attack? She was not privy to how her father had died, but did it matter? She knew he would have died well, if such a notion existed. He would have been brave. He would have been selfless. He would have given his life quietly – or resolutely.

When she looked back at the kitchen clock, she realised she had been lost in her thoughts for more than half an hour and soft tears had fallen and dried against her cheeks. Looking again at the letter from her father, she could now see splotches on the page where the lead of the pencil blurred slightly.

So he had been weeping too as he wrote. Curiously, this made her heart ease slightly. Here was evidence that his emotion had broken through, spilling onto the page. He had not tried to wipe it away; it had simply dried as he wrote. A little starburst of emotion exploding on the page to demonstrate just how desperately sad he was.

It felt like their tears were communing. Violet covered the tear stain with a finger as though touching him, and then she placed that finger to her lips to kiss him goodbye.

She put his letter down and looked at the two others, hating them. She hated the people who had written them in the belief that their words of remorse or sympathy might bring comfort. Well, they wouldn't! They had stolen her father, and this Raphael had caused his death. Why would he presume she might want to hear from him? She didn't want his condolences or his apologies.

And, yes, in case you're wondering, Raphael, she thought angrily, *I do wish you'd died instead of my father.*

She caught her breath at the viciousness of this sentiment and quickly banished the thought; it somehow debased her father's letter and the life he had given to save Raphael. It didn't stop her hating the son of the champenoise, though.

She opened Sophie's letter, not caring that she bent the quality stock as she did so. The purple of the ink against the obviously expensive paper was vivid; it spoke of wealth and status. Violet felt an inner sneer erupting. Was Sophie hoping to impress her?

She snapped her attention to reading the words.

Violet, you don't know me, but I suspect you know of me. I have experienced much sorrow over the course of both the great wars, but I have found myself in an emotionally torn situation only twice in my life because it involved a man I barely knew, our time spent together was fleeting and he represents an overwhelming rush of feeling I find inexplicable. This feeling is a mix of joy and guilt.

When my eldest son, Leo, was lost to this war, my whole body felt broken, but I've allowed myself to be consoled slightly with pride at his sacrifice on behalf of France. My husband has been imprisoned twice over our marriage and that has brought its own sorrows, but also a sort of fierce resilience that he defies his jailers by staying alive. I shall never stop missing Leo or wondering how his life might have shaped up if he hadn't been cut down in his prime and I continue to hold the greatest hope that my husband will return to me.

But this guilty, joyous feeling in my heart involves your father, Captain Charles Nash. He is, without doubt, one of the most courageous and selfless men I have had the good fortune to know. He will claim I saved his life, but let me assure you that he saved mine at a time when I was lost, alone and grieving. Our friendship – and yes, our affection for each other – has spanned decades, and yet we could count the time we spent alone in hours. You must know we both respected the sanctity of our marriages. Just in case you wonder, your father adored your mother and you beyond everything... you especially. He spoke to me with only pride and awe about you.

I don't know what the British War Office will tell you, but I am guessing they might choose their words carefully because your father was a spy. I'd rather be blunt about this, because it takes such deep reserves of courage for someone to work alone and in the shadows, forever wondering if today is the day their identity might be revealed, and there is no mercy, or prisoner-of-war status, for spies and resisters from the Germans. They are simply executed.

Which is why I too am weeping on the other side of the world to you, because I have lost my great and loyal friend – one of the best people to have crossed my path – and you have lost the most precious of people, your father. I share your tears, Violet, for he was a wonderful man and at the end he was selfless – as he always has been – because he gave his life to save another: my son, Raphael, who would surely have been executed alongside him if your father had not protected him. And I must tell you that I asked him to offer this protection. He was in constant danger with his decision to return to France in the role he did but my plea certainly put him in the path of the enemy. The decision was his but I fear your father would always walk into the path of danger on behalf of others and especially because of my urging.

I don't know how to show my gratitude, though I can imagine it is quite an empty sentiment to read. I realise you must hold us keenly responsible for your father's death and I cannot change the fact that we have lost this special man, but I invite you to come to France, when you can. Please. Visit us at Épernay. I want to show you something important, and I want to answer every question that may be burning within you.

He tells me you are beautiful, intelligent and extremely talented as a distiller and blender of whisky. Maybe as two women, both working in a man's world, we may find common ground, even friendship. You know, some of the most powerful Champagne makers were strong, resilient women, and I know that strong, resilient women were also instrumental in distilling some of the best whisky in Scotland. For that alone, the two of us have something in common – and then there's both of us adoring the same man. Surely we might contrive to meet? I promise it will be on common ground.

As I write, the Germans are fleeing eastward. Good riddance to them all. Happiness is not the right sentiment. Relief is probably the only one I can offer up at this time, so I will let the celebrations wait until peace is ultimately and finally announced. When that peace arrives – and it is not far away – please come, Violet. We shall share grief at Charlie's loss, but also joy as we celebrate his life. We shall share Champagne in his name, and maybe we might find friendship in his name too.

Sophie

Violet trembled as she read, but not in anger as she'd antici-pated. She once again began to weep at the kind words and graciousness of Sophie Delancré. She wanted to hold a grudge, but this woman spoke so tenderly of her father, her mother and of her that it would fly in the face of all that she was and all that her parents had raised her to be if she didn't accept this olive branch with the same grace.

Sophie wanted to meet her. Common ground... what did that mean?

Violet shook her head and took a slow breath as she reached for the third letter. This was a single sheet, written on just one side in slanted navy ink. It was a bold and confident hand, but this time she was sure she could hate its author and maintain that loathing.

It was written in English, as his mother's was. She was vaguely impressed.

Sophie, I'm not sure if I have any right to send you this note. My mother asked me to post her letter to you with your father's note, and I have taken the very great liberty of enclosing one from myself, although I fear I might be giving offence by the very presence of my handwriting.

I'm sure by now you know your father's death is a consequence of my immature determination to give something back to the people of this region, to defy the Germans who have held us prisoner for nearly five long years.

I will make no excuses. I accept that I have brought you pain and the worst form of sorrow by my actions. My only defence is that I had no idea that your father would step in as he did and suffer the consequences that should have been mine to bear. I would have borne them gladly – I was in a frame of mind to waste my life in the defiance I so wanted to show. Instead I wasted his. I am inconsolable, but I can only imagine this is a fraction of how you feel.

I don't know what else to say to you. I dare not ask for forgiveness, but I do offer myself to you in any and every way that I might serve, should you ever have need. It is not enough. I know this. But I have no idea how to engage with a stranger on the other side of the world who probably hates me. That we have your father in common is all I can say. And for his sake and for what he did for me, I think hate is the last thing he had on his mind. He gave his life instead of mine because of his friendship with my mother and to prevent another young life being given too easily.

I can't thank him. But if you ever need help of any kind – at any time and anywhere – I will give you that help. This offer will stand until the day I die, hopefully peacefully and having done something good to live up to your father's gift of life.

I know my mother has extended an invitation for you to visit. I would like to add my wish to that, although I understand if you would prefer I not be present. Please do agree to meet with my mother, though. She has things to say and to show you.

Sincerely, Raphael Méa-Delancré

Violet set down Raphael's letter, laying his mother's over it and then her father's on top of both, and placed her hands across them all. She breathed out shakily.

What was she expected to do?

Or – did it really matter what was expected of her? There was no one in control now. There was no one she owed any allegiance or courtesy to. In fact, she didn't care what anyone thought. All that mattered here and now was what *she* thought she should do.

The answer came quickly. She didn't need time to ponder or consider her situation. The fact was, she was intrigued by Sophie's offer to meet. And, as much as her grief wanted her to ignore it, her character prevented her from behaving in this way. It would give entirely the wrong impression of who Violet Nash was: the daughter of plucky, cheerful, practical Ellen Nash and of courageous, slightly island-like Charlie Nash, with whom she shared so many qualities. He had always met his dangers head on and had never been too scared of any situation to stand up or stand out, to be counted.

Well, that's who she was too. She would meet the woman her father had loved. There was nothing to forgive; there was only acceptance that her parents had lived lives long before she'd arrived and claimed all their attention. A child believes her parents' universe is focused on them, and as an only child, she forgave herself for believing the same. If anything, the realisation that her father had a secret life in his imagination added a dimension that she found rather fascinating.

And Sophie's mention of wanting to show her something, as well as her son's, was irresistible.

She straightened. She had made her decision.

She would go to France.

'What have you got to lose, Violet?' she asked aloud. 'At the very least, you can ask them to send you oak Champagne barrels.' She smiled wryly; she'd often wondered after her father's discussions about Champagne how those barrels might enhance a whisky blend. At least she wouldn't have to die wondering.

She left the table and moved to her father's small bureau, from which she took some writing paper. He'd left his fountain pen behind; this was the first time she'd noticed it sitting quietly in the drawer. Well, she would fill it with fresh Indian ink – nothing so fancy as Sophie's French violet or her son's rich blue, but plain old black writing ink – and sit down to craft a letter of acceptance.

But first, she needed to write to the people who'd sent her father to his death, because she would require the War Office's help; as with the Champagne barrels from the Méa-Delancrés, this was the least they could do for her.

TWENTY

HOBART

December 1944

Violet was seated across from John at the busy tea rooms in South Hobart beneath Mount Wellington. They were on the top verandah of a vast double-storey timber house, overlooking their growing city, which was now beginning to show a genuine sprawl, with new suburbs clinging tightly to the shoreline of Hobart's marvellous bays and harbour. Plenty of people were out enjoying the warm weather; Violet was happy they were in the shade of the vast wraparound verandah. John had taken it upon himself to choose the venue and book a prime table.

Waitresses were in constant motion, stepping briskly around the customers to take or deliver orders, and Violet marvelled at their long, crisply starched aprons; they looked like white butter-flies dancing between tables.

'I used to come here as a boy,' John said, interrupting her thoughts as they gazed out across the immediate landscape.

'Really? It's so pretty.'

'My nan used to bring me because it was one of her favourite places to visit as a younger woman – a threepenny ride on the tram, she told me. It's been around as long as she can remember. Day-trippers would come by train to the terminus and picnic, finishing up in the tea rooms for all sorts of treats. The original owners used to light the gardens at night with fairy lights, and there was lots to explore: bird aviaries and winding paths that led to fern groves and a bridge over the Hobart Rivulet. I gather that the early owners were florists in town and brilliant horticulturists. People would come from far and wide just to admire the garden and have a pot of tea afterwards. And the owner after that was just as talented with flowers – he was the one who illuminated the gardens and used Chinese paper lanterns. I think it even used to have an entertainment area – a stage – that he could move around and put on shows for visitors, with a bandstand.' He smiled softly. 'Oh, that's right. When I came as a really young lad, they had a peacock called Priscilla, who apparently could tell fortunes for a ha'penny.'

Violet laughed.

'They had a snake handler and a ten-foot-high lucky Buddha statue. That's all gone now, but its history is wonderful, and I hold it close to my heart.'

'I love it, John. Thank you for suggesting it.'

'I'm just glad to see you, Violet. I've been worried.'

She nodded. 'I know, and I am sorry that I've been so elusive.'

'I understand, of course. Who wouldn't. But—'

Violet covered his hand with hers. 'I know.' She sighed, not wishing to discuss her father's death. 'But this pain is mine. I'll deal with it, because I have no other choice, but John, before your generous manner starts to suggest you'd like to help, you can't. My way is to turn inward, not outward to friends.' She searched his face; she could tell he respected what she was saying but didn't really understand. Time to be straight with him. 'I'm planning to travel to France.'

He looked at her quizzically. 'What do you mean?' Rather unnecessarily, he added, 'There's a war on.'

Their cream tea arrived. Burnished scones in a small basket, steaming beneath a napkin. No plump sultanas due to rationing, but even so, the scones brought the smell of domesticity and comfort, and the waitress set down bowls of rich whipped cream and two colours of jam that glistened in the afternoon sun. 'This is a yellow plum conserve from last year, and a raspberry jam from this year's fruit from our gardens,' the girl said, in a way that suggested she was trained to provide this information. It didn't matter that the offerings were small; everyone was used to rationing.

Violet smiled. 'Thank you. Your gardens are beautiful.'

'And so are your scones,' John added, peeking beneath the napkin.

'Thank you, sir, thank you, madam. Your pot of tea is just coming. Enjoy your afternoon.'

The tea arrived almost immediately on a tray from another waitress, who set down cups and saucers while the silence lengthened and began to feel brittle between them.

Finally they were alone again.

Violet cleared her throat. 'I realise we're still at war, but we're at its end – I think we all feel that. Paris is liberated. The whole of eastern France is being cleared as the German Army retreats at speed. By the time I get there it will be safe enough.'

'Safe enough? How did you get permission?'

She shrugged. 'I don't need it. I'll sail to England and take a ferry from there. The French are returning, and many English families are being repatriated now, so there are plenty of crossings.'

'Good grief, you've got it all worked out.'

Violet nodded. 'I have. And I have to go, John. I have to go where my father lies in the ground. I don't know where yet, but I'll find it.' Her eyes watered with emotion.

It was his turn to nod. 'I'm sorry, I don't mean to upset you.'

'Don't apologise, please. You're far too accommodating.'

He frowned slightly. 'Is that a criticism?'

'No... yes!'

He laughed. 'All right,' he said, in neutral.

'Let's not allow the scones to grow cold,' she said, wanting to smooth over the tension.

They began to eat, making pleasurable sounds at the delicious food, agreeing on the perfect tartness of both jams. She poured them each a cup of tea.

'What did you mean,' John said, wiping a napkin across his mouth, 'by no, and then yes?'

Violet smiled sadly and began stirring the milk into her tea. 'Just being honest.'

'About us?'

Violet wanted to say that there was no us, but hurting this lovely man's feelings was not her intention. 'John...'

'Oh dear,' he began with an embarrassed smile.

She put down her spoon. 'Listen to me, please. There is nothing easy about me. My mother told me that, when I was tiny enough to sit on her knee, and my father never stopped referring to my tricky ways. I have opinions, I am driven by my own instincts, I sometimes flare up, either with anger or enthusiasm, while other times I go inward and silent. Both extremes are probably frustrating. I'm just...'

'What?'

'Very contained.'

John studied her. 'What do you want, Violet?'

'All the usual things,' she said softly.

'Marriage? Children? A dog? A peaceful life?'

'All of it,' she admitted.

He waited a beat. 'But not with me,' he finished for her.

She met his gaze. 'Not with anyone I've met yet. Perhaps something's wrong with me; I've said as much to my father.'

He didn't respond, so she felt obliged to continue.

'But he said I just hadn't met the right man. I know that sounds dismissive, but the way he said it, and when he said it, I trusted that he was sincere. He was warning me, I think, to take my time, even if I'm feeling anxious about being left on the shelf.'

'Are you anxious about that?'

'Now and then.' She grinned self-consciously.

'Violet, you know I would do anything for you. And'—he ignored her trying to quieten him with a hand over his again—'no, it has to be said. I'm in love with you. I have been since the day you came to the brewery, full of ideas and opinions. I loved you for them. I loved your honesty and your no-nonsense attitude.'

'There's a difficult flip side to that, John,' she tried.

'I don't care. Couples argue, it's natural. People can't expect to see eye to eye on everything all the time, or we'd be boring.'

'How true.'

'So?'

'So, no, John. We are not a match, you and I. You're like someone I knew in my childhood. He was every bit as wonderful as you... as full of kindness and a gentleness that most women would pray to find. But what I saw in Angus is what I see in you: a best friend.'

He winced and made to speak, but she kept going.

'No, please hear me out. My mother told me that her knees used to tremble a bit to see Dad after a day of work – these were the early days, mind,' she said wryly. 'I heard my mother give Dad a piece of her mind often enough, but I also saw how in love they were. They were inseparable. They could speak without moving their mouths or making a sound – they just knew each other and what the other needed. As a child, it's wonderful to be surrounded by that kind of love. But John, we've never so much as kissed – that's not your fault, it's my choice. I don't want to ruin what we have by trying to make it something it can never be... because I don't feel it. I feel a great tenderness and friendship for you, but there is no romantic urge as my mother described.'

He nodded, clearly hurt. She'd tried so hard to convey her thoughts without causing pain but anyone in an unrequited love situation was always going to feel pain, she reasoned, and that was not her fault. Honesty was the only way.

'I'm sorry,' she began.

'No, don't. You've never done anything to give me false hope.

All the romantic feelings have been driven from this side of the table. I've never met anyone like you before, Violet, and probably never will again. Your independence is as frightening as it is amazing. I admire you in every way.'

'Thank you. If you will allow it, I would like to know I have you as a friend.'

'Always,' he said, then gave her a deeply sad smile and sighed. 'So, now to cheer up and enjoy your company. Let me pour this time,' he said, surprisingly bright.

She offered him her cup and saucer, smiling. 'And I have something to discuss with you.'

'All right. Clearly not what I'd hoped, but I'm intrigued.'

Violet added a drop of milk to her tea and stirred, thinking how to begin. 'It's about France.'

'I should think so. How will you make that work with everything going on here?'

'Well, you've been learning about the processes leading to whisky for a while now.'

'And I have enjoyed every minute.' His gaze told her his words had a double meaning.

'So I want to give you the farm, John.'

'What?' He blanched and put his cup down, perplexed.

'I've thought about it long and hard.'

'Violet—'

'No, please listen. I'm going to France, as I said. But first I'm going to England. My grandparents left me their house, everything in it, as well as their money. They lived frugally, so they had a fair amount of savings, and it's all become mine, which is lovely and sad at once. But I need to get over there and sort things out. And after France, I'm going to Scotland. I have to, not least to walk the streets of my childhood and visit my mother's grave, but to keep a promise to my father. And that all takes time, so I sense I shall be in no hurry to return to Australia.'

He read between the lines well enough, it seemed. 'You mean you're not coming back?'

'I don't know. I may not. With all due respect, I have one person here that I care about – that's you. And we're friends, so we can write, and you can visit. You will need to continue your education... perhaps in Scotland?'

That made him smile. 'What about Jimmy?'

'Ah, Jimmy. I don't plan on leaving him behind.'

'You're taking him with you!' John looked shocked.

She shook her head. 'Not immediately, no. I shall send for him, though, if he wants to come. I need him to grow up a little more, and I think being around you will help him. He's only got his grandfather and his mother, and I think he would benefit from your influence in his life. Maybe when he turns seventeen I shall send for him, organise passage, and get him working at a distillery in Scotland so he can learn as much as he can. Then he can make choices.'

'Choices?'

'To stay over there, or to come back here and run Glen Corbie in Australia with you.'

He looked at her in shock. 'What?'

'John.' She took a deep breath, realising she needed to explain her thoughts better. 'I know you've held some hope that we might be partners, and I realise that today I have shut that hope down, but I'm wondering how you might feel about being a different sort of partner.'

He met her gaze. 'In business?'

'Exactly. Be my business partner in Australia. Run the farm. You can do it with your eyes closed. Jimmy's a great help and so is old Ben.'

'A lad, an old man and me, a cripple?'

She shrugged. 'I don't see it that way – I see three people with a talent for what they do. Ben knows malting as well as anyone, while you know farming. And Jimmy is a sponge – he learns fast, and he remembers everything he learns. But I am going to give him that opportunity abroad, so if you need to bring in help, do it. It'll be your decision.'

He looked back at her, mouth still open in shock. 'But...'

'The farm is yours, John. You do not have to pay me a cent – except for a token amount, to make it official – but if I could just hand it over I would. Dad didn't leave me penniless by any stretch, and with my grandparents' estate, I can live independently. Let me pass it on to you.'

'What about the house?'

'Well, you'd prefer to live in Hobart, am I right?'

He nodded, still looking as though he was struggling to take all of it in. 'So keep living with your nan and father, but you can use the house as you please. There are going to be times – at harvest, for example – when you cannot commute to Hobart. Or feel free to bring your dad and nan to live with you in Richmond. I make no rules.'

'And France, when do you go there?'

She shook her head. 'That's the part I can't fully wrap my mind around yet. It will take me a while to get everything in order, and I'll go to England first. Perhaps being back in Britain will help me to find my way. I will go – I have to go – but as to when, I shall decide once I'm on the other side of the world.'

'Where is home for you, Violet?'

She put her cup back on the saucer and regarded what was left of the scone. She neatened the crumbs in the side plate as she considered his question. 'I don't think I have one, to tell the truth. I love Richmond and Hobart, I love London, I love Knockando in Scotland. They've all been part of my life and yet each has its sorrows. I think maybe I have to find a new home – one I create myself that is based around my own happiness... somewhere I settle down into because I have found a measure of contentment – happiness even – not because I have to.' She looked up and gave him a wide smile. 'I'm a grown-up and I'm alone for the first time in my life, so I'm going to make selfish decisions and see what happens and where I find myself.'

He smiled back. 'You make selfishness sound highly desirable.'

'Well, it can be, if it's coming from the right place and for the right reasons – and doesn't harm anyone else. So what do you say, John? Ready to be a barley and wheat farmer? It's a good business selling to the brewery; your product will be in greater demand when the war is finally, officially over.'

'What about the distillery – your whisky?'

'Ah, now. I will take two of the barrels that are ready with me, and I shall do some blending in Scotland. Glen Corbie still exists in Speyside – it's just locked up, like a ghost distillery. Hopefully all our equipment there is intact. I am going to present the single malt Dad made here, which I'll call the Soldier's Dram, in his honour, to anyone who will taste it.' She grinned. 'I know someone in London – a hotelier – who may be open to buying what I can offer from those two barrels.'

'You'll bottle in Scotland?'

'Yes. It's more expedient. So for now, the distillery here will sit dormant. Jimmy will understand that I plan to continue his training. He needs to be patient and help you around the farm for now – it won't hurt him a bit to learn every last piece of knowledge about how these cereals behave while growing.'

'So, just for clarity, Violet, you are giving me your farm, and will sell it to me officially later for a small amount?'

'Yes. I will find out whether I'm allowed to hand over my land. Either way, it's yours to farm and reap all the benefits from. I do not want anything from it, other than perhaps some malted barley down the track.'

'If and when you return?'

She smiled. 'If and when we reopen Glen Corbie Australia. The remaining barrels I will organise to bring to Britain when they're ready. They've got some years to go, especially that spirit in the applewood. When that's ready, that's our true all-Tasmanian whisky.'

He blew out his cheeks. 'I don't know what to say.'

'Just say yes. You aren't in love with your role at the brewery, I could tell the day we met. You're proud of what you achieve, but you're a farmer at heart.'

He nodded. 'I am.'

'So say yes.'

Their gazes locked. 'Yes,' he said. 'All right. I'll look after everything until you return.'

'If and when,' they both qualified at the same moment, making them laugh with affection.

PART FOUR

TWENTY-ONE

FRANCE

May 1945

Hitler was dead. The coward had killed himself in his birthday month, leaving his armies rudderless and on the run. To the end, he still believed Germany could win this terrible war and had urged his people to fight, not at all ashamed to enlist children to pick up weapons.

General Eisenhower, the supreme commander of the Allied Expeditionary Force in Europe, had decided in February to relocate his headquarters from Versailles to the city of Reims, from where he would command eight armies: five American, one English, one French and one Canadian, plus three American air force divisions. The Allies kept this move and the headquarters' location in rue Jolicoeur discreet, not wishing to trigger German intelligence services. However, with Berlin in ruins and in the hands of a vengeful Red Army, and with most of Germany in a chaotic state, there were partial surrenders.

After attempts to stall, Hitler's successor, Grand Admiral Dönitz, was forced to send his emissary – General Jodl – to Reims to agree to Germany's unconditional capitulation, signed in the smallest hours of the night of 7 May, which put an end to World

War II in Europe. This occurred in a landscape famous for its cathedral, where many French kings had been crowned, and for the vineyards that produced the king of liquor, the drink that the world used for celebrations: Champagne.

When the news broke of the surrender, Sophie Delancré opened several bottles for her workers, her friends and her son and they wept and laughed and toasted France and her allies.

Stalin was not so willing to accept the formal surrender and demanded it be ratified in the ruins of Berlin, where the Russian Army held command.

On the other side of the world, Violet listened with full attention to the news of more defeat for the invaders. It was inevitable that Stalin's enemies would fail. Already the terrible, inhumane camp – which was surely hell on earth but went by the name of Auschwitz – had been evacuated; that cruel man Himmler didn't want inmates alive to tell their tale, so he'd ordered the concentration camps emptied and many of its inmates taken on death marches far from the frontline. But the Soviet Army had reached the concentration camp at Lublin and liberated the ill and dying there. The full horror of the death camps had begun to reveal itself.

Meanwhile, on every front, furious battles were taking place to force the retreat of the German forces who had not yet received news of the surrender, and the Japanese, who had brutally occupied so much territory in Asia and the Pacific. The Germans still held tightly to Dunkirk, but the news that everyone wanted to hear was finally confirmed on 8 May.

The whole of Europe erupted in a gloriously happy celebration. After nearly six long years of aggression, famine, poverty and death at every turn, as well as courage and sacrifice, there was at last victory.

Someone needed to tell the Japanese that the war was over, Violet thought, but much of the devastation had finally ended. Until now, she had taken her time, making plans, getting her barrels packed for their destination in Scotland. She had completed all the paperwork and signed all the documentation needed by the lawyers to formally give the farm to John. And she had spent the summer working furiously with Jimmy and John on the harvest so that the barley was in. She was free now to follow her heart and make her next move, which had been building in her imagination since she'd read the letter from Sophie.

Violet's mission, just as her father's had been, was to enter France, except she would do so in peacetime. Her aim was to sail to England at the close of the Australian winter and be ready to sail onwards to France before its autumn had fully arrived. She knew roughly when harvest of the vineyards might occur, so her plan felt just about right; she would arrive after the harvest, in late September. She had plenty of savings, between what she had earned from the farm before handing it over to John and the inheritance from her grandparents, and so she had decided she would travel comfortably and in surrounds that would give her space and calm. She knew at the end of this journey she would have to confront the full reality of her father's death at German hands.

After arriving in London, Violet went to her grandparents' home and spent a few days reacquainting herself with it. A flood of good memories as a very young child washed over her. The place was dusty and the garden overgrown, but all it needed was some care. It still smelled the same, once she'd opened up the windows and gone over it with a familiar feather duster and her grandmother's mop. It was so old she remembered hanging on to its wooden handle as an infant, laughing as someone she loved pushed it back and forth.

No, she wouldn't sell the house, as she'd originally planned. This place was a cocoon of memory and should be preserved, if just as a safe, welcoming hug. She hired a team of cleaners and, together with her efforts, the old home shone again. All the dust was banished, the windows sparkled, and every surface was polished and now smelled of wax and her love. A gardener had spent five days mowing, weeding and redefining beds and said he could be back at the end of autumn to start pruning, if she'd like him to.

'Actually, I will pay you for the upkeep of this garden. How about I pay you three months' wages upfront to visit regularly and keep an eye on it?'

He looked back at her in surprise.

'Can you do that, Mr Donaldson? Mow, weed, water, trim, whatever needs to be done?'

'I can.'

'Very good. Please let me know your fee this week. I shall be leaving England shortly for France, and I wish to pay you before then.'

'France? Is it safe?'

'Yes. I gather many of the French have been returning to their homes, or what's left of them, since Paris was liberated. Plenty who fled have been sailing back across the Channel since around June. Peace is with us again.'

'You must have good reason to be going, Miss Nash.'

'I do.' She smiled but said no more. 'Thank you for helping with the garden.'

For the time being at least, this house would remain hers and she would give it the love it needed to become a happy, thriving space again. Violet was feeling an urgency to get to France, to walk the ground her father had. She allowed herself to believe she might catch a wisp of his presence if she found where he'd fallen or his final resting place. Scotland would wait for her; she'd sent her barrels on to Speyside to be stored until she arrived.

She left London, surprised to notice a slight spring in her step. It wasn't seemly, she thought, but it was starting to feel like there might be a future for her that wasn't all about bleak grief and looking backwards. A home in England would provide a new frame upon which she could gradually build a new life, whether it was predominantly spent in Australia or she moved her operation to this side of the world.

It didn't seem wise to make any hasty moves; the world wasn't yet used to peace. Rationing was still keeping everyone wary, soldiers were only now beginning to dribble home, and London especially had to be cleared, parts demolished and rebuilt. Now that the joy of peace had suffused the population, the reality of what lay ahead was weighing on many. Not every returning soldier or brave nurse came home whole, in body or mind.

Some, like her father, didn't come home at all.

She focused on her journey to France. The ports of Dover and Folkestone were still busy with military transport, but the passenger ferries were leaving from Newhaven in Sussex and reaching Dieppe in France. A lot of the ferry vessels had been acquired by the navy during the war, and some had been seized by the Germans, but hers was called the *Isle of Thanet*. Its summer route, pre-war, had been between Southampton and St Malo in Brittany, but the war turned it into a troopship, Violet learned, and then it was requisitioned as a hospital ship based at Dover, successfully taking part in the Dunkirk evacuation before the navy used it for everything from target duties to assault group headquarters, and in exercises as an infantry landing ship.

This brave old ferry, which had suffered so many collisions and refits and repurposing, had only been handed back to Southern Railways a month ago to recommence commercial services. Violet felt a tingle of pride as she boarded, knowing how loyally the ferry had served the Allies during the war.

She felt anxious to arrive in France, and had wondered how she would journey from Dieppe to Épernay. Polite letters had been exchanged with Sophie making it clear how delighted she was that Violet had taken up her offer to visit France, insisting that it would be more enjoyable for her if she continued on to Gare du Nord in Paris, where Sophie would meet her on the platform.

Violet had written to say that meeting her was unnecessary and she would make her way to Épernay independently, but Sophie short-circuited that thought with an urgent telegram to say she would do no such thing:

I WILL BE THERE.

And be there she was. With the French SNCF train still sighing after its journey between Dieppe and Paris, Violet emerged from the cloud of steam and looked down the platform. Through all the other milling people she saw a tall, lean woman lifting a hand in greeting. Violet nodded at the porter, who was politely waiting for instructions, to follow her.

She held her breath momentarily; there was no doubting this was Sophie. She was so much more striking than she'd imagined, with warm green eyes and hair that had once been golden but was now streaked with tendrils of grey. As they approached one another, Violet had time to study the older woman, imagining how her father might have viewed her nearly thirty years ago. Sophie's modest yet tailored russet dress suited perfectly the mood and the season, being neither celebratory nor sombre. Her shoulders were accentuated but only in a small way, and a simple round-necked jacket followed her slim figure, cinching at the waist but not flaring; rather, it curved in a most malleable fabric, with deliberately draped folds, to the slimmest of skirts. The whole ensemble was exquisite, even from a distance. Violet could see that people were noticing Sophie, but Sophie had eyes only for her.

She felt momentarily unnerved in her own olive-green travelling suit, beneath which she wore an audaciously orange blouse. The suit was new, bought in London, and indeed echoed the modern shape of Sophie's, so perhaps they'd both made an effort for this first meeting. Violet's lacked any decoration, but she'd teamed her outfit, as the mannequin had, with tan shoes, a tan hat and gloves, and she felt neat and polished.

As the two women drew closer, Violet counted eight buttons to Sophie's throat, around which she wore a platinum rope with a diamond pendant hung daringly to one side, large enough to double as a brooch. She held a simple fur-trimmed chocolate-brown felt hat, fashioned like a neat bucket, and draped over the same arm was a rich chocolate-coloured shawl, also fur-trimmed. Her make-up, Violet noted, was scarce, just a soft hint of red at the lips. She was a picture of restraint: elegant and helplessly beauti-ful, and she moved confidently, but not with any superior air.

Seeing Sophie for the first time, Violet could imagine her father falling in love in an instant. She knew from Sophie's letter that it hadn't been like that but, even so, when he'd overcome the shock of his injury and realised who was nursing him, surely he would have surrendered to feelings of attraction.

Ellen had been pretty. But Sophie was stunning. Violet hated to admit it, but she now understood perhaps, just a little better, the hold this woman had had over Charlie Nash.

Now Sophie was upon her, smiling with so much warmth. 'Violet!' she declared, tears evident in her eyes. 'Your father told me you were the double of your mother, but I saw only him when you stepped off that train. I knew it was Charlie Nash's daughter the moment I caught a glimpse of you.' She spoke perfectly in English with a delightful French accent, especially on *Sharley*.

Violet nodded, unsure what to say. 'I'm happy to hear that.' She held out her hand in an effort to be gracious, but Sophie surprised her by pulling her into an embrace.

'Forgive me, I have to hug you. I simply have to. I am honoured by your presence.' When she let Violet go, Sophie was openly crying.

'I promised myself no embarrassing tears,' Violet said, feeling awkward.

Sophie shook her head. 'Impossible. Tears for joy as much as sorrow. I am feeling both.'

'Your English is very good,' Violet said.

'Do you have any French?'

Violet nodded. 'Yes, I learned it at school, though it's very rusty right now. I've only spoken English since I was about sixteen.'

'We shall sweep it up, as you English say.'

'Brush it up,' Violet corrected, helplessly enchanted in spite of her sorrows.

Sophie smiled. 'Ahh, I must remember that. Come, you must

be tired.' She urged the porter to follow them towards the concourse, thanking him.

'Not really,' Violet replied. 'The travel has energised me, to be honest. I've spent years in a sleepy town in a sleepy place.'

'Well, Épernay isn't much different, but we have so much to talk about, there will be little time for sleep. How long will you stay?'

'A couple of days, I thought.'

Sophie looked startled. 'Nonsense, Violet. You must stay longer. I have so much to show you, to discuss.'

Violet didn't know what to say to that, or how long she wanted to commit to staying somewhere that might bring pain and grief, so she shifted topics. 'Um, is your son going to be at Épernay?'

Sophie cut her a look of enquiry. 'Not if you don't want him to be, and no one would think less of you if that is your preference. I know you are grieving, and it is so brave of you to come. He is terrified to meet you, I admit it. But as the mother who loves this boy, I would appreciate it more than you can imagine if you would agree to meet him. You will like him, I truly believe this, in spite of whatever your thoughts are right now. Raph is impossible not to like.'

I doubt it, Violet thought, but she kept her face neutral. 'Well, I too am frightened, but I believe I need to look him in the eye, if just for my father's sake.'

Sophie paused as they reached the station concourse. It was busy and people streamed around them. The porter, trailing with Violet's trunk, waited patiently several steps behind.

'Yes, of course. I am not asking you to forgive him, Violet – I doubt you can... certainly not at present when it is all still so raw. I am simply hoping that you will allow him to meet with you, to show you that in time he might prove he is worthy of your father's faith and sacrifice. I won't try to speak on my son's behalf. The mistake of ambition and misplaced heroism is his, and he alone can seek forgiveness from you. But I would be filled with gratitude if you would give him a chance to talk with you. Otherwise I fear that your father will have saved him only for a lifetime of regret and recrimination. He is feeling stuck, I can tell, struggling to believe there is life beyond this unholy war we've come through, because he feels angry that his passion directly caused the death of someone I adored.'

Violet swallowed. It was hard to ignore Sophie's plea. She had never intended to come all this way just to snub the family holding out their olive branch, but she would be lying if she didn't admit to harbouring anger and an unresolved despair. She explained this to Sophie, ending with, 'I will give him that chance.'

Sophie's features relaxed. 'That is gracious. You are indeed your father's girl; it would be just like him to take this attitude, so I shouldn't be surprised. I ask no more,' she said, clutching Violet's wrist in thanks. 'We can organise a car, or the porter will walk with us to Gard de l'Est – that's the station for the train to Reims. Do you think a ten-minute walk is all right?'

'Of course.' Violet smiled. 'I am in comfy shoes.'

'Excellent. Shall we?' Sophie gestured and they walked to the exit to make the short journey to the station that serviced the east. 'It will take us a couple of hours to get to Épernay,' she continued, falling into easy conversation. 'I did think about driving, but the roads aren't yet fully operational and there's a lot of debris. The train is faster.'

'I'm amazed they've got the train lines working.'

'Oh, yes, very quickly too, although not all of them just yet,' Sophie said. 'The railways were a constant target for everyone, friend or foe. Our resisters were sabotaging them to prevent the enemy transporting goods and men, while the Germans blew up everything behind them as they fled.' She gave a sound of disgust. 'Paris wasn't even bombed, but it's a mess. At least all the hateful Nazi flags have been torn down.'

'No Nazi flags ever flew in London, but the devastation after the Blitz is horrific,' Violet replied.

Sophie cast her a look of sympathy. 'We appreciate everything the British people did for ours – and the Australians, of course. How do you see yourself, Violet? Are you English or Australian?'

'Both.' She gave a smile. 'Scottish as well. I left a good chunk of myself in Scotland, but I've just taken over my grandparents' house in London – it was mercifully untouched by bombs – and it has brought back so many fond memories that I realise I am still English. And yet my work, my passion, is still in Australia.'

Sophie nodded. 'Good. You are the new generation and we shall depend upon those like you, who will forge strong international relations. Women like you will not permit war ever to happen again.'

Violet smiled, realising she was already under the spell of Sophie Delancré.

On the train to Reims, she came face to face with the shocking aftermath of war. The passing landscape showed broken vehicles, twisted metal where it should have been bursting with autumn colours. Instead, like supplicants, trees reached broken limbs heavenward, scorched and naked, and the earth was a rusted brown, no doubt from continual explosions, or being carved up by machinery. But even as she noted this she saw grass struggling through, nature fighting back. Even some brave wildflowers dancing in the breeze as the train chugged by.

They were not going fast. The line had only recently been repaired, Sophie explained. 'The priority this year was to get Paris moving again, as so many of the French railways were destroyed. Getting lines out of Paris to the major cities was paramount.'

'Of course,' Violet replied.

They watched military vehicles move around columns of cheerful soldiers, tooting their horn or blowing kisses when they saw the women staring back from the train window.

Sophie waved back. 'Americans,' she qualified for Violet.

'Hope you have enough Champagne for the celebrations.'

Sophie gave a laugh. 'Champagne we have. But fuel shortages and not having locomotives and carriages in working order add more constraints.'

Violet nodded, realising now that for all the wireless and newspaper reports, she had had very little idea of what Europeans were facing in terms of rebuilding their lives.

'Passengers, goods and postal services all needed to be reconnected. I'm relieved to say that Reims was considered strategically urgent to re-establish the rail network to, and that began as soon as Paris was liberated. There was an acute shortage of coal and people were living through severe cold. Our minister of public works halted steam passenger trains on the entire network to help conserve it. To Reims we began travelling with what we call Autorails de Liaison, which were electric traction trains... but wait, I am surely boring you?'

'You're not. I was just thinking, though, that I have been so protected from the reality of what everyone here has been trying to survive. I'm sorry to be so ignorant.'

'Don't apologise. I wish with all my heart that all our sons and daughters could have been living away from the carnage. I worry for the youth – what they've seen and survived... and must now learn to live with.'

Violet nodded sadly. 'You cannot forget what you've been through.'

'Exactly. All of us, but especially our children, have survived six terrible years. They've lost friends, or seen friends weeping at the loss of parents, and they've had the whole trajectory of their lives shifted. They've been hungry all these years, feared for their loved ones all these years. They've had nothing to smile about, couldn't just be children for all this time, and I include my son in this. He's an adult but he's missed out on these stolen years, which should have been about learning and growth... of wonder and falling in love.' Sophie paused. 'What about you, Violet? Is there a handsome young fellow waiting for you?'

Violet shook her head with a rueful smile.

'You jest, surely. They must be banging at your door!'

That made Violet laugh. 'No, I scare men away.'

Sophie frowned. 'And why is that? You must know. Tell me.'

'I suppose...' Violet sighed. 'I think I want too much. I don't mean dresses and furs and jewellery, I mean that I'm too ambitious for most men my age. They find it...'

'Threatening?'

Violet lifted one shoulder in an embarrassed shrug. 'I don't know, but I unnerve them, I suspect, because I don't sound to them as though I want marriage, children... to settle down, as they say.'

'You don't want those things?'

Violet laughed. 'That's the curiosity. I do.'

'But you want them on your terms.' Sophie smiled, amused.

'Yes, I think that sums it up.' Violet smiled back, a little self-conscious. 'And so, rather than let them down or settle for less than I want, I've just avoided getting involved with men.'

Sophie nodded; it felt to Violet that she truly understood. 'But you can't avoid them forever. Your very presence attracts attention. I sense you are modest, which I applaud, but you must be aware of the effect you likely have on men. I can see how a driven woman can be a challenge, but it shouldn't make you avoid men... you just have to find the right one.'

'And who's he?' Violet asked archly, but she smiled to show she meant it with humour.

'Well, he's going to have strong opinions of his own, which you'll likely appreciate,' Sophie replied. 'I can already tell you don't want a man fawning over you, but you want his respect as much as his love. I imagine you want someone strong who can match you in his drive.'

Violet nodded. 'Exactly. There was someone nice, but I told him it wasn't to be, because he would have been hurt by my pushy ways.'

'Nice is not enough, my girl. You need to be swept away.' Sophie told her about Jerome and soon they were chuckling together about how he'd stolen her heart.

Violet knew she had to ask. 'And my father?'

That straightened Sophie's expression. 'Oh, Charlie Nash was one of a kind. He was like a lost child and yet this strong, enigmatic man at the same time. He needed no one, and yet he was looking for someone. Does that make sense?'

Violet nodded sadly. 'I think I'm like that.'

'I think you might be. Your father and I met at the wrong time. If it had been another time, another place, another...'

'World?'

Sophie laughed. 'Yes, an alternative world – perhaps we might have been together. But I loved my husband and the moment I saw him again after the first war, I realised just how much I needed and wanted him, over all others. But'—she lifted a hand and placed it over her heart—'your father lived here, that lonely soul who got under my skin, crept in here and never left. I felt privileged to meet him again, all these years later, and you know, Violet, he hadn't changed. He was still quite hard to reach.'

'That's Dad,' Violet said, smiling sadly. 'I don't know if those are good qualities, but I sense them in myself.'

Sophie took her hand and squeezed it warmly. 'When you meet the right man, Violet, give all of yourself to him. Don't hold back. There's nothing to fear in love.'

TWENTY-TWO

ÉPERNAY

September 1945

Violet likened House Delancré to a castle from her childhood books. Only a fairytale princess would live here, surely, with its tall and ornate stone-gabled windows. It felt classically European; while some of the other houses she saw on the avenue de Champagne were ostentatious and modern, Sophie's home sat quietly in a class of its own. Stylish, peaceful and whimsical, and for that it seemed welcoming.

Violet was shown to a comfortable room on the top floor that overlooked the back walled garden and Sophie's workers. Beyond the Delancré grounds were the tiny dots of houses, but the landscape was dominated by rolling hills covered by vineyards for as far as the eye could see.

After washing up and changing into a simple dress with three-quarter sleeves, Violet went downstairs to find Sophie waiting for her. Her host had also changed, looking magnificent once again in a white dress Violet was sure she recognised.

Maybe Sophie sensed her curiosity, because she looked down at her clothes. 'It's not an exact replica, but something I had made to entertain our community a couple of years back. We put on a show where I was playing Ingrid Bergman and my barrel room manager was Humphrey Bogart, starring in our own comedy version of *Casablanca*.'

'It's wonderful,' Violet breathed. She was genuinely delighted by the dress, with its nod to a sailor theme; it had striped short sleeves and matching stripes peeping through the bodice.

'But you look like a beautiful picture, Violet. And, may I say, every inch Hollywood glamour.'

Violet laughed. 'Thank you.' It was a lovely compliment, which she appreciated given she'd made an effort with the dresses she'd allowed herself to buy in London. It was a soft peach, which complemented her skin, with a knotted belt of the same fabric and mother-of-pearl buttons to the hem, which was bordered with a creamy flower pattern. Border dresses seemed to be the rage right now. It was ridiculously pretty, and it helped her to feel confident in this unnerving situation.

'Are you hungry?' Sophie enquired, sounding hopeful.

'Not at all.'

'You look thin.'

'We all are, aren't we? It will change when food feels plentiful again.'

'Did you have rations in Australia?'

'Nothing like here or England. It really only began three years ago, first with butter and then sugar, tea and meat. My understanding is that it was more about ensuring that everyone had access to what they needed – you know, equitable sharing – rather than truly meagre supplies. Plus, we were providing regular supplies of food to Britain and our soldiers.' Violet gave a momentary grimace. 'But, to tell the truth, I haven't had much of an appetite since...' She looked down.

'Of course. I understand. But I'd be failing as a host – and as a mother – if I didn't insist on feeding you up.' Sophie gave a nod. 'Well, I hope you brought some comfortable shoes, because I'm going to ask you to walk with me.'

Violet looked down at her feet, which were encased in a neat pair of stacked heel Oxfords in a bone-coloured leather with a sweet perforation detail. 'Are these suitable?'

'No. Far too nice. Although the ground is still firm enough, we're walking slightly uphill. Let's not ruin those heels. May I lend you a pair of my working shoes? I'll be wearing the same, I promise, so we can look slightly odd in our nice frocks and working shoes together.'

Violet laughed. 'Can I admit now that I prefer my loose trousers, old shirt and work boots anytime?'

'Never admit that aloud near Paris, Violet,' Sophie cautioned archly in a highly amused tone, making them both laugh. 'Come.'

'Where are we going?'

'You'll see.'

After changing into working shoes in the boot room, she followed Sophie obediently out of the back door, down the garden and through the gate that led to the working area.

'Your father convalesced here in the staff quarters,' Sophie said. 'He was very happy here.'

'How bad were his injuries?'

'Nothing too serious – it was more his spirit that needed to heal. He was always going to recover from the physical injury to his arm. Did he ever favour it?'

Violet showed her surprise. 'Sophie, I didn't even know he injured his arm. All I knew was that my mother attended to a head wound.'

'That sums up the man I knew. He was hardly someone who went looking for sympathy. He barely looked for conversation.'

'Except with you,' Violet said, unable to help herself.

Sophie cut her a glance. 'I suppose. I think I was a surprise for him. I took an interest in him and his knowledge of science, and especially in his return to good health. I don't know what would have happened if they'd moved him out of the hospital at Reims, or where he would have been sent. Épernay was the reason he recovered, I'm sure of it.'

'I think *you* were the reason he recovered.'

'Well, I made sure his wound was—'

'I don't mean that.'

Sophie paused. 'Violet...'

'It's all right. I'm not accusing you of anything – it's simply a fact. I have made my peace with it, because what you had with my father was before my parents had experienced any romantic exchange – not much more than a few words, I'm told, before Dad was moved on from Mum's hospital tent. You two met before I was born, before they were married.'

'Yes – and it was wartime. We use that excuse to explain a lot of things, but we were all so sad. All anyone wanted was to be with their family again, and some of us, like Charlie, who was so alone, and me, believing my husband dead – well, I think any human connection was precious. Your father and I connected first over the need for him to commit to getting well.'

'Was he reluctant?'

'Yes. I think Charlie tried to die out there on the battlefields. It's still a wonder as to how he emerged, a single soldier coming from behind the enemy lines to end up in the French section. My cousin, Gaston de Saint Just, who was leading the French Arab forces, brought him to me.'

They had left the house behind and were walking past a small village, where Sophie raised a hand and offered salutations to various people before leading Violet into a vineyard. 'It's just up here. Watch your step. We must avoid the field and follow this path.' She didn't explain why and Violet didn't ask.

Instead she followed her host obediently. 'Where is your cousin now?'

'He survived too, I'm pleased to say. The last I heard he was in the Free South, working with the Maquis. Have you heard of them?'

Violet frowned. 'Resistance?'

'Yes, a very particular kind of French resister who hid out in south-eastern France. The terrain was rough and inhospitable, frozen in winter, hellishly hot in summer. It was called Maquis, and so they took their name from this landscape. They were tough and they made a difference; some of them were brilliant at taking Allied spies over the Luberon and French Alps safely and into places like Lyon so they could infiltrate the cities, especially Paris. I met one once. His name was Luc Bonet – such a handsome man. He was originally a lavender grower from Provence. I met him a couple of years ago.'

'What was a lavender grower from the south doing in the north?'

'A long story – but a romantic one. He was given the mission of getting a young British woman across. She was parachuted into the south and he got her safely to Avignon, but then they were picked up by Gestapo. They were strangers falling in love with one another, pretending to be friends.' She shook her head with a smile. 'Somehow they escaped the hideous Gestapo and she made her way to Paris to become a spy.'

'Is that it?'

Sophie shook her head. 'Luc told me her role was to get close to a particular German colonel, find out information for the Allies.'

'Gosh, how brave.'

Sophie nodded. 'Her nerves must have been made of iron.'

'So tell me how you met them?'

'Well, he was part of the Paris resistance – I know this because I was privy to some of their missions and offered assistance whenever I could help. I gather Luc was meeting with our group, but he was probably keeping an eye on the woman he loved too. He came here to Épernay to pick up some supplies and we spent half an hour talking in the cellars. Upstairs, the colonel and Luc's love were together.'

'How could he stand her being with the colonel?'

Sophie shrugged. 'I don't know. The war asked a lot of all of us.'

'Where are they now?'

'I have no idea.'

'I wonder what happened to the colonel.'

'I'm not sure I care. He seemed like a gentleman compared to some of the German officers, but he still wore the uniform proudly.'

'It's sad, isn't it, that war makes good people do bad things. I do feel like an interloper; I've not been exposed to any of this, and if I think of that spy and the tremendous courage she showed, I realise I have done nothing in my life worth speaking about.'

'I don't wish that courage and sacrifice on anyone,' Sophie said, regarding Violet sadly. 'I am happy you have been shielded from the horror of war, but this is why I live in the hope that you will find a measure of understanding – if not forgiveness – for Raphael. He was acting out of his desire to do something to help the people of this region. At its heart it was brave, though I didn't want him to go. Had his troupe not been betrayed by a treacherous conspirator, he might be able to feel proud of his efforts. Instead he lives with the guilt.'

Violet fell quiet as they walked towards an enormous tree, although she felt as though Sophie was waiting for some sort of response. Finally, she spoke. 'As I say, I know little of my father's first war, and almost nothing of this one. The most revealing he ever was with his thoughts was in his letter from the grave. I do recall one story he told me about his time in France during the Great War, when he and a German soldier made a pact not to kill each other. It would have been a fight to the death apparently, but they were both exhausted, injured, tired of the war, of the killing. They made friends in the few minutes that they both hid under an upturned boat and then Willi told my father to go, promising he would not draw attention to him. But I never heard what happened next, and so I'm grateful you can share some of it, helping me to piece together bits of his life.'

Sophie nodded, her face solemn. 'I don't think anyone spoke about the war on their return. In this I think he's like most of the returning soldiers. But look how important it is for children to know what their parents' past looked like – it provides so much clarity and understanding.'

'Does Raphael know about you and my father?'

Sophie actually blushed. 'There is nothing to share. Nothing happened, Violet. Just words.'

'Words are powerful, though... and so is intent.'

The older woman nodded. 'You're right.' She sighed. 'His father is alive. What would you have me say to Raphael? That just for an instant I believed myself to be in love with an English soldier who I met by chance in an underground hospital in nineteen eighteen?'

'*Did* you fall in love?'

Sophie's countenance twisted into one of despair. 'I don't know what to say, Violet; it was so long ago and I wasn't so much older than you are now. I am not making excuses, but to understand properly is to appreciate the circumstances. I was young, alone, with no family to speak of and barely days into my marriage when my husband went off to war and was lost for years – I was told he was dead. I did all in my power to find proof of his death, and I was shown witness statements by the authorities I trusted, confirming where he fell. And while all of this was in the balance, his villainous brother was trying to insert himself into my life—'

'Oh, really?' Violet couldn't help the disgust in her voice.

'Louis was so conniving. He had the kindest, most generous brother in the world in Jerome, and yet he was doing everything he could to destroy everything his brother owned and loved, including me.'

'So Dad was, what... convenient?'

Sophie gave her a look of shock. 'No! He was a saviour. He appeared in my life to help me realise that I could still allow myself to dream of a better life beyond war... to start to understand that loneliness would not be my companion forever, that I could smile again. Your father gave me faith in myself again. Yes, I loved him, and I could imagine making a life with him—'

Violet opened her mouth to speak but Sophie stopped her, continuing.

'—until I saw my husband again. I told you, everyone impressed upon me that Jerome was dead. I never fully believed it, but others made me realise I was being delusional. They had proof! But when Jerome walked back into my life that day, your gracious father simply stepped away. I can't imagine what it took, but I know he loved me enough to let me go. Your father was not convenient, Violet. He was my lifeline and my hope – and perhaps the best friend I've ever had. Jerome, your mother... the geography that separated us and even now this great chasm of life and death will never change how much I adored your father. I have only respect and love for him, and for the family he loved – which is now you.'

Sophie took a breath and Violet waited, sensing she had more to say. She was right.

'I think, if Charlie were standing here before us now, he would urge you to consider Jerome's and Raphael's feelings in this, and what might occur if you insist on us discussing the depth of the relationship I had with him.'

Violet considered how her father had kept his friendship with Sophie entirely separate from his family. To the best of her knowledge, he had never done anything to try to rekindle the relationship with Sophie – Violet had specifically asked the SOE people in London about Charlie's placement in France to satisfy herself. She'd met with a senior man there, who had assured her that his operatives did not choose their missions.

'Absolutely not,' he'd said, frowning.

'Then why was this region chosen for him?'

'Why do you ask?' he muttered, his face clouding with suspicion.

'Mr Johnson, I've just lost my father. I don't even know where his body is, and I'll probably never know. He assured me he was simply an adviser, handling liaison, he said. I knew he was going to be some sort of spy, but he laughed at the idea that he would be, as you might say, "hands-on". His role was support only, he told me, nothing active in the field. Now I discover he died in that very field, during a parachute drop of clandestine goods in Occupied France. He was in the open, defying the enemy, and all on behalf of the British Government. I realise he is one of many brave fallen and I'm not singling him out as some sort of hero, but I have questions and I think the least you can do is answer them.'

The man had a file on his desk that she presumed was about her father, but he didn't open it. He simply sighed. 'Miss Nash, your father knew this region extremely well. He had lived in and around Reims and Épernay during the Great War, and perhaps you know that he remained on after peace was declared to help with the clearing parties.'

'I do.'

'Your father also spoke excellent French and, combined with his knowledge of the region, this meant he was perfect for the role of liaison officer working with Silversmith circuit in the north-east. He seemed rather surprised, I recall, when he learned where had been chosen – I think he had expected to go south.'

'He never said anything about knowing people there?'

'No, not a word, although I will admit that there was strategic presumption on our part that he likely would, despite the years that had passed. We anticipated that he might, if needed, rekindle former friendships, but it was not discussed. People in your father's situation have to make their own decisions in the moment. We can only warn of dangers, provide as much background to their roles as we can, and then hope their own sense of danger will keep them safe, and their bravery will guide their decisions about what is achievable.'

Violet hadn't known how to react to this information. 'I see,' was all she'd said.

'I hope I have answered your questions to your satisfaction. I understand that with a loss like this, there is little information to help bring peace,' the man had continued, his eyes softening with kindness. 'Good luck, Miss Nash. I hope you find what you're looking for in France.'

Those words rang in her mind now. What was she searching for exactly? She didn't know the right questions to ask or why there were any questions at all, but she had to learn what she could about her father's death, simply to start to put this behind her.

Sophie interrupted her private musing with a gentle hand on her arm. 'We're here, Violet.'

TWENTY-THREE

Here? Where? Violet looked around. They were standing close to the outer reaches of an enormous oak tree.

'Your father loved this oak,' Sophie said, looking a little wistful. 'He called it a giant. I told him that I climbed it as a child and my father did the same, and that I suspect my grandfather used it as his special lookout too.'

'I see a treehouse of sorts,' Violet said, gazing up into the old limbs of the oak.

Sophie smiled. 'Built by Jerome. Both Leo and Raph spent many a happy summer playing among its branches. Charlie once told me, in what I thought was my new widowhood, that my children would enjoy this tree. I desperately wanted to believe him, but I couldn't imagine anything further from my life than that type of joy.'

The tree's leaves looked as though they would turn within a month or so. It had a gnarled, ancient beauty, Violet thought, and, reaching to touch its bark, she felt as though she was somehow connecting with her father as a younger man. 'It's a sentinel, watching over your vineyards and your house... your life.'

'My guardian,' Sophie murmured softly. 'Also watching over your father,' she said, clearing her throat.

Violet's slightly misted awareness, which had been lost in admiration of the tree, suddenly snapped to attention, her gaze riveted on Sophie. 'What do you mean?'

Sophie pointed at the earth just beyond the wide oak. 'I took the liberty of finding him and having him buried here.'

Violet gasped, following her companion's gesture. She only now noticed that the slightly higher ground nearby looked newly grown over.

'If your father ever expressed a desire for how he was to be cared for after his death, I will help you to make that happen.'

Violet could hear Sophie's voice but barely took in her words; she was holding her breath, eyes watering as her legs buckled and she found herself on her knees at her father's grave.

'I would have put him right beneath the tree if I thought its roots would tolerate it. He is still somehow...' Sophie's voice sounded choked and she cleared her throat gently. 'He's still within the giant's embrace, though.'

Violet leant down further and placed both hands on the ground as Sophie continued.

'I couldn't bear for him to lie beneath bare earth, so I had my people transplant some grass here, and it has taken well.' As Sophie spoke, tears dropped from her cheeks to water the grass. 'It may not flourish, though, competing with the oak, so I want to create something to grow above your father instead. I have a close friend who is a talented gardener, and she has designed something. If you trust me, I will make this a wonderful little Eden for your father to rest in.'

Violet understood that if Sophie hadn't found her father's body, he might have rotted into the soil of that field, or been found, tagged presumably, and either put into a communal grave or buried somewhere far away. At least she knew exactly where he lay, that he was in a place of beauty and his grave would be tended. She sobbed and finally spoke. 'Thank you for finding him.'

Sophie knelt at her side, holding Violet as she allowed the tears to flow. She had thought she might feel embarrassed to let go in front of a near stranger, but she didn't; she couldn't regret crying for the man she loved above all others.

Sophie wept with her. 'He will rest happily here, I promise. He faces the vineyards and will nourish the soil of Épernay, which he loved so much. Flowers will always smile above him in spring.'

Violet leant into Sophie's arms. It had been a long time since she'd felt the embrace of a mother. 'I've never felt more alone,' she admitted, hunting for her handkerchief. 'Forgive me my tears. I thought I was done with them.'

Sophie sat back on her haunches. 'Tears are human. You don't always have to be strong, Violet.'

'I feel I must. I've had to be strong since I was seven. Strong for Dad, so he didn't know how much I missed Mum, and also because I know how much he missed her.'

Sophie regarded her. 'You know, many people never find a love like that.'

Violet met the older woman's gaze. 'Was he lying, though? Was it always you?'

Sophie shook her head firmly. 'No, Violet, no. You must never think like that. Your father and I were just a dream... and dreams are important in times of war, because they feed hope, and hope is everything. We gave each other the optimism that there was life beyond all the bloodshed and death, right here in these fields.' She swept a hand in a wide arc. 'But it wasn't real. Perhaps we both sensed that – I don't know. I won't lie, I have always held your father close to my heart, and if he thought of me, it would have been in the same way. We got each other through a moment of tremendous despair, and then reality stepped back in and we stepped away. Everyone's allowed a private dream life, Violet, but that doesn't mean that by glimpsing it now and then you are being unfaithful to your loved ones.'

Violet bent fully to kiss the earth. 'I miss you, Dad. Sleep in peace.'

They helped each other to stand, Sophie giving a soft groan of effort and then a small, mirthless chuckle. 'I must stop making that noise. Makes me feel old.'

Violet smiled – her father used to say something along those lines when he straightened his back from gardening. This woman was not what she had expected, with her humour and warmth, and Violet liked her, despite every reservation she had arrived with. She had wanted to find her haughty in her beauty, or miserly in her wealth, or lacking education because she had grown up on a farm. But all of Violet's suppositions – and indeed hopes – were obliterated. Try as she might, she found no cracks in the champenoise. She was outrageously beautiful even in her mature years, sophisticated in her outlook, and clearly very well educated – far more than Violet. And she was gracious in every way: generous, sentimental, empathetic and kind to all, apparently.

Beneath the oak tree, Sophie took Violet's hand. 'With your approval, Raphael would like to organise a headstone. He waited for you so that you could oversee what might be carved into it.'

'That's thoughtful,' Violet said, choosing her words carefully. She didn't want anything from Raphael, but she could see this was important to Sophie.

'Oh, here he comes,' Sophie said, looking down the hill.

'Uh, what?' Violet stammered, following her gaze, swiping at her tears with the handkerchief. The man who had killed her father was here, just seconds away. Could she avoid this somehow? She gave a small shake of her head. No. She would not let him see her undone; she would not give him even the sliver of an opportunity to seek her forgiveness.

'Please meet him.' There was a strong tone of supplication in Sophie's voice. As Violet hesitated, she felt Sophie's cool hand on her wrist. 'Please.'

Good sense, pragmatism, manners – whatever it was that prevailed in that moment to quell her anxiety and keep her firmly in place, Violet watched the man approach. She didn't have to like him, she told herself. She didn't have to be magnanimous, but she knew her parents would have demanded politeness and at the very least for her to be reasonable in all her dealings, even with this coward.

His shirt hung loose across broad, square shoulders, flapping in the breeze as he approached in long strides. Dark but reddish, unruly hair flicked wildly at his ears, and he had the beginnings of a beard; either that or he cared little for his presentation. She decided it was the latter as he came nearer, because his trousers were slightly torn, only adding to the dishevelment. Clearly he wasn't trying to make a good impression.

Sophie could read her mind, it seemed, for she said, 'And as usual he's made no attempt to be neat and tidy. He's so like his father. In fact'—she paused, and Violet saw a smile she perhaps didn't mean to share—'he is his father all over again.'

'No wonder you love him, then,' Violet said. It seemed the right comment to make.

Sophie smiled more broadly. 'Leo was a lot like me. But this boy – he is Jerome of three decades ago. He looks like him, walks like him, laughs like him... Although I haven't heard that laugh from either of them in a while. He even wears his farm clothes like his father does.'

And suddenly Raphael was there, standing much taller than both of them. His gaze felt hot against Violet's skin... or was she blushing? She certainly felt a warmth through her body that wasn't there a moment ago and her throat felt tight. How could this be? She hated him. And now she hated herself for thinking him attractive, because she did, she realised with disgust. She schooled her features not to betray her surprise.

She was still holding her handkerchief but was pleased her tears had subsided. A tentative smile tried to curve out of his squarish face, which was tanned from the sun, but it disappeared quickly at what must have been a wooden expression from her.

'Good morning. I'm Raphael,' he said, his voice soft but deep and clearly uncertain about how welcome he was. He spoke in French.

She replied in his language. 'I'm Violet, the dead man's daughter.' Oh, it was harsh, and it looked as though it landed on Sophie like a stone being thrown. Violet gave a soft sigh of regret.

He nodded, accepting the barb, instantly solemn, waiting for her next move, which was – to Violet – equally alarming. Given her attitude, it struck her as strange that she would hold out her hand in greeting. She really hadn't been sure she had that grace within her, but it seemed something else was driving her; there was a quality about his presence that had immediately broken through the wall she'd built. She felt fragile and decided to no longer hide that, moving into English so she could express herself properly. 'I am hurting and incapable of tempering my pain just at this moment. You will have to look past that.'

She felt Sophie release her arm and suspected she might feel a sense of relief that at least Violet was going to be civil.

'My English is not as good as my mother's,' Raphael said, apologetically.

'And my French is not as good as her English,' Violet replied, again in his language. Her tone was neutral.

He frowned momentarily, working out what she meant. Then, in spite of himself, he let out a laugh that filled the space over the grave they flanked.

Violet really wanted to hate him. Her mind was reassuring her of this. Her treacherous body, however, was reacting differently; she felt hot in places that made her feel uncomfortable. She wanted to run down the hill, flee from Épernay, but, no, she would face this trial because her father lay in his grave before her. His spirit was listening.

Remember what this man did, she told herself, furious that her wall was down and the ice had melted. The desire to know more about him was erupting within.

Sophie looked irritated to be interrupted as a young lad came scampering up the hill's path.

'What is it, Jules?'

'People to see you, Madame Méa.'

'People,' she tsk-tsked. 'Which people?'

'They have English and American accents,' the lad offered and shrugged. 'They're at the bottom of the vineyard.'

Sophie squinted. 'Run down ahead of me, Jules. You know visitors, and especially strangers, are not allowed in this vineyard.' She huffed but looked back at Violet in apology. 'Forgive me. I'd better see what this is about.'

'Of course,' Violet nodded, wanting to scream. She didn't want to be left alone with the son, who hadn't taken his gaze from her. Had Sophie planned this to leave them alone?

They both watched her leave with the lad.

'What's wrong with this vineyard?' Violet asked, speaking French, needing to fill the silence. She only now noticed that the vines were still laden with their fruit, and presumed it must be some sort of late harvest.

'We can't go in here to collect the grapes.'

'Why?'

'The Germans left us a parting gift.' When she frowned, he continued. 'There are mines through here.'

'Mines?'

'Landmines, you know...' He mimicked the sound of an explosion, his hands moving apart.

'Oh,' she said, instantly alarmed.

'It's fine up the pathway we all use, and the Americans and British will send in their team to find them and defuse them soon, we hope.'

'Gosh, how dangerous.'

'How cruel.'

She blinked, unsure if he was going to continue his explanation, but he simply looked back at her.

'She's something special, your mother,' Violet said, needing to fill the awkward pause. She had returned to English; it was easier.

'In this region she's like the oracle,' he admitted, replying in

French, which was likely easier for him. 'Everyone comes to her first, including the officials.'

'Is it because she's wealthy?' she asked. She sounded so inflammatory, but she had no intention of allowing him to feel comfortable around her.

He barely flinched. 'No,' he said airily. 'I personally believe it's because she was a hero for the people in these parts during the first war – they have long memories. And of course she's been instrumental in helping so many to survive during this war. My mother shares all that she can, and she works with her hands right alongside everyone else. She was also defying the enemy in every way possible.'

'She's marvellous,' Violet said, almost allowing her true self to shine through.

'So are you.' He'd returned to English.

She grimaced in shock.

'The fact that you're here speaks to your courage,' he explained. 'Thank you for coming.'

'I didn't come for your apology, Raphael.'

'I'm not here to offer you one,' he replied evenly, which shocked her further. 'I don't know what else I can say. Anything would sound contrived. I bared my soul in the letter I sent you, and that is everything I needed you to know. You surely understand how I feel and how much despair I wish I could take away from you. I would gladly bear all your pain.'

She stared out across the vineyard, a small, truce-like silence stretching between them. She sighed, her shoulders softening slightly. 'It's very beautiful here,' she said. 'I can see why my father was seduced.' She wished she hadn't used that word and hoped he didn't know it.

'Your father was a great help to my mother back in nineteen eighteen. Did he tell you about the sugar... blockade?' he said, frowning as he searched for the word in English.

She shook her head and felt something give a little inside when he smiled, continuing.

'It was so clever. You see, no sugar could get through from the Caribbean or Africa. You can't make Champagne without sugar.'

'How did your mother manage?'

'It was Charlie's idea. He was a chemist, is that right?'

Violet nodded. 'Yes, he trained as one in his youth and worked as one until he went to war the first time.'

Raphael shrugged. 'So he used all that knowledge and realised that we had something else we could use: a liqueur, a by-product of Champagne, that all the producers have. It goes by the name of ratafia. Have you heard of it?'

'No.'

'Well, ratafia is sweet. It serves as an... aperitif. You drink it slowly in small quantities.' He gestured sipping. 'Nice before dinner, or after with cake or dessert, or a small drink when someone visits. Everyone makes a form of it around this region, some in their back gardens.'

Violet actually smiled, enjoying the story.

'Clever Charlie suggested using the ratafia in place of the sugar.' Raphael shook his head. 'So clever and simple... and it worked. It's not as refined, and it needed a lot of balancing – fortunately my mother had the skill to achieve this – but at least she was able to make her Champagne.'

'Brilliant! I love innovation. In fact, I'm trying something a bit wild for—'

'Wild?'

'Er, inventive?' Violet tried.

'Ah, I see. Go on.'

'I make whisky, and the barrel you put it in to develop its flavour is just as important as the grain and the water you begin with.'

Raphael gave an expansive shrug. 'This is the same with Champagne. Every house is different, of course, but the time in oak matters to the cuvée. You would have passed part of our cellars on your way here? Within, we have our own coopers to make our barrels.'

'That's impressive.'

'My mother is fifth generation. We've had time.'

'That makes you its sixth,' she remarked, looking back over the vines. 'Quite exciting.'

'I've never wanted to take over the Champagne house.'

'Why not? Following in my father's footsteps was all I ever wanted.'

Raphael's eyes darkened, and Violet watched his face grow sombre. 'I had a brother. Leo was the eldest. It was his role to take on the brand of Delancré.'

She nodded thoughtfully. 'Did that ever bother you?'

'That it was his, you mean? No. I loved my brother. He was the sensible one – never got into trouble, always reliable. I realise now that I depended on him for so much.'

'I never had anyone to rely on, other than Dad, so we just looked after each other. You are fortunate to have some family to lean on.'

He stared at her. 'Violet, I'm sorry you've lost your remaining family member. Your father arrived into my life as a man called Pierre Dupont. He said he was an itinerant vineyard worker, a lie supported by my mother for a brief while.'

'He was a spy.'

'I didn't know that, though. He spoke fluent French and my mother trusted him, but she didn't trust me enough to tell me the truth about him. It was Charlie who told me, once he discovered I was going to help the resisters in our region, who were being aided by the Allied spies.'

'Like my father,' she murmured.

'Yes. Because my mother had told me I could trust this stranger, I told him I was going out on a mission with some of the resisters for a *parachutages*.'

Violet didn't know this word. '*Parachutages*?'

'A night drop of supplies from the Allies.'

'But it wasn't his mission, was it? Why was he involved?'

'I didn't ask him to join me. Behind my back he told my

mother, and I suspect she insisted he watch over me. I've had to find a way to... to put myself in her shoes and understand why she would risk Charlie like that.'

'Because you were more precious to her than he was.'

'That's one way of looking at it, I suppose. I think she would say that she trusted him over all others to make sure I didn't get myself into trouble.'

'He shouldn't have been there!' Violet said. 'He was old, he was meant to be behind a desk somewhere.'

'He never showed his age, Violet. He was strong, he was a leader, and ultimately he was the bravest of all of us.'

'Why do you say that?'

Raphael looked down. 'He could have got away.'

Violet let out a gasp. She had barely drawn breath to question him further when he continued.

'We were betrayed by one of our own, who conspired with the Gestapo, but the Germans only knew seven of us would be there. Your father had turned up unexpectedly to watch over me, and we welcomed his help, because it made everything faster to have an extra pair of hands. But the Germans didn't know an eighth man was there, so when it all went wrong, he could have hidden. They would never have known. Instead—'

'Instead he hid you,' she said, all of the story fitting into place now. She could imagine her father doing exactly that, ensuring the younger man, who meant so much to Sophie, was safe, while he put his life on the line.

Raphael nodded, his eyes watering, and then he looked away. 'I fought him on it, but he made me promise on my very life, which he was saving, that I would look out for you, tell you this story and make you understand that he did not sacrifice his life because he had nothing better to do with it, but because he wanted to save mine, a young life that had years to do something good with. I am not saying I agree with him, Violet, but I am keeping a promise to a man I knew so briefly and yet owe everything to.'

She was crying again. Oh, she hated these tears that weakened her. She allowed the soft breeze blowing through the leaves of the vines to dry her face, while Raphael was silent, letting all that he'd said sink in. When she finally looked back at him he had more to say.

'He gave me no choice. If I'd defied him, we both would have been shot that day. But this way he believed his death had value. And there was no way he was walking away from it – I pleaded with him in the little time we had.'

'You were ready to give your life?'

He nodded.

'Why?'

'Because I felt…' He searched for the word and ended up spitting it out in French: '*impuissant!*'

Violet had not heard the word before, but it sounded similar enough to English for her to translate it: impotent.

Raphael was still speaking. 'My father, my brother, both doing their bit for France, but me… I was sent home injured and was just here, working in the vineyard. It has to be the same reason that Charlie left Australia to come here. He must have felt that everyone else was contributing and he, a former hero, was just standing back and observing.'

Violet nodded. 'I think that sums it up perfectly. But he left me, and now…' She opened her palms.

Raphael regarded her with soft eyes. 'Is there no one for you to go home to?'

'No.'

'I find that hard to understand.'

'I'm not that easy to like. Perhaps you've discovered that,' she said wryly.

He shook his head. 'I like you.'

'Why? I've been horrible to you. Deliberately so,' she admitted.

Now he smiled. 'I give you permission to be horrible – I deserve it. But I'm not asking for forgiveness, Violet.'

'I'm not giving it, either,' she said, narrowing her eyes. 'But I shall try to stop hating you for hate's sake. Hate is what started this war in the first place, what took my father's life. And he loved so much about life that I think I would shame his memory if I didn't find it within myself to live my own life to its fullest. I can't let it be filled with regret and recrimination.'

'I applaud that sentiment.'

A thought occurred to her. 'I have another question. You said you were betrayed that night?'

Raphael nodded. 'Yes. The traitor was not within our group, but someone who found out about our plans. Brave men, family men, patriotic men – including your father – died that night because of one man's greed.'

Violet swallowed hard. 'Who is he?'

'A man called André. He was a collaborator who took money from the Gestapo to report on any activity by the Resistance that he heard about. I gather he overheard a conversation in his cousin's bar about the drop, and he gladly betrayed the resisters to a much-hated German man called Klaebisch, who in turn let the Gestapo in the region know of a possible drop by the Allies.'

'I see. You said he *was* called André.'

He nodded. 'He hanged himself in his barn.'

Violet's hand flew to cover her mouth. 'What?'

'I'm sure he had some help,' Raphael said. 'When my mother first learned of his involvement, she urged everyone within her safe circle to get the word out, and then she travelled secretly to meet with one of the leaders of the Resistance in our region. Even I don't know where she went or who she met, but I believe she made sure revenge was exacted on behalf of the good men who died. All the families of the men who gave their lives were grateful when they heard he was gone.'

'Your mother is certainly a force,' Violet said, helplessly impressed.

'Something broke inside her when she heard about your father,' Raphael said, searching Violet's face. 'I know she felt responsible, and she needed to make his life count, and not let the treachery go without any form of retribution.'

'His life counted, I promise you,' Violet said. 'I am devastated he is gone, but I can see why he did it.'

'I'm grateful you say that,' he said, smiling softly.

It irritated her enormously that they were being so civil. More than civil – friendly. She wasn't ready to feel so comfortable around him; she wanted to hold on to her hurt, and take some time to make better sense of it all, now that she'd met the two people she held responsible for it. She turned away to stare at the vineyard for a moment, then turned back. 'Raphael, why are you here?'

He looked taken aback. Perhaps he too believed they'd found some middle ground. 'It was for the headstone,' he replied.

'Your mother and I could have sorted out a headstone. I don't need you to help with that.' It sounded so unkind, and still she pressed on – her mouth set in a thin line and her eyes filled with mistrust. 'You said yourself you barely knew him.'

He nodded, watching her. She pushed a hand through her hair, feeling uncomfortable under his gaze. Could he tell that he'd disarmed her? Could he see that her discomfort wasn't purely from being in the presence of the man who'd caused her father's death? Why did he, of all people, have to make her feel like this? It was inexplicable.

Could she hate herself more in this moment? She didn't think so. Her conscious mind was reprimanding itself, but her unconscious mind was certainly engaged in treachery. And over this she had no control; whatever was between them was like a current. His body gave off a familiar aroma of the earth, which was comforting. Those large hands, with their small scratches and tiny wounds, spoke of the work they did. She blinked as she realised she was already imagining them holding her face and—

'Would you like me to go?' His voice was shaking.

'Yes,' she said, too fast.

He looked injured. 'Er, well, I will go from here, but I can leave Épernay altogether for a short while, so our paths don't cross.'

Violet's stomach dropped. 'I have no business asking you to leave your home. I'm the one who should go. Frankly, I no longer know what I'm doing here anyway. I wanted to meet your mother, and...' She looked again at the grave.

'You came for him,' he said softly, pain in his tone.

'I did. But it's done. I can't bring him back to life,' she said, almost savage. 'I've seen where he rests, and I approve. And now I must go.' She left him at the oak tree, hurrying back down the path, but he soon caught up with her.

'Wait, Violet!'

She pressed on, needing to get away from him, needing to get away from here. She would not repeat her father's mistake.

'Violet!'

'What?' she said, in French this time because it sounded slightly less rude. Even so, it was just short of a yell as she stopped in her fury.

'Don't go.' He shook his head. 'Let *me* leave for a few days. Have some time with Maman. She will be deeply upset if you leave in anger, and over me. She doesn't need to know we had this... this talk. Wait here a little longer and I'll be gone before you get back.'

She shrugged gently. 'I'll be gone too. I can't stay. I don't wish to.'

'Where will you go?'

'I really don't know.' Violet rubbed her eyes. 'I would have gone to Paris, but I imagine it's chaotic. I'll come back and see it one day.' She nodded. 'I shall go to Knockando.'

He looked baffled. 'Where is this?'

She gave a mirthless smile. 'It's in Scotland – in Speyside, where whisky comes from. Speyside is like Épernay, but for whisky... a beautiful little enclave where the finest spirit is made and permitted to be called Scotch.'

'Ah, Scotch. But you make whisky in Tasmania. Is it the same thing?' He looked confused.

'Close. But don't say that to someone from Scotland.' She chuckled genuinely now, surprised she could after the pain of a few moments ago.

'What is the name? Knock...?'

'Knockando. It's a translation from Gaelic – perhaps not a good one, but essentially it refers to the "black hill", or "little hill of black", I think. We lived there when I was a small child, and my father dreamed of having his own Scotch distillery. It's where I remember being at my happiest, swinging on the gate of our front garden, waiting for him to kiss me goodbye before he left for his work day.' She drifted slightly in her thoughts. 'And there was one place where I felt complete.'

'Where?' He was smiling at her musings.

She came back to the present, slightly embarrassed. 'Oh, the blending room, where I would watch my father taste all the spirits from the barrels and begin using his magic.'

'I can see how much it enchants you. I wish you that sort of happiness again, Violet.'

'You too,' she replied, wanting to leave him on a positive note. 'Make my father's sacrifice count.'

He nodded. 'I'm glad we met, even if you aren't so sure. I shall remember you looking windswept and sun-kissed in your pretty frock and gardening boots.' She looked down as he gave a soft laugh. When she met his gaze again, still scorching in a way she didn't entirely understand, Raphael gave a small bow. '*Au plaisir,* Violet,' and she watched him stride back down the hillside, relieved that she didn't have to look upon his face again, with those eyes, or those hands.

His farewell had not been final, though. His words essentially meant *until next time.*

There would not be a next time if she could help it.

She was certain she wasn't strong enough to resist becoming friends if she stayed and they had a chance to find more common ground. He was the enemy, a little voice inside kept reminding her. He might as well have loaded the gun that shot her father dead.

That notion had begun to erode in the past few moments, but she refused to let it go. She needed her bitterness to survive if she was going to rebuild her life.

TWENTY-FOUR

When Violet returned to the house, removing her boots at the door, Sophie met her with a sad countenance and showed her into a small, private salon. 'Forgive me. Raphael has left rather hurriedly, and I'm not sure when he will return.'

Violet waved away the apology. 'It's fine. He told me he had to be somewhere.'

'Did he say where or why?' Sophie asked. She looked puzzled, but Violet didn't have the heart to explain. She noticed the champenoise had changed out of her sturdy boots, her feet looking small and neat in a pair of cream brogue-style walking shoes.

'Er, no,' Violet replied. 'I didn't think it polite to enquire when I barely know him.'

Sophie tilted her head, studying her. 'I wish you did. You would have a higher opinion of him.'

Violet had nothing to say to this, so she pressed on with the matter at hand. 'I plan to leave too, Sophie. I'm sorry, but I can't stay.'

Her host looked injured – almost the same expression that Raphael had given her.

'This is too hard for me. But I assured Raphael that we could plan a headstone inscription between us.'

Sophie nodded slowly. 'Of course. I'm really very sad that I can't persuade you to stay longer. Are you sure? We could—'

'I am sure, thank you.' Violet avoided the older woman's eyes.

'All right,' Sophie replied. 'Do you have any special words in mind?'

Violet frowned slightly. 'Something like... *Here lies a soldier, who was also a husband, a father and a friend. Too well loved to ever be forgotten.*'

'Violet, that's perfect.'

'Is it?'

'Of course. You've managed to include all of us in that, which is gracious of you. Please do write that down.' She gestured for Violet to sit at a small desk.

Reaching for a pencil and a sheet of paper, Violet noticed a fountain pen and a bottle of violet ink, which Sophie must have used to write to her. She began to print the inscription in clear letters. 'I'm leaving him in your care, Sophie,' she said. 'To be honest, I can't think of anywhere he'd like more to rest. We both loved Australia, but it was never truly home. In London he felt unfulfilled after the war. In Scotland he was happy, but by the time we left, I think he felt like a stranger there. The Depression alienated him because the Scottish distilleries protected their own. He was always the Sassenach.'

'What is this word?' Sophie looked alarmed.

Violet laughed. 'Sorry. It's Gaelic slang – it means someone from England. It makes one feel like an outsider, even when no insult is meant.'

'Sassenach,' Sophie repeated. 'You should call his whisky this.'

It felt like an awakening to hear it. Of course Violet should use this name on a product! The first release of Nash whisky that she'd made from scratch herself and blended alone should be called the Sassenach. And then if it worked, her own single malt would be called the Boireannach, another Scottish Gaelic word that loosely translated to 'womankind', or maybe Ban-Sasannach – woman of England. Her mind was spinning with possibility.

'Oh, I nearly forgot,' Violet said in a rush. 'I brought you something.'

Sophie looked surprised. 'You didn't have to bring—'

'I know, but this is important and you'll like it. Let me fetch it from my room.'

Violet dashed upstairs and returned with a bottle of rich amber liquid. 'It's not the final bottling – that's yet to be done in Scotland – but I've got this down to the alcohol proof I need. We need small, slightly tulip-shaped glasses if you have something like that? And a small jug of water.'

Sophie's smile stretched wide. 'I have just the thing.' She disappeared momentarily, returning with two squat glasses not unlike the shape of the old still Violet's father had used in Scotland to make his first Scotch. They felt like a romantic link to him.

'Perfect. This is for you; it's his first whisky made in Tasmania, which I have tinkered with a little, so we are both in here. I call it the Soldier's Dram. I plan to bottle it in glass shaped like a hip flask – the sort soldiers might have carried on the battlefield for a wee dram.'

Sophie looked enchanted and confused at once. 'Wee dram?'

'*Wee* means small in Scottish. And *dram* is a measure of alcohol. It tends to refer to whisky specifically.'

Sophie smiled. 'How large is a dram?'

'That depends on who's pouring it,' Violet said, laughing now. 'The common agreement is a mouthful, but it's personal.'

'I see.' Sophie smiled. 'I have heard the saying in English of "How long is a piece of string?"'

'Exactly.' Violet held out the bottle of whisky. 'We made this single malt together. I'd love to use it in a blend too, in an ode to the one constant in my life, the man I gave all my love to. He was brilliant at blending and I can only aspire to that skill. In here lies his magic, though. May I?' she asked, her hand ready to open the bottle.

'Please. I'm intrigued.'

Violet poured a finger of the honey-coloured whisky into each glass and was immediately swept away by the superb balance of aromas as the spirit tasted the air: sweet, spicy and savoury all at once. She handed one of the glasses to Sophie.

Sophie smiled but did not raise it to her mouth. 'What do you smell? Tell me first.'

Violet closed her eyes and breathed in over the shot of whisky. 'Oh, that's easy. I smell my father,' she said, and her voice broke a little.

Sophie lifted her glass to follow suit, inhaling with closed eyes.

'Tell me, what do *you* smell?' Violet asked softly.

'Mmmm. It's deep. I smell honey... um, vanilla?'

'Go on,' Violet said, enjoying herself for the first time since setting foot in France.

'Er... fruit. I would say orange, perhaps, but also plums.'

'Good. What else?'

Sophie sniffed again, her eyes still closed, and Violet could see how stunning she must have been in her youth. She could see why her father had been attracted to Sophie, and why he had fallen under her spell, just as Violet might, if she let herself. Sophie was a brave, generous woman.

Her eyes suddenly flew open.

'What is it?' Violet asked.

'May I taste? I want to check what my senses are telling me.'

'Of course. You may want to add a little water – it helps disperse the flavours in your mouth.'

'No, I want to taste it pure, as you and Charlie made it.'

'He always used water,' Violet assured her, but Sophie was already sipping.

She licked her lips and then gave a sighing sound, closing her eyes and sipping again, taking her time to allow the spirit to move around her palate. Violet knew there was little she could teach Sophie about tasting, but perhaps she could educate her on the complexity of whisky.

'I can't get away from it,' Sophie said, eyes wide and shining with some private amusement.

Violet frowned slightly. 'What are you tasting?'

'Christmas!' she said, almost gleeful. 'Plum pudding, nutmeg, cinnamon, even a hint of ginger. I taste bonfire and butterscotch and toffee apples.' She glowed with suffused pleasure. 'I taste Charlie too. He told me he loved Christmas, because it made him feel like a child again.'

Unable to hold back happy tears, Violet clapped. 'Oh, brava, Sophie. He would be so proud of you.'

'Yes?'

'Yes!' Violet said, putting down her glass and moving over to hug her. 'I know how much he adored Christmas. He always made it such fun for me when I was growing up, and after my mother died, he redoubled his efforts to make it the happiest day of the year. In Australia it was all so upside down, with Christmas Day being so hot, in the middle of summer, but he never gave up on the dream of those gorgeous, snow-laden Christmas celebrations in Scotland, when we had no sadness in our life, only the joy of the family.' Violet wrapped her arms around herself and smiled sadly. 'What you describe are the clear notes of Dad's Australian whisky, including that marvellous bonfire – that's the merest hint of some Tasmanian peat that he used to gently smoke some of the barley. I didn't really want to add that smoky note, but I did it for him because he loved it, and he was right – it adds that extra special layer to the taste. He is the master, and I the apprentice.'

'No, Violet. He told me you would surpass his blending skills very quickly – he had innate faith that you would become a tour de force, as he called you, on the world's stage for whisky.'

Violet felt a grin spread across her face. 'He said that to you?'

'Without a shred of shame at telling me how amazing his daughter is.' Sophie laughed. 'And now you've proved that. This is incredible,' she said, raising the glass to look at the liquid, the light streaming through it. 'So succulent and so full of...'

'Memory,' Violet finished for her.

Sophie glanced at her with a soft, intrigued frown. 'How romantic.'

Violet nodded. 'Whisky is memory – that's what Dad always told me. It can be social, but it becomes something romantic and whimsical that one sips in the quiet of the night – a private dram. It cannot be rushed. The notes must be savoured slowly, and this gradual tasting leads one to contemplate... to remember.' She sighed. 'And the more you sip, the more the vault of the mind releases and you can drift... back to events, back to childhood, or back to one's first love,' she said, then paused. 'Maybe Dad thought of you as he made whisky.'

She hadn't meant to say that. It just flowed from thought into spoken words.

Sophie didn't overreact to the remark, but nodded thoughtfully. 'Charlie was learning about wine, and particularly Champagne's capriciousness. I believe when he left here that he too wanted to make alcohol that could bring people pleasure. I know he never wanted to return to a laboratory or be involved in making weapons again. But the science of taking fruit and turning it into wine intrigued him.'

That made sense to Violet. 'He worked with beers and ales first, and while the hops intrigued him, he realised it was spirits, especially Scotch, that truly interested him.'

'Whisky comes from cereal, am I correct?'

'Yes, the purists in Speyside would say barley, specifically.' Violet chuckled. 'But the blenders use other grains too, like wheat or rye, even maize.'

'And those grains bring with them the memories of the field they grew in,' Sophie mused. 'What ran through it, what flavoured it, which weather conditions affected it over years. Nature is a form of memory after all.'

Violet smiled. She loved that Sophie understood her father's private rationale.

'Champagne, though, is the opposite of whisky, but no less romantic. It doesn't make you thoughtful, or wistful, or even vaguely nostalgic,' Sophie continued. 'Champagne is the now. Champagne is the moment. It is the joie de vivre, and is perhaps about *making* memories rather than observing them. It is a celebration that should echo laughter, conversation, music and the enjoyment of being in good company. Champagne should never be drunk alone.' She smiled. 'Maybe one day, if you return, we'll share some.'

'Maybe,' Violet replied. It sounded inviting, but right now she needed to get away, to press on her own thoughts. Why did she feel so nervous around Raphael? And why, in moments, did she feel jealous of Sophie? 'I'm going to leave this with you,' she said, nodding at the flask of whisky. 'Perhaps Raphael will try it too, and you can educate him about this drink.'

'He knows his cognac, so I imagine he'll want to taste your product. Especially because it's yours... and because you made it for your father.'

Violet looked down. 'He doesn't know either of us well enough to think like that.'

'Oh, Violet, you don't have to know a person a long time to decide if you like them. It can happen over time, yes, but it can also occur the moment two people meet.'

She nodded. 'Mum fell for Dad in that moment.'

'There you are. And I was in love with Jerome, even though I wouldn't accept it, from the second he blustered into the room, straight out of the vineyard – with no care for his dishevelment,' Sophie said, smiling at the memory. 'And I have no doubt that Raphael liked your father.' She paused. 'If you'd only give him more time, I think you'll discover that the two of you have more in common than you think.'

Violet didn't reply to this remark.

'But I respect your wishes,' Sophie continued, reaching out to put her hand on Violet's arm. 'I'm sorry to see you go.'

Violet nodded. 'I'll pack' was all she could think to say, and very swiftly was ready to leave. She had only brought a small suitcase to France; most of her belongings she'd left back in the London house.

When she returned downstairs, Sophie was waiting. 'Where will you go? France is not in a good way.'

'Nowhere is,' Violet admitted. 'I'll stay overnight in Paris and then go back to London, I think. My grandparents' home has become mine.'

'Perhaps you can leave that address? I would like to send you some Champagne... and also some ratafia. It is a special drink that always reminds me of your father.'

Violet smiled. 'Actually, Raphael told me that story.'

'Oh, good.' Sophie chuckled. 'Charlie saved us that year.'

'You saved *him*, Sophie, and for that I will always be grateful.' She stepped forward to embrace her, but Sophie shook her head.

'No goodbyes yet. I'll come with you to the station. The car is ready with the driver.'

Settling into the back seat next to Sophie, Violet looked at the fairytale house, like a tiny romantic castle, and sighed. 'You have a beautiful home, Sophie. I'm glad I've seen it.'

'Thank you. I hope that Raphael marries and it hears the sound of laughter and love and children again.'

'It will have love and laughter when Jerome returns. He can't be long now, surely?'

Sophie gave a shrug. 'Oh, it's frustrating how long these things take, but I haven't received a letter in some time.'

Violet frowned. 'You're not worried, are you?'

'It would do me no good if I were. No, Jerome is like a cat with many lives. He'll swagger in one day soon and scoop me up and twirl me around as though we are still young.' Sophie closed her eyes for a moment, the hint of a dreamy smile on her face.

'I'm going to keep that happy image in my mind and wish you exactly that on his return,' Violet said.

Sophie covered her hand. 'I wish you a love like mine too. He will come.'

'Will he? I feel I'm entering old spinster territory now.'

Sophie's laugh filled the car. 'Don't be ridiculous. Just let him in, Violet. You're like Charlie – you are very complete within yourself. That's tricky to navigate for someone who wants to love you.'

Violet nodded at the truth of those words.

'But who knows,' Sophie added. 'You may have already met him. You just have to accept he's right for you.'

'We'll see,' Violet said, wanting to close off that topic of conversation. 'How are the grapes this year? Are you expecting a good vintage?'

'This may sound ridiculous, but I think it will be an extraordinary year.'

'Really?'

'Absolutely. It's uncanny, as though the vines knew the torment of the land was ending... that France would be released. Nature knows.'

Violet was fascinated. 'How do you know it's going to be so good?'

Sophie shrugged. 'Experience. The buds broke early, and although we got spring frosts that caused damage and wiped out a lot of the emerging buds, a small harvest meant the vines could take on more nourishment – less fruit to support.' She frowned, evidently thinking back over the year. 'The vines flowered slowly, and we had some incidences of disease, like berry moth and grape worm, but they seemed to stay in one region. We began harvesting at three in the morning on September eighth.'

'Gosh, that's specific,' Violet remarked, impressed.

'Oh yes, I all but sleep in the fields during that time period, when I know we are about to shout to the heavens, *time to harvest!*'

Violet laughed.

'Then every last person, including the children, gets busy, but it's a very happy time bringing in the harvest. This one was the happiest of all because we had peace. The crop was exceptional in every way – the yield alone was mightier than expected, and the average alcohol content had the potential to be close to eleven per cent, which is extraordinary.'

Violet chuckled. 'You know, when we put our raw spirit into the barrels, we anticipate more than sixty per cent alcohol.'

'Sixty per cent!' Sophie gave a soft shriek of alarm.

Violet nodded, laughing again. 'My job is to bring that right back to around forty to forty-three per cent, let's say.'

'Hmm, Violet, this is a different world.'

'Not so different. We still all need those precious oak barrels.'

'Precious? Are they hard to come by for you?'

'Yes,' Violet replied. 'They have been. I've been experimenting with other types – applewood is my latest.' She remembered the idea she'd had after reading Sophie's first letter. 'I don't suppose you have any spare oak barrels?'

'I'm sure we do. We have some that are very old, actually.' Sophie smiled.

'Do they still hold flavour? I mean, have they been used so much they've simply become a vessel?'

'Not at all. I'm quite choosy about how much oak flavour is in my Champagne. It's a talking point for many makers. Some of us, like me, don't want so much that we stamp out the flavours of the terroir. It's so important to the character of my product.'

'Sophie, if I used an oak barrel that has held Champagne, it would cast a new flavour to the whisky. If you sent me some, I could try it.'

'Oh my. And this has not been done before, I suspect?'

Violet shook her head. 'Not to my knowledge. It will be innovative. Dad was way ahead of his time, I think, as he thought a lot about how to give our whisky personality. I don't mean the spirit itself – we knew we could make a superb whisky – but how to present it to potential buyers.'

'Ah, now, you speak of branding... the modern way of thinking,' Sophie said, as though this wasn't the first time she'd had a conversation on the topic. 'This concerns all of us who take anything to market. We haven't been able to focus on it lately, for obvious reasons, but this is one of Raphael's great passions. He is always talking to me about the Delancré brand and how to protect it, how to keep it unique and so on. I'm too old for these discussions. I just want to make high-quality Champagne – what comes out of the bottle speaks for itself.'

'No, Raphael's right. When you think of all the different Champagne makers, how do they broadcast to a customer that theirs is the one they seek? It's not always about the best... sometimes the buyer looks for other qualities. I presume most of the Champagne from this region is going to hit a certain quality – it's the same in Speyside with Scotch – but what makes each special? There are lots and lots of little distillers making whisky in Scotland, and so it's how you sell the whisky that matters. There's an... an emotional factor now, and we have to talk to those emotions. That's why I plan to bottle Dad's in a glass hip flask. While it is an ode to him, I hope the Soldier's Dram will speak to all the men who are demobbing and returning to civilian life. It's their drink.'

Sophie smiled. 'I'm going to leave that to your generation to work out, but I am impressed, Violet. That's very clever what you are doing. I'm afraid Champagne must be bottled in the way it is currently.'

'Well, if I try ageing my whisky in Champagne casks, I'm going to think about marketing whisky to women. Traditionally they don't drink it – maybe in a cocktail at a pinch – but if I can somehow make something round, maybe faceted to look like a large perfume bottle, I might catch their attention.'

'The party whisky,' Sophie said, clapping her hands in delight.

'Exactly!' Violet said, eyes shining.

'Where do I send the barrels?'

'Scotland – I'll write it down. I'll need to make arrangements.'

'Good. Please do. I'm thrilled to be able to do something that makes you smile – you are so beautiful when you do.'

Violet sighed. There really hadn't been much to smile about, but this new project was filling her imagination. 'Were those people who came this morning here about the landmines? Raphael mentioned you couldn't harvest the grapes because of them.'

Sophie's eyes darkened. 'Yes, they're organising the clearing team. The Germans had to do as much damage as possible, it seems, as they fled. Apparently that madman wanted scorched earth. I haven't been able to let my workers go anywhere near that field, other than the narrow path we took. The vineyard has had to look after itself, and those grapes will probably shrivel and dry on the vine.'

'Nothing to be done?'

'Not until winter, when the team will have better visibility through the rows. It's a slow, anxious process, I'm told, and they need quiet and stillness. They definitely do not want the vines themselves causing obstacles. I have to let that crop die.'

'I'm so sorry, especially as you think it will be such a good year.'

Sophie nodded. 'Well, Charlie gets to share that resplendent vineyard for the rest of autumn. And that's all right with me. We've had a good harvest. Ah, we're here,' she said, as the car pulled up outside the station.

Sophie walked with Violet onto the platform. It was a small station, and they both checked their watches. It was the last train to Paris.

'Another fifteen minutes. You don't have to stay,' Violet said. She didn't want a long goodbye.

'I want to. I'm glad we had the time in the car – it's fascinating to hear you speak about whisky. We're two generations of women working in worlds that are populated mostly by men, and I know how tough that can be. I may have it a little easier than you, Violet, because we have a history of women in Champagne, so I can claim I belong.'

'Ah, well, you need to hear the story of a woman called Helen Cumming, which Dad told me. At the turn of the previous century, she was running her own illicit whisky enterprise.' Violet explained how Helen had lured taxation agents to her farm with scones, and while they were enjoying them, she hoisted a red flag so all the other illegal distillers could hide their equipment and product.

Sophie's eyes grew bigger, along with her grin. 'I do know that women were important in whisky's early years, but I didn't know this story. She threw flour over herself? How marvellous she is to even think that way!'

'She was clever for sure,' Violet said. 'Tax was so ridiculously high in the early eighteen hundreds, and it was only when those tax laws were reviewed and relaxed that the distillery openly showed itself and gladly paid taxes, and her husband, John, became registered as a distiller of malt whisky. Cardhu Distillery, it was called.'

Sophie was entranced. 'What happened next?'

'Their son, Lewis, took over the business. It was the smallest legal distillery in Scotland, but it made an exquisite product by all accounts. Helen outlived Lewis and at ninety-five years old encouraged her daughter-in-law, Elizabeth, to take it over.'

'My goodness. And she did?'

'Elizabeth proved to be an outstanding businesswoman. She was among the first to understand that blending whisky was the future, and that the single malt that had ruled until then would become a more specialist product. As the story goes, her small enterprise couldn't keep up with demand. She needed to expand, so she sold the old distillery at the height of its popularity to William Grant and its new whisky Glenfiddich – a fledgling business. Then she bought herself four acres and built a much bigger distillery called New Cardhu. But the burgeoning business soon became too big for her and in her mature years she sold it to wealthy grocers in Scotland, John Walker and Sons.'

'I've heard of Glenfiddich.'

'Glenfiddich is enormous now. The name means "valley of the deer". And our tiny distillery in Scotland was Glen Corbie – the valley of the ravens.'

Sophie gave a soft sigh of pleasure. 'Violet, that's so romantic.'

'It's still there – Dad never sold it. We just locked it all up and left for Australia. Dad used to work for Cardhu, which produced the famous Johnnie Walker brand, before he struck out alone. Him and me.'

'Is there anything left for you in Australia?'

'A distillery, a farm, a barrel house...'

'A life?'

Violet shook her head. 'Not without Dad. I loved Tasmania, but it's not the same for me.'

'Did you love Scotland?'

'With all my heart. That's why I think I'll go there next.'

'Then you must get Glen Corbie started again. The Soldier's Dram can be your first release, no? And after that some other special lines including the one for women – that's an inspired way to use the Champagne casks I'm going to send you. I can easily get them to Scotland.'

Violet could feel her imagination taking flight again. This was the most excited she had felt in years. Scotland was there and waiting for her. She would never be a big producer, but she could be a specialist distiller who blended unique lines for afficionados of Scotch. And it would be actual Scotch – authentic at last. Yes, Glen Corbie deserved its moment in the sun.

They heard the train at the same moment and were suddenly hugging.

'Go and heal, Violet, but come back sometime, promise me. We have much to share.' Sophie's gaze was firm.

But Violet couldn't promise. She doubted she would have any reason to return here anytime soon. 'I hope Jerome comes home swiftly and you are a family again.'

Sophie touched her cheek. 'We shall never be complete without Leo, but thank you. I know I have much to be grateful for with a husband and a son at my side. Go to this place, Knockando,' she said, mangling the word Violet had written down for her, 'and find a good man to love you. Your life will change into something entirely different and in the best possible way. I'm going to think of you opening those distillery doors again and dreaming of your new life, your bridal veil fluttering across the barley fields.'

Violet nodded. It was a lovely image. 'Goodbye, Sophie.'

'No, not goodbye. It's too final. I shall say "until next time".

And next time you come, there will be a headstone over your father's grave.'

The train arrived, passengers bundled on and soon Violet was waving farewell to the woman she helplessly liked and admired, who had started to break down the walls she'd built around her heart in grief. Her reversal on Sophie was complete; of course she understood her father's affection for her. Sophie was very easy to love.

TWENTY-FIVE

KNOCKANDO

October 1945

Scotland still smelled the same. The aroma of fermenting barley was on the air, combining with the scent of pine and the lush woodiness of heather. Vast tracts of the wild purplish pink flowers tumbled in mounds down the hillside towards the glen, and Violet fancied for a moment she might be borne away on the drift of shifting pink.

She could see pillows of steam from the trains in the distance, chugging along the railway track that connected Dufftown to Drummuir and onwards to Keith. She knew that journey well: it passed through a spectacular landscape where the red squirrels ran freely and the deer roamed, the tracks snaking through dense forests of pine near the valley where the River Isla wound its way.

She sighed. She was on her way home to Glen Corbie, which had never really had a chance to get going. Her mother's death, the world's financial crisis, which soon found its way to the tiny hamlet, and her father's agreement to whisk them to the other side of the world had made Glen Corbie a ghost. She wondered again how he was ever able to leave this all behind – it was everything he'd worked so hard for – but her father had been an enigma in life and remained so in death. All she could comfort herself with was the thought that he'd loved her mother so much that he couldn't face life here without her.

Strangely, that *was* comforting to her, but the move to Australia had changed her life so dramatically that she no longer belonged here. He'd moved her from London, where she had been born and raised in her early years, and Scotland became her true home. But their move to Tasmania had forced her to embrace a new way of life, in a new country, with all of its challenges and different smells and sounds and creatures. And if he hadn't gone off again, she would have made that her life. She would have been an Australian.

Now she was just confused. Where was her true north? She didn't know. But she would begin here, where she remembered endlessly warm summers and a cottage where her parents were in love and loved her wholly.

Someone else lived in the cottage now; it belonged to the Johnnie Walker distillery, whose Scotch was gaining a reputation for its instantly recognisable label and now a royal warrant from the King. How clever the Striding Man branding was. It inspired Violet to imagine what she might create.

She made her way to the small buildings that formed Glen Corbie. Her father had been so proud. It had been a ghost distillery when they'd bought it, and they'd turned it into one again when they abandoned it. But she set her jaw as she dug in the pocket of her tapestry bag; now that she was here, she was finding confidence, beginning to formulate a plan for her life ahead.

It began here.

She looked at the heavy key in her hand and then the padlock, which was so dusty she imagined no one had even thought about it since they'd left. After all, war had banished all thoughts of new undertakings.

She twisted the key and felt the lock give.

It was time to step into her future.

The door creaked as she crossed the threshold and was suddenly flung back to her teenage years. The copper still was dulled by dust, and her father's blending table and shelves were hung with cobwebs. There was only one barrel; they'd sold the rest before they left. But those from Australia would be waiting at the Glenfiddich warehouse; they'd kindly agreed to store them as she hadn't been sure when she'd arrive. The shed held no barley, but if she closed her eyes and inhaled, she could recreate its smell and imagine two men raking it over the heated floor. Would she return to the old ways or source her barley already malted, as she had in Australia? She didn't know yet, but being here in Speyside – the true home of Scotch – she felt a need to be pure, almost religious, in her approach to production if she went ahead. That meant the old ways: barley grown nearby, warmed by coal or peat and turned by hand. She just wished she had someone to share this new dream with.

'Violet?' She swung around at the voice. 'You're home!'

'Angus!' she breathed, then laughed, then ran towards her friend. 'Oh, Angus!' She was in his arms, wide smiles on both their faces as they pulled back to stare at each other and then hugged again.

'Well, well, Violet Nash. You're the most beautiful lassie in all the world. You always were.'

'Oh, hush. Look at you, though, Angus. You became a man!'

He let her go and bent his arms to flex his muscles. 'I did. I'm a blacksmith now. I work with the coopers at Dufftown.'

'And are you married?'

'Yes, to the love of my life, Rhona.'

'I thought I was the love of your life, Angus,' she teased.

He laughed. 'You were, when we were mooncalves.'

She couldn't rein in her smile. 'I told you then I wasn't the one for you, and now you have someone special.'

He nodded. 'I worship her, Violet. She's very pretty and so are our daughters.'

'Girls? You clever thing!'

'Yes, Sorcha and Isla. Together with Rhona, these three lassies own my heart.'

'You deserve them. I'm very proud of you.'

'And you?'

She shook her head. 'I haven't found him.'

He nodded and left it at that. Her best friend had grown wise, it seemed, withholding platitudes. 'I heard about your father, Violet. I'm sorry. I always liked him. He was one of the best, and it seems he was also one of the bravest too.'

'Thank you.' Violet looked down for a moment. 'I haven't told many, just a few who asked after him, but I guess word travels faster than me walking up the hill.'

'Ooh, that reminds me. The postmistress just happens to be my wife, and she said some post had come for you. I said I'd deliver it.'

Violet frowned. 'Post? But no one knows I'm here.'

He shrugged. 'Well, someone surely does.'

'Ah,' she thought aloud. 'I spent a couple of weeks in London before I came here, and I asked the local post office to forward all mail to me here at Knockando. Must be bills.'

'Here we go.' He handed three envelopes to her and she tossed them into her bag for later.

'So where do you live now, Angus?'

'Same house. I inherited it after Mam went, and so I'm raising my own family at Knockando now, Violet. You must come share a meal with us. I'd love you to meet them all.'

'Of course I will,' she said, squeezing his arm in sympathy. 'It's so lovely to see you, Angus. Gosh, we have so much to share, don't we?'

He grinned again and she could see the boy was still there. 'I have to get back to the house now – I'm just off my shift and the girls will be walking home from school, so I like to be at the gate waiting for them.'

'Of course, off you go. You know where to find me.'

'Where are you staying?'

'I've taken a room in Archiestown, so I'll be close.' It was just a couple of miles, an easy walk.

'Good. I'll speak to Rhona and we'll organise when to have you over. I'm looking forward to hearing all about your exciting life.' He kissed her on the cheek and left.

As the place returned to its former stillness, Violet could hear the ravens talking to each other and the soft wind blowing through the leaves, which were beginning to crisp and change colour. And although it felt so comforting to be back here among the memories of her happy childhood, her friend's words echoed.

Her exciting life.

Had it been exciting? All that anticipation and dreaming... Had she acted upon all of that ambition? Although she'd suggested Australia, they'd had no choice on the other side of the world but to grow barley to survive and fulfil their promise to be farmers, and then just as the distillery and its product were coming to fruition her father had smashed that dream and left her.

It wasn't his fault.

Sophie's words danced in her mind. Two women in much the same pursuit within what was traditionally a man's world... and yet both of their industries had been pioneered by women. Sophie was telling her to be a pioneer. That she should never compromise her dream. That was why she was sending her the barrels, making sure Violet continued her exploration of whisky flavours and dared to be different, to work at the edge of what people might rail against until it became normal. Women making whisky... whisky from applewood barrels or oak that had held Champagne. Violet had to dare to dream and to stand alone.

And she was not oblivious to the fact that, through Sophie's Champagne barrels, the next generation of Delancré and Nash might find a way to keep the relationship alive, even if it was cordial, rather than loving.

The image of Raph, appearing through the fields, his hair unkempt, suddenly returned to her. Loving him wouldn't be that hard if she could find forgiveness.

Violet took a breath, shocked at the thought. Why was she thinking such a thing? *Me love him?*

Yes, why not? a small voice began, *he's no pushover. And you hate pushovers.*

Violet took a low, frustrated breath, but the voice continued.

He's nothing like John. You liked John just as you like Angus – they're lovely men, but they're not the kind of man you want. You see, Violet, you want someone strong who will take you on and argue back and refuse to be bossed around. He will walk his own path, and make decisions – good or bad – without hesitation. But you also want the man you commit your life to sharing to be tender, to be generous, to be intelligent and, above all, to consider you a prize worth fighting for.

Was that truly what she searched for? She didn't think that person existed.

He might, the voice said. *And that's your fear. You fear that Raphael Méa-Delancré might embody all of those qualities and present great potential as your soulmate.*

'*Pfft!*' she said aloud. 'What a lot of cock and bull.' That had been one of her mother's favourite sayings.

Wanting distraction, she took the letters out of her bag. She should check there was nothing urgent within them that needed attention. The first was a bill, as expected, which would be easily fixed through the bank. Next she opened a letter from her solicitor, which was passing on information about her grandparents' estate: the house was officially hers and in her name.

She pushed the paper and envelopes aside for the final piece of mail, which she presumed was unimportant, until the navy of the ink caught her attention and her breath.

Only one person she knew wrote in that colour.

Why was Raphael writing to her? She hoped it wasn't another outpouring of apology, but even as she thought it, she knew it wouldn't be. He had been very firm that he had bared his soul in his first letter and had no intention of apologising again. They had said goodbye on civil terms. What could he possibly have to say and have gone to the trouble of writing for?

She ripped open the envelope. Suddenly feeling warm and

claustrophobic – why was he having this effect on her, even from afar? – she stepped outside, walking into the adjacent field to sit among the heather, while some hairy coos chewed in a nearby paddock, watching her. She paused a moment to look into their placid faces; she wanted to hug them. She wished she had someone to hug.

The envelope sat in her lap. She sighed and lifted the single sheet, dated the week she'd left France.

Dear Violet,

I write this to you from a deep and inconsolable sadness.

It seems your life and mine mirror one another's, for I have lost the two remaining members of my family in the same seventy-two hours.

Violet stopped, held her breath, and then gasped. What was he talking about? She read the opening paragraph again, hardly making sense of it. How could this be?

She read on, frightened.

After you left – the next day, in fact – my mother received a visit from a gentleman who had information about the camps where the French workers had been held. My father had been doing his compulsory work service in a German camp as a farmer somewhere close to our French border in Alsace– Lorraine. He knew beets well enough, and apparently he was put in charge of a work contingent. That's about all the man was permitted to tell us.

The last letter we received from Papa said that they were hopeful of their freedom, as word had got through that Paris had been liberated and then the peace treaty was signed in May in Reims. We were under the impression that he and the others were in the process of being liberated, to be returned across the border. It was a slow process, and we were asked to be patient.

However, according to my mother's visitor, my father was one of the men who tried to protect his fellow French as German soldiers began to flee eastwards and back into Germany via Strasbourg. There was fighting, not that I imagine the French workers had any weapons other than their farming tools, and the German soldiers opened fire on them.

My mother was told that my father was cut down and buried in a mass grave weeks ago, and this was why we had received no word. The authorities have only just recently discovered this group, fifteen workers who were not accounted for at the camp where they had been held for the past year or so.

People tried to reach me, but got to me too late, and so I am very sorry to inform you that my mother, unable to cope with another death – especially after the war was won – has taken her final breath. It is impossible to imagine, but Maman walked out into the vineyard – you'll know the one – and died. I think she deliberately chose that vineyard, but she died of a heart attack, mercifully.

At this point Raph's writing had become shaky, almost illegible, and he'd smudged the ink in places.

I believe her tormented mind, especially after your father's death, which she felt so responsible for, simply could not take yet more heartbreaking news and grief.

I know this is hard to bear, and I despise that of all people I am the person who is the bearer of this news. But I doubt there was any other way that you might find out, as I imagine you have no reason to visit anytime soon, if at all. You deserve to know of her fate because you were so recently with her. I know she was very excited *to meet you and had high hopes that our families might find friendship, and I know she made a promise to you.*

She left me a letter in which she asked me to send you some of our oak barrels, which I have made arrangements for.

I feel, if nothing else, that you and I are now kindred spirits in that we have no siblings, no parents, no grandparents... We are individual boats on rough seas, and I will take your lead and try to find a way to navigate them, to make the very best of my life – a gift from my parents and from your father, who protected it with his. I tell myself that I have been left behind for a purpose. I just hope I can find it.

In sorrow, but also in respect to you and your own recent loss,

Yours, Raph

The letter dropped into her lap as Violet made two fists, pushing them against the ground where she sat, and screamed her anguish across the glen.

'But, Violet, you've only just arrived.' Angus looked at her, baffled. She'd interrupted the family's evening meal. Two little girls, aged perhaps five and three, stared back at her from their table. The elder had flame-coloured hair and the younger looked out from beneath a mop of curly reddish-gold hair. Their mother had been speaking to them softly, no doubt asking them to behave themselves in front of the visitor, and now regarded her with a bemused expression. Rhona was indeed pretty, with golden hair and huge, intelligent eyes, as deep in colour as a sapphire.

'I know, but I have to go.' Violet had sat in that field for an hour, perhaps two, or more, numb and yet electrified. Sophie gone. What could she do?

'Why? Where?'

'It's an emergency.'

'What sort of emergency? Are you all right? Are you—'

'Angus, leave the poor woman alone, would you?' Rhona said, in an accent Violet immediately recognised as from the Shetland Isles, with its soft, lulling manner. She'd once met an old barley maltster from the Isles, and she had loved listening to him. Rhona seemed to have the same lilt, although living with Angus here at Speyside had begun to change it. 'I'm Rhona,' she said, wiping her hands on the apron hanging on the back of her chair and offering one in greeting as she pushed her worried husband gently aside. 'Angus told me all about you, but I didn't expect to meet you so soon.'

'Forgive me, interrupting your supper—'

Rhona shook her head. ''Tis no trouble, Violet. Won't you join us?'

'I won't this evening, but I will soon, that I promise. Right now, I have to go to France.'

'France!' they said as one.

They were a well-matched couple and she wanted to express that, but now was not the moment. 'A friend in need.'

'Can we help?' Rhona asked.

She nodded. 'It's why I'm here. Angus, can I trouble you to take me down the hill? I have to get my things, get to the station and, if I'm lucky, get on the last train to Inverness and then the overnight to London.'

'Of course. Rhona?'

'Yes, yes, go. I'm sorry for your friend, Violet, and hope to see you soon.'

Violet cast the girls a smile that was difficult to muster and gave a small wave. 'Hello, pretty girls.'

Both shyly waved back.

'I'm so sorry,' she said again.

'Don't,' Angus warned. 'Come on, I've got a motorcycle now. You don't mind riding pillion?'

Violet almost found another smile at the image. 'No, not at all. I'm very grateful.'

A few minutes later she was holding on to the waist of her old schoolfriend, both of them wearing goggles and roaring down the hill towards Dufftown.

'I'll wait for you to grab your stuff,' he yelled over his shoulder. 'And I'll take you to Huntly. You can take the train to Edinburgh and onwards to London.'

'Thanks, Angus,' she said, close to his ear, and he gave her a thumbs up and pressed on fearlessly. She wanted to close her eyes, feeling momentarily scared by the speed, but the sun was setting into a glorious bath of the most luminescent golden pink, and she couldn't tear her gaze from its beauty.

In this wild frame of mind, with thoughts cannoning off one another, a single big question reverberated: *What are you doing?* The dying sun replied deep into her frantic mind: *Only your presence will bring Raph comfort. You need each other right now.*

It was ludicrous – pure whimsy at best, and madness at worst. They weren't even friends; they'd parted on awkward terms, glad to be rid of each other. But they now had so much in common that Violet believed she was someone who could fully understand what he was going through and what he now faced.

She was determined to find some grace within herself over Raphael's part in her father's death. Raph didn't ask him to die for him. Raph didn't pull the trigger either.

She needed to let him know that Charlie Nash made his own decisions. And that she was making one too – to forgive Raph for his part in Charlie being there that night and to forgive Sophie for asking Charlie to go.

Forgiveness was the mark of the strongest soul, her mother had always said. Violet was going back to Épernay so that he might forgive himself and also that she, in her forgiveness, might set herself free.

TWENTY-SIX
ÉPERNAY

October 1945

Violet didn't want to think about the journey she'd just made, with its difficulties and the hellish expense of hiring someone to drive her from Gard du Nord in Paris to Épernay. The train to Reims would have required her to wait hours and she didn't want to linger.

She'd slept on the train to London and on the ferry across the English Channel, which had been so rough it was a mercy to sleep away its unpleasantness, although her dreams were ugly and upsetting. She had been the last passenger to secure a sailing, and only because she'd pleaded with the ticket master that it was for compassionate reasons. Given that the whole of Europe needed compassion right now and every person had a tale of woe, she hadn't thought it would work, but he was a kind soul and he allowed a moment's pity at her genuinely broken expression.

It was a cold autumnal morning in northern France and she didn't focus much on what was passing by her window. The driver asked if she spoke French, but she lied and said she didn't, preferring not to engage in conversation for the hours ahead on the road. It would only have been about the war anyway. They'd agreed on a price and she paid him upfront, so there was nothing more to be said. By midday, they were driving down the avenue de Champagne.

She wore her orange blouse and a cardigan over her baggy slacks, and a car-style coat for a layer of warmth, and had nothing with her except a couple of changes of clothes in her tapestry bag. Her hair hung loose, unstyled, but it was clean. She wore no make-up and felt scruffy, but she wasn't here to make an impression.

She was here for... what exactly? She blinked in the car as it crept down the large but quiet avenue. What did she think she could do for Raphael?

She would offer sympathy, because she understood his pain. But would he want that from someone who had been so hostile towards him?

If the driver could hear her internal conversation he would probably laugh at her.

'Trust your instinct,' her father had said time and again. 'It always serves you true.'

Well, instinct was all she had now, and it was telling her that Raphael would welcome her presence – that he needed it, in fact. And she knew that her parents would approve of her empathy.

She thanked the driver and entered the courtyard of the fairy-tale house, which felt still and silent. Its windows, which last time had struck her as pretty eyes onto the world, were now shrouded with black behind their glass, and a cloth had been wrapped around the door knocker. She didn't know how to rouse anyone inside, but one of the staff must have seen her, because the door opened softly as she reached the steps to its portico.

'Mademoiselle Nash?'

It was the housekeeper she remembered alongside Sophie. She had been cheerful and smiling then, but there was no sign of that now in her expression.

She shifted to French. 'Er, it's Jeanne, isn't it?'

'Yes, mademoiselle.'

'I've come to see Raphael.'

Jeanne opened the door slightly wider. 'Mademoiselle, I have to tell you that—'

Don't say it! 'I know. I've heard.'

'Did you not leave for London?'

'I did. But Mr Méa-Delancré wrote to me,' Violet said.

'Oh.' The door opened. 'He is not here.'

Violet frowned. 'Is he away?'

'No, he is...' Jeanne pointed behind the house. 'Up the hill. You can wait—'

'He's at the tree?'

She nodded. 'But you mustn't go there – that's the vineyard with the mines.'

'I know. But I also know the safe path. My father is buried up there.'

The woman looked worried. 'Let me get some help.'

'There's no need, I assure you. Please let me just leave my bag.' Violet didn't wait for an answer, but placed it inside the doorway and shrugged off her coat, knowing it would be a burden up the hill, and handed it to the housekeeper. 'Thank you,' she said as kindly as she could. 'I can find my way.' And then, before the woman could respond, she was down the stairs again and heading around to the back garden and through the gate, following the route she remembered vividly.

She walked fast, then broke into a jog and finally just short of a run. It wasn't excitement or nervousness but a surge of energy, urgency. She needed to get to him as fast as she could, now that she was within reach of him.

She passed all the familiar sights and then suddenly she was into open country in the vineyard, its leaves even more rusted red since she'd been here; some had even turned a crisp brown, others had already fallen. Some had blown across her pathway and they crunched beneath her swift footfall, which began to slow as the hillside ascent became tougher. Her breathing wasn't laboured but it was challenged, coming a little harder than was pleasant because of her haste.

And then he was there. Head bent, hands clasped around his knees, sitting near her father's grave.

Oh, she knew that position, had imitated it in her bathtub in Tasmania, feeling weak, needy. He was lost in his shock as she had been, and she knew he wasn't thinking anything: there in body but his spirit in a deep mist. His thick wavy hair was being teased by the autumn breeze, but she suspected his winter was already upon him.

He didn't seem to hear her careful approach. His back was angled towards her.

'Raph,' she said softly.

He raised his head very slightly at her voice but didn't turn, perhaps presuming she was one of the staff, checking on him. 'I said for you all to leave me alone. Go away, please.'

'Raph, it's me, Violet Nash,' she said in English and watched his head jerk up and twist around, his mouth open in surprise.

He hauled himself to his feet and she noted he looked even more dishevelled than when she'd last seen him. He mustn't have shaved since his mother died, his eyes were red-rimmed and he'd shrunk in ways she couldn't fathom.

They simply stared at one another, but she felt it, as surely he did; her difficult breathing and the sudden warmth in her body was nothing to do with her physical effort to reach him. She felt a new pound in her chest like a single drum marking a beat, and it seemed to drown out all other sound, adding to the tension of the moment.

It was his presence having this effect on her, she knew. The taut silence lengthened further as they looked at each other, and Violet wondered whether he was moving through similar thoughts, trying to reach the decision she did in this heavy heartbeat. It was a profound dawning for her. And Violet, who prided herself on control and rationality in every situation, suddenly closed the space between them; she would never know if she didn't take the risk.

He had the slightly higher ground but his arms reached out and held her. He leant them back against the old oak tree and buried his face in her neck. She could feel his body trembling against hers and then – in a moment that felt like a surrender – he began to slide down the tree, taking her with him until she was curled on his lap and they were both weeping in each other's embrace.

'Thank you for coming,' was all he said, his voice muffled and broken.

'I had to. I had to be here with you.'

'She got the visit just after you left – I wasn't here, because I was trying to give you some space.' He paused. 'I think she lost her mind to grief. Jeanne said my mother suddenly left the house, grim-faced and as white as a bedsheet, without any explanation. No one knew what the man had said to her. But he'd given her a written report, which they found later.'

Violet was shaking her head in disbelief. 'What happened? When you said she walked out into the vineyard... I was initially terrified that she'd been killed by the landmines.'

He shook his head. 'I personally think it was heartbreak, Violet. But she had a heart problem she never spoke about – I only knew because Papa told me when he was leaving that I had to look after her because of it. I was shocked to learn that but she waved it away when I asked her about it. Maman never put herself first, and I suppose she didn't want to worry any of us with her health issues. My Papa told me that her doctor had said it would kill her eventually, and I think the shock of the news of my papa's death simply hastened her end.' He rubbed his eyes, then looked at her. 'Everyone she loved was gone in that moment, including both of us. I'm not blaming us, but I think the tension was deeply upsetting in addition to how your father had died – and then the news of my father. I think her heart simply broke... her mind, her resilience, the power that had sustained her through her life. Did you know she lost her parents and brother when she was very young to the Great Flood of Paris?'

Violet shook her head.

'I think the years between the two wars were her only years of true happiness. All her life she needed to be stoic and look after others, which she did. I think losing my father, after everyone else, took away her hope. Maybe she was coming here to tell your father what had happened. She had nearly made it to the oak tree.'

Violet's hands flew to cover her mouth.

'Maybe she knew her end was near and she wanted to die close to him because she couldn't have Papa.'

'Raph, I'm so sorry.' Violet pulled him close again and they remained like that for what must have been the longest minute of her life. Through it she experienced a tumble of emotions, mixing with random thoughts, like a waterfall through her mind. She felt slightly ashamed about one, given the circumstances.

This felt right.

She was where she should be.

That was confusing. She was here out of kindness, wasn't she? She had some helpless attraction to this man, but he was still the person who'd caused her father's death, if indirectly. She wouldn't stay – just until she had reassured herself that he would be all right, that he would get through his early shock and grief, as she had.

Don't lie to yourself, the voice inside accused. *Why are you so comfortable in his arms... in his lap? Why are you clinging as hard to him as he is to you?*

'Violet,' he groaned, interrupting the interrogation from her inner self. 'Don't leave me.' He shifted his head to look at her with a bruised expression.

She was sure she had worn an identical one when the telegram had come, except she'd had no soft, warm body to cling to. But was that all she was to him? Someone to hold close?

'In fact, please don't ever leave me again,' he murmured, looking into her eyes. He took her hand, threading his fingers through hers.

She breathed out, looking at their hands. 'What are you saying, Raph, I don't—'

'Yes, you do. You knew the last time we were on this hill together and you know it now, even though you're scared to admit it. We're both feeling it.' A new light seemed to erupt in his eyes. 'I thought I was imagining it when we met. In fact, I was so confused by my feelings... not just confused but conflicted. I told myself I shouldn't be having romantic thoughts about you, the daughter of the man whose death I brought about by my actions. You hated me. I could see it in your expression, hear it in your tone—'

'I didn't hate you. I wanted to, it's true, but I was... confused too. I couldn't make sense of how I was feeling. I had one vision of how I'd react to meeting you, but the reality was the opposite. And I was angry at this.'

'I could tell.' His gaze fell so softly on her now and all it did was warm her even more. 'Why did you come?'

She sighed. 'You're in shock. I know this feeling. I thought you could use the presence of someone who understood completely.'

'*Why* did you come?' he repeated, more urgently.

'Because I didn't have anyone when I went through this, and suffering alone is a terrible thing.'

He shook his head. 'I am not alone, though. I have plenty of people here who have known me since I was a child and who certainly worshipped my mother. But I wish they'd all leave me to my grief, because they can't bring my brother, father or mother back.'

'No. But they can bring *you* back from your sorrow, in time.'

He regarded her. 'Is this why you're here?'

'In a way.' She looked down, escaping the intense stare from those soulful eyes. She realised he was gently stroking the skin on the purlicue of her hand. How did she even know this word? Her thoughts were tripping over each other, trying to move to the safety of facts and science, but they weren't winning; the pervading thought was that she was enjoying his touch. Such a simple motion, so innocent, and yet it was setting off what felt like electrical charges through her body.

'I'm here because of your loneliness,' Violet said, finally finding the words to articulate herself. 'I've been where you are, in despair, and I am testimony that life goes on. I've had to heal alone, but you don't.'

She moved to stand and he helped her; she needed to stop this thrum of desire, and at the very least say what she had come here to say. Deliberately but gently, Violet pulled her hand away from his, regretting instantly the loss of his touch.

'The danger, Raph, is allowing yourself to believe that your grief is any more painful than anyone else's.'

As he opened his mouth in reply, she put the same hand up to stall him. 'What I mean is that I made that mistake too. Yet I suspect that every single person in every single village here and around Épernay, all the way to Reims, has lost someone they love, probably more than one person. Their pain is no more or less than yours, and yet they have to find a way to survive it, as you must.'

She paused to draw breath; she couldn't tell if her words were getting through to him, but she had more to say. 'I'm not saying it will get better now, or even next month. But I needed to tell you this – that the old and vexing adage that time heals all is true. It sounds so empty, but it holds only the truth. It will heal your pain, but first you have to stop fighting it. Surrender to the sadness. Wade through it. It took me a while to learn this, but eventually I did just that. I let it nearly drown me, but the human instinct is to survive at all costs. I came through it, at least well enough to function normally, to be with people again, to consider a path ahead. It's not easy, but we all can survive. You can too.' Violet swallowed and looked down. 'That's all I came to say, because no one said it to me – I wouldn't let them. Whether it would have made a difference in the moment, I don't know, but I'm trying, because I know exactly how you're feeling and... because I felt I should. I'd just been with you, just been with your amazing mother. I had to come in person and acknowledge your loss.' She raised her eyes to his again, and immediately felt his heated gaze.

'And that's all you came to say? That's very generous,' he said, although his tone said otherwise, on the border of sarcasm.

Gosh, they were alike, Violet thought. She would have taken a similar attitude, always ready to defend herself with a quick, sharp rebuke couched in a polite response. She licked her lips, unsure how to proceed; she was rarely lost for words. 'It felt right,' she admitted truthfully, but hoping she was hiding that truth sufficiently. 'It felt... important, as though I was being guided back here.'

He didn't look away. 'So a kindness, then?'

She blinked. He had her measure, though he wasn't baiting her, she could tell. He was simply giving her the opportunity for honesty, for her to admit something that would allow him to be honest with her.

Do it, Violet. Take a chance. Let go of control, all that you've trained yourself to be, and give in to instinct, the universe pleaded with her.

'I came because I needed to...' Her voice faltered.

He waited, his expression encouraging.

'To be with you. I needed you. Need you.' There, it was said. The strangest words she'd ever heard herself utter, so alien to her independent spirit, but they were the truth.

His features relaxed slightly, even though his gaze didn't let her off the hook. 'Given that a few minutes ago I simply wanted to be alone,' he said, finally breaking her gaze to look out over the vineyard, 'I couldn't be gladder that the one person interrupting my solace is you.'

'Why?'

'You... got under my skin.' He shrugged. 'When you stomped away, angry and glad to be rid of me, I felt a fury that I'd let you go. I didn't really understand why, and I couldn't think of anything to make you stay. I couldn't think of a single reason to say to you that was rational. I had only an irrational thought... about my heart.'

Violet stared at him. 'You couldn't say what was in your heart?'

'I didn't trust it! I was so shocked. I knew you despised the very thought of meeting me, so I didn't know what to do with these feelings towards you.'

'Which are?'

He regarded her for what felt like an age. 'That I'll never let you turn your back on me in anger again. That I don't ever want you to walk away from me again. I want you here, in my life.' He shook his head. 'We can't replace them, I know that. But we can step into the void their deaths have created and make a life together.'

It was so shocking, she would have sworn her heart stopped its beat just for a couple of moments. It made her light-headed.

'I've never met anyone like you, Violet,' he continued. 'And before you say I barely know you, I realise that. But it's your very presence that disrupts and dismantles me. The way you look at me with all that power and fury and confidence, it gives me a sense of invincibility.'

She gave a strangled laugh and he joined her.

'I barely know what I'm saying, but I'm saying it anyway. This is what's in my heart. I've lost my mother, but she brought you to me. You lost your father, but perhaps he gave me to you through his death. Can we ever find a way to look at what we've lost through that lens?' He searched her face for agreement.

Violet thought about it. It was such a beautiful sentiment, allowing something so wildly romantic to grow over something so full of despair. She willed herself to respond. To not be afraid... to no longer be alone. Here *he* was. This was the one. Her mind hadn't seen it, but her heart knew it from the second he'd swaggered up the hill, nervous to meet her and yet determined to confront her and allow her hate to wash over him. He'd come with the faint hope that maybe she'd allow him to emerge as a friend.

Neither of them could have imagined they were both looking at their future. But here he was. Her future – if she allowed it.

Take it, Violet, her father and Sophie whispered on the wind.

We both approve.

'Yes, I can see us through that lens,' she said softly.

He took a moment to double-check that he'd heard correctly, and then he swept her up into his arms, hugging her hard, before pulling back to look into her face. 'May I kiss you?'

She nodded, laughing. 'I don't know why it's taken so long.'

And she felt the lips of the man she knew she loved join hers. It was impossible, beautiful, incandescent all at once. The life she'd hoped for but never sought out... the one she dreamed about but never allowed herself to consider.

Death follows life, which follows death. It was the circle. The ultimate truth.

They parted, smiling at each other.

'Is it too soon to say that I love you?' he asked.

Violet shook her head, suffused with astonishment and love herself. She gazed at the ground, taking it all in. It was only now she noticed that the earth by her father's grave was newly laid. 'Did you bury your mother here?'

Raphael took her hand. 'Is that wrong?'

Violet searched his face. 'Doesn't she have a family vault or something? She's one of so many generations of Champagne makers. I would have thought the family had—'

'It does. But I couldn't bear the thought of her in the church's crypt. I wanted her here, among the vines.'

'You think she's happier next to my father? Wouldn't she want to be beside yours?'

Raphael looked sombre. 'My father will never come home. He's buried with the people he tried to shield, who had shared his life for years. My mother would otherwise lie in a cold, dark place. Here, it pleases me that she's next to someone she clearly loved. She was coming to him as she was dying. She wanted to be with him, perhaps tell him her troubles. I know it feels awkward... and yet somehow...'

'It's kismet?'

Confusion filled his eyes.

'Destiny,' she offered.

Raph nodded. 'Yes, fate decided that they could not be with their beloved. And it also decided that...' He shook his head.

Violet understood. 'While they couldn't in life, they would lie beside each other in death.'

He nodded. 'That's it. How does that make you feel?'

'A bit odd, and yet it's so romantic I could weep. But they did love one another. My father once said that in a different life they might have been together,' she said. 'And curiously, your mother said much the same thing when I met her. "In an alternative world," I think her words were. These were the closest two people could be as friends, and it does feel right that they have each other here.'

Raphael nodded, then frowned. 'I hate that the strong, resilient mother I admired so much would have her life end in heartbreak.'

Violet squeezed his hand. 'It wasn't weakness. Never think that of her. She was looking forward to life after war. She was excited to send me the barrels and what it might mean to link our two houses through her Champagne and my whisky. She'd survived two wars, and had helped ensure the safety of many people through both of them. She'd lost the man she adored to both wars, and then he was murdered. They still took his life, even after peace was declared. How close she came to that reunion – imagine it. And she'd already given a son to the war, and countless friends no doubt, including my father, and she was in absolute fear of losing you too, in your desire to prove yourself worthy.'

'Is that what I was doing?'

She took a breath. 'I don't know, Raph. I barely know you.'

'You know me,' he insisted. 'And you can love me, I believe, as I believe I can and do love you. That's what matters now. Neither of us can change the past, but we can shape the future, can't we?'

She smiled. 'Fighting talk.'

'Then stay with me. Forever.'

She paused. 'Is that a proposal?'

He caught her gaze again, taking both her hands now. 'I'll do it better at a more appropriate time, but here, in front of our parents, with the vines surrounding us and the wind blowing through your hair, and me looking untidy as always, which I know irritated my mother but she said it reminded her of Papa, will you say yes to marrying me?'

Violet couldn't stop her mind from racing ahead, even as her heart was shouting yes. 'How do we do that, though? Where will we live? I was just about to start a new life in Scotland.'

He gave a soft sound of vexation. 'Don't put anything in the way of what you want, Violet. If you want me, say so, and together we will work out how to make our lives and our businesses work. I'm not going to stop you in your ambition – I'll give it all the oxygen you need. Your father told my mother that one day you'd be not just the best female blender in all of Scotland, but one of the best in the world, man or woman.'

She felt pricks of tears at her father's relentless pride.

'I will not get in the way of that, I promise.'

'Then yes,' she said simply. 'I am yours forever.'

He took her in his arms again, but instead of sinking to the ground, this time he picked her up and twirled her around. Her feet arced over two graves, and she would have sworn the dead were sighing.

EPILOGUE
KNOCKANDO

Early September 1952

The beautiful young Elizabeth, eldest daughter of George VI, had ascended the throne and was waiting to be crowned Queen, but this was nothing compared to Violet's toast over breakfast.

'Cheers, everyone! We can soon drink as much of this as we choose, because I have it on good authority that tea rationing will finally end next month.'

Violet's two girls cheered, unsure why this was so important but loving the fun, while their father raised his wide-rimmed cup of coffee – more of a bowl, which he'd insisted on bringing from France – and laughed. '*Santé*, I suppose. I'll never understand you British and your love of tea.'

'Tea is life, Raph! Tea is appropriate in every situation.'

'I'd like to see tea getting a party started the way Champagne does,' he challenged.

Violet laughed. 'Well, there you have me. For a party, only House Delancré will do.' She blew him a kiss across the table and their daughters giggled.

'Papa, do you have to go?' Charlotte asked.

'I do, *ma petite biquette*.'

Both girls erupted into laughter; they loved it when their father mixed English with French.

'I am not a goat,' she admonished him.

'I said *baby goat*,' Raph countered. 'Quite different.'

'What am *I* today, Papa?' her younger sister wondered.

'Well, now, Gisele, today you are *mon petit poussin*.'

'A chick?' She found this very funny, but then she was only five years old.

Her older sister left the table to hug her father. 'Don't go.'

Violet smiled, loving how close the girls were to their loud and gregarious father. This was a quality she hadn't noticed in their early meetings, but then they'd met under such torturous circumstances. His true personality was this: fun, boisterous, always ready to break into song, of all things; he said his father had been like this too. She wished Sophie was alive to see him so bright and cheerful. 'Girls, it's nearly harvest time. You know your father has to be in France during September.'

'Why can't we all go?' Charlotte moaned.

'Because I want to get your sister at least started in her new school,' Violet said. Her eldest pulled a face, but it was one of resignation. 'Come on, let's get dressed so we can see your papa off at the station.'

They now lived in Knockando's old church manse, its stunning walled garden overlooking the local hills and pretty valleys and the mountains in the far distance, snow-capped through winter. She had known and loved the house from childhood and pinched herself regularly that when she'd mentioned to Raph that it had come up for sale, he'd bought it for them. It was a surprise that took her breath away and now she called it home, a sprawling three-level Gothic house with so many rooms she barely knew what to do with them all. She and Raph had one floor to themselves, while the girls' bedrooms, playrooms and bathroom were on the top floor. *How lucky we are*, she often thought, recalling the tiny cottage, not too far away, where she and her parents had lived and loved. A pastel drawing of Sophie's, of the garden at House Delancré, hung on the wall, reminding them of what they'd loved and lost, as well as the place that had brought Violet and Raphael together. Raph had found it rolled up with a note to send it to Charlie. He'd brought it instead to Violet.

Working out their lives together had indeed proved tricky but somehow they were making it work. There were periods in the year when Raph needed to be in Épernay – like now – and there were other periods of the year when Violet had to be in Speyside. So far they had juggled the to-and-fro between France and Scotland admirably, but it was becoming harder as the girls grew up and schooling became more important.

One fact they were both adamant about was that the family could not split up for any long period. Short bursts were fine, but a month was their boundary. Violet knew the whole month of September would mean separation because Raph couldn't foresee the exact date of harvest. It was capricious, the grapes tested daily until just the right ripeness and colour signalled that it was time. These days, in Scotland, she sourced her barley already malted so her life was not governed by nature's demands quite as strictly, but there were still important times to be on site.

Now was one of them, and not just because her younger daughter was starting school. While both girls would attend school mostly in Scotland, they would also attend in Reims if the family was together in France. There might come a time when they would need to choose between them, or board the girls if they liked the idea, but for now this was working. Charlotte and Gisele would make that decision for themselves, but Violet suspected her eldest would not venture far from her mother's side. While Gisele was all sunny and laughs like her father, with an easy disposition that allowed her to go along with most family decisions, Charlotte – named in honour of her grandfather – displayed the Nash streak. Violet's elder daughter was more serious, with an alarming intelligence that regularly gave both parents pause. She was already beginning to challenge their decisions, forcing them to explain everything, and she tested boundaries, at times frustrating her teachers with her precocious attitude. But, above and beyond all, she understood whisky.

From the early weeks of her birth, Violet had put Charlotte in a sling and 'worn' her child everywhere. People had nicknamed her Joey, after learning from Violet that this was the term for a baby kangaroo in the pouch. Charlotte didn't seem to mind, answering to the name of Joey at school – everywhere, in fact, except within the four walls of their home, where her pretty name needed to be heard, Violet felt. The nickname certainly spoke to the fact that the two of them were mostly inseparable; where Violet went, Charlotte went too, whether it was to the malting shed, to see the coopers, to check the still or the blending room. And she learned fast, because Violet had never stopped talking to her about the preparation and distillation of whisky, its maturation period and its blending, since long before Charlotte could speak. By the time Charlotte was of school age, she knew just about everything there was to know about not only the making of Scotch but also the making of Champagne. Raph often joked that one girl could take over House Delancré and the other could take on the Nash Distillery.

'World domination in Champagne and Scotch, you think?' Violet had laughed one day recently.

'No, world domination is for you, *ma chérie*,' he'd said, stroking her face and smiling proudly.

He was referring to her entry of Glen Corbie's blended whisky into the World Whisky Prize, an annual competition for any whisky from any country. Violet was quietly confident of some recognition for her work, though she knew she had some stiff competition. The winners were to be announced that day.

At the station, having kissed and hugged his daughters many times, Raph now turned his attention to Violet. 'I'm sorry it's today I have to leave.'

She smiled, not at all offended. 'I won't win, Raph, so I think the Champagne harvest is more important.'

'Don't be negative – you know your entry is superb.'

'It is. Even without the recognition of my peers, I am very proud of it. It's truly my best work.'

'For all sorts of reasons.' He gave a bittersweet smile. 'I'll telephone when I get in. And I will miss you until I hear your voice.'

'Don't be soppy,' she said, but she was smiling.

'I thought I was being romantic,' he replied, feigning an injured tone.

'Kiss me, Raph, and miss me. Come home soon. By the way, there's something I want to do soon. It may involve going to Germany.'

He looked shocked. 'Whatever for?'

'There's someone I want to try and find. He saved my father's life once, a long time ago, and I'd like to meet him. To let him know that Dad's gone, but also to thank him. Dad always wanted to see him again, and I'll do it for him.'

'Do you know if he's alive?'

'No. But I shall do my utmost to find him or meet his family; he had a daughter, Dad said, who wouldn't be a lot older than me now. Your mother once told me it was up to our generation to heal the world. This could be a step, couldn't it?'

'You're full of surprises, Violet.' He kissed her long and lovingly, Gisele skipping around while Charlotte made sounds of soft yet happy disgust that her parents would publicly embarrass her so.

When the final whistle blew, Violet let go of Raph and took her elder daughter's hand. 'You'll kiss someone as wonderful as your father one day, Charly.'

'Will I?'

Her mother nodded. 'Yes, but you have to be patient and wait for the right one.'

'What about me, Mummy?' Gisele asked.

'Oh, all the men are going to fall for you, my darling. You'll be fighting them off.'

Gisele skipped away happily, yelling to her father to watch her attempt to balance on one leg until the train left.

'Am I pretty?' Charlotte asked.

'Of course. With your raven-coloured hair and blue eyes, you're beautiful. But, Charly, always know that your mind is your power,' she said, touching her child's temple. 'You'll scare off some because you're so clever. But someone like your papa will come along and he'll adore your intelligence as much as your beauty, I promise. You must be very choosy, to be sure you're a perfect match. Do not settle.' She paused as her father had. 'Never. Trust Mummy on this.'

The train squealed and they began waving frantically to Raph, who was blowing them all kisses. They watched until the back end of the train had curled around the tracks and disappeared out of sight.

Violet sighed. 'Let's head home, girls. I gave you a day off school, Charly, but we'd better not show off or the headmistress might want to talk to me.'

'Can we go into the distillery today?' Charlotte asked as they began walking to their car, Gisele trailing a few steps behind.

'Yes, well, I do have to go in, actually.'

'I want to watch you work.'

'No work today, Charly, although we can certainly test one of Papa's Champagne barrels.'

'Can I taste?'

'Er, you're six – still a bit young for alcohol.'

'I'm not talking about drinking it.'

Violet laughed at the disdain in her tone, but her child's face was earnest.

'I want to taste and learn,' Charlotte continued.

'You'll hate it.'

'*You* didn't.'

Violet blinked, more than aware of why her daughter's teachers might find her frustrating. She suspected this was how she'd behaved too – constantly questioning, constantly pushing to know more. 'Well, I suppose age is irrelevant,' she answered.

'Then I would like to taste and learn what we're looking for in the spirit.'

Violet sighed. 'Why can't you talk to me about the things that fill the heads of other girls your age?'

'Like what?'

'Oh, I don't know – what they want for Christmas, perhaps.'

'Well, that's still far away but it's easy, I already know.'

Violet laughed. 'I see. And what is that?'

'I want my own spirit thief.'

Violet paused in shock. 'What?'

'I'd like a doll's tea set, Mummy, please,' Gisele announced in great earnest, joining the conversation.

Violet smiled at her youngest to let her know she had heard, but she returned her gaze to Charlotte. 'A spirit thief?'

Charlotte nodded. 'It's all I want. I want to make whisky, Mama.' Her tone sounded as though she thought her mother was a bit daft. 'I'm going to follow you and Grandad. I want to work at Glen Corbie. But I want to go to Australia too and see Glen Corbie there. We've never been, and you keep promising.'

Her mother sighed. 'I want to as well.'

'So when? Uncle John keeps writing and asking you to visit.'

'Perhaps January, for the harvest. You need to see Australia when its land is golden and its skies stretch to infinity, in the most incredible blue you can't imagine until you see it. We'll go to sandy beaches that go on for miles and where the ocean crashes to the shore.'

Charlotte's face was alight with hope. 'Is that a promise?'

Her mother nodded. Yes, it was time to go back and fall in love with Tasmania again, to show her girls and her husband a place like they'd never seen before and to help them understand that it too had shaped her into the person she was today. She'd talk to Raph about it soon.

'Good,' Charlotte said. 'Because I want to see the distillery. I want to learn more about the applewood whisky.'

Violet had called it Devil's Dram, with an image of the distinctive Tasmanian devil on the label. It was every bit as delicious as she'd hoped – lighter of colour, softer in flavour and beautiful on a summery night with soda, like a cocktail, or sipped neat with a dash of water.

Charlotte was swinging her mother's hand happily as they walked, and Gisele grabbed Violet's free hand to copy her.

'I'm going to invent a Scotch one day like you,' her older daughter said. 'I'm going to be the world's best female whisky maker – after you, of course.'

Oh, where had she heard that before? Violet's heart felt like it tilted momentarily and made a strange thump in her chest. She had to swallow the resulting lump that seemed to surge into her throat. 'That's impressive, my darling. Hold to that dream. Come on, girls, there's the car,' she said brightly, sniffing away the emotion of her daughter's announcement.

'If Charly's going to make whisky, Mummy, then I'll make Champagne with Papa, shall I?' Gisele enquired, so sweetly that it was heartbreaking in the happiest possible way.

'Yes, why don't you, Gisele? And then you can be a seventh-generation champenoise.'

Her younger daughter screwed up her nose. 'I don't know what that means.'

'It's okay, darling. You can just be a little girl for a long time and not worry about anything.'

Violet piled the girls into their recently acquired Hillman Minx Series V, which she loved driving, although Raph was now threatening to purchase a Rover, which she didn't think they needed. When they got home, she could hear the phone ringing.

'Oh, quick, quick, Gisele. I'm going to get that. It could be Papa. Charly, help your sister out of the car and come inside.'

Violet ran indoors and grabbed the heavy receiver just in time. Even as she'd said it, she knew it couldn't be Raph, who'd just left, and it was probably Charlotte's teacher, wondering why she needed the day off from school. Violet was already preparing to explain that she'd thought it important her daughter be there to wave her father off, since he wouldn't be home for a month.

'Hello, Violet Nash speaking.'

But it was a man's voice that responded to her greeting. 'Ah, Miss Nash, good morning.'

'Actually it's Mrs.'

'Pardon me?'

'I'm married, but I go by my family name when it comes to work.'

'Oh, how modern.'

'Well, you'd find my married name of Delancré even more quizzical, perhaps. Um, is this about the distillery?'

'It is, sorry. Let me begin again. Hello. My name is Charles Furber, and I am the chairman of the World Whisky Prize based in London.'

'Oh, good grief.' Violet hadn't expected a call about the prize so early, if at all. 'Um, Mr Furber, hello, how can I help?'

'Well, it's what we can do for you. I come with the happiest of tidings. Your magnificent Glen Corbie's Sassenach has won this year's World Whisky Prize.'

Her mouth fell open: no words were coming, and her mind was fizzing like a glass of Raph's finest cuvée. 'I'm speechless,' she finally pushed out, after a long pause.

'I can hear.' Mr Furber chuckled. 'And I'm pleased you are momentarily lost for words. I can tell this means plenty to you.'

'You simply can't imagine the whole of it.'

He laughed delightedly. 'And I'm sure it will thrill you – as it does all of us – that you are the first woman to take out this prize, which has been running for the past fifty years.'

'There are some illustrious and talented women behind me, and I stand on their shoulders, Mr Furber.'

'Indeed,' he agreed. 'Well, we'd like to invite you to London to collect the award and to learn all that it entails. For example, you may now add the award to your labelling, among other wonderful news.'

'There's more?' This seemed incredible.

'Well, I'm probably not supposed to say anything just yet, but our new Queen plans to award a warrant to a Scotch producer, and I know she favours Speyside. The royal family has had an affinity for Scotch for generations, but she is also the Queen of the Commonwealth, as you know.'

'I do.'

'So I think your Sassenach whisky has strong appeal for Her Majesty, because she has learned that it includes spirits you made in Australia, which you have blended with Scotch your father made in Knockando.'

Violet felt a delicious shiver go through her, hearing the recognition of her special blend. 'That's correct. I feel it is the best of two generations of whisky blenders.'

'And will there be a third?'

'I think so, Mr Furber. Certainly if my daughter has her way.'

'Marvellous. Well, you don't know that about the Royal Warrant, Violet, but I suspect by the time you journey to London the news might be appropriate to make public. My most sincere congratulations – you pipped a lot of fine blends from all over, and I suspect many of your colleagues from Speyside will be gnashing their teeth tonight when the announcement is made. I hope your family feels very proud, and I'm so pleased for you, Violet. My secretary will contact you with arrangements very shortly, so if you have any questions, contact her, and we'll look forward to meeting you in London next month. Bring the family.'

Violet thanked him, her mind dizzy with excitement.

Her tears were all happy, she assured her alarmed girls, who found her sobbing, her hand still on the phone's receiver. 'Your grandad would be so proud,' she said, hugging them and explaining about her award.

That night, when the girls were asleep and the house was still, Violet found herself restless, unable to sleep. She presumed it was the excitement, or perhaps that she hadn't been able to share the news with Raph yet. But even despite that sensible thought, there was more... she felt that something was calling to her, something more spiritual – a pull, or an invitation, from far away. She slipped a dressing gown around her nightie, imagining she would tiptoe downstairs and warm some milk, perhaps adding a dash of whisky to help her sleep, but she found herself moving first to the drinks cabinet, where she poured herself a small shot of the Soldier's Dram she'd bottled for herself, before taking the glass on to the boot room to pull on her gumboots.

The night was cool but not yet cold. She smiled into the dark, realising her blood had adjusted back to the Scottish climate, and pulled her gown closer around her and tied its tatty belt; it was her father's old one that he'd loved and refused to give up. She liked to pretend it was his arms around her and that she could still smell him on it, and that sensation felt strong right now, more real than ever. She smiled into the inky night and warmed the glass in her cupped hands, yet to take a sip. She heard an owl hoot mournfully and turned at the mellow sound, unable to pinpoint the source, and that was when the first flash glowed.

Violet blinked. What *was* that? She stared into the thick velvet of the night sky over Speyside and it seemed to quicken again, from glittery coal to a radium green.

And then the celestial dance of the angels began.

Plumes of luminous green surged against purple and red and blue, sometimes pink. The green was constant, while the other colours glowed or pulsed across the sky's dome and the merry dancers celebrated for her.

She realised her cheeks were wet with more happy tears. 'There you are, Dad,' she murmured in relieved joy. 'I knew you'd find me. We did it. Glen Corbie's name is now known... your dream has come true, and now you can sleep in that place where you are happy and we can visit you. I love you, Dad.'

The sky seemed to rip upwards into the empyrean domain, brightening momentarily as though acknowledging her. 'Rest, finally in peace, Charlie Nash,' she said and raised her dram to the heavens.

A LETTER FROM THE AUTHOR

Thank you for reading *The Soldier's Daughter*. I hope you enjoyed it!

Would you like to know when I release new books? Here are some ways to stay updated:

Be the first to know about my latest releases with Storm here:

www.stormpublishing.co/fiona-mcintosh

Join my personal mailing list:

fionamcintosh.com

Your time spent with these pages means the world to me. If you found yourself caught up in the story, I'd be incredibly grateful if you could share your thoughts in a review. Even just a few words can help other readers find their way to these pages. Every review is like a conversation between readers, and I treasure each one.

I write in silence and isolation, so knowing you've joined me on this adventure and that my story has reached out of that distant place to connect with you is extremely satisfying, and I'm excited to share that there are many more tales waiting in the wings.

Fiona x

KEEP IN TOUCH WITH THE AUTHOR

fionamcintosh.com

instagram.com/fionamcintoshbooks

bookbub.com/authors/fiona-mcintosh

ACKNOWLEDGMENTS

I've been under reader pressure since 2019, when *The Champagne War* was released, to continue the story of Captain Charlie Nash, for whom most readers felt devastated at the end of the book. I must admit to feeling badly for him too, but I don't plan, so the characters make their own decisions. After several years of avoiding it I finally succumbed to the requests and carried on the tale. Because I don't lay out my stories beforehand, the characters often walk down paths that are unexpected and change the trajectory of their journeys. But what has never happened before in all the books I've written is that I got the timeline wrong in the early chapters of my first draft.

More than halfway into the writing of this book I realised I'd made a spectacular miscalculation and for me to have Charlie's daughter, Violet, of an adult-enough age for the story, then I found myself in the late 1930s, staring at WWII. I had hoped to avoid war for this book, given *The Champagne War* was set in WWI throughout, and keep Charlie's story within the interwar years but oh dear, I got it wrong.

I was staring miserably at the notion of having to backtrack through 65,000 words and work out how to avoid this impasse, and then the idea struck — send Charlie back to war. I was so shocked I stopped writing for a couple of days to think it through, but I realised I could return him to France and not just that... but Sophie, a character we all loved, could return into these pages. The idea that I could have Charlie meet Sophie, the love of his life, once again after a quarter of a century has passed, felt irresistible and set the story off on a new tangent that was both exciting and tense. I couldn't see ahead, though, and that's the life of a gunslinger writer like me. I didn't expect it to become the highly emotional story it has, and maybe I should start apologising to readers all over again.

Anyway, it was such a pleasure to craft this tale, but while a writer's life is a lonely one, you never write without help and I received expert help from so many places.

A huge thank you to Kristy Lark-Booth, who handcrafts spirits 'from garden to glass' in Tasmania and upon whom I began to fashion Violet. Kristy taught me about whisky-making and her pedigree as the daughter of Bill Lark, the godfather of whisky in Australia, meant I was learning from someone who, like Violet, learned at her father's knee. Please visit Kristy's operation, Killara Distillery, whenever you're next down Richmond way in Tasmania – a prettier place would be hard to find. Whisky, gin and other exciting spirits are made here, and it's fascinating to learn about the local botanicals being grown on the property that go into Kristy's gins.

Tasmania has quite the burgeoning whisky industry, and I was surprised to be able to do several whisky tastings at some amazing establishments, including Lark Distillery, Launceston Distillery, Old Kempton and many more. Please treat yourselves to a visit and learn about this spirit. It is a challenge to begin with, but its following around the world knows few equals.

When I went roaming to Scotland for this novel, I stayed at the gorgeous Cardhu Country House next door to Johnnie Walker Distillery, where our hosts were Colin Corson and Sarah Stewart. Colin is quite the whisky connoisseur and collector, and I spent many hours in his company being educated about Speyside – the home of fine Scotch – and learning how to taste and appreciate its exquisite product. And now I quite often add a splosh of whisky along with cream to Ian's winter porridge after watching Sarah do the same for our breakfasts.

Colin introduced me to many helpful people, including whisky curator and historian Andy Fairgrieve from Glenfiddich, who taught me plenty and, walking around the Johnny Walker

Distillery, opened my eyes to the fact that women were as instrumental in the advancement of scotch whisky in the early days as they were for champagne in France. It gave me a perfect platform for Violet Nash and her journey in the book.

Others who must be thanked... my old friend David Harrison, who continues to teach me about a spy's life during WWII, and Simon Godly, who knows absolutely everything there is to know about the Allies in northeastern France during WWI and WWII. Simon runs brilliantly crafted tours of the region, and you can contact him here: simongodly@orange.fr

Of course my thanks to fifth-generation champenoise Sophie Gonet, who first allowed me to rummage through her family's home, their history and their knowledge to craft *The Champagne War*, and to use their Champagne house in Épernay once again for this story.

There's Carol Cane in Hobart, who just loves researching local history, and she was a magnificent help to me when I felt lost. Together we did a wonderful tour of Cascade Brewery, and Carol has been a constant support in finding out bits and bobs that enrich this story. I'd like to thank Liz Wells too, the editor of Grain Central, who helped me right when I needed some critical information on barley in the region and in the era of the 1930s.

Pip Klimentou, who works fast and pulls no punches, thank you for always being ready to drop everything and read my early draft quickly.

Thank you to my publishing team, led by Ali Watts, who wanted this whisky book for a long time, and to my editor, Amanda Martin, who makes the interminable task of the many drafts so easy for me. Couldn't do these books without these two fab women in my writing life. And to the greater team at Penguin Random House – there are so many involved in the production and marketing of my books and so big thanks to Holly Toohey, Hannah Ludbrook, Anna Tidswell, Heidi Camilleri, Veronica Eze, Jo Baker and her team, Janine Brown and her fab sales team around

Australia and everyone else in-house whose expertise has touched *The Soldier's Daughter.*

Booksellers – print, digital, audio – we can't do this without you. Thank you for being such terrific supporters of my books, especially those wonderful people who hand sell and recommend eagerly, placing books into the hands of customers they know will love their recommendations. I am on the receiving end of that support and love regularly, so thank you. And the same goes for our network of librarians. What would we do without our amazing libraries in Australia? Thank you.

And of course family – nothing at all gets achieved without their support. Endless gratitude to my husband, Ian, who reads the many books I buy to educate myself about a topic and points me in the right direction through that tower of books, and to Will and Jack, our sons, who came on the whisky journey into Tasmania and took turns as designated drivers so I could focus on the story. And Will especially for coming along on that first journey for the book to scour the State Library of Tasmania and roam around Richmond. It was so helpful to have you alongside. Thank you, boys. Fx

VIOLET'S WHISKY SHORTBREAD

This is my own take on a shortbread recipe from Cardhu House in Knockando, Scotland. Truly delicious!

Ingredients

200g unsalted butter at room temperature (but on the cold side)
110g caster sugar
30g cornflour
310g plain flour (lower protein is good)
A generous pinch of salt (around half a teaspoon)
As much vanilla paste as you dare (but at least one teaspoon)
A splotch or two of good whisky

Method

Preheat your oven to 180 degrees Celsius and line a couple of baking trays with baking paper.

Violet would have mixed her shortbread by hand, but I tip everything into a food processor and whiz until it starts to clump. Then I tip that out onto a lightly floured surface and bring it together into a dough with light fingers.

Roll out the dough and cut into desired shapes. I tend to do thin discs (approximately 3 mm thick), using the smallest round cutter I have (around 5–6 cm wide). But please don't get too scientific or worried about this. Just roll to a thickness that you're comfy with and cut into any shape you like.

Put your biscuits onto the prepared trays. You can, if you wish, sprinkle them with some granulated sugar. It adds some crunch and sparkle when the biscuits have cooled.

If your biscuits are a similar thickness to mine, then you'll bake them for 20 minutes. Please keep an eye on them, because they can go from light to dark in a blink!

Let them cool on a rack. Once cool, you can dust with icing sugar if you wish. I do so liberally because I find it helps them stay fresher for longer, but it's not essential or traditional. But then Violet is not traditional!

BOOK CLUB NOTES

1. 'I'm tired of fighting, my love. I seem to have done it for a lifetime.' In what ways has Charlie been fighting all his life?

2. Of his experience in the war, Charlie declares: 'I count myself lucky to have survived with a healthy mind.' In what ways does Violet perceive otherwise?

3. When Charlie and Violet arrive in Australia, do they find it to be 'the land of opportunity' that had been promised?

4. Do you understand and/or respect Charlie's motivation for returning to Épernay?

5. '*Give me time and love*, her whisky replied... *We could become very good friends*.' Are you a drinker of whisky? What makes it so special?

6. 'War makes good people do bad things.' Discuss in relation to this novel.

7. Do you agree with Violet's mother, Ellen, that love is overwhelming? In what ways do we see this idea played out in *The Soldier's Daughter* and its prequel, *The Champagne War*?

8. Violet wants to hate Raphael, but life has other ideas. What is it about him that attracts her? Do you think he's a better match for her than John, and why?

9. *The Soldier's Daughter* is full of dramatic moments. Which surprised you the most?

10. Where do you think Violet feels most at home – England, Scotland, Tasmania or France – and why?

11. Of Charlie's many sacrifices, which was the greatest?

12. 'Never be a sheep, Violet,' Charlie had counselled. 'You may not be popular, and you may unnerve others, but you will always be happier if you stay true to yourself.' In what ways does Violet heed this advice? Does it lead to happiness?